THE DARKNESS DEEPENS

THE DARKNESS DEEPENS

the seven trilogy
book two

SARA DAVISON

ASHBERRY LANE

THE DARKNESS DEEPENS

Published by Ashberry Lane, a division of WhiteFire Publishing
13607 Bedford Rd NE, Cumberland, MD 21502
www.ashberrylane.com
Printed in the USA

Canadian spelling is frequently used.

Published in association with the literary agency of Wordserve Literary Group, www.wordserveliterary.com.

ISBN 978-1-946531-52-0

Library of Congress Control Number: 2016935830

Cover design by Roseanna White Designs
Photos from www.shutterstock.com.com
Edited by Rachel Lulich, Christina Tarabochia, Kristen Johnson, Sherrie Ashcraft, Andrea Cox, and Amy Smith

FICTION / Christian / Romantic Suspense

Praise for The Darkness Deepens

"The second book in the Seven trilogy is more exciting than the first. Davison does a wonderful job at further developing the main characters by diving into their backstories and unpacking the things from the past that have helped shape who they are in the present. The suspense is well-placed and the timing is spot on, giving readers enough breaks to not be overwhelmed while never losing the tension."

—*RT Book Reviews*, 4 Stars

"Sara Davison's second book in the Seven trilogy, *The Dragon Roars*, brings together all the essential elements of a good suspense read—compelling story, fast-paced action, and believable characters. *The Dragon Roars* is a riveting, well-written novel with an engaging storyline that draws the reader into futuristic world where it's dangerous to be a follower of Christ. Davison is a master at weaving the faith elements of the story into a beautiful tapestry that highlights rather than detracts from the underlying message of survival in a dangerous new world of unbelief. Readers will not be disappointed in Davison's second book in the trilogy; it delivers!"

—LUANA EHRLICH, Author of *Titus Ray Thrillers*

"Sara Davison is a terrific storyteller. She takes the truths of the Bible, the what-ifs of an end-time's scenario, and populates her story with unforgettable characters to create a world that is terrifyingly possible. The Dragon Roars is an edge-of-your-seat romantic thriller that will give your emotions a roller coaster workout."

—BARBARA ELLEN BRINK, Author of *Roadkill*,
Double Barrel Mysteries, Book 1

"I love reading novels about strong and courageous heroines of faith and heroes who are equally matched in determination and bravery. *The Dragon Roars* delivers on this big time in the characters of Bible smuggler Meryn

O'Reilly and Captain Jesse Christensen, as they fight for their love and faith, and to do what's right against growing, seemingly insurmountable odds. *The Dragon Roars* brings something special to the ambitious genre of 'End Times' novels in that it tells a story about the unfolding Apocalypse through relatable and emotional relationships between sweethearts, parents, siblings, and friends. Sara Davison's vision of a dystopian Canadian future has refreshingly smart and courageous characters with a lot of heart."

—MAGGIE K. BLACK,

Author of over 8 novels including

Tactical Rescue and *Kidnapped at Christmas*

Praise for The End Begins

"The first book in Davison's Seven trilogy grips the reader from page one and holds on until the very end. Meryn O'Reilly is a believable character, and—though dreadful—the story is plausible. The events unfold in a forward-moving way that allows readers to sympathize with Meryn and Jesse and understand the dilemmas they face. Thought-provoking, relevant and suspenseful, *The End Begins* is a must-read."

—*RT Book Reviews*, 4 ½ Stars, *Top Pick*

"What would you do if the government outlawed the Bible? *The End Begins* depicts the response of a bookstore owner, the army captain duty-bound to arrest her if she breaks the law, and the family, friends, and enemies in their lives. It's a compelling and scary read you won't soon forget."

—SANDRA ORCHARD,

Author of the Award-Winning Port Aster Secrets series

"Sara Davison takes 'what if' to a chilling level that is all too real. Yet wrapped in love, both human and divine, this novel gives us hope. Book Two can't come out soon enough."

—NANCY RUE,

Author of *One Last Thing* and *The Merciful Scar*

To Julia, my only daughter and ally in a house of boys. It is a joy and privilege to watch you grow into the beautiful woman you are becoming, and to witness you facing life's challenges with humour, determination, and quiet strength. I thank God for the blessing of you.

To my brothers and sisters around the world who truly know what it means to suffer for the cause of Christ. May God comfort and sustain you until the end.

And always and above all, to the One who gives the stories and who has promised to never leave us or forsake us. It is all from you and for you.

Then war broke out in heaven.
Michael and his angels fought against the dragon,
and the dragon and his angels fought back.
Revelation 12:7

Chapter One

Captain Jesse Christensen pushed open the back door of the old cabin and stepped onto the rickety porch. *Where is she?* Clouds drifted across the moon, obscuring the opening to the woods. Did Meryn have a flashlight? He scanned the trees, straining for a glimmer of light.

The sound of an approaching vehicle tightened his stomach muscles. Meryn wouldn't try to drive here, would she?

Jesse edged to the corner of the building. The ancient wooden boards groaned under his hiking boots as he peered around the corner of the cabin.

A green army jeep whizzed by the end of the driveway.

He ducked back out of sight. She better not come that way. Even the half-mile drive from her farmhouse, the next property over, put her at risk of being caught out after curfew. As a convicted felon, the army would come down hard on her. And this time not even he or Caleb, his best friend and commanding officer at the base, would be able to help her.

A twig snapped.

Instinctively, he reached for the Glock in the back of his jeans. It wasn't there. He measured the distance from the porch to the jeep he'd parked behind the cabin. Could he get to it in time?

Relax. It has to be her.

He crossed over to the stairs. A spring thunderstorm had passed through the area that afternoon and the mingled scents of crushed wildflowers and damp earth hung in the air. The cracking of branches and rustling of grass grew louder as he approached the trees. A hard thud made him wince. "Meryn?" he whispered her name as loudly as he dared as he made his way down the path.

"Coming."

The clouds parted. Her long dark hair, pulled back in a ponytail, gleamed in the moonlight as she limped toward him.

Jesse pulled her into his arms. "Are you hurt?"

"I'm fine. Just didn't see a branch lying across the path."

"Don't you have a flashlight?"

"Yes." She stepped back and pulled the small silver tube out of the pocket of her windbreaker. "I didn't want to use it, though, in case someone saw the light."

"That's smart, I guess." He glanced down at the torn knees of her jeans, then reached for her hand. "Come inside. I can assess the damage better there."

She followed him up the stairs and into the cabin.

Jesse let go of her and swung the door shut.

The room plunged into blackness.

Meryn inhaled sharply. "Jesse?"

"Just a sec. Don't move, okay?" He felt in the thick dark for the lamp he'd set up in the corner of the room. His fingers brushed against the shade. "Almost have it." He pushed the button and soft light flooded the cabin.

Meryn clasped her hands in front of her. "We have power? How?"

He waved a hand at the machine humming in the corner. "Solar generator. There's heat too." He nudged another small machine with his foot. "So we're all set."

Meryn walked across the room toward him. The smile on her face made all the work he'd done to try and make a cozy room out of this old shack worthwhile. "But won't someone see the light?"

"Nope." He gestured toward one of the windows. "I covered all the glass and any chinks in the wall I could find with black paper. From outside it still looks like an abandoned wreck of a building."

Meryn stopped in front of him. "Seems you've thought of everything."

"Everything except how to get you here in one piece." He looked her up and down. "You're bleeding and covered with dirt." He gently traced a line of red slashed across her cheek. "What happened to your face?"

"I took on a branch somewhere in the middle of the woods and lost."

Meryn looked down at the rips in the knees of her jeans. "I'm okay. It was a little tricky coming here, that's all. I'm going to have to hike through in the daylight sometime and see if I can find a better path."

Jesse sighed and placed his hand on her back. "Come sit down." He guided her to a wooden table in the middle of the room and pulled out a paint-flecked chair. When she settled on it, he turned another one to face her and sat down. "I'm sorry we have to meet this way, Meryn."

"It's not your fault. We both knew it would be like this when we agreed to try and keep seeing each other."

"I guess, but ..."

She touched his arm. "It's fine. Actually"—her gaze traveled around the room—"it's a lot better than fine. I can't believe what you've done in here. It's like our own little world that no one else on the planet even knows exists."

Not yet, anyway. Jesse pushed back the thought. Their time together would slip through their fingers like water. He didn't want to waste a second of it worrying about what might happen in the future. "That sounds good to me. I wish we could stay in this world forever, but I promised Caleb I'd be back on the base by ten. Any later than that and someone will start asking questions."

"It's okay. I know you have to be careful."

He turned her hand over in his and rubbed his thumbs over her palm, brushing off the dirt. "We both do." He finished with that hand and reached for the other one.

She searched his face. "What is it?"

"What's what?"

"What's bothering you? Has something happened?"

Of course she would see it in his eyes. He'd never been good at hiding what he was feeling, especially from her. And new laws seemed to be passed every week. Almost all were designed to oppress Christians after a radical group, "The Horsemen," had carried off a deadly terrorist attack on 10/10/53, six months earlier. She probably expected something like what he was about to tell her.

Jesse blew out a breath and reached inside his jacket to pull a slim, white box out of the inside pocket. "I wasn't going to give you this right away, but since we can't stay long, maybe it's best." He held the box toward her.

Meryn reached for it. "You got me a present?" She started to lift the lid.

He stopped her by covering the box with his fingers. "No."

Surprise flickered in the ocean-blue eyes that met his.

When he spoke, he couldn't keep the coldness from his voice. "This is not a gift. And it is definitely not from me."

Chapter Two

Meryn set the box down on the table.

He gave her a moment, then flicked his fingers against the back of her hand lightly. "It's not alive," he teased. "I didn't put a snake in there or anything."

The irony of the words struck her, given that the revulsion on his face when he handed it to her had suggested it might be something conceived in the pit of hell.

"Then what is it?"

"Open it and see."

Meryn studied his face for a moment, then turned back to the box and lifted the lid. She picked up the slim grey bracelet. Turning it over in her hands, she examined both sides, ran a finger over the hard plastic face of it, across the *3* etched into the band. "What is this?"

"It's an identity bracelet. *Your* identity bracelet, to be exact."

"Mine?"

"Yes. The computer chip inside has been programmed with your personal information—physical characteristics, job, contact information ... anything the government considers relevant."

"What about religious affiliation?"

He hesitated. "That's not programmed in, no."

"Why not? I thought the government considered that extremely relevant these days."

"They do, but it's not necessary to program in the fact that you're a Christian."

Icy fingers danced up and down her spine. "You mean they'll know that because of the bracelet, right? It's only for the Christians. To keep track of them."

"To 'protect them' is the official party line. Because there have been so many attacks against Christians since 10/10, like the one on your store."

She winced, the memory of the brick smashing through the window of her beloved secondhand bookstore, the deafening crash and the glass that had showered down on them both, pummelling her like a fist.

"The government claims this is the best way to keep the Christians safe. There is a button to push in an emergency, and if anything extreme happens and someone with a bracelet disappears, the army could use the embedded GPS system to track the missing person down, so in a way I guess it could be used for safety."

"But it's not the main purpose, is it?"

"No. I suspect that's just a smoke screen."

"So they'll know where I am at all times. Even here." Fear crept into her voice.

"The tracking will be done by a handful of soldiers at a few centres scattered across the country. And millions of people will be wearing the bracelets. Unless you do something to draw attention to yourself, it's unlikely anyone will be tracking your movements. But you will have to be more careful now than ever."

Meryn pushed back her chair and stood. For a moment she paced at the end of the table. "Will they use this to keep us from buying and selling merchandise?"

"Not yet."

She wandered over to the worn, tiled kitchen counter in the corner and turned to lean against it. The bracelet shook in her fingers.

Jesse got up and crossed the room to stand in front of her.

Meryn traced the number in the band. "What does this mean?"

"It means, once you put this bracelet on, you'll be classified as a level-three Christian."

She looked up. "Level-three?"

"Yes. Number five means you have never been in trouble with the law. Four means you have been suspected of a crime but there hasn't been enough evidence to arrest you, or you've been arrested but not convicted.

Three is for those who have been arrested and convicted of a hate crime other than terrorism. Level two is reserved for suspected terrorists, and number one is for terrorists who have been arrested and convicted. That number will go into their official records, but they'll never have it etched on their bracelets."

"Because ...?"

"They'll be dead."

Meryn drew in a long, slow breath. "So everyone will have a bracelet already pre-programmed with their information in it?"

"Everyone suspected of being a Christian, yes. Basically, if you have ever been affiliated with a church or if we've found a Bible in your possession or you have acted in a way that suggests you are either a believer or in sympathy with believers, you're on a list, and there is a bracelet with your name on it. I grabbed yours from the pile so no one would show up at your door with it, but soldiers will start delivering them tomorrow. Once the bracelets are secured, they cannot be removed. They are waterproof and virtually indestructible. Tampering with the lock or attempting to cut through the plastic will set off an alarm at Headquarters. Then they will use the GPS that will go live at the end of the day tomorrow—when all the bracelets are activated at the same time—to track you down in minutes and arrest you."

She bit her lip, absorbing that information. "Wow. It's moving fast, isn't it?"

"I'm afraid so."

"What about you?"

"I'm not on the list, so they don't suspect anything. Not yet, anyway."

"That's good."

"Is it?"

"Of course it is. As long as they don't suspect anything, you're safe."

"That's just it, Meryn. Why should I be safe?" His voice was harsh and she blinked. Jesse ran his fingers through his hair. "I'm sorry. It's just that it's getting harder and harder to stay hidden away in my quarters, avoiding the treatment all the other Christians are getting. Even having to order some of it or carry it out myself. It just doesn't feel right."

Meryn set the bracelet on the counter beside her. "You aren't hiding.

And I was wrong to use the word *safe.* But as long as you're there and no one suspects you of being a believer, you can help us. Especially now that these bracelets are going to make it a lot easier to restrict our movements and our access to goods or services."

"I guess."

"Should I warn Kate and Ethan about this?"

Jesse shook his head. "No, don't. If your message gets intercepted, there'll be trouble, since no one is supposed to know about this ahead of time. I brought their bracelets with me, and I'll take a chance and stop by there tonight."

"Is this happening all across the country?"

"Yes. Your brothers will have to get theirs out west, before they move back here."

Meryn tilted her head and looked up at him, a small smile on her face.

"What?"

"I'm not sure I like that you always know what I'm thinking."

He shrugged. "You're the one who wanted to be more transparent, lady. It's not my fault that I can read you like a book now."

"A good one, I hope."

"Definitely one of my favourites. Dickens, at least."

"I'm sorry, *one* of your favourites?"

Jesse laughed. "Slip of the tongue. I meant my absolute, better-than-Shakespeare favourite of all time, not even a close second."

She grinned. "Better than Shakespeare. I can live with that." She moved closer and laid her head on his chest. When Jesse wrapped his arms around her, she inhaled deeply, breathing in the faint scent of citrusy musk and feeling a peace she hadn't felt in days at least, maybe months. She looked up.

He lifted his hands to her face and pressed his lips to hers.

The feel of his mouth, of his strong fingers against her skin, filled her senses and the rest of the world faded away. Everything that was happening outside of these walls, outside of their perfect, secret place, felt imaginary, dream-like, as though the two of them were the only things that were real. It was an illusion but she slid her hand to the back of his neck to pull him closer, deepening their kiss to keep everything else at bay a little longer. After a moment, she stepped back with a sigh.

They couldn't keep everything else at bay. Couldn't even keep the evil out of this place, apparently.

She reached for the band and held it up between them. "Do I have a choice? About putting it on, I mean?"

"Oh yes." Bitterness tinged his words. "That's the great thing about living in a free and democratic nation. You always have a choice." Jesse reached into his back pocket and withdrew his i-com. "You can put on the bracelet or you can sign this." He turned the screen, the now-familiar gold-and-red government logo swirling across the top, toward her. "It's a sworn statement saying that you renounce Jesus Christ and the teachings of the Christian Bible." He slid the stylus from the side of the device and held it up in his other hand. "Simply sign this, and as soon as I submit it tomorrow, you'll be free to go, no questions asked."

Meryn scanned the words. When her gaze met his, the fear was gone. Without a word, she offered him the bracelet and held out her other arm.

Jesse replaced the stylus and dropped the i-com back into his pocket before taking the bracelet. He snapped it around her wrist, then wrapped his fingers around both. "Congratulations, Meryn O'Reilly. As of April 8, 2054, you are officially a Christian in the eyes of the government of Canada."

Chapter Three

The i-com in Jesse's back pocket vibrated as he climbed out of the jeep. Emotionally drained from leaving Meryn, then taking the bracelets to Kate and Ethan, he'd hoped to sneak into his quarters, spend five minutes on his laptop removing Meryn, Kate, and Ethan from the list of identity bracelet recipients, and go straight to bed. Judging by the message that flashed across the screen, it was going to be a while before that happened.

My office. Now.

If he was lucky, the urgent tone was the result of a breaking national or international crisis. If he wasn't, Caleb had already found out he'd delivered some of the bracelets early.

Jesse strode across the parking lot and entered the old stone building that had once been a psychiatric hospital. It now housed a company of soldiers sent to enforce the martial law that had been indefinitely declared in Canada after the terrorist attacks of 10/10. That was six months ago, and there were no signs that the mission would be wrapped up any time soon. The military was even more firmly entrenched in running the country, under the authority of the Prime Minister and the administration of justice by the Canadian Human Rights Commission, than it had been immediately following the series of deadly explosions.

His neck muscles tight, Jesse approached Caleb's office and knocked lightly on the door before pushing into the room.

Caleb rose to his full six-foot-four-inch height as Jesse approached the desk.

"You wanted to see me?"

"Yes."

Jesse's apprehension level elevated. Usually he had a fairly good idea of what his friend was thinking, although he didn't have Caleb's uncanny ability to read his every thought and emotion. Tonight the major was giving nothing away.

"I want to go over tomorrow's plans to make sure we're ready to carry out the operation quickly and efficiently."

"Okay." He drew out the word, trying to analyze Caleb's posture for clues.

Caleb clasped his hands behind his back. Not usually a good sign, but his features remained even. "In fact, I had hoped to go over them with you a couple of hours ago, but I stopped by your room and you weren't there."

The noose was tightening. "No, I wasn't."

"Were you somewhere on the base, the gym maybe, or the library?"

Jesse sighed. Why did Caleb insist on asking Jesse questions Caleb clearly already knew the answers to? "No, actually. I went out for a bit. I wasn't aware that I needed to let you know every time I ran an errand."

The flippant comment was a tactical error.

Caleb's blue eyes grew hard and cold, and he fixed the laser-intense gaze on Jesse that regularly sent prisoners cowering into submission.

He lowered his gaze. "Sorry."

"Hey." Caleb ground the word out between clenched teeth and waited until Jesse looked up to continue. "You are not required to inform me of your every move, no. However, these are extremely uncertain times, and you have made decisions in recent weeks that have put not only yourself but me, as your sole ally here, on extremely shaky ground. If you let me know when you leave the base and when I can expect you to return, I can cover for you. Is that asking too much?"

He swallowed. "No."

"Good. Would you care to tell me where you went?"

No, I would not care to. Not one bit. Since Caleb had probably already figured it out, though, there was no point in antagonizing him further. "I saw Meryn. And then I dropped by to talk to her friends Kate and Ethan."

"Why?"

"Because I hadn't seen her in a few days and I missed her."

He jumped when Caleb slammed his laptop shut and stalked around the desk. "We have important work to do tonight and you are wasting my time. Why did you see Meryn and her friends?"

Jesse resisted the urge to take a step back. Caleb hadn't been this furious with him since the day Jesse arrested Meryn and brought her to his quarters instead of taking her to prison. It was possible he had overestimated how understanding Caleb was going to be about tonight's activities. "I took them their identity bracelets."

Caleb's jaw worked. "Are you trying to get us both court-martialled?"

"No."

"Because if you are," Caleb said as if Jesse hadn't spoken, "I hate to disappoint you, but as of this afternoon that is no longer an option for the type of crime you just committed."

"Crime?"

"Yes. Information about operations like the one we are carrying out tomorrow is considered classified. And anyone leaking classified information, particularly to a person convicted of a crime under Bill 1071, will now be held liable under Section 47 of the Criminal Code."

Jesse choked on the breath he'd just taken. "Treason?" If that was true, if anyone else found out what he had done, he could be sentenced to life in prison or even given the death penalty.

"Yes. A new bill passed today moves Section 47 over to the Terrorism Act and broadens the definition of treason to cover a number of previously relatively minor offences. What I could have brushed off yesterday as foolhardy behaviour on your part—or just another day in the life of Jesse Christensen—is now an indictable offence that could cost you your life."

The warmth drained from his body. "I'm sorry, Cale. I didn't know."

"Would it have stopped you?"

"Maybe."

"Maybe isn't good enough. I need you to promise me something, Jess."

"What?"

"That you'll let me know from now on when you're planning to pull a stunt like you did this evening so we can discuss it. You can't just go off half-cocked anymore. There's too much at stake. Can you do that?"

It was a reasonable request. Purely out of loyalty, Caleb had already risked his career, and now he was offering to risk his life as well. All he asked was that they work together. "I will. I promise."

Caleb exhaled and ran a hand over his blond crew cut.

Jesse relaxed slightly. The worst of the storm had passed. In this room, anyway. Seemed like it raged more violently than ever outside these old limestone walls.

Caleb waved a hand toward the two leather armchairs in front of the fire. "Let's sit."

Shaken, Jesse followed him across the room and sank down on the deep-brown chair facing his friend. "Did you know?"

"Probably. Did I know what?"

"That I had taken the bracelets."

"Yes. At least I knew you had taken Meryn's. When I realized you'd left the base, I checked to see if her bracelet was missing. I had intended to send all the lists tonight to the soldiers that had been assigned to them, but I held off until you could tell me if you had taken any others so I could remove their names as well."

Jesse massaged his neck with one hand. He'd assumed the lists wouldn't go out until the morning. If Caleb didn't know Jesse as well as he did, he'd have sent the lists off and someone would probably have already figured out that three of the bracelets were missing. He'd come that close to being discovered, and he hadn't had any idea. "I guess I owe you one."

Caleb snorted. "One? I've lost count of how many you owe me, but I do know it would take you several lifetimes to pay me back."

"At least you've bought me a little more time to try."

"Make it count." He crossed an ankle over a knee. "How is she?"

"Meryn? She's good." Jesse studied the flickering flames in the fireplace. "Not crazy about having to put that bracelet on, but she didn't think twice about it when she heard the alternative."

"That doesn't surprise me. Those bracelets will separate the people who really believe what they say from the ones who don't. From what I know of Meryn, her faith is deeply real to her."

"Yes, it is. And her friends are the same. They didn't hesitate to put them on, either."

"Would you?"

"Not for a second."

"Well, let's hope it doesn't come to that. No one, and I mean absolutely no one, can suspect that you have crossed over. Gallagher is your biggest threat, of course. You can't do anything to arouse his suspicions, since nothing would make him happier than to bring you—and preferably both of us—down."

"I know." In spite of the warm fire, a cold chill slithered through him at the thought of the lieutenant who had hated Jesse since he had been promoted to captain three years earlier. Gallagher and his cronies looked for every opportunity to undermine his and Caleb's authority.

"One more thing."

"I don't think I can handle one more thing."

"Nevertheless, here it is. The WHO is warning about a potential Red Virus outbreak."

Jesse's eyes widened. "Here?"

"Yes. Five people have been hospitalized in Ontario. Test results haven't come back yet, but it doesn't look good."

"I thought that had been eradicated."

"Most health experts did too, but there have been a few lone voices warning the world not to get too complacent, that the virus may have been banked but was still smouldering. It looks like those voices were right. If so, we could be facing an inferno."

The chill running through him deepened. He and Caleb had both contracted the Red Virus, known simply as Reds, three years before in a hospital in Austria where they'd been sent after Jesse had been diagnosed with PTSD and Caleb had been injured on a tour. Although it only lasted forty-eight hours, it had nearly killed them both. Thankfully they were both immune now, as Reds had one of the highest person-to-person spread rates of any virus in history.

Jesse pressed the tips of his fingers against both temples to push back the headache throbbing there. What a night. The only good thing was that he'd been able to see Meryn. He worried about her even more than Caleb worried about him. At least her brothers would soon be around to keep an eye on her. He lifted his head. "So you know, I need to go out again sometime in the next few days. Meryn's two older brothers are moving to town, and she wants me to meet them."

"Do they know about you?"

"Yes, she told them."

"Everything?"

Jesse sighed. "Unfortunately, yes." His stomach churned as the image of the whip in his hand, cords flecked with blood, flashed through his mind.

A smirk crossed his friend's face. "Ooh, I wouldn't want to be in your shoes, my friend. Although I wouldn't mind being there to see how that meeting goes down."

"You don't have to look so giddy about it."

"I think I do. After all, if you'd stayed away from her like I told you to from the start, none of this would be happening."

That was true. Jesse shifted in his seat. "Didn't you mention something about us having work to do tonight?"

Caleb grinned and slapped both hands down on the arms of the chair to propel himself to his feet. "Yes, we do. Let's get at it so we're not up half the night. Tomorrow's going to be a long day."

Jesse's throat tightened. He definitely was not looking forward to pounding on doors and putting Christians in the position of having to decide on the spot just how much they were willing to sacrifice for the cause of the Christ they claimed to follow. By the end of the day, everything would have changed in their country. Again.

And then he had the encounter with Meryn's brothers to look forward to. Jesse followed Caleb over to his desk. Better to concentrate on the task at hand and not worry about the future. Jesse'd have to be completely focused and alert from now on.

As of today, his life literally depended on it.

Chapter Four

Meryn set the last of the glasses on the top rack of the dishwasher and closed the door. "Thanks for dinner, Kate. It was amazing."

"How would you know?" Kate nudged Meryn's shoulder before squeezing water from the dish cloth and hanging it over the tap. "I don't think you ate three bites."

"I'm sorry." Meryn leaned back against the counter with a sigh. "It wasn't the food, honest. It was … everything, I guess."

"You mean the bracelets?"

"The bracelets, the sneaking around, the curfew. It's all starting to get to me a little."

"Since it looks like none of the above is going to change anytime soon, it's better to focus on other things. Come help us tuck the kids into bed."

Meryn followed, the heaviness in her chest lightening at the sound of Matthew and Gracie giggling in their bedroom. Which was exactly why she had sought solace at Kate and Ethan's place this evening.

Kate looked back at her as they climbed the stairs. "It was good of Jesse to bring us our bracelets last night so we didn't have strangers pounding on the door today demanding we decide on the spot if we were going to put them on or not."

"Yes, it was. I hope he didn't get in trouble for it."

"Me too." Kate opened the door of the room.

Ethan chased the kids, already in their pyjamas, around the room, holding both hands in front of him, fingers curled.

Kate glanced back over her shoulder and rolled her eyes. "The tickle monster is on the loose."

Meryn grinned. Was there anything more healing than the carefree laughter of children? The sound of it pushed back the darkness that had crept to the periphery of her consciousness after she had left the cabin, and Jesse, the night before.

"Come on, guys, story time." Kate scooped a giggling Gracie into her arms and nodded toward the rocking chair.

Meryn walked over and sat down in it, then held out her arms. When Kate handed her daughter off, Meryn pulled the little girl to her, burying her face in the soft, red curls.

Gracie snuggled down in her lap, and Kate tossed a knitted blanket over the two of them.

"All right, little man." Ethan pulled back the covers of Matthew's twin bed. "You heard Mom. Into bed."

Matthew scrambled under the covers, his flannel pyjamas, covered in stars and planets, disappearing under a pile of blankets.

Kate settled on the edge of Gracie's bed as Ethan grabbed the thick book of Bible stories off the shelf and held it up. "What story are we reading tonight?"

David and Goliath, Kate mouthed to Meryn.

"David and Goliath," Matthew called out, voice muffled by blankets.

Meryn laughed.

Ethan pulled the blankets away from his son's face. "David and Goliath again? You know there are lots and lots of other good stories in here, right?" He tapped the hard cover of the book.

Meryn studied it. The soldiers who came for their Bibles last year must not have been worried about the book of stories, since it wasn't an actual Bible.

"What about Jonah and the whale, or Noah's ark, or Jesus feeding five thousand people with a couple of loaves of bread and some fish?"

Matthew popped out of the mound of blankets. "My teacher says we're not supposed to say *Jesus*."

Meryn and Kate exchanged a look.

Matthew's brown hair was mussed up, and Ethan ran a hand over it to smooth it down. "When did she say that?"

"A few days ago. I was telling Ryan about Jesus walking on the water, and she heard me. Mrs. Greening said that I shouldn't talk about Jesus because he isn't real, and I could get in big trouble if I told the other kids he was. But he is real, isn't he, Dad?"

"Yes, son. He is very real. And even if Mrs. Greening doesn't believe in him, he loves her and he loves Ryan too. If your friends ask you about Jesus or you want to talk about him, you should. But maybe talk about it outside at recess so you don't get in trouble with your teacher, okay?"

A tight knot formed in Meryn's stomach. Ethan's advice was wise, but it had to be difficult for him and Kate to know what to tell their children. Neither of them would ever deny their faith in public, no matter what the consequences. But to ask their children to speak up and talk about something that could bring them ridicule, or a lot worse, was a whole different matter.

Matthew flopped back onto his pillow, and Ethan tucked the covers around him again before opening the book. "Fine, David and Goliath. But something else tomorrow night, okay?"

"Okay." Matthew sounded drowsy.

Meryn stroked Gracie's hair. She was so tiny, so innocent. And so completely unaware of what was happening in the world around them. Meryn's chest squeezed as she pulled the little girl tighter. She loved these kids so much, and she felt for Kate and Ethan with the burden they must feel over all that was going on around them.

And the growing awareness that they had so very little time to teach their children everything they needed to know to strengthen their faith before the world did everything it could to rip it from them.

Chapter Five

Meryn took a deep breath of the steaming cup of coffee Ethan set in front of her. She really should be getting to work, but everything that had happened the last few days had filled her with an overwhelming desire to be with the people she cared about the most. Kate must have felt the same way, judging by how she had grabbed Meryn's hands and pulled her into the house when she had shown up on their doorstep that morning.

"Thanks." Meryn poured cream into the dark liquid and swirled it absently with her spoon. "You don't think these things have cameras, do you?" She lifted her arm to examine the bracelet.

"Man, I hope not." Ethan shot a look at Kate, who bit her lower lip as a tinge of pink appeared on both cheeks.

Meryn lowered her arm back down to the table. "I see you two recovered from the trauma of all this quickly," she said dryly.

Kate lifted a shoulder, clearly unrepentant. "It's called making the best of a bad situation, Mer."

Ethan laughed. Planting both palms against the wood, he leaned across the table and kissed Kate. "And you were definitely the best, love."

Meryn squeezed her eyes shut and covered her ears with both hands. "Really don't need to hear this."

Air brushed past her face. Before she could move, soft lips touched hers.

Her eyes flew open.

Ethan had lifted Gracie up to Meryn for a kiss.

Meryn laughed and held out her arms.

"Didn't want you to feel left out." Ethan grinned as he handed over his daughter.

"I doubt she feels left out in that department." A smug look crossed Kate's face. "She did see Jesse before he came to our house the other night."

"It wasn't a completely social call, remember?" Meryn held up the bracelet again.

"Not completely doesn't mean not at all. Tell us everything."

Ethan closed his eyes and covered his ears with his hands. "Really don't need to hear this."

When Kate and Meryn laughed, Gracie giggled and Meryn pulled her close. Such sweet innocence. With all the chaos and evil in the world, spending time with her was like soaking up sunshine in the eye of a deadly storm.

Ethan kissed Kate before grabbing his jacket from the back of a kitchen chair. "I'm off to work. Meryn, are we still having dinner with you and those crazy brothers of yours Saturday night?"

"Yes. They fly in late tomorrow. They're looking forward to seeing you."

"Looking forward to seeing them too." He pulled a cap down over his sandy-brown hair as he headed for the hallway. "Have a good day, everyone."

Meryn waited until the front door clicked shut behind him before she turned to her friend. "You got a good one, Kate."

"I know." Kate held up a finger. "But no changing the subject. I want to hear how things are going with Jesse. I'm sure it was great to see him, in spite of the circumstances."

"It was." Meryn set Gracie up on the table and started playing patty-cake with her, loving the feel of the soft, chubby hands clapping against hers. She tried to focus on the game, but Kate's eyes were on her.

"What is it?"

Meryn sighed. "I don't know. When I'm with him, everything is wonderful. There is nowhere else I want to be and no one else in the world I want to be with. Then, the second he leaves, the doubts start pouring in."

"You've got to find a way to let it go, Mer."

"You're right, I know. And when I'm with Jesse, it feels like that's actually something I can do. Then he goes back to the base and I can't see him or contact him, and it all gets confusing again."

"Do you want him to leave the army?"

"Yes. No. I don't know." Meryn exhaled loudly. "See?" Lifting Gracie's palms to her mouth, she blew raspberries into them until the toddler shrieked with laughter.

Kate got up, grabbed a lidded cup of milk from the counter, and handed it to her daughter.

Meryn pulled Gracie back into her lap and cuddled her as the little girl lifted the cup to her mouth. "I have moments of weakness where, yes, all I want to do is ask him to leave the army so we can be together without skulking around and meeting in secret. I know that's wrong and that he's where he's supposed to be, but I'm scared that one of these times I'll forget how wrong it is and ask him anyway. Ahh." Meryn rubbed the side of her hand hard against her forehead. "I can't believe how weak I am."

"You're not weak. You care about him. Of course you want to be able to see him and not have to hide what you feel. That's completely normal."

"I hope so. Because nothing feels normal anymore." She unrolled one of Gracie's curls and let it bounce back against her head. "I'm glad Shane and Brendan are coming. They'll be a good distraction."

"And you won't be alone out there in the country. That's a positive thing."

Meryn rolled her eyes. "Now you sound like Jesse."

"I'll take that as a compliment. He's a good one too, Mer."

Her throat tightened. "I know." She glanced up at the sunflower clock on the opposite wall and made a face. "I better get going. The store's supposed to open in a few minutes." She gave Gracie one more squeeze before handing her over to Kate. "Thanks for the coffee. And the confirmation that I'm not completely crazy."

"There's a fine line between being in love and being crazy. Sometimes it's hard to tell the two apart."

"Kate."

"I know, I know. You're just figuring things out. You're not in love. Blah, blah, blah."

Meryn laughed. "That's right. Don't forget it."

"Don't you forget it. Because I'm pretty sure Jesse forgot it a while ago. And if I know you, and I do, you're in pretty grave danger of that little fact slipping your mind too."

Meryn shook her head and rose. Clearly she was losing either her heart or her mind, and Kate was right.

Sometimes it was next to impossible to tell the difference.

Chapter Six

Headlights arced across the trees lining the driveway, and Jesse moved back quickly into the shadows.

Meryn parked her little white Ford Kev in the driveway. On Fridays, the store was open late, so she had a pass to be out after dark.

In the strange light of night vision goggles, Jesse watched her as she started up the cement walkway toward him. He waited until she passed by, then he jumped out from behind the oak tree in the yard and caught her around the waist.

Meryn started to cry out.

He covered her mouth with one hand and leaned in close to whisper, "It's okay. It's me." When she relaxed, he loosened his grip.

She turned in his arms and smacked him on the chest. "You scared me."

Jesse laughed. "Sorry. I couldn't resist."

"What is all this?" She waved at the night vision goggles.

"I had to park a couple of kilometres down the road and make my way here in the dark. Since I do have all this military equipment at my disposal, I thought I might as well use it."

"Am I green right now?"

"Yes. Completely. And here's something you may not know about yourself—you're still beautiful, even with green skin and hair."

She brushed several wayward strands from her face. "I doubt that. I've spent the day unpacking books and dusting shelves. I'm sure I'm an absolute mess."

Jesse pulled off his goggles and tightened his hold on her. "Trust me on this. You are more beautiful every time I see you." He started to lean in, then stopped, eyes narrowing. "You're shaking. Did I scare you that badly?"

Meryn stepped back and he let her go. "Sorry. A bit of an overreaction, I know. I guess I thought ..."

"What?"

She glanced around the yard before looking back at him. "Have you ever come here before and not told me?"

"No, of course not. Why?"

"It's just ... every once in a while I hear something, a rustling in the bushes. I'm sure it's nothing—the wind maybe, or some kind of animal—but it always makes me feel kind of creepy, like someone is spying on me."

Jesse pulled the goggles back on. He scanned the trees and bushes lining the driveway and the rail fence at the top of the hill leading down to the pond.

Nothing lurked in the shadows.

Still, every one of his senses went on high alert at the idea that anyone could be watching Meryn. "You know I've never liked you being out here by yourself."

"I know. But I'm not here by myself anymore. Not for a while anyway. Brendan and Shane are here. Is that why you came? To meet them?"

"I mean it Meryn. If you won't move ..."

"I won't."

His jaw tightened. *So stubborn.* As concerned as he was about her safety, there were times when he could just throttle her. "Then you need to be careful. You could use more lights in the yard, for one thing. If your brothers can put some up while they're here, that would be great. Otherwise I'll come and do it. And you should keep your door locked too. All the time, day or night."

Meryn bit her lip.

He didn't like the hesitation.

"I will."

Jesse gripped her arms lightly. "Promise me."

"I'll try to remember. I promise."

"Good. Thank you."

"You're welcome. Now come and meet my brothers." She grabbed his hand and took a step toward the house.

Jesse didn't move.

Her eyes were laughing when she turned back to him. "Come on. It'll be fine."

"I know, I know." Jesse glanced at the softly lit windows of the house. Shadows moved on the other side of the blinds.

"How big are they again?"

Meryn wrinkled her nose.

"Great."

She squeezed his hand. "You are a trained, professional soldier. I'm pretty sure you can hold your own."

"Don't forget decorated."

Her eyes widened. "You have a medal?"

"Four of them, actually. I don't usually mention them, but for some reason I feel the need to remind myself at the moment."

"So you'll be fine. Let's go, then." She tugged on his hand and he followed her up the walkway to the bottom of the stairs leading to the porch.

The light shining beside the door blinded him for a second, reminding him he still wore the goggles. "Wait." He let go of her and removed them. After tossing them on the ground beside the stairs, he unzipped the camouflage jacket and slipped it and his wool hat off, then added them to the pile. He ran a hand over his short, dark hair. "There. Do I look presentable? I want to make a good—"

She stared at him.

Jesse glanced down at his clothes. "Why are you looking at me like that? Do I have leaves all over me or something?"

Meryn shook her head. "No, nothing like that. You look … very presentable." Her voice had gone husky. "That shirt really … the colour … it brings out the green of your eyes. It's … you look …"

The corners of his mouth twitched. "Meryn O'Reilly, you're stammering."

"Excuse me. I'm still recovering from the shock of being leapt upon in the dark. I think I can be forgiven for stumbling over a few words."

His smile widened. "Leapt upon? Really? And is that actually the reason?" He moved closer, until they were almost touching.

She swallowed hard. "Of course. What else …?"

Jesse slid a hand to the back of her neck and pulled her to him. His mouth found hers and he savoured the feel of her lips on his and the taste of her cherry lip gloss. Maybe they could just stay out here a while longer. This was far better than …

The front door crashed open. "Meryn. What is taking you so—? Oh."

Jesse let go of her abruptly. *Definitely not the first impression I wanted to make on her brothers.*

Meryn winked at him before turning and climbing the porch stairs.

Jesse started up after her. From the pictures she'd shown him, he recognized the huge, linebacker type in the doorway, face set like granite, as Brendan, the younger of her two brothers. Also the one Jesse needed to be most careful of, as Meryn had told him about Brendan being a bit of a hothead.

"Brendan, this is Captain Jesse Christensen. Jesse, my brother Brendan."

"Nice to meet you, Brendan. Meryn's told me good things." Jesse stuck out his hand.

Her brother waited a full five seconds before he reached out and took it in a point-proving grip.

Jesse forced himself not to wince.

"She's told us things about you too."

He didn't hold Brendan's hostility against him. When Meryn had been arrested for distributing Bibles and sentenced to fifteen lashes, Jesse had been forced to carry out the punishment. It was the hardest thing he'd ever done. She understood why he'd had to do it, but he wasn't sure her brothers ever would. Maybe it had been a bad idea, coming out here unannounced. Probably should have given them a little more time to settle in and get used to the idea of him being in Meryn's life. Jesse had to brush by Brendan to follow Meryn into the kitchen. He caught her brother's look as he did, and repressed a sigh. Better to face this head on. Something told him that, unless he did, they were unlikely to get used to the idea of him at all.

Meryn marched through the kitchen and into the living room.

Jesse followed her.

Shane tossed a magazine onto the coffee table and stood up when the three of them came into the room. His expression didn't change when Meryn introduced them, although his dark eyes did harden slightly. He shook Jesse's still-throbbing hand firmly, but not so firmly that Jesse was tempted to sink to his knees.

Meryn attempted small-talk, but when none of the others responded, her words trailed off.

No one spoke for a moment, until Shane broke the awkward silence. "Meryn, why don't you put on some decaf?"

When she didn't move, Jesse touched her arm. "I could use some, if you don't mind. It's pretty cold outside." Which was true, although it was considerably colder inside, in spite of the flames roaring behind the glass in the woodstove.

She exhaled loudly. "Fine." As she turned to go, she shot a look at Brendan. "Try not to be a Neanderthal, for a change."

"Who, me?" He offered her a small smile that disappeared the second her back was turned.

Jesse faced the two brothers. Shane was about his height and build. Brendan was only an inch or two taller, maybe six foot four, but with his size, at least 250 pounds of solid muscle, he dominated the room. The two of them side by side, black hair gleaming in the firelight, made a formidable sight. Both stood with their arms crossed over their chests.

Jesse desperately wished he could do the same, but he kept his arms hanging loosely at his sides. He met their penetrating stares steadily. When neither of them spoke, he lifted a hand, palm up. "Go ahead. I promise you there's nothing you can say to me that I haven't said to myself a thousand times."

"You hurt our sister." Brendan flung the accusation at him like a rock.

"I know. I'm sorrier for that than I can say."

"We should take you outside and rip you apart."

"I wouldn't blame you."

Brendan took a step forward.

Jesse braced himself, but Shane shot out an arm and stopped his brother with the back of his hand against Brendan's chest. "Why didn't you just refuse to do it?"

"If I had, the lieutenant on base would have done it, and he's as close to a pure evil human being as I've ever met, other than ..." Jesse stopped and cleared his throat to cover up the fact that he'd been about to name their half-sister, Annaliese, an informant for the army, who went by the well-deserved code name Scorcher.

Annaliese had always hated Meryn and had turned her in to the army when Meryn broke the law by smuggling Bibles. Although Annaliese was the most stunningly beautiful woman Jesse had ever met, the image of her that flashed through his mind now made his skin crawl, and he pushed the mental picture away roughly. He had enough to deal with at the moment.

"The only other option was to leave the country and take Meryn with me. I tried to talk her into that, but she refused to live her life on the run. Believe me, if I could have come up with an alternative, I would have grabbed it."

Both men studied him in silence.

Jesse didn't look away under the intense scrutiny.

Shane uncrossed his arms. "What are your plans?"

"Plans?"

"Yeah. Meryn says you're a believer now. But you're still with the army." He glanced at Jesse's bare wrists. "How does that work?"

"Meryn convinced me that I could be of more use if I stayed. It's tricky, I admit, but so far I don't think anyone suspects anything, other than my superior officer, Major Donevan, who knows everything. Fortunately, while he's not a believer yet, he is sympathetic to the cause. He's also my best friend and willing to help, so I'm not completely alone there."

"That's good. I don't imagine it will go over well if they find out where your loyalties lie. Is it wise for you to come here, given that that's the case?"

"No, it likely isn't. I don't usually, but I took a chance tonight, so I could meet the two of you."

Brendan's arms remained firmly crossed. "It's dangerous for Meryn to see you anywhere. Don't you think it would be better, for her sake, not to see her at all?"

A loud thud stopped Jesse from answering.

All three of them looked toward the doorway.

Meryn had carried the pot of coffee and four ceramic mugs into the room on a tray and banged it down on a small wooden table. Clearly she'd caught Brendan's last words.

In spite of the treatment Jesse had received from him, he felt a twinge of sympathy for the man.

Eyes blazing, Meryn stalked across the room and stopped inches in front of her hulking brother. She jabbed her right index finger into his massive chest. "Brendan, don't you dare come into my home and start telling me who I can and cannot see. You are not my father, and I am not a child. Jesse and I are well aware of the danger, but we have decided to see each other anyway. So you can just back off and keep your big nose out of our business." Her left fist clenched.

As happy as Jesse was to see her fighting for them, he did wonder if he should try to stop her before she took a swing at her brother.

Before he could move, Brendan stopped her himself by laughing. "All right, kid. All right. Ouch." He uncrossed his arms, finally, and wrapped his hand around her finger to pull it away from his chest. "You've made your point."

"Good. And don't call me *kid*."

Brendan grinned and pulled her into a bear hug.

Meryn gave him a few seconds before extricating herself and smoothing down her hair. "I'm glad that's settled. Now can we all sit and have a cup of coffee like civilized people?"

"I'll get it, assuming the cups survived your wrath better than Brendan did." Shane waved a hand in the direction of the couch. "Sit, Jesse. If you and Meryn are going to be together, and apparently you are, we should get to know each other better."

Laughter that verged on hysteria welled up in Jesse, but he reined it in as he sat down on the couch beside Meryn.

Brendan pulled an armchair closer as Shane set the tray down on the coffee table and handed Jesse a steaming cup.

"Thanks."

"You're welcome." Shane's eyes were still guarded but considerably warmer as he took the chair across from Jesse.

Meryn's older brother appeared to be a man worth getting to know. Brendan too, for all his bluster. He clearly cared deeply for his sister and would do anything to keep her safe. Something he and Jesse had in common. Hopefully, with their first meeting over, the three of them would be able to put the past behind them and move forward.

Chapter Seven

The Red Virus, so named because of the flushed, fevered skin of its victims, hit Canada with the force of a Category Four hurricane, terrorizing everyone in its path. The death rate topped fifty percent, far higher in areas where Ribometh, the most effective treatment, was in short supply or unavailable. The schools had locked their doors three weeks earlier, at the beginning of May, and non-essential businesses were starting to shut down. Everyone was ordered to stay home as much as possible.

Jesse sat on a kitchen chair as Meryn roamed around the cabin, picking various items up from counters and shelves and replacing them without seeming to have taken note of what they were. Something was clearly up. She appeared to be working her way toward telling him, so he was trying to be patient and wait her out. The bouquet of daisies he'd brought her lay on the table in front of him, and he absently fingered the petals on one. *She loves me. She loves me not …*

Meryn set a jar of brightly coloured buttons back down on a crumbling wooden bookshelf. Several mouldy books dotted the shelves, and she ran a hand over their spines, no doubt sickened at their state. "I closed the store."

Jesse nodded, even though she was turned away from him. "Probably a good idea."

Meryn didn't look at him.

He sighed as he tipped the chair onto its back legs and rested it against the wall. It made sense that Meryn would close her store to limit her exposure to people like so many others were doing. *So what's on her mind?*

Finally she turned around. Her hair, so dark it was almost black, flowed down over a blue sweater that heightened the colour of her eyes. "They're desperately short-handed at the hospital. More than a third of the staff members have gotten sick, and the ones that are left are being run off their feet."

He studied her face. *What aren't you saying?* "Yeah, I heard that. They requested help from the military, and we sent a team over, but we're overextended too, trying to enforce the curfew and the quarantines and all the closures."

"They've sent out a frantic plea for volunteers."

A cold, hard ball formed in the pit of his stomach. She wasn't going to offer to help, was she? For once he did want her out in the country, as far from what was going on in the city as possible. What she was talking about was the complete opposite, heading straight into one of the most dangerous spots on the planet at the moment—a building filled with a deadly, airborne virus. "You don't have any medical training."

"I know. They don't care about that anymore. They're just looking for people to sit with the sick, to apply cold compresses to try and bring down fevers, and to notify medical staff in case of an emergency or …"

"Or what?"

"Death."

His throat tightened. "Please tell me you're not thinking about doing it."

Meryn rubbed both palms over her jeans. "Someone has to."

The front legs of the chair hit the floor with a thud as he stood up. "That someone doesn't have to be you."

"Why not me?" Her voice faltered as he walked toward her, but she lifted her chin, clearly prepared to do battle.

Well, he was a trained soldier. Battles were what he knew. *Bring it on.* "Because it's not safe." He stopped inches from her and drew himself up to his full height. He wasn't particularly proud of using the stance to intimidate her, but he was desperate enough at the moment to employ any tool at his disposal.

Meryn looked at him and he read in her eyes what she was going to say before she said it. "Why should I be safe?"

Jesse's fists clenched. Using his own words against him was low.

Effective, but low. *Because I want you to be. Because I need you to be.* His shoulders slumped. Not good enough arguments. Unfortunately, no others would come to mind.

Meryn's face softened as she reached for his hands. "These times aren't about being safe, Jesse. They're about doing the right thing. Doing what we are called and compelled to do, whether or not it's dangerous. And persevering to the end, no matter what we face along the way. I'm a better candidate than most people. I have time now, with the store closed. I don't have any children who need me to be there for them. And, not that I think it will come to this, but if it does, I am ready to die."

"But I'm not ready for you to die. And you may not have children who need you, but you have plenty of other people in your life who would be devastated if we lost you." He pulled his hands from hers. "Have you told Shane and Brendan what you're thinking of doing?"

She looked away.

A tiny flicker of hope ignited inside him.

"I haven't yet. I wanted to tell you first."

Tell him, not talk to him about it. "They have a right to know. Your going to the hospital and coming back home will put them in danger too, you know."

She swung her gaze back to meet his. "Is that really why you want me to tell them? Or are you hoping they'll join forces with you to try and talk me out of it?"

His jaw tightened but, since she wasn't wrong about his motivation, he didn't answer.

"Fortunately, they've gotten work with a construction company and they're away a lot. I won't see them much and, if the worst happened and I did get a fever, I'd go to the hospital before the cough developed. I should be okay, though. There are strict procedures in place for putting on protective gear before going inside and for removing it afterward."

"And yet a third of the staff members have come down with the virus," Jesse said bitterly.

"They probably got sick outside of the hospital. They're extremely cautious there."

His eyes narrowed. "How do you know all this?"

Meryn bit her lip.

The cold ball in his gut hardened to ice. "You've already signed up, haven't you?"

"Yes."

"So this isn't really you and me discussing a possibility. It's you informing me that you've already decided to go ahead and risk your life without any input from me."

"I'm sorry you don't like it, I really am. I don't want to go against you in this, but I know it's the right thing to do. The only thing is ..."

"What?"

"I don't want to put you at risk. So I don't think I should come here for a while."

He didn't want to make this decision any easier for her, but he wouldn't lie to her. "You don't have to stop coming here. When Caleb and I were in a hospital in Austria three years ago, we came down with the virus during the first Reds outbreak. We survived, if barely, so we're both immune now."

Relief flashed across her face. "That's good. I'm glad to hear you're not in danger from this."

He grasped her arms. "No, I'm not in danger now. But that immunity came at a high cost. It was awful, Meryn. The original SARS was bad enough, but this genetic mutation is far worse. It strikes hard and fast. For the first few hours, before I lost consciousness, the pain was so bad I wished I *would* die. I'd never want to see you go through that. Never."

"I'll be careful." Her words were quiet but threaded through with steel.

Jesse let her go. "I don't suppose it would make a difference if I ordered you not to do it?"

A faint smile played at the corners of her mouth. "I'm not one of the soldiers under your command."

"I know. Sometimes I really wish you were." He ran a hand over his head. "There's nothing I can say to change your mind?"

"No. I'm sorry. This is something I have to do."

"Stubborn Irishwoman."

Her smile broadened. "You might as well know now."

Jesse snorted. "Believe me, lady, I've known that from day one."

"So you're okay with this?" She had such a hopeful look on her face he couldn't bring himself to respond in the negative as vehemently as he would have liked to.

He shook his head. "No. But I will, under duress, admit that I am proud of you. As much as I hate the idea, this really is brave of you, and selfless. Do not tell your brothers I said that, though. We have just barely made it onto firmer footing, and I'm sure they wouldn't appreciate me encouraging you in any way."

"Well ..." Meryn moved closer and wrapped her arms around his neck. "They might not, but *I* appreciate it."

"Really?" His eyebrows rose. "How much?"

"This much." She pulled him down to meet her and pressed her lips to his.

Conflicting emotions coursed through him as his arms circled her waist. Love. Desire. An almost paralyzing fear of losing her that he had to push back firmly. *She isn't mine.* She belonged to God and had to answer to him first. Still, an equally strong urge gripped Jesse, to hold her like this, where she was safe, forever. Then she lifted her head to meet his eyes, and he sighed.

He couldn't hold on to her forever. He had to let her go. Something he should be getting used to by now but never would.

She gripped his forearms. "I better get home."

"When can we meet again?"

"Friday?"

"That should work." He reached for the royal-blue windbreaker she'd hung on the hook by the door and held it up for her. "What do Shane and Brendan have to say about you sneaking out at night to come over here?"

She slid her arms into the sleeves of her jacket but didn't answer.

"You haven't told them? How have you managed to keep that a secret?"

"They've been away a few of the times. When they're home, they tend to go to bed early, so I wait until they do before I leave. Like you said, you've just gotten on solid ground with them, and I don't want to do anything to threaten that, either. But I will tell them, soon." She zipped her jacket and gathered up the bouquet of daisies.

Jesse grasped her arm. "Meryn."

She turned to him.

"You'll be careful?"

"I told you I would be."

"I need to hear it again."

A faint smile lit up her eyes. "All right. Yes, I will be careful. I'll follow procedures exactly, and I won't take any unnecessary risks. I promise."

"Thank you." That was the best he was going to get. Now he'd have to put her in God's hands and trust him to keep her safe. *Easier said than done.* "Can I pray for you?"

"Yes. Please."

Jesse took her face in his hands and prayed a blessing over her, asking God to protect and keep her, and to watch over all those they loved. He ended with a plea for healing for those who had already fallen ill, and for peace to overcome fear, not only in their country, but around the world.

When he finished, she covered his hands with hers. "Amen."

Jesse kissed her again, then forced himself to let her go.

"See you Friday?"

"I'll be here."

"You better be." Meryn flashed him a grin before slipping out the door. She crossed the small clearing and entered the woods.

Almost immediately she disappeared from sight, but he stood, straining to hear the crunching of leaves and cracking of small branches beneath her hiking boots that told him she was still nearby. Then those, too, faded, swallowed up by the thick, silent darkness of the night. Only then did he go back inside and extinguish the light they had used to keep that darkness at bay. Not that it had done them one bit of good that night, or any other night for that matter. He stabbed at the button to turn off the generator.

In spite of their best efforts, no matter how many lights they lit, the darkness always seemed to come for them.

Chapter Eight

Meryn held her double-gloved hands under the running water and scrubbed them hard. She shook off the moisture and turned around with both arms held out from her sides. Goggles protected her eyes as the doffer sprayed her from neck to foot with chlorine. After pulling off her apron and outer gloves, Meryn washed her hands again and submitted to another dousing of chlorine. When the zipper of her yellow overalls had been liberally sprayed, Meryn pulled it down and wriggled out of the suit, careful not to touch the outside of it. After every step, she held her hands under water and washed the gloves thoroughly—at least ten times throughout the extensive process. Then she dropped the goggles she'd been wearing into a bucket of bleach as they, along with the apron and boots, would be reused. The rest of the protective gear would be tossed into the incinerator.

After eight hours in the hospital with the sick and dying, Meryn gulped in the fresh, warm late-May air as though it were food she could consume. She had intentionally parked her car several blocks away to give herself time to clear her head. After working five shifts, she had developed a routine. With every block she walked, she shed the stark, heart-wrenching images of the day like she shed the protective garb she wore in the hospital—slowly, deliberately, a layer at a time.

For the most part, she was able to leave the memory of patient after patient writhing in pain or gasping for air or growing still as death claimed them, in a discarded pile behind her, like the tainted clothing. Some still clung, though, casting a shadow over her waking hours and driving her to bolt upright in bed at night, sweating and shivering as the last vestiges of a nightmare slowly faded. Although she'd only been helping out for a week, she'd gained a much deeper understanding of the post-traumatic stress disorder that haunted soldiers returning from a war zone.

The same stress that still haunted Jesse.

Meryn stopped on a street corner and braced herself against the side of a brick building to catch the breath that had hitched at the thought. What had Jesse seen and done on the battlefield? After what she had witnessed the last few days, she couldn't imagine any greater horror, but that had to be exactly what he had experienced.

I'll spend the rest of my life trying to bring him joy to make up for all that sorrow. The intensity of the vow startled her, and she pushed away from the building. Where was her car? Jesse would be waiting for her at the cabin in a couple of hours. She smoothed her hair, tangled from the mask and goggles, back from her face. *I need some time to get ready before I see him.*

Brendan and Shane had been gone all week on a construction job, so she still hadn't had a chance to tell them that she was helping at the hospital or that she was meeting with Jesse regularly after dark. She wasn't looking forward to either conversation, but she couldn't keep those facts from them much longer. If she was lucky, she would get one more reprieve, as they usually came home exhausted from their trips and may already have gone to bed, especially since her shift at the hospital had lasted longer than usual that day. Dusk was already settling in. She'd have to hurry if she was going to make it home before curfew.

Meryn spotted her car halfway down the block and started toward it. A toddler in a bright-yellow sundress, red curls tumbling almost to her shoulders, stood barefoot on the cold cement sidewalk twenty feet in front of her.

Meryn's chest clenched. *Gracie.* She started for the girl, but stopped when she got closer. Of course it wasn't Kate's daughter. Not out here alone.

The girl's cheeks were flushed bright red and tears streamed down her cheeks. Both tiny hands pushed against her chest as her little body was seized by a paroxysm of coughing.

Oh no. Meryn searched the area wildly. Where were the girl's parents? Why was she out here without an adult?

Meryn's heart sank. Reds orphans were becoming far too common a sight on the streets. Child Services couldn't begin to keep up with the numbers, and they wouldn't take in any children who had been exposed to the virus, anyway.

There were few other people on the streets. Those who had ventured out wore masks and hurried by the child, skirting widely around her as they did.

The coughing stopped and the little girl reached out to a man passing by.

He lunged away to avoid her grasp.

The toddler slipped off the curb and tumbled onto the concrete road.

Meryn glanced down the street.

A truck and several cars headed in their direction. They'd only be a couple of feet away from the child when they sped by. If she moved at all, she would crawl directly into their path.

Jesse. The promise she'd made to him, to be careful and not take any unnecessary risks, flashed through her mind.

Vehicles hurtled closer, rapidly closing the space between them and the child.

Wailing loudly, the little girl flipped over onto her hands and knees. Another spasm of coughing gripped her.

Meryn touched her fingers to her mouth. What if that actually were Gracie? And what if no stranger passing by would help, just allowed her, sick and suffering, to wander into traffic?

It was unconscionable. Meryn couldn't leave her there.

The child's life wasn't worth less than her own.

The little girl struggled to her feet.

The truck was half a block away.

Terrified eyes met Meryn's and held them.

The last of Meryn's resistance crumbled when the girl held up tiny arms toward her. *God, help me. Keep us both safe.* Shoving back her fear, she hurried toward the toddler. When she reached her, Meryn slid her hands under the child's arms and swung her away from the road.

A blast of hot air pummelled them as the truck roared by.

Meryn cradled the child to her and half-turned to protect her from the grit that flew up from the wheels of the truck.

The child coughed again and Meryn pressed a hand to the soft curls, tucking the girl more tightly against her chest.

A woman scurried by, casting a dark look back over her shoulder as she did.

Ignoring her and the other people on the street who scuttled away from them like wild animals from a torch, Meryn tightened her grip on the child and, almost at a run, retraced her steps to the hospital.

Chapter Nine

Jesse paced back and forth in front of the fireplace in his quarters. Something wasn't right. An unsettled feeling had kept him from eating much dinner in the mess hall, and he'd come straight back to his room afterward to avoid having to make conversation with anyone. For the twelfth time since he'd returned, he glanced at the antique clock on the mantel.

Still a while before he could leave the base and go to the cabin to meet Meryn.

He couldn't be away for more than a couple of hours without raising suspicion, so it didn't make sense to head over early and waste precious time waiting for her to arrive. He'd give anything to be able to contact her, but the risk of interception was too great. His i-com was secure, but he couldn't count on hers not being tapped. Unless he knew for sure there was a problem, he couldn't take the chance.

Likely everything was fine. She'd been at the hospital all week but had promised to be careful. He shook his hands, trying to get rid of the excess adrenaline powering through him. *What is the matter with me?*

Until he saw her and knew she was okay, he couldn't stay in his quarters, not without losing his mind. Jesse grabbed the keys for his jeep and headed down the long hallway toward Caleb's office. When he reached it, he knocked lightly on the door and pushed it open.

Caleb looked up from his computer when Jesse closed the door behind him. "Hey."

"Hey, Cale." Jesse wandered over to the huge wooden desk and dropped onto one of the leather chairs. "Has anything happened?"

"What do you mean?"

"I don't know. All evening I've had this feeling that something's wrong. I can't put a finger on it, it's just this sense I have. Is something going on?"

Caleb folded his hands together on the desk. "Seems like something is always going on these days. This Red Virus thing has everybody on edge, of course, but that's not new. I did get a bulletin a couple of hours ago about another attack on a mall in the States today. Five gunmen stormed the place and killed twenty people. Not sure if that's what's affecting you."

Jesse winced. Caleb was better than he was at compartmentalizing these things and not letting them get to him. Although similar reports came in with alarming frequency, they never failed to sicken Jesse. "I don't know. Maybe. I might have caught a bit of that on the news in the mess hall, and it didn't really register until now."

"Are you still going to see Meryn tonight?"

"If it's okay with you."

Caleb tented his fingers in front of him. "Do you think something's happened to her?"

He shook his head. "I'm sure she's fine or I would have heard. I'll feel better after I see her, though."

"I'm sure." Caleb grinned. "Yeah, it's okay, as long as you're careful. I put it on record that I was sending you into town on curfew enforcement tonight."

"Good. I'll leave now and drive around a bit, see if I spot anyone out who shouldn't be. Then I'll head over and see Meryn before I come back."

"Sounds like a plan." Caleb waved a hand toward the door. "Message me after you see her to let me know she's okay."

"I will. Thanks, Cale." He started for the door.

"Don't do anything I wouldn't do."

Jesse stopped, his hand on the doorknob. "Since that doesn't restrict me too much, shouldn't be a problem."

"I mean it, Jess." The teasing was gone from his friend's voice, and Jesse looked back to meet his serious gaze. "Be good and be careful."

"I'm always careful." Jesse shut the door behind him and covered the distance to the end of the hall almost at a jog. He stopped abruptly when he turned the last corner before the exit and nearly ran headlong into another officer. "Lieutenant."

Lieutenant Gallagher nodded, but the smirk that seemed a permanent feature on his face undermined any hint of respect. "Captain." He flicked a finger toward the keys in Jesse's hand. "It's late to be heading out, isn't it?"

"I guess it is, but of course it's tricky to do curfew checks before curfew actually starts." The comment slipped out before he could stop it, and Jesse mentally kicked himself. Rising to the lieutenant's bait only caused trouble, and Jesse always regretted it.

Gallagher's eyes gleamed, as if he knew he'd just scored a point. "Going out patrolling alone? I'd be happy to accompany you if you need a partner."

"Thank you, Lieutenant, but as you said, it's late and I know you've put in a long day. I don't want to add to your duties. I'll be fine."

His subordinate offered him a mocking salute. "Of course, Captain. Good night, then."

"Good night." Jesse stepped around him and walked to the exit. That was rotten luck, running into the lieutenant, of all people. Although there were no windows on this side of the building, the chilling feeling that the lieutenant's dark gaze still followed Jesse stuck with him long after he had climbed into his vehicle and driven out of the parking lot.

Chapter Ten

When Meryn entered the large gymnasium-type room that served as an admitting area for those with Reds symptoms, the rank oppressiveness hit her like a slap across the face. The patients she was used to dealing with had already been admitted and treatment begun. Although most were in pain or dying, health care workers or volunteers had taken some measures to comfort them and to sanitize the area around them. No such measures had been taken here.

Everywhere she looked, people, flushed and glassy-eyed, huddled in misery on chairs, against the walls, or on the floor. She had to step over several bodies to reach the figure sitting at the admissions desk.

"Can I help you?" The person was so covered in protective gear Meryn didn't know it was a woman until she spoke, voice harried and exhausted.

No doubt this was the short-straw assignment, working with the most wretched and desperate people in the city.

Through the goggles, the woman glanced at the grey band on Meryn's wrist and her pale-blue eyes hardened.

Meryn pulled the girl closer. "She's not mine. I found her wandering the streets."

The woman's eyes softened when the girl coughed into Meryn's shoulder, her little fingers gripping Meryn's shirt. "Do you know anything about her? Her name? Address? Where her parents are? Anything?"

"No, sorry."

The woman sighed. "Of course you don't." She waved a hand toward the room behind them. "Take a seat. We're still taking kids, anyway. Someone will come and get her."

Meryn found an open wall space and sank down on the floor, pulling her knees toward her to hold the child firmly in place. Every second in this room increased Meryn's chances of coming down with the virus, but she couldn't leave the little girl here alone.

The child gradually sank into sleep, or possibly unconsciousness. For what felt like hours, Meryn sat against the wall, praying fervently for the life of the girl and for those around her, afraid to shift to a more comfortable position and disturb the toddler even though Meryn's arms and back ached.

Finally, a man dressed in protective clothing walked over and crouched in front of them. He rested a gloved hand on the child's crimson cheek. His eyes, dark with sadness, met Meryn's over the little girl's head. "I'll take her."

She held out the little one, and he slid his arms beneath her and pulled her to him.

The girl didn't open her eyes as he lifted her.

Meryn watched helplessly as he carried her out of the room. A tear slid down her cheek, and she brushed it away with the back of her hand as she struggled to her feet.

This time, the air outside felt not only refreshing but life-giving. Meryn waited until she was a couple of blocks from the building before she allowed herself to breathe deeply. Reds symptoms usually came on within a couple of hours of exposure. She took stock of how she felt. No trouble inhaling and no pain in her chest. She touched her palms to her cheeks. *They're cool.* Maybe God had protected her, and she would be spared this illness.

Two soldiers, a man and a woman, strode toward her, frowns on their faces. Meryn looked around. Night had fallen while she was in the admitting area with the girl.

She held up a hand. "Wait."

They stopped several feet in front of her. The woman rested a hand on the butt of the pistol in the holster at her waist.

"I know I'm not supposed to be out, but I got held up when I found a sick little girl wandering on the sidewalk and took her to the hospital. When I did, I was exposed to the virus. My car is right there." She gestured toward the Kev, the only vehicle parked on the side of the deserted street.

The soldiers glanced at each other before the man pulled an i-com out of his pocket. "Name?"

Her chest tightened. Would they arrest her? If they didn't believe her story, they might take her into custody, and not only would she face another sentence, but she could infect dozens, maybe hundreds, of soldiers. "Meryn O'Reilly." Her voice rasped and she cleared her throat.

Both of them had moved farther away from her. They must at least suspect she was telling the truth.

The man touched the screen and studied it for a moment before shoving the device back into his jacket pocket. "You have been officially warned about being out after curfew. One more infraction and you will not get off so lightly. Is that clear?"

"Yes."

"I made a note on your record, so if you get stopped along the way, they'll see that you have been cleared to be out. You have fifteen minutes."

The woman jerked her head toward Meryn's vehicle. "Go straight home. If what you said is true, you should quarantine yourself for the next twenty-four hours to avoid infecting others."

The drive out to her place in the country took eleven minutes. Meryn gripped the steering wheel tightly, hoping she wouldn't get stopped again, in spite of the clearance she'd been given. Every contact with another human being increased the risk of passing along the virus. A chill passed through her as she pulled into her driveway and parked in her usual spot. Now what? She couldn't go inside and risk infecting Shane and Brendan or contaminating the house. She glanced toward the spot under the tree where they parked their work truck and her heart sank.

They weren't home yet.

Headlights down the road reflected off the rearview mirror.

Meryn ducked down in her seat. That had to be her brothers. She couldn't let them see her. They always came home tired and went straight to bed. If they saw her vehicle in the driveway and didn't hear her moving around in her room, they might assume she was already asleep and wait until morning to knock on her door.

Meryn slouched lower in her seat as the black Ford F-250 turned toward the house. She bit her lip as light sliced across her vehicle and the trees lining the driveway. Whoever was driving cut the engine, and in the sudden silence her ragged breaths sounded deafening. She stayed absolutely still as both truck doors slammed. Her throat tightened at the sound of her brothers' voices. She'd give anything to jump out of her car and run to them, tell them what was going on and let them deal with the situation. Instead, she waited until the screen and then the heavy wooden front door banged shut behind them. She sat up and fixed her gaze on their bedroom windows.

Two minutes later, a soft glow emanated from both.

Meryn rested her head against the back of the seat. If her brothers suspected she wasn't home, they would come outside to find her. If they did, she wouldn't be able to convince them to stay away. They'd insist on taking her to the hospital where, after what she had just gone through, she had no desire to go.

She waited a few minutes, then twisted her wrist to check the time.

Jesse would be at the cabin soon. It would take her fifteen minutes or more to make her way through the woods to him. She needed to go.

Meryn glanced back toward the house. Brendan's light had already gone off, and as she watched, Shane's window went dark too. It should be safe for her to get out and head over to the cabin.

A lock of hair fell over her eyes, and Meryn reached up to push it away. When her fingers touched her forehead, she yanked them back. She pulled down the visor to look at her cheeks in the mirror.

They were flushed bright red.

Chapter Eleven

Terror clawed at Meryn's throat, but she pushed it back. What should she do? From what she'd observed in the hospital, she didn't have a lot of time. She dropped her hands. *Jesse.* She had to get to him. He was the only one who could help her now.

Reaching across the passenger seat, Meryn fumbled with the glove box until the lid dropped open. She yanked out a sheet of paper from the pile inside and grabbed the stubby pencil she kept in the pocket of the door. After scrawling a few words across the page, she set it on the dash and rummaged through the glove box again until she found a thin black flashlight. She shoved it into her pocket, then yanked on the door handle and scrambled out of the vehicle. Before she headed toward the woods, she placed her thumb on the pad below the window and waited until the locks clicked.

When Shane and Brendan found her vehicle in the morning, they wouldn't be able to get inside and touch anything she might have contaminated.

Meryn made her way across the top of the hill leading down to the pond. The moon shone brightly, illuminating the opening in the trees, and she plunged through it and started along the path through the woods.

Leaves formed a nearly-impenetrable canopy overhead, blocking out most of the light.

Meryn fingered the flashlight in her pocket. She didn't want to use it, but the woods seemed thicker tonight, darker than usual. More ominous. She'd only gone a hundred yards or so into the trees when she tripped and caught herself on a log, the rough wood scraping along her palms.

Blood pounded in her ears and the world spun around her. When it slowed, she pushed herself away from the log. A chill swept over her.

Meryn stumbled another hundred yards, bracing herself often against the trees that lined the rough pathway. A sudden stabbing pain drove her to her knees, and she gasped as she pushed the heel of her hand against her chest. *Father God, I can't do this on my own. I need you. Please help me get to Jesse. Please.*

An image of the red-headed girl, little hand pressed to her chest the same way, flashed through her mind.

Focus, Meryn.

She looked around wildly. *Where am I?* The pain seared through her. She struggled to her feet and concentrated on placing one foot in front of the other along the overgrown path.

Her feet seemed so heavy all of a sudden, as though her sandals were weighted down. Another stabbing pain brought tears to her eyes, but she rubbed her hand over her chest and kept moving.

A sudden fit of coughing seized her.

Bending over, Meryn gripped her knees as her entire body convulsed. When she was able to draw in a breath, she straightened and took a few more steps. *It's so dark.*

Even the thin glow of the moon that managed to work its way through the branches seemed to be weaker and hazier, as if a veil of smoke had drifted across it.

Cold fingers of fear grazed her spine. She had to make it to Jesse. If she collapsed out here, he might not be able to find her until morning, and by then it could be too late. *My i-com.* She patted the pockets of her jacket, feeling for it, until she remembered she'd left it in her bag in the car. She felt something hard and round. *The flashlight.* She fumbled for it, no longer caring if anyone saw her. It tumbled out of her trembling fingers as she yanked it from her pocket, and she dropped to her hands and knees to feel around the dank forest floor.

Another fit of coughing seized her. When it passed, her ribs ached and the pain in her chest was almost unbearable. Tears dripped down her cheeks and onto the leaf-strewn ground. She made one more attempt to feel for the flashlight, and this time her fingers closed around the metal tube. Shaking with relief, she pushed the button, illuminating a small circle on the ground in front of her.

Meryn gasped for air as she pushed to her feet. Sweeping the flashlight over the path in front of her, she took another ten steps forward.

The light flickered and dimmed before brightening again.

She blinked, trying to clear her vision, but the light continued to waver. The ground suddenly pitched downward, and she reached for another tree to steady herself. She took one more step, but a loud, rushing noise filled her ears, and she sank down to her knees again. *Father, help me. I'm not going to make it.*

Meryn leaned back against the trunk of the tree. *I just need to sit for a minute to catch my breath.* She turned her face to rest against the pitted bark.

The cool, damp wood soothed her burning cheek. The stabbing pain in her chest made it difficult to draw in air. She coughed again and the flashlight slipped from her fingers.

The darkness the meagre light had kept at bay swept over her.

Meryn closed her eyes.

Where is she? Jesse touched the button to illuminate his watch. 9:25. Meryn was supposed to meet him at the cabin at nine, and she'd never been late. They didn't have a lot of time together, and neither of them wanted to waste a second of it. He yanked his i-com out of his inside jacket pocket and checked for messages again, but his inbox was empty.

She was spending long days at the hospital and was likely exhausted; it was possible she'd taken a nap after work and forgotten to set an alarm. He shook his head. Something in his gut told him that wasn't what had happened. There was only one way to find out.

Jesse spoke a command into the device and waited. After a moment a voice, thick with sleep, came through the speaker. "Hello?"

"Brendan?"

The urgency in his voice must have shaken Meryn's brother awake. When he spoke again, his voice was much clearer. "Jesse? What is it? Is something wrong?"

"Probably not, but can you do me a favour? Check to see if Meryn is home?"

"Of course she's home. It's after curfew."

"Could you look in her room and make sure?"

Jesse waited through the long exhalation of breath. "Just a sec."

Footsteps padded across the floor, followed by the creaking of a door.

Jesse drummed his fingers on the kitchen counter. *Come on. Come on.* Several rapping sounds told him Brendan had reached his sister's door. Jesse strained for a response from the room but heard only silence until another door creaked open.

"Meryn?"

More silence, then Brendan's voice came across the line again, worried now. "She's not here. What's going on?"

"Is her car there?" Jesse couldn't wait for Brendan to check. Keeping the i-com against his ear, he crossed the cabin to the door.

"Her car's in the driveway, but she's not in the house. Do you know where she is?"

"I have a pretty good idea. As soon as I find her, I'll let you know. Message me if you hear from her, okay? That's safer than calling."

"But—"

Jesse disconnected the call and yanked open the cabin door. Branches tore at his clothing as he struggled to follow the overgrown path in the dim light filtering through the trees. No wonder Meryn had looked so bedraggled the first time she'd done this. He'd have to get her a pair of night vision goggles for the next time she ... His chest squeezed. *Please God, let there be a next time.* Pushing back the thought, he kicked at the fallen branches in his path and used both arms to shove away the twigs and brambles that scratched at his face.

Where was she? In this light, he could walk right past her and not see her. Of course, she'd hear him, the way he was crashing through the woods. Unless she was unconscious or ... He couldn't finish that thought, either. Jesse stopped and turned in slow circles, looking for any sign that Meryn had come this way.

A harsh, rasping sound broke the stillness of the woods.

What was that? He held his breath until he heard it again.

Coughing.

It didn't sound too far away, but he wasn't sure which direction it had come from. When he heard it again, the hacking both terrified and relieved him. She was just ahead.

Jesse took a few cautious steps, then blinked and squinted into the trees to his right. Was that a light? He pushed forward another twenty feet, eyes never leaving the soft glow.

Finally he saw it. A flashlight lay on the ground, its battery almost dead.

In the faint light, he could just make her out, sitting on the ground slumped against a tree. "Meryn."

She didn't move.

Jesse scooped up the flashlight and dropped to his knees. He shone the beam in her face, heart sinking at the sight of her flushed skin. The tears that glistened on her cheeks ripped him apart. How long had she stumbled through the trees, frightened and in pain, trying to get to him? He forced himself to tamp down his emotions. He had to think, had to get her to the hospital. Jesse grasped her arms and shook her lightly. "Meryn?"

Her head slumped forward.

He shoved the flashlight between his teeth and clamped down, hoping the dull glow would offer him at least a little resistance against the vines and branches that would threaten to trip him up. Regaining his feet, he bent down, slid one hand under her knees and the other behind her back, and swung her up into his arms.

It was only two hundred yards back to the cabin, and Meryn wasn't heavy, but by the time he staggered out of the woods, the dead weight in his arms was killing his back and shoulders.

Jesse made his way to the jeep and set her on the seat, then slid in after her. Wrapping an arm around her, he gunned the vehicle down the overgrown driveway and sped toward the hospital, praying the same words over and over as he drove.

God, help me get her there in time.

Chapter Twelve

Jesse parked in an alley two blocks from the hospital. Away from the jeep and dressed in jeans, a navy T-shirt, and a ball cap, he wasn't immediately recognizable as a soldier. Not that he cared too much at this point, but if he was caught taking Meryn to the hospital and identified as military, nothing but trouble could come out of it.

The admissions area of the hospital was as depressing and terrifying a place as he had ever seen, and he'd been to some of the darkest places on earth on his tours. The horror and despair were palpable as he wove through prostrate bodies and headed for the desk.

Through goggles and a mask, a nurse looked up at him, her eyes weary from more than just exhaustion.

"My friend is sick. She needs help immediately."

The woman's gaze flicked to Meryn's wrist. She shook her head. "We're full. I'm sorry."

Shock rippled through him. "You're full?"

She waved a gloved hand at the room behind him. "Yes. We can't take anyone else. As you can see, we can't even help the people who are already here waiting."

"But she's dying. If she doesn't get help now, it will be too late." Panic tore through his gut and came out in his voice.

From the look on her face, the woman remained unmoved. Likely she'd faced enough panic this day alone to immunize her for life.

"She's been volunteering here, risking her life to help out. And now you're telling me no one will help her?"

Her gaze swept over Meryn again. When her eyes met Jesse's, they were hard. "There's nothing I can do. I'm sorry."

For three seconds he thought about charging through the doors behind her and demanding that someone do something to help Meryn. That was unlikely to do him, or her, any good. Although he suspected the nurse of baser motives, she probably was telling the truth.

Jesse felt sick. He couldn't take Meryn home and let her die. But what recourse did he have? Biting back a string of curse words, he spun on his heel and picked his way carefully through the crowded waiting room and back out into the cool night air. He'd think of something. Maybe her doctor, Rick, the one who'd taken care of her after she'd been flogged, could help them somehow. Jesse wouldn't stop trying until …

"No luck?"

He gathered in his whirling thoughts.

A man in protective gear stood behind a truck that had backed up to the delivery entrance of the hospital.

"No. They said they were full."

"Tough break. Hopefully this load of Ribometh will help a bit. I'm waiting for someone to come and take it inside."

Jesse glanced into the open back of the truck.

Boxes were stacked up at the edge, waiting to be unloaded.

He looked back at the man.

"I'm going to fill out the last of the paperwork before they come for it." He tilted his head almost imperceptibly toward the stack of boxes before walking along the side of the truck to retrieve a clipboard from the front seat. He stood, his back to Jesse, and started writing on the form.

Jesse wasn't going to get a better offer than that. A quick glance around the area confirmed that no one else was in sight. He shifted Meryn in his arms and reached for the nearest box. After tearing open the lid, he grabbed two of the small aerosol cans, shoved them into his pocket, and tightened his grip on Meryn again.

Not wanting to put the delivery person in any further danger, he walked around the back to the other side of the truck. Although he couldn't tell the man how much the risk he'd just taken was appreciated, Jesse breathed a quiet thanks as he strode away.

As soon as he reached the jeep, Jesse set Meryn on the seat. He yanked the lid off the can and cupped his hand in front of her face as he sprayed a cloud of the Ribometh into her nostrils. "Breathe it in, love.

That's it." He waited a few seconds before pulling his hand away and snapping the lid back on. That was all he could do for her for now. He slid the can back in his pocket and started the vehicle.

Outside of town, he let go of the wheel long enough to grab his i-com, speak a command, and set it on his leg.

"Jess? What's up?"

Just hearing Caleb's voice eased some of the tension of the last hour. "I need your help."

"Is it Meryn?"

"Yes. She's sick."

Caleb exhaled. "I'm sorry. Is she in the hospital?"

"No. I took her but they wouldn't admit her. They said they were full."

"Oh man. That's not good. So what's your plan?"

"I'm taking her to a cabin on the property next to hers. I'll take care of her there. I was able to get my hands on some Ribometh, thankfully, so I'm giving her that."

There was a long pause on the other end of the line.

"Cale?"

"Sorry, just trying to work all this out. I'll have to come up with a plausible reason for you to be gone for a few days. What do you need?"

"As much bottled water as you can bring me. Clean sheets and towels. Some food, I guess. Basic toiletries. That should do it."

"Where do I bring it?"

Jesse gave him directions, praying his line was still secure.

"On my way."

"Thanks, Cale."

The cabin was coming up on his right.

Jesse glanced in the rearview mirror.

No lights broke the solid wall of darkness behind him. If there was a bright side to the pandemic, it was that there were far fewer people out for him to worry about.

He pulled behind the cabin. "It's not exactly a state of the art facility, but it's going to have to do," he murmured in Meryn's ear as he carried her toward the back door. He prayed that what he had told her the night he had given her the identity bracelet was true, that unless she had done something to draw attention to herself, it was unlikely anyone would be tracking her movements. They should be safe here for a few days.

She didn't stir in his arms.

Jesse unhooked the latch with one hand and kicked the door open.

He hated to put her down on the musty old bed in the corner of the room, but until Caleb arrived with the sheets, the dingy mattress would have to do.

He rested his hand on her head. "Fight, Meryn. That's all I ask. Don't give up without a fight." With a deep sigh, he turned and crossed the room to grab a kitchen chair.

When he returned, she hadn't moved. Jesse sank down on the chair and reached for his i-com again. Time to keep a promise, although he wasn't looking forward to it. He switched from voice to audio message mode. *It's safer.* He shifted on his seat. *Coward.* When he spoke, the machine transcribed his words to writing.

Meryn's with me.

Thank God.

Brendan must have been sitting on his device, waiting to hear from him.

Are you bringing her home?

No, I can't. She's sick.

Long pause. *Is she in the hospital?*

No. They wouldn't take her. Too full.

Another long pause before a curse word slashed across his screen in bold caps. Before Jesse could reply, another word appeared, small letters this time: *sorry.*

Don't be. I totally get it. I have some medicine, and I've already started giving it to her.

Where are you?

Jesse hesitated. Her brothers wouldn't like it, but he didn't have a choice. Slowly, he spoke the words *I can't tell you,* then closed his eyes and waited.

When the device vibrated, he looked down and read a single word that tore at his heart: *Please.*

Shoving back the urge to give in, he shook his head. *I'm sorry.*

After another long pause, more words appeared on the screen. *When this is over, I am ripping your head from your body.*

He smiled grimly.

Now there was the Brendan Jesse knew and loved.

Fair enough, he answered. He wasn't too concerned. If Meryn survived, her brothers would forgive him. If she didn't—he stopped and bent forward at the pain that ripped through him at the thought—if she didn't, her brothers could do whatever they wanted to him and it wouldn't matter.

Take care of her.

You know I will. And I'll keep you updated.

Please.

That word again. Amazing how six little letters could portray such anguish. His heart heavy, Jesse ended the connection. He sent one more message, to Ethan and Kate, deeply aware of the alarm he would cause with every word, then tossed the i-com onto the small bedside table.

Meryn started coughing. The harsh, rasping cough that might have saved her life in the woods now sounded like it could end it at any minute.

Jesse turned her onto her side and rubbed her back in an attempt to get the cough to loosen its grip on her.

After what seemed an interminable length of time, it finally did and she stilled.

Heart pounding, he lowered her gently back to the mattress. While he waited for Caleb to arrive, he moved the solar generator and the lamp across the room and set them up closer to the bed. He wished he'd asked Caleb to bring him a book from his room. Sitting there listening to Meryn struggle to breathe was going to drive him out of his mind. He repented of the thought as soon as it crossed his mind. Better to hear her struggle for breath than for her to stop breathing altogether.

As long as she was struggling, she was fighting, just like he'd asked her to do.

Jesse reached for her hand, alarmed at how hot it was beneath his fingers. Clasping it tightly, he leaned in closer to her. "Don't give up, Meryn. This time I need you to be the stubborn Irishwoman I know you are and refuse to give up."

He studied her. Although he searched desperately for some kind of acknowledgment that she had heard him, nothing flickered across her face.

"That's okay. You rest. I'm not going anywhere. Rest and get better, and when you're ready to wake up and talk to me, I will be here."

Chapter Thirteen

"Thanks, Cale, I really appreciate this." Jesse set the last of the sheets, blankets, towels, food, and bottled water inside the cabin and pulled the door shut.

Caleb propped a shoulder against the post at the top of the rotting porch stairs. "No problem. Just so you know, you've taken a few days of leave for personal reasons."

"Okay, thanks."

Caleb jabbed a thumb in the direction of the cabin. "How is she doing?"

Jesse ran a hand over his head. "Not good. I've been giving her the medicine since we got back, but so far it doesn't seem to be doing much. She's still burning up, her breathing is shallow, and every time she coughs it feels as though she'll never stop."

"I'm sorry."

Jesse lifted a hand in the air. "How did this happen? After everything we've learned about preventing and controlling pandemics, how could this possibly have gotten out of control so fast?"

Caleb didn't answer.

Jesse's eyes narrowed. "You know something, don't you?"

"It's classified, Jess. And largely conjecture. I'm not supposed to discuss it with anyone."

"Please. I need to know."

Caleb exhaled loudly. "No one knows for sure why the Red Virus has spread so quickly this time, but there is a great deal of suspicion and some slowly emerging evidence that it wasn't all natural. That it was helped along, sort of like an accelerant to a fire."

Jesse blinked, trying to process that information. "You mean they think this was done deliberately? As in biological warfare?"

"Maybe. Like I said, it's mostly conjecture at this point. No one has claimed responsibility for it, but it is looking more and more like a possibility."

"Who would do that?"

Caleb shrugged. "Any number of radical groups would have done it if they could have. Most of them don't have the capability, though, and wouldn't keep silent about their part in it if they did. Based on that, CSIS is focusing on a new group."

Jesse shook his head. Another new group. Decades of fighting radical extremist groups, and every time the Canadian Security Intelligence Service rooted one out, and they and the military managed to shut it down, ten more sprang up to take its place. "Tell me about them."

"There's not a lot to tell at this point. They're different in that they work outside the grid, in person instead of online. That makes it difficult, if not impossible, to track their movements and predict what they will do next. Recruitment-wise, they don't focus on disenfranchised youth, either, like most of the groups do. They target high-level politicians and wealthy business people, the type with actual power and money and the connections to leverage both. And I said they were a new group, but only because their existence has just recently come to light. They've likely been around for years, maybe decades, slowly growing and acquiring networks and wealth until they were finally in a position to pull off an attack like this."

"For starters."

"That's true. If they could plan and carry out something this huge almost completely undetected, who knows what else they're capable of."

"Do they have a religious affiliation?"

"Not that they advertise."

"What's their motivation, then?"

"Who knows? World domination, maybe. Annihilation of the West, probably. Like I said, we don't have a lot of information on them yet."

Jesse cocked his head. "You said *almost* undetected. So we did have some knowledge of them before this happened?"

"A little. About eighteen months ago, CSIS got wind of them, and two agents managed to infiltrate one of their pods. They're the reason we know as much as we do about them. They fed us everything we have on the group until ..."

"Until what?"

"The transmissions stopped."

"Ah." His shoulders slumped. "Does this group have a name?"

"They call themselves Thrakon."

Jesse looked at him.

Caleb grinned. "I see that, as usual, much of what I'm saying is Greek to you. This time you have an excuse though; it actually is Greek. Ancient Greek, to be exact."

"For?"

"The dragon."

"Hey"—Jesse leaned against the wall of the cabin—"there's no chance they're responsible for the 10/10 bombings instead of that Horsemen group, is there?"

"Could be. I think it's wise to keep every possible option open, especially since, other than that one unsubstantiated claim right after the explosions, no evidence has verified or even pointed to the fact that Christians blew up those mosques."

Jesse waved a hand through the air. "So everything that has happened since then—the military taking over, the identity bracelets, the curfew—has all happened because of one unsubstantiated claim from a group that may or may not even be Christian?"

"Or it's all been the unfolding of some greater plan."

He stared at his friend.

"What?" Caleb shrugged. "I told you I like to keep every possible option open."

The sound of a hacking cough kept Jesse from responding. He went into the cabin and rubbed Meryn's back until the coughing eased. When he came back out, Jesse pounded the side of his fist against the weathered cabin, sending strips of grey paint spiralling to the ground. "I feel so helpless, Cale. Like there's nothing I can do for her."

Caleb shoved both hands in his pockets and stared out into the dark woods. "Do you remember being so sick in the hospital?"

"Of course. I'll never forget it."

"It was an awful time for both of us, with everything that had occurred. When we did finally leave the hospital, we never really talked about what went on there."

"No, I guess we didn't." Jesse gripped the railing.

"Can you remember anything that happened when you were unconscious? I mean, do you recall hearing anything, even while you were out, like voices or people working in the room?"

Jesse thought back. Caleb was right. It had been a terrible time. Other than when Jesse's brother, Rory, died in combat, those weeks in the hospital, first being treated for PTSD and then coming down with the virus, were the worst of his life. He wasn't sure he wanted to go back there even now, but Caleb obviously had a reason. Jesse pushed through the haze surrounding those dark days until pinpricks of memory started to return. "Yeah, I guess I did. Strange, distorted voices, like I was hearing them underwater, but I definitely did hear them."

"I was a lot sicker than you were."

That Jesse did recall with shocking clarity. He'd responded to the medicine and improved fairly quickly, but Caleb hadn't. After Jesse had come to and could sit up in bed, weak but conscious, he'd asked the doctor how his friend was doing. He had ignored the man's reassuring words and heard, far more clearly, what his eyes said—that Caleb's life hung in the balance. For another twenty-four hours, some of the most agonizing and frustrating ones Jesse had ever known, that had been the case. "I remember."

"So do I, Jess. I remember everything as if it happened yesterday. After I lost consciousness, I woke up in this sort of alternate reality. I could see vague images around me, but no colour. Everything was grey and shimmering like mirages. Every step felt like wading through the knee-deep mud of a trench. As time went on, the greyness became darker. The images faded around the edges, became less defined. Even the air around me grew heavier, as if it was pushing down on me. It got harder and harder to take a breath, harder and harder to take a step. Finally I stopped and dropped to my knees. I couldn't go on. If the darkness wanted to crush me or annihilate me, so be it. I wasn't going to fight it anymore. And then I heard it."

"What?"

"A voice. I didn't recognize it at first, but in the midst of all the darkness, that voice sounded like light and hope and happiness. It sounded like home."

"Natalie." Jesse smiled faintly at the memory of Caleb's wife. Sadly, she had died of cancer a year after Caleb had nearly lost his battle with Reds.

"Yes. She'd flown to Austria and was sitting by the bed talking to me, calling me, begging me to come back to her. I heard her, faint and distorted, but gradually growing clearer and clearer. I resisted for a while. It seemed so much easier to give in to the darkness. But the voice came again and again. She wouldn't let me go. I finally struggled to my feet and started toward it. I stayed focused on that voice every step, all the way to her."

Jesse's throat thickened. "And you woke up."

"I woke up." Caleb reached out and clasped Jesse's shoulder. "That's what you can do for Meryn, Jess. You can be there for her. You can talk to her. And you can bring her back."

Chapter Fourteen

Prickles of electricity tingled over Kate's arms. "Meryn's car is here."

Ethan opened the back door of their van and undid the seatbelt that secured Gracie's car seat. He lifted her up into his arms. "Yeah. Shane said it was here last night too. Obviously she left the property another way."

"How …?" She froze. The pieces clicked together in her mind like the combination of a safe.

Ethan rounded the back of the vehicle and opened the door so Matthew could scramble out. "Here." He held their daughter out to Kate. "If you take her, I'll grab the …" He slowly lowered Gracie to the ground. "What is it?"

"Nothing."

Ethan shot a look at Meryn's car and back at her. "Matthew, take your sister up to the house, okay? We'll be right there."

"Come on, Gracie." Matthew grasped her elbow and tugged her up the walkway toward the front porch.

"Kate."

She met her husband's gaze.

"You know where she is, don't you?"

"Not for sure, but I have a pretty good idea."

"Where?" Ethan held up a hand. "No wait, don't tell me. I don't want to know. Just promise me you won't try to go there."

"I won't. There's nothing I can do, but it helps, just knowing."

"Good." He glanced toward the house. "I wouldn't let Shane and Brendan know you suspect where she is."

"No, that would be a bad idea. I don't want to lie to them, though."

Ethan handed her a suitcase. "Well, hopefully they won't ask." He grabbed the other bags and followed her to the house. They caught up to the kids near the top of the stairs.

"Welcome, Williams family." Shane held the kitchen door open for them.

"Hi, Uncle Shane." Matthew held out his hand solemnly.

Kate was struck, as she was more and more lately, by how like a little man he was becoming. Her heart squeezed. Life really did fly by too quickly.

Shane shook her son's hand. "Good to see you, sir."

Matthew's freckled face split into a grin. "You too."

Shane reached for Gracie, swinging her high up into the air until she squealed with delight. "And how's my favourite redhead?"

"Hey," Kate protested, as she and Ethan walked into the kitchen.

He laughed as he set her daughter down. "It's a tie." He kissed Kate on the cheek before turning back to the kids. "There are toys in the living room."

"Did you get out the train set?" Matthew asked eagerly, suddenly a five-year-old boy again.

"Yep. Uncle Brendan and I set it up this morning." Shane's smile faded as the two kids trotted from the room.

Kate touched his elbow. "How are you holding up?"

He ran a hand over his face. When he dropped it, dark circles shadowed his eyes. "It's been hell, to be honest. Just sitting around waiting to hear how she is."

"I know. It's incredibly frustrating."

"It really is. Every time the i-com buzzes, I think ..." He blew out a breath. "Like I said, it's been hell."

"Where's Brendan?"

"In the barn taking out his frustrations on the punching bag. I'm pretty sure he's beaten the stuffing out of the thing by now, but it's keeping him out of trouble, anyway."

Kate grinned wryly. "That's always good."

The sound of children's laughter drifted in from the other room. Shane shoved his fingers through his hair. "Look, I should have discussed this with you before you came over, but I hope it's safe here for the kids. We really don't know what happened with Meryn last night between when she drove home and when she took off again. We've been in her room and in the kitchen and living room most of the night and we're fine, so I'm assuming she didn't come in the house and touch anything—"

"She didn't."

All three of them turned as Brendan pulled open the screen door. His grey T-shirt was soaked with sweat and his dark hair was tousled.

Kate's chest tightened at the wild look in his eyes. *Glad he's got a punching bag to take the brunt of that pent-up aggression.*

Shane's brow furrowed. "How do you know?"

"She left a note on the dashboard of her car. I couldn't get in because she locked the door, but she said she loved us both and she was sorry she had to go, but she was sick and needed to get help. She also wanted us to know she hadn't come into the house."

"That's good, I guess."

"Is it? If she had, we would have known she was sick, and we could have helped her."

"And gotten sick ourselves. That wouldn't have been a whole lot of help to anyone."

Some of the fire left Brendan's eyes. "I know. Sorry, Kate, Ethan. I've been going a little crazy."

Ethan clasped Brendan's shoulder. "We're all going a little crazy. It's hard to sit around waiting for news when we'd rather be doing something to help."

Kate nodded. "Speaking of which, what can we do? Have you eaten lately?"

Shane and Brendan looked at each other as though that was something they hadn't even thought about for a while.

Ethan pulled open the fridge door. "If you have eggs, I'll make omelettes."

Kate started to follow him. "I'll put on coffee. You both look like you could use some."

Shane stopped her with a hand on her arm. "Thanks for being here. It helps more than you can know."

She covered his hand with hers. "We couldn't be anywhere else. We'll get through this together, okay?"

"Okay."

"I'm glad you're here too." Brendan wiped beads of sweat off his forehead with the sleeve of his T-shirt. "And I'll show you my appreciation by not giving you a hug. Not until after I hit the shower, anyway."

Kate waved toward the hallway. "Thank you. Go ahead and do that now if you want. Breakfast will be ready when you get back."

"Sounds good. But after breakfast it's train time with my nephew."

"He'll love that."

Brendan crossed the kitchen and headed out the door.

Shane watched him go.

Kate squeezed his arm. "He'll be okay."

"I know. It's just that doing nothing is not his strong suit. It's good the kids are here. It'll take his mind off everything."

"Yeah, they're good for that." Ethan cracked an egg and emptied the contents of the shell into a bowl. "Why don't you sit down and relax, Shane?"

"Yes, sit. I'll get you a cup of coffee." Kate planted her palm between his shoulder blades and gave him a gentle push toward the table. "I'm guessing you didn't get a lot of sleep last night."

He shrugged as he pulled out a chair and dropped onto it. "Not a lot, I guess."

"Have you heard anything from Jesse?" She poured water into the coffeemaker and reached for the can of grounds on the counter.

"He sent a message this morning saying Meryn had made it through the night. She's still unconscious and has a high fever and that terrible cough, but she's hanging in there. He promised to let us know as soon as there's any change."

"She's strong, Shane."

"I know." He sighed deeply. "I'm clinging to that."

"Have you talked to your parents?"

"Yes. I called them this morning. They're pretty upset. They really want to come, but it's not safe to travel right now. I told them I'd keep them updated."

The smells of coffee brewing and bacon sizzling in the frying pan filled the big farm kitchen. Kate handed Shane a yellow-and-white-checked mug and sat down across from him. By the time Brendan came back, in a clean red T-shirt and navy track pants, his hair still wet from the shower, Ethan was lifting omelettes onto plates.

Shane and Brendan had clearly eaten as little as they had slept since discovering Meryn was missing. They inhaled Ethan's breakfast. A warm, late-spring breeze set the lace curtains dancing above a glass vase filled with daisies on the windowsill.

It was good to be here, surrounded by her adopted family. But it was odd too. Kate felt her friend's absence much more keenly here. *I've never been in this house when Meryn wasn't.* The idea, when it came to her, was like a loose thread in a sweater. She couldn't help tugging on it, playing with it, trying to tuck it away out of sight but only succeeding at unravelling her thoughts further.

The moment Shane and Brendan were done eating, Gracie and Matthew dragged them into to the living room to play.

Kate rested a hand on the back of a kitchen chair and watched them go. She'd never really had family until she met Meryn. Her dad had left when she was eight. She had nothing but wispy, half-formed memories of him that hung in her mind like puffs of smoke from the cigarette dangling perpetually from his lips. Her mother had been devastated and sought solace in a crystal meth-induced oblivion. Kate mothered her for a few years until the latest boyfriend in a long string told her mom it was either him or the kid. Then she'd been kicked around the system for a while, clinging to what little ambition she could muster and every last penny she could save until she was able to flee to Kingston and the university.

A month after she arrived, she ran into the library to borrow a book she needed to finish an assignment. The older lady at the counter, hair tinged with blue, had pointed an arthritic finger toward an aisle.

Kate found the shelf and started running her hands along the spines of the books, searching for the right code. When she spotted the book, she reached for it. Before her fingers could touch it, someone else grabbed it. Kate straightened up quickly to face the girl with the long, nearly-black hair standing in the aisle holding *her* book. "Hey," she snapped. "I need that. I have an assignment due tomorrow."

"So do I," the girl answered, clutching the book tighter. They argued about who needed it more for a couple of minutes, until the other girl's bright-blue eyes lit up. "Look. We can share it. Come home with me and we can both work on our assignments tonight."

The word *home* held nothing but negative connotations to Kate. "I don't think so. I don't even know you."

The girl shifted the book to one arm and held out her hand. "Meryn O'Reilly. We're in the same psych class, and I've seen you around campus a lot. That red hair is hard to miss."

Kate thought about being offended, but the girl's words were as warm as her smile, and it seemed a waste of energy to get mad.

Meryn laughed. "It's a compliment. Your hair is gorgeous."

"Oh." Kate racked her brain, trying to remember a time when someone had offered her a compliment without trying to get anything in return. "Then thank you." Reluctantly she shook the girl's hand. "Kate Thompson."

"There." The smile broadened. "Now we're not strangers. And they're about to close the library." She tapped the back of the book. "Are you coming with me or—?"

"Hey."

Kate started, yanked from the past as Ethan came up behind her and massaged her shoulders. His hands were strong and warm, and after he'd worked for a couple of minutes, the tight knots in her muscles loosened. She turned to face him.

He had a dish towel slung over his shoulder.

She looked over at the sink. The breakfast dishes had been washed and put away. "I'm sorry. I meant to help with those."

"No worries. I was happy to have something to keep me busy. You were a million miles away. What were you thinking about?"

She shot a glance in the direction of the living room. The excited chatter of her children and the laughter of Meryn's brothers reverberated through the house. "I was thinking that sometimes the family you choose can be a lot closer than the one you're related to by blood."

"I believe that." He touched her face. "I chose you."

A small smile crossed her lips. "Would you do it again?"

"In a heartbeat."

Tears pricked her eyes. "I can't imagine a world without Meryn in it."

"I know." He kissed her and pulled her close. "God, you know how much Meryn and Kate mean to each other, how much Meryn means to all of us. Please watch over her, help her get well, and bring her back to us. Amen."

Kate smiled up at him. "Thank you."

He pressed his lips to her forehead, then nodded toward the living room. "Let's go check on the kids." He took her hand.

Kate's gaze stayed locked on him as he led her out of the kitchen. Meryn's parents and brothers had made her feel, from the moment she walked in their door, that she was part of the family. If they hadn't become the anchor that had been missing in her life, she would never have understood their faith, or been able to open her heart to Ethan when she met him in her final year of school.

She and Ethan settled on the couch to watch Shane, Brendan, and the kids playing with the train set. Even with the distraction of the kids laughing and enjoying themselves, the morning passed slowly. Kate's thoughts strayed continually to Meryn.

Ethan always seemed to know when she had drifted away, and would squeeze her hand or brush a finger across her cheek, bringing her back. *What would I do without him?* She glanced around the room, at all the people, except one, that she loved the most in the world gathered together. *What would I do without any of them?* She rested her head against the back of the couch. *Father, help Meryn. I know she's strong, but she needs your help now to fight. Help her get through this, please.*

Shane made them all sandwiches for lunch. After they cleaned up, the three men went out to use the punching bag and the rest of the home gym in the barn, Matthew traipsing along at their heels. Kate took Gracie upstairs.

"We sleep in Aunt Meryn's room, Mama?"

Kate hesitated. The kids had their own room in the farmhouse, like she and Ethan did. *She needs to feel close to Meryn.* So did Kate. She nodded. "All right, sweetie. Just this once."

She had meant to tuck Gracie into bed and leave her, but felt the need to crawl in and snuggle close. A new appreciation for the fragility of life and the preciousness of time spent with the ones she loved welled up in her. She'd hardly closed her eyes the night before and didn't expect her racing thoughts would let her sleep now, either, but she surprised herself by waking up two hours later.

Gracie still slept in her arms, and not wanting to disturb her, Kate stayed where she was and looked around the room.

The window was cracked open slightly, and a warm breeze drifted through the room. Nearly every item on Meryn's dresser brought back memories of their years together. A framed picture of the two of them at their university graduation, wearing caps and long, black robes, was propped up against the mirror beside a photo of her with Meryn, Shane, and Brendan, posing under a tree at their parents' fortieth anniversary celebration a couple of summers ago. There were several photographs of the four of them, and some with Meryn's parents as well, hanging on the walls. Kate really had become part of their family.

Annaliese was conspicuously absent.

Kate shook her head. How anyone could turn their back on this family and reject the love they had tried to give was beyond her. Meryn's mother still tried. She still reached out to her older daughter. Still hadn't given up hope. A shudder moved through Kate and she pushed aside all thoughts of Meryn's half-sister, wanting to focus only on good memories today.

Gracie stirred and rolled over. For a moment, confusion flickered in her brown eyes—the exact colour of Ethan's—as she looked at Kate, then around the room. "Aunt Meryn's room?"

Kate brushed the back of her fingers over her daughter's little round cheeks. "Yes, honey, this is Aunt Meryn's room."

"Is Aunt Meryn here?"

Pain shot through her chest. "No, she's sick, remember? She has to get better before she can come home."

Gracie pressed dimpled hands together and squeezed her eyes shut. "I pray."

Tears pricked Kate's eyes as she covered her daughter's hands with her own. "Yes, sweetie. You pray for her. Pray very hard."

"Dear Jesus, please make Aunt Meryn better so she can come home and nobody will be scared anymore. Amen." She pulled her hands from Kate's and scrambled off the bed. "I go find Uncle Bennan." She disappeared out the door.

Smiling at the way her little girl said Brendan's name, Kate sank back on the pillow. She'd thought the adults had done a good job of hiding their distress from the kids. No wonder Gracie had been Brendan's shadow all day. She must have sensed that something was wrong and drawn comfort from his towering strength.

The smell of meat cooking wafted into the room from outside. Kate sighed and got up, straightening the blankets as well as she could before going downstairs and into the kitchen. She stopped at the window.

All the men in the family, including her young son, were gathered around the smoking barbeque. Gracie had found Brendan and wrapped her arms around one of his legs. His hand rested on her head as he flipped burgers with the lifter in his other hand.

Several of the daisy petals in the vase on the sill had turned brown, and Kate plucked them off. The bouquet looked much fresher after she had tossed the petals into the garbage. It was silly, but she couldn't let go of the thought that, if she kept those flowers alive, maybe Meryn would be okay too.

After a supper of salad and burgers, the six of them retired to the living room to watch a classic Disney movie. The catchy strains of *The Lion King* soundtrack kept the mood in the room light until, halfway through, Shane's i-com vibrated.

For a few seconds, the adults all stared at the device on the coffee table. Then Shane snatched it up. "It's from Jesse." A frozen silence descended on the room as he scanned the message. "He says there isn't much change. She's coughing less now but he isn't sure whether that's a good sign or not. He'll keep in touch."

Every bit of energy Kate had mustered to get her through the day left her body, and she slumped against Ethan. His arm tightened around her. She rested her head on his shoulder, not sure how much more of this she could take.

Shane must have felt it too, the stripping of the lightness from the air. He stared at the TV for a few more minutes, then excused himself to go to bed.

Ethan kissed the top of her head. "The kids should go too."

Matthew leaned against her on the other side. His eyelids looked heavy.

Ethan got up and came around to pick up their son.

Gracie had snuggled up with Brendan on his La-Z-Boy chair. He grabbed a book from the basket on the floor. "I'll read to Gracie while you get Matthew settled."

Kate climbed the stairs behind Ethan and Matthew.

They had packed the Bible story book, and Ethan pulled it out of the suitcase and flipped through the pages as she helped Matthew change into his pyjamas and brush his teeth. Ethan didn't object this time when their son requested David and Goliath.

Kate stretched out on the bed, her arm around her son, as her husband read. The story struck her as appropriate for this night. Meryn was fighting the giant of Reds, while the rest of them wrestled with fear and letting go and trusting God to help them win the battle with the few small stones they had in their bag. The odds seemed insurmountable, yet young David had brought down the mighty warrior. Courage and hope seeped back into her slowly as she listened. *Father, be with Meryn. Please help her get well. Make our pathetic little stones fly straight and true as only you can.*

By the time Ethan finished reading, Matthew's eyes were shut and his breathing had deepened. Ethan closed the book and set it on the bedside table, and Kate padded after him silently as he went out of the room and back down the stairs. When they came into the living room, Ethan took her arm and inclined his head toward the La-Z-Boy. Both Brendan and Gracie had fallen asleep. Her head rested on his chest, and his arms circled her and held her tight. In the warm glow of the flickering fire, both their faces were relaxed and serene.

"Leave them be," Ethan whispered in her ear. "Brendan needs something to hold on to tonight."

Kate watched the two of them for a moment and felt the love and warmth emanating from them wrap itself around her like a soft blanket. Giving thanks for the small mercies of rest and peace, she turned and followed her husband up to bed.

Chapter Fifteen

Jesse jerked awake and looked around the room. Where was he and what had woken him up?

"Tell me!" Meryn thrashed from side to side on the small metal bed.

Reality came thundering back. What was she dreaming about? Jesse grabbed the seat of the chair and slid it closer to her. "Meryn."

Distress flashed across her face. "You have to tell me," she repeated, head whipping to one side.

Memories of the night in his quarters when he'd been tangled in the grip of a terrible nightmare and she'd calmed him with a hand on his arm flooded through him. He pushed up the sleeve of her pink shirt so he could touch her skin. His breath snagged at the heat radiating from it, and he rested his other palm on her forehead.

She was still burning up. If anything, she felt a little hotter than she had the night before.

Jesse kept his hand on her arm until she stilled and the nightmare seemed to have passed. Then he went to the kitchen area to grab a couple of water bottles and refill the bowl he'd found in the cupboard. The room was dark, and he tore several of the black sheets of paper off the windows, trying to inject not only light, but a bit of life into the place. When he'd settled himself on the chair again, he dipped a facecloth in the water, wrung it out, and folded it. He draped that one across her forehead and wet a second one to apply cool water to her lips and neck and arms and wrists. He'd give anything for ice, but he hadn't thought to ask Caleb to bring it and didn't have any way to keep it from melting, anyway.

Ribometh and water were her two best defences against the ravages of the virus. Thankfully he'd been able to get the medicine into her, since she could breathe that in. He was too afraid to try to get water down her throat in case it went into her lungs. He carefully pinched a bit of skin on her arm, his heart sinking when the skin didn't settle back into place. She was getting dehydrated, an effect pretty much impossible to avoid since she'd been burning up with a fever for almost forty-eight hours. Something needed to happen, and soon, or she would slip away from him and there wouldn't be a thing he could do to stop her.

Jesse reached for Meryn's hand. Ever since Caleb had shared his experience in Austria, Jesse had been talking to her. For two days he had spoken to her about everything she had to live for and the plans they would make when she got better. He had described in detail the house he wanted to build for them, the one he had told her about in a story the night before her sentence was carried out. He'd even talked about the dog lying on the rug in that house, imagining what breed it would be and what they would call it. Dickens, of course, in honour of the conversation in her bookstore that had sparked a deep connection between them. She hadn't responded to anything he had said, but he pressed on, encouraged by Natalie's refusal to let Caleb go.

Jesse leaned in close to her ear. "Can you hear me, Meryn?" He stroked her face, brushing back the damp locks of hair that fell across her flushed cheeks. "Come back to me. Don't leave me, please. I need you." He murmured to her for several minutes, then half-turned so he could fold an arm under his head and rest it on the back of the chair. He'd dozed off and on since they'd arrived but hadn't slept for more than an hour or two in a row. Physical, emotional, and mental exhaustion assaulted him now, tugging him down into a dark abyss. Jesse closed his eyes. *I'll just rest for a few minutes ...*

When he woke again, the sun that had streamed through the window earlier had softened. Pale light bathed the room in a rosy glow. Evening was approaching. He'd slept for a few hours.

Meryn lay completely still on the bed.

Once that fact registered in his consciousness, he froze, terror darkening his vision like an eclipse of the sun.

Then she drew in a shallow, ragged breath, and he expelled the one he'd been holding. He propped his elbows on his knees and rested his forehead on their clasped hands. "Meryn, please. Come back. I don't want to live my life another minute if you're not in it. Please come back to me. Don't go yet. It's too soon. I need you." He tightened in his hold on her hand. "I know there's pain here. And fear. And uncertainty. But there is joy too. And love. So many people love you, Meryn. *I* love you."

A slight pressure on his fingers brought his head up sharply. Meryn's eyes were open and the ocean blue of them, the slight crinkling at their corners as a faint smile played on her lips, the long, black lashes that framed them, painted the most beautiful picture he'd ever seen in his life.

"Meryn." He touched his hand to her forehead. Her skin was cool beneath his, and he almost wept with relief.

Her lips moved as though she was trying to say something.

He bent down close to her mouth.

"Thirsty," she whispered.

"I'll bet you are." He let go of her hand, reluctantly, resting it on the bed before getting up and striding to the kitchen to grab a bottle of water. When he reached the side of the bed again, he slid an arm behind her back and helped her sit up a little so she could drink. "Slowly," he cautioned, not sure how much her body could handle after being deprived of fluids for so long.

After several sips, she turned her head.

He lowered her back onto the pillow. His legs were weak and he sank onto the chair. "You scared me, lady."

Her eyes scanned the room before coming back to his face, confusion wrinkling her forehead. "What happened?"

"You got sick, remember? At the hospital."

Her eyelids flickered, like she was trying to recall, then her face cleared. "No, not the hospital."

"Not the hospital? Then how ...?"

"The girl."

"What girl?"

"On the street. Little girl with red curls. Crying and coughing."

Ah. Suddenly what had happened made sense. "She reminded you of Gracie."

"I had to help her. I'm sorry."

"Don't be sorry. I understand."

She clutched his sleeve. "My family."

"They're all together. Ethan and Kate are staying at your house until they know you're okay. I should message them to tell them what's happening."

"Tell them … I love them."

"I will." He rested a hand on her head until her eyes closed, then he bent down and kissed her forehead. "You sleep. When you wake up, I'll be here."

Her lips turned up slightly, but she didn't open her eyes.

Jesse watched her for a moment. Joy coursed through him so powerfully he thought he might explode from the force of it.

He picked his i-com up off the table and touched his finger to the screen.

Chapter Sixteen

Kate watched Brendan closely during supper. He snapped at Shane a couple of times but otherwise didn't say much. Pressure was building inside him. *When and how is that going to come out?*

The Red Virus worked its way quickly through the body. Either the fever broke and the patient woke up or, just as often, they slipped deeper and deeper into unconsciousness and died within the first forty-eight hours.

No one mentioned that fact, but as the relentless hands continued to circle the clock on the kitchen wall, the ticking sound seemed to grow louder and more ominous.

After they ate, they all went back into the living room, and Ethan turned on a kids' show for Matthew and Gracie.

Brendan jabbed at the fire for a bit before tossing the poker back into the holder with an angry *clang*. "I need some air." He stalked across the room and into the hallway. Seconds later, the screen door slammed shut.

Shane lifted Gracie off his lap and settled her on the couch. "I'll go check on him."

After he left, Kate shot a worried look at Ethan.

Matthew sat on the floor with his back to the couch.

Ethan ruffled his hair. "Watch your sister, okay, son? Mom and I are going outside for a couple of minutes."

Matthew nodded, his attention on the screen. Gracie was watching the TV too, and neither of them moved when their parents got up and headed out of the room.

Dusk had settled over the property. Tendrils of fuchsia and orange trailed across the western sky, and crickets chirped loudly in the long grass around the pond.

Under other circumstances, Kate would have sat down on the porch swing and settled in to enjoy the beautiful evening.

Brendan paced up and down the driveway. Shane leaned against the truck a few feet from him. Ethan and Kate joined him as Brendan stopped pacing. "It's been two days. Why aren't we hearing anything?"

Shane shrugged. "There's no sense in Jesse continuing to send us the same message over and over. As soon as he has something new to tell us, he will."

Brendan locked his hands together behind his head. "How did she get sick, anyway? I thought she closed the store. How could she have come into contact with someone who had the virus?"

Kate's stomach knotted. Obviously Meryn hadn't had a chance to tell them what she had been doing with her time. "She signed up to volunteer at the hospital."

Both of the brothers spun around to look at her.

Shane lifted a hand. "What? Why? And how long has *that* been going on?"

"All last week. They were short-handed and desperate. She figured that since the store was closed, she had the time, and she felt compelled to help out in some way."

Brendan shook his head. "You've got to be kidding me. Didn't you try to stop her?"

"Of course I did. So did Jesse. But she had made up her mind."

"Don't they have procedures to keep their volunteers safe? How could she have gotten infected so quickly?" A vein throbbed in Shane's forehead.

"They do. Meryn said they were extremely cautious, so I don't know how she got sick."

For a long moment no one spoke, then Brendan blurted out, "I'm going to find her."

Shane kicked at the gravel with the toe of his running shoe. "Where are you going to look? You don't have any idea where she is."

"I do have an idea."

"How could you?"

Brendan gestured toward Meryn's car. "She didn't drive anywhere. It doesn't take a detective to figure out she didn't go far."

The knots in Kate's stomach tightened. "Jesse might have picked her up and taken her away. She could be miles from here."

Brendan's gaze swung back to her. "But she's not, is she, Kate?"

"Why are you asking me? Meryn didn't message me after she got sick."

He took a step closer to her, and Ethan moved to her side. "That doesn't mean she didn't tell you something before she got sick. Jesse said he doesn't usually come here, because it's too dangerous, and she sure doesn't go to the base to see him, so where do they meet, Kate?"

"What makes you think she told me?"

"Oh, I don't know. The guilty look on your face. The fact that Meryn tells you every little thing that's going on in her life. The way you're doing everything you possibly can to avoid answering my questions." He shoved his hands in the pockets of his jeans as if he was afraid of what he might do with them if he didn't. When he spoke, he ground the words out between clenched teeth. "Tell me where they meet."

"Take it easy, Brendan," Ethan warned in a low voice.

Brendan's eyes bore into hers for another few seconds before he stepped back. "Fine. I'll find her myself. There's nothing to the south of us for a couple of miles, so if she left here on foot, she must have headed north, through the trees. When we were driving back from town, I noticed an old cabin just down the road. My guess is that's where the two of them are, so I'll start there."

"No, you won't." His back still against the truck, Shane slid over until he stood in front of the driver's side door.

"Get out of my way, Shane."

"I don't think so. I know this is killing you. It's killing all of us. But we can't go to her."

Brendan closed the space between them. Shane held up his hands, and Ethan started toward him but stopped when Brendan slammed both palms against the truck on either side of Shane's head. "I can't stand this. She could be right there, a half mile from us, dying as we speak, and none of us are there with her."

"Jesse's there. She's not alone." Shane grasped Brendan's forearms. "She doesn't want us there, Bren. That's why she didn't say where she was going. And that's why Kate's not telling you where Meryn is. You have to respect her wishes."

For a moment, Brendan didn't answer. When he did, his voice was tired, defeated. "I know. But if something happens to her ..."

"Then we'll deal with that together. But until we hear otherwise, we can assume she's alive. Jesse's doing everything he can to save her. We can't give up hope."

Brendan drew in a long, deep breath and pushed away from the truck. "You're right. We can't." He turned to her. "I'm sorry, Kate. I shouldn't have talked to you like that."

Her heart aching for him, for all of them, Kate went to him and he wrapped his arms around her and pulled her close. She drew comfort from the warm, solid strength of him, and the heaviness that had pushed down on her all day lifted slightly.

The i-com in Shane's shirt pocket buzzed. He pulled it out and touched the button to light up the screen. After a couple of seconds, he squeezed his eyes shut and slumped back against the vehicle door.

Kate couldn't draw in a breath. "Shane?" The word came out in a tortured whisper.

He held up a hand. "No, it's good news. She's ..." His voice broke and he handed her the device.

Kate read the words out loud, voice trembling. "Fever has broken and Meryn is awake. The worst is over. She sends her love to all of you and will message you herself tomorrow." Her knees buckled and she might have dropped to the ground if Ethan's arm hadn't come around her waist.

Brendan pressed both palms to his forehead. "Thank God."

"Mama?"

Gracie stood on the walkway, her eyes wide. "Why is everyone sad?"

Matthew had stopped behind her, a troubled look on his face.

Kate went to them and sank to her knees, gathering them both in her arms. "We're not sad, Gracie. We're happy. We just found out Aunt Meryn is better and she'll be coming home soon."

"I know." Her daughter's voice was muffled against her shoulder.

Kate pulled back to look at her. "How do you know, sweetie?"

A puzzled look crossed her daughter's tiny, round face. "Because I prayed."

Chapter Seventeen

Jesse drove the jeep up the farm lane and stopped at the end of the walkway. Meryn rested against him, and he put the vehicle in park and touched her knee. He hadn't been able to stop doing that—touching her—since she had woken up the day before. Her arm, her hair, her face, anything to reassure himself that she was still there, still with him. "I'll walk you to the door, but then I'll go, okay? Everyone will want to spend time with you, and I don't want to get in the way." He was surprised they weren't out there already, although he hadn't told them when he would be bringing her home.

She sat up. "You won't be in the way. They'll want to see you too. Please stay, just for a little while."

Jesse glanced in the rearview mirror. "I shouldn't sit here too long. Anyone passing by can see the jeep."

"You can park it inside the barn and close the doors."

He thought about it. He did want to go in, pretend that he was part of the family and that he belonged there with all of them. Caleb would appreciate having him back on the base too, though, sooner than later.

Meryn ran a finger along his jawline. "Please."

He caught her finger. "That is not playing fair, lady."

She laughed. "So you'll stay?"

"For a bit." He put the jeep in drive and pulled around the yard, through the big double barn doors.

Meryn climbed out of the vehicle after him and swayed on her feet.

He put his arm around her, waiting for her to regain her equilibrium. "Are you okay?"

"Yes, I'm fine. Just ready to be home."

"I'm sure your family is ready for you to be home too." Except for a moment when he was swinging the doors shut and dropping the board down into the slots to hold them in place, he kept his arm around her as they headed for the house.

When they reached the porch stairs, Meryn started up but Jesse didn't follow.

She stopped on the second step. "What is it?"

"I just remembered something. When I wouldn't tell Brendan where I had taken you, he told me that when all this was over he was going to rip my head from my shoulders." He started to turn around. "Come to think of it, I really should be getting back to the base."

Meryn grabbed his arm. "Don't worry about Brendan. He's a big teddy bear."

"A *really* big teddy bear."

"I'll protect you, don't worry." She smiled, but weariness dimmed the usual brightness in her eyes.

Jesse climbed up beside her and slid an arm around her waist to help her up to the porch. "I'll hold you to that."

Instead of walking to the door, she rested her head on his chest, and he wrapped his arms around her. Neither of them moved for a moment, until she lifted her head. In the soft glow of the porch light, her skin was pale, almost translucent. "If I don't get a chance to tell you later—thank you, for everything."

"Thank *you* for coming back to me."

"You didn't give me a lot of choice."

"That was the idea."

"Aunt Meryn!"

Jesse let her go and moved back.

Matthew pushed open the screen and tumbled onto the porch, Gracie at his heels. When they flung themselves at her, she stumbled back a step.

Jesse steadied her with a hand on her back as she pulled both of them into a hug.

Kate and Ethan came out the door behind them. Kate's hazel eyes shimmered as she pulled Meryn close. "I was so scared."

Meryn offered her a wan smile. "Me too."

"Come inside. There are a couple of other people anxious to see you."

When they reached him, Ethan pulled open the door and kissed her on the cheek. "Welcome back, Mer."

"Thanks, Ethan. It's good to be home."

Jesse's eyes narrowed at the exhaustion in her voice. She needed to go to bed soon or she would collapse.

Kate dropped her arm as Brendan filled the doorway.

He didn't say a word, just pulled Meryn to him, lifting her slightly off the ground before setting her back down.

When he let her go, she was breathless and laughing but braced herself against the doorway before following him into the kitchen.

"Hey, kid." Shane took her face in his hands and studied her as though he needed to convince himself she really was okay.

She leaned against him heavily as he led her to the living room.

Kate touched Jesse's elbow. "Jesse. We'll never be able to thank you for what you did. You saved her life."

Ethan held out his hand. "She's right. We'll never forget what you did for Meryn. It's possible you've even won over her brothers, and that's not an easy thing to do."

Jesse grasped his hand. "I'd have preferred to find an easier way to do it, but still, I'll be happy if you're right."

Ethan clapped him on the arm before letting go of his hand.

Jesse followed him and Kate into the living room and sat down on an armchair in the corner, his eyes on Meryn.

She'd taken a spot on the couch and reclined on the cushions.

Matthew and Gracie came to say good night.

Matthew hugged her, then rested his hand on her shoulder. "Want to play trains with us tomorrow, Aunt Meryn?"

She smiled. "I'd love to." She ran her fingers over Gracie's red curls.

Is she thinking about that little girl on the street?

After Kate and Ethan had taken the kids upstairs, Jesse decided to give Meryn's brothers a few minutes alone with her. He asked where the washroom was, and Meryn pointed to a hallway that ran along the back of the house. She winked at him as he walked past the couch, and a rush of warmth flowed through his chest. What would he have done if he had lost her? Jesse rubbed the side of his hand hard against his forehead. He couldn't even think about that. And thankfully he didn't have to. Not tonight, anyway.

When he dried his hands and came out of the washroom, he took his time meandering back down the dimly lit hallway. Family pictures lined the walls. From the way Meryn had described them, he identified her parents in a lot of the photos. There were quite a few of the four siblings growing up, although by the time Shane, Brendan, and Meryn were in their teens, Annaliese had disappeared from any of the shots. There were other pictures too, of people he didn't recognize. A young blond boy appeared in several of them. He looked vaguely familiar, but Jesse couldn't quite place him. He'd have to ask Meryn who he was sometime.

Ethan's and Kate's voices mingled with Shane's and Brendan's in the living room.

Now was a good time to go back in and say good night to everyone. He'd love to hang out with all of them a while longer, but Meryn needed rest and he didn't want her staying up for him. Wiping the last of the moisture from his hands on the front of his jeans, Jesse started for the end of the hallway.

A new voice stopped him in his tracks. "Well. Isn't this a cozy family gathering."

He ducked back into the shadows. *Annaliese.* Just the sound of her voice sent cold waves shuddering through his body.

A mirror hung on the wall at the end of the living room, capturing most of the room inside its large frame.

From his vantage point, Jesse had a view in the glass of Annaliese dressed all in black, her blonde hair caught up in a loose knot at her neck.

Brendan jumped to his feet.

Jesse couldn't see his face, but from the set of his shoulders Jesse could imagine the look Brendan was giving his half-sister as he advanced toward her.

"What are you doing here?"

"I came to see how my sister is, of course. I heard she was sick and I was very concerned."

The couch creaked as Shane stood too. "And how did you hear that? Are you still spying on her?"

"What are you talking about? Mother told me she was ill. And I have never *spied* on Meryn—I've only kept an eye on her so I could help her if she got herself in trouble."

Shane let out a cold laugh. "Got *herself* in trouble? You're the one who turned her in to the army. Are you trying to tell us that was an attempt to *help* her?"

"Of course." Somehow she managed to sound hurt, as though she couldn't believe he would suspect her of having ulterior motives.

Jesse rolled his eyes.

"And how exactly did you think having her arrested and flogged was helping her?" Brendan practically sputtered as he took a step closer, fists clenched.

"I wasn't the only one who knew she was giving out Bibles, you know. Word was starting to get around. I was terrified that the wrong person would find out and she would be turned over to someone who would demand the maximum sentence for her. Desperate to save her, I could only think to go to the captain. I knew he cared about her, and I thought he had some influence with the major and might be able to help. Unfortunately, I overestimated the amount of influence he had, and she ended up with a harsher sentence than I had anticipated. But it did achieve the result I had hoped for. Meryn stopped breaking the law, and I could rest easy, knowing she was safe."

Shane shook his head. "If that were true, you could have just gone to Meryn and warned her to stop handing out Bibles."

Annaliese tilted her head to one side. "Because we all know it's so easy to get Meryn to stop doing something once she's made up her mind to do it. Like volunteering at the hospital."

Jesse winced. Meryn's sister had just scored a direct hit as the sudden silence in the room attested. In the glass, he glimpsed Meryn rising to her feet and walking toward her sister. His hands fisted. He didn't want her anywhere near that woman, and it almost drove him crazy to stand back helplessly and watch as she stopped right in front of her.

"Thank you for coming, Annaliese. As you can see, I'm much better now. I appreciate your concern."

"I'm just happy that you're okay." Annaliese touched her lightly on the arm.

Meryn didn't pull away, but she did stiffen slightly. At least she hadn't been completely taken in by the web of lies her sister had tried to spin around them all.

Shane moved to stand beside Annaliese. "I'll walk you out to your car."

"All right. See you later, Brendan, Meryn." She turned and zeroed in on Kate and Ethan. "Kate, it's good of you to look in on *my* sister. I appreciate you watching out for her, and I'm sure my brothers do too."

Jesse gritted his teeth. Annaliese was staking out her claim, shoving Kate to the outside, even though she was far more of a sister to Meryn than Annaliese had ever been.

Before Kate could respond, Annaliese turned and stalked toward the kitchen with Shane following along behind her.

Jesse waited until he heard the kitchen door close behind her before he came out into the living room.

Meryn turned around. If her face was pale before, it had gone ashen now.

He rounded the couch and stopped in front of her. "Are you okay?"

Her lips quivered, as though she was attempting a smile but couldn't quite manage it. "I'm fine. I think I'll head up to bed now, though. It's been a long day."

"I'll walk you to the stairs."

Casting a quick glimpse around the room, she raised her hand slightly. "Good night, everyone."

Her fingers trembled and his stomach tightened. Tonight hadn't been the right time to confront Annaliese, but one of these days he was going to find a way to get her out of Meryn's life permanently. Jesse took Meryn's elbow and guided her to the stairs.

She paused at the bottom and looked up.

The small sigh that escaped her told him a lot. "Here." He bent down and picked her up.

She wrapped her arms around his neck as he carried her up the stairs. "Which room is yours?"

"Second one on the right."

Jesse pushed open the door with his shoulder and set her on her feet on the oval, multicoloured area rug in the centre of the room. Someone had left the lamp on beside her bed, and a warm, yellow glow draped over the room.

"Thanks." She attempted another smile. "I appear to have run out of steam."

"I'm not surprised. You've been through a lot the last couple of days. And having your sister show up probably didn't help."

"No, I guess not."

He would have liked a more adamant response than that. Jesse reached for her hands. "Meryn. Tell me you didn't buy anything that woman was trying to sell tonight."

She lifted her shoulders slightly. "I don't know. Maybe she really was trying to help me."

He tightened his grip on her hands. "I know you want to believe that. I know you want to think there is some good in her. But you can't let your guard down. She is dangerous. She turned you in for the same reason she does everything—because it suited her purposes. And if it will help her reach one of her nefarious goals, I promise you she will betray you again. Do you understand that?"

A tear glistened on her eyelashes, and Meryn pulled her hands from his and swiped it away. "Yes, I do. I'm sorry. I'm just so tired, I can't even think straight."

"I should let you get some sleep."

"Wait." She reached out and gripped his arm. "Can you stay for a minute?"

He really shouldn't. "Okay. For a minute. Much longer than that and I'm pretty sure I'll hear about it from your brothers."

"I'll be right back." Meryn turned and disappeared into the washroom off her room. "I'm shutting the door this time," she called out as the latch clicked behind her.

Jesse laughed. When Meryn had been a prisoner in his quarters, the bedroom window had bars on it but the washroom one hadn't. He'd given her strict instructions to leave the door open an inch or two when she went in there, so he could hear if she tried to escape. She may have run out of steam tonight, but somehow she'd managed to hold on to her sense of humour.

While she was gone, he wandered around the room, looking at the photos and other items scattered around on the dresser and walls. It felt deeply intimate to be here in her bedroom, surrounded by her things. He cleared his throat and turned as the door opened behind him.

Meryn's hair fell loose around her shoulders, gleaming in the soft light of the lamp on the bedside table.

For a moment he couldn't speak.

She managed a small, self-conscious smile as she brushed a strand back behind one ear. "I really need to soak for a few hours in the tub, but this was the best I could do in one minute."

He crossed the room to her. "You're beautiful. As always."

She swayed on her feet again and reached out to grab his arm.

"Come here." Jesse took her hand and led her to the rocking chair in the corner of the room. He sat down and pulled her onto his lap. Meryn rested her head on his shoulder, and he wrapped his arms around her and pulled her close.

For a few moments, the only sound in the room was the soft creak of the rocker rolling back and forth over the wooden floor.

Then Meryn straightened up. "I don't want you to go."

"Believe me, I don't want to." It had been hard enough to walk away from her before. Now that he had almost lost her, he honestly didn't know if he could do it. He brushed the back of his fingers across her pale cheek. "Meryn." He waited until her eyes met his. "Do you want me to leave the army?"

Her lips trembled as she shook her head. "Please don't ask me that question. Not tonight. I'm not strong enough to say no."

A tear slid down her cheek, and he wiped it away. "Okay. I won't ask you tonight. But I will ask you one day soon. Because I don't know how many more times I can walk away from you."

"And I don't know how many more times I can let you." She tilted back her head, and he bent down and captured her mouth with his.

For a few glorious seconds he pretended he didn't have to go. Then the hard truths about their situation—that Caleb waited for him back at the base, risking everything to lie about where he was; that her brothers were downstairs, no doubt less than thrilled that he'd been up here, in her room, as long as he had; and that she was exhausted and needed time and sleep to recover from her illness—crashed in and stole the moment from them.

She lifted a hand to his face, her thumb stroking his cheek. He turned his head to kiss her palm, and she smiled faintly. "You have to go."

"Yes."

She sat up.

He helped her regain her feet before standing up himself. "I'll ask Kate to come up and help you get ready for bed."

"Thank you." She gripped the top of the footboard. "Will I see you soon?"

"I hope so. Caleb's put himself on the line to cover for me the last several days, so I don't know when I'll be able to get away again, but I'll message you when I can. In the meantime"—he cupped her face in his hands, and she covered them with hers—"rest and get better, okay?"

"I will."

Jesse pressed his lips to her forehead. "Good night, Meryn." He pulled his hands from hers and forced himself to turn away, knowing if he didn't leave that moment, he might not leave at all.

Chapter Eighteen

Halfway down the stairs, Jesse stopped when the conversation from below reached him.

"You can stop glowering any time now, Brendan." Paper crumpled, followed by a whooshing sound, as if Shane was starting a fire. "They've been together for three days, a few more minutes isn't going to make a big difference."

"Not to mention the two of them spent a week in his quarters a while back, when they were both perfectly healthy," Ethan added, a hint of laughter in his voice.

"And they're alone for a few hours every week," Kate chimed in.

"All right. Not helping." Brendan practically growled the words.

Jesse grinned. They were baiting Brendan. It was kind of fun to hear someone else receiving the treatment Jesse had grown up getting from his older brother, Rory, and Caleb.

"She is an adult, you know," Shane said. "And in case you hadn't noticed, she has a mind of her own."

"Oh, I've noticed," Brendan said dryly. "That doesn't mean I have to like it."

Kate laughed. "It's not like she's never—"

The stair creaked beneath his foot, and Jesse kicked himself. He'd give almost anything to hear how that sentence was going to end. Unfortunately, the opportunity had passed. He came down the rest of the stairs and into the living room.

"Kate, can you go up and see Meryn? She's beyond exhausted and I told her I'd ask you to help her."

Kate got up from the couch, amusement still glittering in her eyes. "Sure. I'll go check on her."

"I'm going up too." Ethan walked over to stand behind her, resting both hands on her shoulders. "I have to get back to work in the morning."

"Actually, Shane and I are supposed to head out again too." Brendan frowned. "Should we change that?"

Kate shook her head. "No, don't. You just got that job, and you don't want to lose it. The kids and I will stay here while you're gone. We need something to do, anyway."

"Thanks, Kate." Shane tossed a piece of wood into the stove and closed the metal door with a *clang*. "It will be good for Meryn to have family here while she recovers."

Jesse's admiration for the man grew. With just a few quiet words, he'd restored to Kate what his half-sister had tried to steal from her.

From the look in her eyes, Kate was touched, but she just nodded and turned toward the stairs.

Brendan yawned and stretched, his fingers almost touching the beams above his head. "Guess it's time for me to go to bed as well." He lowered his arms and held out his hand. "Jesse. It doesn't really seem adequate, but thank you for everything you did for Meryn."

Jesse gripped his hand. "So, not ripping my head from my shoulders?"

Brendan's booming laughter bounced off the walls and ceiling. "Not tonight." He let go of Jesse's hand and slapped him on the shoulder.

"Glad to hear it. I'm sorry I couldn't tell you where we were."

"No problem. I completely understood."

Shane snorted.

Brendan shot a dark look at his brother, who had leaned a shoulder against the doorframe, before turning back to Jesse. "Anyway, it's water under the bridge. I know you were doing what was best for Meryn, and as long as you always do that, your head can stay where it is."

"I'll keep that in mind." Jesse looked at Shane. "I need to get going."

"I'm sure you do." Shane pushed himself away from the doorway. "How were you able to be away from the base for so long?"

Jesse followed him across the kitchen and out onto the porch. "Caleb gave me a few days leave for personal business."

"Ah. It's great the major's on your side."

"I couldn't stay there if he wasn't."

Countless stars gleamed white against the night sky. The only sound disturbing the hot summer stillness of the evening was the deep croaking of bullfrogs in the pond at the bottom of the hill. As much as he didn't like the idea of it, sometimes he could understand why Meryn loved living out here so much.

"Did you park in the barn?" Shane started down the porch steps.

"Yeah. I thought it would be a good idea to stay out of sight." Jesse went down after him. "What was that visit from Annaliese all about, do you think?"

"Who knows? Some kind of reconnaissance mission, no doubt. It's safe to say she didn't just drop by to see how Meryn was doing."

"I didn't think so. Although Meryn wasn't completely convinced of that."

They reached the end of the walk. Shane bent down to pick a rubber ball up off the driveway and toss it back onto the lawn. "She's a lot like our mother that way. They're both determined to see the good in Annaliese, which I cannot comprehend since she has never given either of them anything but grief." He kicked at a small stone in his path. "She might have been looking for you, actually. It's good she didn't see you."

"Yes, it is. That would have been very bad. I'm sure she would have felt it was her duty to *help* me by turning me in too."

The barn loomed in front of them. Shane chuckled as he walked up to the entrance and lifted the bar. Both of them grabbed a door and pulled it open.

Jesse stopped at the side of the jeep. "You have my number. Message me if there's anything you need, okay?"

Shane rested a hand on the hood. "Listen, Jesse, Brendan's right. Thank you seems like a completely inadequate word to offer you after everything you did for Meryn. For all of us, really. I doubt she would have survived if you hadn't been there to help her, and the rest of us likely would have gotten sick too." He shook his head. "I really don't know how to express to you how deeply grateful we are."

"You don't have to. I care about Meryn, a lot, and I care about all of you as well. If there's anything in my power I can do to help any of you, I'm happy to do it."

"Well, I'm not in as good a position to help you, but if you ever need anything, I hope you won't hesitate to ask." He held out his hand.

Jesse clasped it tightly. A look of understanding passed between them as Shane gripped his arm. Warmth flooded Jesse's chest. Having Shane's trust was an honour, and not one he took lightly. "I won't."

"Good." Shane stepped back as Jesse swung onto the front seat of the jeep. "Be careful out there, my friend."

"You too." He drove out of the barn, feeling Shane's eyes on him as he headed down the lane and onto the road. He contemplated the conversations, the spoken and the unspoken ones, he'd just had with Meryn's brothers. Jesse might not be stationed in a war zone, but he was under no illusions. He was deep in battle and had begun to believe he had no brothers in arms, other than Caleb, who would be willing to stand with him in the fight.

Now it struck him that he wasn't as alone as he had thought. He had no doubt that, if it came to it, Meryn, Brendan, Shane, Kate, and Ethan would stand by his side against whatever foe rose to confront him.

For the first time since his parents and brother died, he felt as though he had a family.

Chapter Nineteen

Meryn had no idea how long she had slept, but she had some vague sense that light and darkness had succumbed to each other more than once since Kate had pulled the blankets over her the night she had come home.

Memories flickered, brightening and fading like the room as a breeze lifted the pale-blue curtains, then let them settle back against the glass. A shadowy recollection of Kate bringing her glasses of cool water and steaming cups of tea. And of Matthew and Gracie standing beside the bed, whispering and giggling through hands over mouths and being shushed and led away.

This morning, though, the sun streaming through the window and the cheerful chirping of birds in the giant oaks surrounding the old farm house summoned her from her cocoon of blankets. Meryn struggled to a sitting position and threw back the covers. She needed a long, hot shower. That and a couple of strong cups of coffee, and she might actually start to feel like a human being again.

The soap and steaming water did wonders to push away the cobwebs still clinging to her jumbled thoughts. She pulled on a short-sleeved yellow blouse and denim shorts, and headed downstairs.

Kate was running a dishcloth over the kitchen counter. She spun around, sending a spray of toast crumbs shooting into the air, when Meryn strolled into the kitchen. "You're up!"

"Finally. I'm scared to ask how long I've been out. What day is it?"

"Thursday."

Meryn gulped. "Didn't I come home on Monday?"

"Yep." Kate grinned and tossed the dishcloth into the sink. "You almost died, Mer. Give yourself a break. A couple of days of sleep were exactly what you needed. You look worlds better than you did when you arrived home."

"I feel worlds better."

"Good." Kate filled a red mug from the coffeepot.

"Where is everyone?" Feeling shaky, Meryn sat down at the table and took the mug.

"Let's see." Kate dropped two pieces of bread into the toaster, then grabbed the broom that had been propped up in one corner of the kitchen and swept the crumbs into a dustpan. "Ethan's at the office, the kids are outside playing, and your brothers have been away working since Tuesday morning. They'll be home tomorrow."

Meryn poured cream from the jug on the table into her cup. The small jug felt as if it weighed ten pounds, and she sloshed some cream onto the table when she set it down. She grabbed a napkin from the holder in the middle of the table and dabbed at the puddle. "It's so strange. I feel as though I have lost days of my life."

"You almost lost a lot more than that." Kate dumped the crumbs into the garbage under the kitchen sink and propped the broom back up in the corner. "You would have if Jesse hadn't been there to take care of you." After washing her hands, she grabbed the toast and set it in front of Meryn, then moved the butter and jam closer to her.

"I know." Meryn gazed out the window, a hazy recollection of her time in the cabin slowly crystallizing in her mind.

"What are you smiling about?" Kate pulled out the chair across from her and sat down.

Meryn blinked. "I'm not smiling."

"You were. Let me guess, you were thinking about Jesse."

"You're the one who brought him up." A chill whispered over her arms. "Was I dreaming or did Annaliese come here?"

Kate made a face. "If it was a dream, we all had the same horrible nightmare."

Meryn set down her mug. "She didn't see Jesse, did she?"

"No, thankfully. She just stopped by, messed with all our heads, and left. Not bad for five minutes' work."

"She does have some kind of gift."

"Yeah, the gift of destruction. She must have gotten that from the king of Sweden, because she sure didn't get it from your side of the family."

Meryn would have laughed at the reference to how ridiculously high Annaliese had built up her biological father, if Meryn didn't feel so sick about the fact that her half-sister could have easily caught Jesse in her home.

He was right, he couldn't come here anymore. It was too dangerous. Unless, of course, he did leave the ...

She sucked in a breath.

"What?"

"I just remembered that the night he brought me home, Jesse asked me if I wanted him to leave the army."

"What did you tell him?"

"I think I begged him not to ask me that until I had slept and had a hot shower and was thinking a little more clearly."

"So, today."

Meryn reached absently for a knife and the jar of blackberry jam and spread some on her toast. Was she ready to answer that question?

"What will you tell him if he asks you again?"

"I honestly don't know. When he first became a believer, as hard as it was to be apart, it was obvious to both of us that the best thing was for him to stay where he was. Now, nothing is as clear as it used to be." She took a bite of toast and chewed slowly. Even that task required enormous effort. How long would it take for her to feel like herself again?

"And why is that, Mer?"

"I have no idea."

"Don't you?"

Meryn set her toast down. "Kate." The bite she'd taken wasn't going down very well. "I've let things go too far, haven't I?"

"That depends. How far did you intend for them to go?"

"Not this far. Not without telling him about my past, anyway." She pressed her fingers to her mouth. "He told me he loved me."

"And what did you say?"

"Nothing. He said it just as I was coming to, and all I could think of then was how thirsty I was. I asked him for a drink and he went to get water and we never came back to it. But if he really meant it, he's going to be upset when he finds out the truth."

Kate's eyebrows rose. "*If* he meant it?"

Warmth flooded Meryn's cheeks. "All right, I know he meant it."

"Then don't assume he'll be upset. I'm sure he'll understand." Kate covered Meryn's hand with hers. "He does have a right to know, though."

"I know." She straightened up in her chair. "I'll tell him the next time I see him."

"Good." Kate patted Meryn's hand before pulling back. "Now eat. You haven't had solid food for almost a week."

She managed to get one slice of toast down but pushed the plate away without touching the second one. "Thanks, Kate. I'll eat more later. Right now I need to get some fresh air."

"Call me if you want anything."

Meryn opened the screen door and blinked at the sudden brightness.

Matthew and Gracie tossed a beach ball back and forth in the front yard.

She propped both elbows on the railing and watched the kids. The two of them laughing and playing in the sunshine was the best medicine she could ask for. She envied them their carefree innocence, their lack of awareness of the evil and chaos in the world around them. Meryn whispered a prayer that they would be spared that loss of innocence as long as possible.

A car drove up the lane. Puffs of dust rose from its back wheels and drifted in the thick, warm air.

Kate came out onto the porch, a dish towel and mug still in her hand. "It's Drew." She glanced over at Meryn. "Do you feel up to company?"

Not really.

Drew, a man they both knew from church, had always been a good friend. Even if she was a little uncomfortable with the fact that lately his feelings for her seemed to have grown beyond friendship, it was thoughtful of him to come and visit. It wouldn't hurt to talk to him since he had come all this way and, she noticed as he got out of the car, had brought her a beautiful bouquet of flowers.

Meryn sighed. "For a few minutes."

"Okay." Kate held out her hands. "Come on, guys, time for lunch."

With groans of protest, Matthew and Gracie left the beach ball on the lawn and climbed the stairs to slide their fingers into Kate's.

Drew followed them up the steps.

Meryn lifted a hand. "Hi. What brings you all the way out here?"

He handed her the flowers, and his golden-brown eyes smiled above a freckled nose that made him look a lot younger than he was. "I hope I don't need a reason to come by, but if I do, I heard you'd been sick and wanted to see how you were doing."

Meryn motioned toward a Muskoka chair. "Of course you don't need a reason. And thank you for these. They're beautiful." She buried her face in the assortment of tulips, carnations, and hyacinth, inhaling deeply before settling onto the swing.

Drew sat down and crossed an ankle over one knee. "How are you doing? I'm sorry I didn't come by sooner, but I just ran into Pastor John this morning and found out you'd been ill."

Meryn set the bouquet down beside her on the seat of the swing. "It's just as well. This is the first day I've been up and starting to feel like myself again."

"You look wonderful, but it must have been scary in the hospital, surrounded by all those sick or dying people."

Her mind raced. Should she let him believe she had been admitted? It would be easier than trying to avoid revealing Jesse's part in her recovery. But if he found out later that she hadn't been hospitalized, things would be far harder to explain. Meryn clasped her hands in her lap. "I didn't end up going into the hospital. They were full and turned me away, so a friend who had already survived the virus helped me through it."

His eyes narrowed. "A friend?"

"Yes." She shifted in her seat. "Actually, I was thinking about you the last time I was in town, and wondering if you've been able to keep the bank open."

"So far, yes. The government wouldn't allow us to close completely, although we have gone down to a skeleton staff. Thankfully, the measures we've taken to protect ourselves seem to have worked. I've just heard this morning that the number of new cases of the virus has finally started to level out, so I'm praying we've turned a corner on this pandemic."

"That's great news. Is that just here or all over?"

"Mainly here and in the States, since that's where this thing started, but other countries are reporting slowing rates as well, although millions of people are still sick and it will be weeks or months before this is all over." Drew ran a hand over his thick brown hair. "It had to happen soon. If the numbers hadn't started to drop, the entire planet might have been wiped out. As it is, it looks as if the average death rate for affected countries is around ten percent of the population. Who could have ever believed something like that was possible with all the medical advances we've made over the last few decades?"

Meryn shook her head. "Those numbers are definitely hard to wrap your mind around. I guess it goes to show we're never really in control of what happens in the world, no matter how much progress we make."

"I guess." Drew waved a hand through the air as though to erase the heaviness that had settled there. "Anyway, I didn't come here to bring you down. I was hoping to cheer you up."

"You have." Meryn's fingers relaxed. "It's good to see you, Drew. It's been too long."

"Yes, it has." His gaze lingered on her face. "When you feel up to it, maybe I could take you out for dinner again. We have a lot of catching up to do."

"Yes, maybe. As long as we can go as friends."

"Of course." His smile was a little tight. "You've made it clear that's all you want for us, and I respect that."

"Thank you."

"I don't like it, but I respect it." The familiar teasing laughter was back in his eyes.

"And I respect that." She returned his smile as she reached over and touched the back of his hand. "Our friendship has always meant a lot to me, Drew. I don't want to do anything to harm it."

"Got it. Are you ...?" He stopped and cleared his throat. "Seeing anyone else?"

"You know I still have a lot to work through from the past. I can't fully commit to anyone until I know all of that is behind me." Had the fact that she hadn't exactly answered his question registered with him? She reached for the flowers. "These really are beautiful. Thank you for bringing them and for coming to see me. I appreciate it more than I can say."

"I'm glad to see you looking so well. I'm sure your family has been taking good care of you."

"They always do."

He stood. "Don't get up. You have the perfect spot there, in the sunshine." He held out his hand. "Let me know when you're feeling better, and we'll go for that dinner."

Meryn slipped her hand into his. "I will."

His fingers squeezed hers briefly. "I'll see you, Meryn."

After he'd gone, she pushed against the wooden slats of the porch with her bare toes to start the swing gently rocking.

The sickly sweet aroma of the flowers Drew had brought hung heavy in the air. Meryn wrinkled her nose, then grabbed the bouquet and tossed it onto one of the wooden chairs a few feet away from her on the porch.

The flowers might be beautiful, but they couldn't compete with the simple bunch of daisies still blooming on the windowsill in her kitchen.

Chapter Twenty

Meryn hadn't seen Jesse in over a month. She stood on the porch and gazed out at the hill surrounding the pond and, beyond that, the dark outline of trees. A shudder moved through her at the thought of going back into the forest where she had nearly died, and she gripped the wooden post at the top of the stairs. She couldn't do it.

Then you can't see Jesse. She lifted her chin. She had to do it. This was the longest they had been apart since she'd left his quarters. He had messaged her twice to tell her that Lieutenant Gallagher appeared to be watching him closely and he didn't feel it was safe to come and see her. Yesterday he had finally let her know that he was coming tonight.

She clenched her fists. The fact that the lieutenant, a man she barely knew, could have that much control over her life and happiness nearly drove her crazy. She needed to see Jesse. And even though she knew that what she had to tell him could affect their relationship, she couldn't wait any longer.

Meryn started across the lawn, drawing in the cool night breeze and the smell of earth still warm from the summer sun. The haunting cry of a whippoorwill filled the air, and she focused on the sound. Her footsteps faltered slightly when the ghostly silhouettes of the trees loomed close enough for shadows to fall across the rough pathway just ahead of her, but she took a deep breath and started into the dank, shadowy interior of the woods.

"I wondered if you'd work up the courage to come." A figure stepped out from behind a tree.

Meryn jumped.

The moonlight lit up Jesse's grin. "Actually, I knew you would. But standing here watching you deliberate on the porch about whether or not you could, I did wonder when."

"I'm glad you knew I would do it. I wasn't so sure."

"I didn't doubt it for a minute. I knew you wouldn't let these woods beat you." Jesse's face grew serious. "How are you feeling?"

"I'm good now. Kate is an excellent nurse. I felt like myself again after a couple of days of bed rest. I've kind of been taking it easy for the past month, but I'm just about ready to open up the store again. Everything's been great, except ..."

"Except what?" He moved closer and Meryn's pulse rate picked up.

"Except I thought you would never message me to say that we could meet."

Jesse closed the remaining space between them and pulled her to him. When he kissed her, Meryn wrapped her arms around his neck. The intensity of his hand on her back drawing her up to her tiptoes, the fingers of his other hand tangled in her hair, the fierceness of his mouth on hers, told her how much he had missed her. She hoped he could feel the same from her, in the way she moved closer, responded to his touch with an eagerness she hadn't allowed herself to express to him before. That she shouldn't now ...

As though he felt the sudden cold that swept through her, Jesse let her go. His emerald eyes searched hers.

Meryn stepped back. "You look like a soldier."

A smile turned up one corner of his mouth. "I am a soldier."

"I know, but when I see you, you usually look more like a civilian."

He glanced down at the camouflage pants and dark-green T-shirt he wore. "Yeah, I came here straight from a meeting. If I took time to change, I wouldn't get over to this side of the woods in time to meet you."

"Why *are* you over here?"

"I wanted to bring you these." He unhooked a pair of night vision goggles from his belt. "And I also figured you'd be a little freaked out about walking through the woods after what happened the last time, so I thought I'd walk through with you."

Meryn took the goggles and slipped them on over her head. Trees, bushes, and fallen logs came into focus behind a veil of green. "This is so cool. I've always wanted to try these things out."

"Stick with me, darlin'." Jesse pulled a pair of goggles over his own head. "It's non-stop new and exciting adventures, I promise you."

Meryn laughed. "Why are they green, anyway?"

He reached for her hand and they started down the path. "Some brilliant scientists somewhere figured out that shapes are easiest to distinguish when they're green, so you see things more accurately than you would with other colours."

Meryn climbed over a branch in her path that might have tripped her if she hadn't been wearing the goggles.

"Also, because the human eye is most sensitive to light wavelengths at that spot on the spectrum, the light doesn't have to be as bright, which conserves battery power. That's something that doesn't matter quite as much in a situation like this, but can be a lifesaver when you're hiking for miles through jungle or across a desert."

"That makes sense." Meryn scanned the forest. Everything that had seemed so ominous during her earlier treks through the woods now appeared fascinating and beautiful, not at all threatening. All that had been needed to push back the darkness was a little bit of light. "I spoke to my parents last night."

"How are they?" Jesse held back a branch until she passed by.

"They're good, I think."

"You think?"

"Yeah." Her ankle turned on a patch of soft earth, and Jesse gripped her hand tighter to steady her. "Their i-com hasn't been working great the last few times we've talked. The sound keeps cutting in and out, so it's tricky to have a conversation."

"Why don't they get a new one?"

"I'm not sure. I asked them that but couldn't make out the answer."

The ground dipped suddenly and every muscle in Meryn's body tightened. This was the spot where she had realized she was not going to make it to Jesse that awful night.

Jesse let go of her hand and slid an arm around her waist. Obviously he recognized the area too, or felt the tension radiating from her.

After they passed the tree she had leaned against and lost consciousness, she breathed easier.

The outline of the cabin appeared through the branches. They had made it through the woods twice as quickly as she had in the past, when she was mostly feeling her way along.

When they came out of the trees, Jesse pointed to the porch along the back of the old building, where he'd set two of the chairs from inside. "Want to stay out here? It's pretty stuffy in the cabin, since it's gotten so warm."

"Sure." Meryn climbed the three stairs to the porch. Now that they were in the cleared area around the building, the full moon bathed them in light, so she pulled off the goggles. "Thanks for bringing these." She held her pair out to Jesse. "What a difference they make. It's like night and day. Literally."

He lifted his hand. "You keep them. I bought that pair for you."

"Really?" Meryn pulled them back, thrilled with the gift. They would definitely make it easier for her to hike through the woods to see him. If, that is, he still wanted to meet with her after she told him what she had promised Kate she would tell him tonight. Her stomach knotted as she set the goggles down on the porch railing.

"Close your eyes."

She looked up. "What?"

"Close your eyes."

"Why?"

He shook his head. "Can't you just trust me for once, lady?"

"I do trust you."

His eyes held hers, the teasing gone. "Good. Then close your eyes."

She did as he asked.

"And hold up your hair."

"What—?"

Jesse touched a finger to her lips. "Trust."

Her eyes still closed, Meryn gathered up her hair and lifted it in one hand.

He moved around behind her.

Something cold touched her throat, and she reached for it.

"Don't look."

His fingers brushed her skin, sending tingles of electricity skittering over her. His breath was warm as he pressed his lips to the back of her neck, to the curve of her shoulder.

Meryn shivered and bit her lip as a low moan rose in her throat. "Are you still working on whatever you were working on?"

"No, I'm done with that." His voice held laughter as he kissed her again. "Now I'm just taking shameless advantage of the situation."

"So, I can let my hair down?" She was achingly aware of him, of his fingers trailing over her flesh as he moved to stand in front of her, of his mouth on her skin again, finding the tender spot just above her collarbone, the side of her throat, before he pulled back with a sigh.

"If you must."

"I really think I must." She opened her eyes to find his on her, the fire still burning so strongly in them she felt almost as though he touched her still. "Which isn't the same as *I want to.*"

He smiled. "I'm glad to hear it."

Meryn glanced down at the object he had fastened around her neck, her fingers trembling as they reached for the small gold heart. "Jesse." She looked up at him again. "It's beautiful. Thank you."

His hands engulfed hers. "I know this has been hard, Meryn. But I want you to know, even when we can't be together, you always have my heart." He kissed her again.

For a moment she tried to let go of everything standing in their way, to surrender herself to the joy of being close to him, the comfort of his strong arms holding her tight. She couldn't, though, not fully, not until she had told him everything.

Jesse lifted his head and captured her face in his hands. "What is it?"

Meryn searched for the words, but thinking coherently was almost impossible when he was looking at her like that, seeing, as always, so much more than she was saying in words.

She reached up and gently removed his hands from her face so she could step back. Could try to think. To find a way to tell him the truth and explain why she had kept it from him for so long.

The i-com in his shirt pocket buzzed.

Meryn nodded toward it. "See who it is. I … need a minute."

He didn't move until it buzzed again, then he grabbed it out of his pocket and glanced down at the screen. "It's Caleb."

"Take it. When you're done, we'll talk." Legs weak, Meryn sank onto one of the chairs on the porch. She propped her elbows on her knees and rested her head on the palms of her hands as she listened to Jesse's side of the conversation.

"Hey, Cale." After a few seconds, he spoke again. "Yeah, those are Meryn's friends, why?"

Meryn lifted her head. Why was the major calling Jesse about friends of hers?

"What?" The word exploded from Jesse's mouth as he swung around to look at her.

She bit down on her thumbnail. What was going on?

"Can you stop it?" A long pause and then, "All right, I'll meet you there." He stabbed at a button and jammed the electronic device back into his pocket. "I have to go."

Meryn jumped to her feet. "What is it?"

"It's Kate and Ethan. Someone overheard Matthew talking on the playground the last week of school and reported that his parents had a Bible and were teaching him out of it even though that's now illegal."

A weight, like a large rock, dropped into her stomach. "What does that mean? Will they be arrested?"

His eyes met hers. The news was far worse than that. "No. But we've been ordered to take Matthew and Gracie away from them."

The words slammed into her. She reached out blindly for the railing. "You can't."

He grasped her shoulders. "We have to, Meryn. Normally Caleb would send someone else on the base to do this, but he decided we would take care of it, since they're friends of yours. If we refuse, Headquarters will order someone else to take the kids, someone who won't care about them and won't worry about trying to find a good family for them to stay with while we work all this out. And they'll arrest Caleb and me, and then there won't be anything we can do to help them."

Horror coursed through her. "Would they let me take them?"

He let go of her. "No. One of the many things having an identity bracelet disqualifies you from is being a foster parent. They would never agree to let another Christian take the kids, especially not one with a record."

"Well, you can't just go over there and rip them away from their parents. You have to stop this." Her head jerked. "You could leave the army."

"What?"

"The last time I saw you, you asked me if I wanted you to leave the army. The answer is yes, I do want you to leave. Tonight."

"I can't just—"

"Yes, you can." She grabbed his hands and held them tightly. "We could go away, all of us. Just disappear. You said yourself that Caleb would help us. Kate and Ethan will have their children, and you and I can be together."

"Meryn, listen to me."

His voice was gentle, but every word stung like drops of freezing rain pelting against her skin.

"We can't run. There's nowhere to go, nowhere to hide. If the six of us tried to stay together, they'd find us within hours of leaving. And if we separated, we might never see each other again. And there are your bracelets..."

Meryn looked down at her wrist, and her heart sank. He was right. If they tried to remove the bracelets, that would set off an alarm, and if they left them on, the army would track the six of them down, probably in far less than the few hours he had predicted. And even if, by some miracle, they did escape, she didn't know what Shane and Brendan or her parents would do if the rest of them vanished. She slumped against the side of the cabin. "There has to be something you can do."

"There is. I can take the kids and find a safe place for them. Then I can use every possible legal channel to get them back, so there is no danger that Kate and Ethan will lose them again."

She pushed away from the wall. "I'm coming with you."

He hesitated, then gestured toward the jeep. "Since it's dark, we'll take a chance, but I can only take you there. You'll have to spend the night afterward and find a way to get home tomorrow. And you cannot interfere in any way."

"Fine."

He started down the stairs, only touching one of them before landing on the ground and striding toward his vehicle.

Meryn hurried around to the far side and slid onto the seat beside him.

Jesse started the jeep and backed up, then spun the wheels on the loose gravel as he pulled forward and out onto the road.

Neither of them spoke for several minutes, until she turned to him. "Do Kate and Ethan know?"

"No."

She felt in her jeans pocket for her i-com and pulled it out.

He glanced sideways at her. "What are you doing?"

"Calling to warn them."

"No." His voice was as cold and hard as it had been gentle before. "Put it away, Meryn."

When she didn't move, he shot out his hand and snatched the device from her grasp. "I told you that you cannot interfere. If you tell them we're coming, there's a good chance they'll take the kids and run. Then we'd have to hunt them down like animals. When we found them—and we would—Kate and Ethan would be arrested, and they would lose the kids forever. Do you want to be responsible for that?"

She didn't answer, just turned away from him and gripped the door handle, blinking back tears of rage and frustration. It wasn't fair, but it felt as though he had become the enemy again, like he had been that day in the church, before she had gotten to know his heart. She fingered the necklace at her throat.

Jesse touched her arm. "Everything's going to be okay."

Meryn shifted away from him.

"I'll get Matthew and Gracie back, Meryn. I promise you."

"You can't do that, can you?"

"I can't what?"

"You can't promise me. You'll try, I know, but in the end, everything you do might not be enough. Some nameless, faceless, godless commission in Ottawa who couldn't care less about a couple of little kids they've never met could make the decision to rip them away from their family forever. Then there won't be anything any of us can do or say about it."

He didn't answer.

Meryn stared out the front window. "Nothing that has happened so far, not the brick through the store window or me being arrested or the curfew or the bracelets, none of it has mattered all that much, because it's happened to the adults. We made the decision not to renounce Christ, and we're willing to live with whatever consequences that brings. But Matthew and Gracie ..." She pounded the dashboard with the palms of both hands. "They're just kids. They didn't choose any of this. They don't have any idea what's going on in the world. And now suddenly they're going to be torn from everything that is safe and familiar and loving, and thrust into the home of strangers. They'll be so scared ..."

"You're right—I can't and shouldn't make absolute promises to you. Except to tell you that I will move heaven and earth to bring Matthew and Gracie back home. I *can* promise you that. Please trust me."

Meryn didn't answer. She felt his eyes on her but refused to look over.

Jesse exhaled loudly as he wheeled onto Kate and Ethan's street.

She straightened up, her stomach in knots. Even showing up at the door with Jesse seemed like a betrayal to her friends.

Jesse turned into the driveway and parked, then set her i-com on the dash.

She seized it and stuck it back in her pocket.

He reached into the backseat and grabbed his camouflage jacket. When he slid his arms into the sleeves and did up the buttons, he not only looked like a soldier, he had become a man in authority.

Meryn went cold.

"I'm sorry about this, Meryn. But I have to do what I have to do."

She yanked on the chain around her neck, and the jewelry fell into her hand. She held it out. When Jesse didn't move to take it, she dropped it onto the seat beside him. "So do I."

Chapter Twenty-One

Another jeep pulled up to the curb, and Major Donevan jumped out. Meryn ignored him and started up the walkway, the thudding of boots on the cement behind her echoing around the quiet neighbourhood.

When she reached the front door, Meryn pulled open the screen and knocked but didn't wait for a response, just turned the knob and pushed into the front hallway.

Ethan came out of the kitchen, an uncertain smile crossing his face when he saw her. "Meryn? What are you doing here so ...?" His gaze lifted over her shoulder and the smile disappeared. He walked down the hallway, his eyes fixed on the two men standing behind her on the porch. "What's going on?"

Kate appeared at the kitchen door. "Meryn?"

"I'm sorry, Ethan." Meryn brushed past him and went to her friend.

Kate gripped her arm.

Ethan pulled the door open wider. "Jesse? Is there a problem?"

"I'm afraid so. Can we come in?"

Kate's hold on Meryn's arm tightened.

"Of course." Ethan moved back as Jesse and the major came through the door. "We can talk in the kitchen."

The thudding of boots that had seemed loud outside was deafening in the narrow hallway.

Kate glanced toward the stairs, as if she was worried the noise would wake up her children.

The soldiers stopped when they reached her and Kate, and the major held out his hand for them to go into the kitchen first. Jesse followed them into the room, but the major stayed in the doorway.

A tendril of steam rose from a mug on the table. Kate sat down and picked up the mug as Meryn sank onto the chair beside her.

Ethan turned and leaned back against the counter. "Can I get you anything? Tea? Coffee?"

Jesse shook his head. "We're here on official business." He pulled the i-com from his pocket, touched the screen, and turned it toward Ethan. "Based on a report we received that you have a Bible in the house and are teaching your children from it, we have been ordered to remove the two minor children from these premises."

Kate set her mug down hard. Some of the hot liquid splashed onto her fingers.

Meryn grabbed a napkin from the holder and dabbed at Kate's hand.

Kate didn't seem to notice. She stood, bracing herself against the tabletop.

"What?" Ethan pushed himself away from the counter, his brown eyes suddenly hard. "We don't have any Bibles. You took them away last year."

"If there's been a mistake, it will all be straightened out by the Canadian Human Rights Commission. In the meantime, we are required to take the children."

"Take them where?"

"They will be placed with a foster family until the commission makes its ruling." Jesse took a step toward the hallway.

Ethan moved to stand in front of him, his back to the major. "I don't think so."

"Ethan." Jesse's voice was low and warning. "You can't stop us from taking the kids. I promise you they will be safe; I'll make sure of that myself." He took another step forward.

Ethan stopped him with a hand on his chest. "You will have to kill me before you take my children." His voice was as hard as his eyes.

A chill moved up Meryn's spine. Although he was practically a brother to her, she almost didn't know the man in front of her. What was he capable of if pushed hard enough? What were any of them capable of?

"Ethan." Kate's voice shook.

He lifted his other hand. "It's all right, Kate. We'll work this out. It's a misunderstanding."

"This *will* all be worked out," Jesse said. "But not here, not tonight. The commission ..."

"Stop saying that word." Ethan shoved him and Jesse took a step backward. "No bunch of bureaucrats in Ottawa is going to decide what happens to my kids."

The major moved closer.

Jesse held up his hands. "Calm down, Ethan."

"Calm down?" Ethan's eyes flashed fire. "You come into my house and threaten to take my children away from me for no reason, and you want me to *calm down*?"

"Teaching them from the Bible is against the law."

"I told you we don't have a Bible."

"So you haven't been telling them Bible stories?"

Ethan's jaw worked but he didn't answer.

Jesse glanced at Kate. "Kate, pack a bag for the kids, just for a few days."

"Don't do it, Kate."

"Ethan, don't make me arrest you."

"Arrest me, I don't care. You can do what you want with me, but Matthew and Gracie aren't going anywhere."

"This isn't helping. We *are* taking the kids, and if you cooperate, your chances of getting them back will increase dramatically."

"What are you saying?" Kate lifted her chin, her eyes blazing now too. "If you take them, we might not get them back?"

"*When* we take them, we will do everything we can to get them back to you as quickly as possible."

"But you might not be able to."

Jesse drew himself up to his full height. "All of your questions will be answered within a few days. For now, if you won't bring the children to us, we will go and get them ourselves." He started to brush past Ethan.

Ethan drew back a fist and threw a punch at him.

Jesse blocked it with his forearm.

Kate cried out as the major grabbed Ethan's arms and yanked them behind his back.

Meryn jumped to her feet.

Jesse looked at her. His face was impassive, almost cold. "Meryn, help Kate pack a bag and wake up the kids. It will be easier for them if the two of you get them ready."

Meryn shifted her gaze from him to Kate. *What should I do?*

Kate pushed back her shoulders. Without a word, she turned on her heel and strode toward the stairs.

"Kate." Ethan struggled, but the major's shoulders tensed and he stopped.

Fighting nausea, Meryn followed Kate up the stairs.

Kate's eyes glistened, but she stayed silent as she pulled a small suitcase out of the closet in Matthew and Gracie's room. Yanking open dresser drawers, she pulled out clothes and dropped them into the case.

"Mom?" Matthew sat up in bed, his hair tousled and his eyes sleepy.

Kate stopped packing and went to him. "It's okay, Matthew." The fingers resting on his head trembled. "You and Gracie are going for a little drive, okay?" She pulled back the covers.

"Where?"

"Captain Christensen is here with his friend Major Donevan. They want to take you to stay with a nice family for a couple of days."

"Why?"

Kate looked at Meryn helplessly.

Meryn sat down on the edge of the bed. "It's kind of like a holiday for you and Gracie, Matthew."

He shook his head. "I don't want to go on a holiday without my mom and dad."

"I know. But it's just going to be you and your sister this time. You'll have fun there, and you'll be back home soon."

He didn't look too sure, but he climbed out of bed and allowed Kate to help him get dressed.

Meryn finished packing the suitcase as Kate walked over to the other bed, where Gracie still slept. Kate stopped in front of the window and gazed out into the darkness on the other side of the glass. Meryn knew what she was thinking. Jesse's words, that there was nowhere for them to run and nowhere to hide, echoed through Meryn's mind. Still, if they weren't wearing the bracelets, she might have helped them try to escape that way anyway.

"Almost ready?" Jesse appeared in the doorway.

Kate turned away from the window and went to Gracie's bed. She ignored him as she wrapped her daughter in the soft, peach-coloured blanket she couldn't go to sleep without and lifted her up.

Jesse went to the table between the beds and picked up the Bible story book. "I need to take this, okay, Kate?"

"Can I stop you?"

He didn't answer as he tucked the book under his arm. "Do you want me to carry her?"

"No." Kate's voice was sharp. "Matthew, go with Aunt Meryn."

Meryn snapped the suitcase shut. She held out her hand, and Matthew slid his small one into it. *I may never feel his fingers in mine again.* Her chest squeezed.

Kate stalked past Jesse and started down the stairs.

When Meryn got to the doorway, Jesse took the suitcase from her. "Here."

Clutching Matthew's hand, she started to move forward.

Jesse caught the fingers of her free hand in his. "Meryn."

She didn't want to look at him. She wanted to be furious with him, to blame him for everything that was happening. Something in his voice, though, made her turn.

Agony roiled in his eyes.

This is costing him so much. As devastated as she was for Kate and Ethan, she ached for Jesse too. They were all innocent victims in this nightmare. Gracie and Matthew most of all, but their parents, her, Jesse, the major. None of them wanted to be here, not one of them had asked for a part in this heartrending drama. But here they all were, forced to play it out to the end.

Her skin burned beneath his. She squeezed his fingers.

His face cleared and he let her go.

Meryn went down the stairs.

Ethan sat on a chair at the table, hands cuffed behind his back. The major stood behind him.

Meryn bit her lip. Had he been arrested?

Ethan's eyes sought out Jesse as he came up behind Meryn. "Jesse, don't do this. Please. You know we haven't done anything wrong."

"I'm sorry, Ethan." Jesse's voice had lost some of its coolness, as if it had been easier for him to deal with Ethan's anger than with his pleading. "I don't have a choice."

"All right, enough." The major jerked his head toward the door. "Captain, take the children out to the jeep now."

Jesse turned to Kate.

Tears slid down her cheeks as she pulled her sleeping daughter closer, and Gracie's hair tumbled over the blanket. "I'll bring her."

"Wait." Ethan's voice was anguished. "Let me say goodbye to them."

Jesse looked at the major, who inclined his head slightly.

Meryn took Matthew over to Ethan. Matthew's eyes were huge as he approached his father, but he didn't speak.

Ethan looked over his shoulder. "Can I give him a hug?"

"No," the major said curtly. "The cuffs stay on."

Ethan sighed and touched his forehead to Matthew's. "I need you to be brave, okay, son? Take care of your sister. Mom and I will see you soon."

"Okay."

Meryn blinked back the tears that pricked her eyes as she and Matthew stepped back.

When Kate held Gracie out, Ethan pressed his cheek to hers. "I love you, sweet girl," he murmured.

Kate made a sound deep in her throat, like a wounded animal, as she pulled her daughter away.

Gracie stirred in her arms and pushed herself upright, her hair a mass of curls. When she saw Ethan, she cried out, "Daddy."

Ethan started to rise but the major clapped a hand on his shoulder and pushed him back down.

"Hey!" Matthew wrenched his hand from Meryn's and charged toward the major. "Don't hurt my dad."

"Matthew!" Ethan's voice was firm, and his son came to an abrupt stop in front of him. "Leave Major Donevan alone, son. He's not hurting me."

Matthew's face wrinkled in confusion. "Then why are you tied up?"

"It's just"—Ethan exhaled—"something that happens to adults sometimes when they don't listen very well."

Matthew's head tilted. "Like a time-out?"

"Yeah. Kind of like that. You ..." Ethan winced slightly, as though the words he was saying caused him physical pain. "Go with Captain Christensen now. I'm okay."

Matthew didn't look convinced, but when Meryn held out her hand, he crossed the room and took it.

Kate turned to go, but Gracie twisted around her, tears streaming down her cheeks, and held out her arms. "Daddy!"

"It's okay, Gracie." Ethan's voice broke, but he didn't try to get up again. "Everything's going to be okay."

Matthew clung to Meryn as they followed Kate to the door.

"Captain." Ethan ground out the word.

Meryn froze and looked back.

Jesse had started down the hall, but he stopped when Ethan called out.

"I swear, if anything happens to either of them, I will hold you personally responsible."

Jesse's eyes met Meryn's briefly. Then he squared his shoulders and nodded toward the exit.

"She needs her car seat." Kate jutted her chin at the front hall closet.

Jesse opened the closet door and grabbed the pink seat before following them down the walkway. He set the seat in the back of the jeep.

Gracie was still crying, and when he turned around and held out his arms, Kate stumbled back a step, clutching her daughter to her. "I can't."

"Kate." Jesse's voice was gentle. "I promise you everything is going to be ..." His gaze shifted to Meryn's. "I promise I'll make sure they go to a safe place. And then I'll fight with everything I have to get this thing overturned."

Tears coursed down Kate's cheeks. For a moment she didn't move, then she kissed the top of Gracie's head and held her out.

She struggled to hold on to her mother, but Jesse took her and set her carefully in her car seat.

Kate crouched down in front of her son. "God loves you and we love you, Matthew. You remember that."

He touched her cheek. "Why are you crying?"

Meryn's throat was so tight she couldn't swallow.

Kate attempted a watery smile. "I'm going to miss you and Gracie, that's all. But you have fun, and I'll see you again before you know it, okay?"

"Okay."

"Captain Christensen will take good care of you."

Jesse helped Matthew into the backseat and strapped him in. When he finished, he straightened up and turned to Kate. "I'll let you know as soon as I hear anything." With a last, quick glance at Meryn, he rounded the front of the jeep and slid behind the wheel.

Meryn wrapped an arm around Kate. They stood like that, watching the jeep grow smaller and smaller until it disappeared in the distance. Kate shivered and Meryn squeezed her shoulder. "Let's go inside."

The major was leaning against the wall behind Ethan when they came into the kitchen. He looked up. "Are they gone?"

Meryn nodded.

He pushed himself away from the wall and came around in front of Ethan. "Stand up and turn around."

Ethan got to his feet and turned so the major could remove the handcuffs.

Meryn let out the breath she'd been holding. He hadn't been arrested, then. Kate had shown amazing strength so far, but there was no way she'd be able to take much more.

The major nodded curtly at Ethan. "We'll be in touch soon."

None of them moved until the front door shut behind the major. Then Ethan dropped back onto the chair and lowered his face into his hands.

Kate sat down beside him.

When she grasped his arms, he lifted his head. Deep lines spoked out from the corners of his eyes. He looked as if he had aged a decade in the last hour.

Not wanting to disturb them in their shared grief, Meryn slipped out of the room and crossed the hallway into the living room.

As dark as it had been before, the world suddenly seemed a much darker place. And no matter how hard she searched for it, Meryn couldn't grasp hold of even the slightest bit of light that she could use to push the darkness away.

Chapter Twenty-Two

Jesse fixed his eyes on the road, trying to block from his memory the look in Ethan's eyes as Caleb held him back. Although Jesse didn't have kids, he could imagine the frustration and helplessness Ethan had felt when his daughter had called out to him and he hadn't been able to go to her.

Gracie still sobbed in the backseat, and the sound of it ripped at Jesse's heart.

Matthew, who must have been as confused and frightened as she was, tried to comfort his sister, patting her hand and saying over and over the same thing their dad had told her. "It's okay, Gracie. Everything is going to be okay."

Jesse's i-com buzzed and he pulled it out of his pocket and glanced at the screen.

Caleb. *Meet me at the base, and we'll take kids to a foster home together.*

Jesse's chest tightened. He really hoped he'd have some say in where they went, since he had promised Meryn and Kate and Ethan he would make sure they were left in a safe place.

Jesse turned into the base and flashed his identification card at the guard, who waved him through. He pulled into his spot and waited. A couple of minutes later, Caleb parked beside him and jumped into the passenger seat. Jesse appreciated the concession, since Caleb pretty much never let him drive when the two of them were together. At least being the one to drive the kids to the place they would be staying gave him some semblance of control, although he knew none of them really had that.

"So where are they going? Is this a good place? What do you know about it?"

Caleb held up a hand. "One thing at a time."

Not a good sign. Jesse's stomach clenched.

"There may be a problem."

"What?"

Caleb glanced into the back seat and lowered his voice. "As you know, the system was already overloaded before the Red Virus swept through, and now things are even worse. A case worker did agree to try and find someone for them, but initially she didn't sound very optimistic. She messaged me a few minutes ago to say she managed to find one family willing to take them, but I get the impression they're kind of scraping the bottom of the barrel."

"That doesn't sound good."

"We'll see." Caleb tapped the screen in the dash. He spoke an address and a map appeared.

Jesse grimaced. Not the greatest neighbourhood in town. He looked in the rearview mirror.

Gracie, her crying having subsided to the occasional hiccup, sucked her thumb.

Matthew's brown eyes met his in the mirror. "Where are we going?"

Caleb turned in his seat to look back. "To the home of a nice couple, Mr. and Mrs. Charleton. They're looking forward to having you and Gracie come and stay with them."

"Do you know when we can go home?"

"I'm not sure, Matthew."

"Is my dad still in a time-out?"

Caleb glanced at Jesse before turning back to the boy. "No, he's not. He and your mom are fine. And I'll make you a deal. If you do your job and listen to the Charletons and help them take care of Gracie, then Captain Christensen and I will do our jobs and try to get you home as soon as possible, okay?"

"Okay."

When they pulled into the driveway of the foster home, the door of the vehicle in front of them opened, and a woman climbed out. One side of her striped shirt was tucked into her black dress pants and the other side hung out, as if she had dressed in a hurry.

Jesse looked at Caleb. "Do you mind staying with the kids while I check the place out?"

Caleb nodded and Jesse got out of the vehicle and walked toward the woman.

She held out her hand. "Emily Dixon, Child Services."

He shook her hand. "Captain Jesse Christensen." He gestured toward the house. "Do you think this is a good place?"

The woman offered him a thin smile. "Define good, Captain. I think they'll be safe here, yes. The parents are decent people."

He definitely would have preferred a more glowing endorsement. "Can I meet them?"

"Of course. They're expecting us." Since the front of the house was dark, she led the way around to the back of the house to a door lit by a dim, spider-web-encrusted bulb.

Jesse looked around the backyard. Lots of grass and all fenced in. Not a bad place for the kids to play.

A man with pale, thinning hair and a belly sticking out between a baggy brown T-shirt and even baggier sweat pants pulled open the door. "Come in." He turned and went up three steps to the kitchen.

Jesse waved the case worker in ahead of him and followed her up the stairs.

A woman in a worn yellow housecoat sat at the kitchen table. Her short grey hair was mussed, as though she'd been pulled from her bed. When the case worker introduced them, the woman turned to Jesse. Her eyes were kind and he relaxed a little.

Jesse nodded to her. "I'm Captain Christensen. It's good of you to agree to take the kids."

The woman offered him a tired smile. "We raised five of our own, so we're used to having little ones around. It's a bit too quiet here sometimes, now that they're gone. We're happy to help out."

Jesse studied the man. His eyes were more guarded than the woman's. Something about him gave Jesse a bit of an unsettled feeling, but nothing he could put his finger on.

The man glanced behind him. "So where are they?"

"I'll get them in a minute." *Why so impatient?* "We just want to make sure this is the right place for them. I have a vested interest in this case, and I need to make sure they will be well taken care of."

The man drew himself up. "Of course they will be. Like my wife said, we've raised five kids, and they all turned out all right."

"It's just ..." Jesse stepped closer. He was a good head taller than the man who, he was happy to see, shrank back a little as he approached. "If anything were to happen to them, I would take that as a personal affront." *Should have strapped on my gun.* The sight of the Glock usually drove his point home pretty effectively when he was talking to someone questionable.

The man seemed to get it anyway. He nodded. "You don't have to worry. We'll treat them like they're our own."

Jesse wasn't sure how comforting that thought was.

The woman rose. "Captain." She ran her fingers through her hair as though she'd just realized how she must look. "I promise you we'll take good care of them. We're glad to have a couple of kids running around the house again. Chief'll be happy too."

"Chief?"

"Our dog. He's a lab, nice and gentle. He loves kids. There's a boy, right? Five or six?"

"Almost six."

"I'm sure he'll have fun with him. Chief'll play fetch with him all day if the boy will let him."

"What about the little girl? She's only three. Will the dog be okay with her?"

"Oh yes. When our grandbabies come around, he stands guard over them as if he's their personal watchdog. He wouldn't ever let anyone lift a finger to them."

Jesse shot a look at Emily.

She shrugged. "The dog has been okayed. There's never been a problem with it."

He contemplated the situation. Not ideal, but hopefully he'd made it clear that nothing could happen to the kids or the Charletons would answer to him. Then Jesse would answer to Ethan. He winced. "I'll go get the kids."

The case worker followed him and he handed her the suitcase. Jesse helped Matthew out of the vehicle and lifted Gracie from her car seat.

Her eyelids looked heavy from crying and exhaustion.

Caleb grabbed the car seat and motioned for them to go ahead.

The man held the door open for them as they went into the house and up the stairs.

A look of delight crossed the woman's face when she saw Gracie. "What a sweetie. Look at those red curls. Will she come to me, do you think?"

Jesse held the girl out.

Gracie looked a little uncertain, but she went to Mrs. Charleton, holding herself back and staring at the woman's face.

Matthew turned toward the hallway at the sound of nails clicking on the hardwood floor. When a big yellow dog came into the kitchen, the boy's face lit up.

The dog padded straight over to him.

Matthew reached out tentatively to pat him on the head. When the dog wagged his tail in response, Matthew grinned.

Emily set down the suitcase, and Caleb propped Gracie's car seat against it.

Jesse's gaze swept the room. For tonight, this was as good as he was going to get. He pulled a card from his shirt pocket and crossed the room to set it on the table. "This is my personal line. Don't hesitate to get in touch with me if you have any questions, okay?"

The woman ran a hand over Gracie's curls. "We'll be fine, Captain."

The case worker inclined her head toward the door, and he and Caleb followed her back to her vehicle.

Jesse stopped at the driver's side door. "You think they'll be all right here?"

"I'm sure they will be. This place is the best we can offer you, anyway. As you can see, we're stretched pretty thin these days. And all due respect, but you're the ones who pulled these kids, who look perfectly fine to me, out of a home we've never had any complaints about, and brought them to us to deal with." She rubbed her forehead with her fingers before looking up at him again. "Incidentally, I hope that isn't going to become a trend. We don't have the resources to deal with a new flood of children in need of foster homes."

"I hope not too." Jesse pulled the jeep keys from his pocket. "Thanks for setting this up. Let me know if there are any problems, and I'll come deal with them myself."

"I will."

He climbed behind the wheel as Caleb slid onto the passenger seat. *God, please let them be all right. And show me what to do to get them back.* The situation was about far more than restoring one family. The implications were huge.

I'm in over my head. Please help me.

The peace that filled him was a reminder—why did he need so many of those?—that he wasn't in control. Not of what was going on with Matthew and Gracie. Or of his relationship with Meryn. Or of anything else that was going on around him.

Someone else was.

Chapter Twenty-Three

The murmur of voices drifted across the hall to the living room. Meryn laid her head against the back of the couch and brushed a tear from her cheek. Where were Matthew and Gracie now? Had Jesse found a good place for them? They must be so scared and confused. *Like the rest of us.*

Kate appeared in the doorway. "I'm making tea, Mer. Come join us."

Meryn hesitated. For the first time in her life, she felt like an intruder in this home. She had brought Jesse here. She was the one who had brought him into their lives in the first place, for that matter. Well, maybe not, but she was the one who had invited him to stay.

Kate rested a hand on her shoulder. "Please come."

"I'm not sure Ethan will want to see me."

"None of this is your fault. He knows that. He doesn't blame you."

"He blames Jesse, though."

Kate squeezed her shoulder. "Come have some tea and we'll talk."

With a heavy sigh, Meryn got up from the couch and followed Kate into the kitchen.

Ethan had been resting his forehead on his clasped hands, but he straightened up when Meryn came into the room.

"I'm sorry, Ethan."

"Don't be. You didn't do anything wrong."

"If it helps, it just about killed Jesse, doing what he had to do tonight."

"But he did it anyway, didn't he?"

"Ethan." Kate set a mug down in front of him.

"Well, he did. He could have refused."

"Then the army would have sent someone else to take the kids. A stranger. Would that have been better?"

Ethan scrubbed his face with both hands. "I don't know. I guess not."

"If it had been someone else, that soldier would have arrested you for taking a swing at him. The only reason you're not in a cell right now is that Jesse and the major let you get away with what a lot of soldiers wouldn't." Kate pulled out a chair. "Here you go, Mer."

Meryn's legs were weak and she was grateful to take a seat. "He'll do everything he can to bring the kids back to you quickly. He promised."

Ethan threw a look at her, as though he considered Jesse's promises to be worth about as much as the used tea bag Kate had just fished out of the pot, but he didn't say anything.

Kate filled Meryn's cup.

Usually the soft gurgling sound of tea being poured, the warm, chamomile-scented steam rising from the mug, comforted her, but tonight nothing could lift the heaviness that had draped itself over her.

Kate pressed her hand against her husband's back as she poured his tea. "And he'll make sure they're in a good place until he does."

He looked up at her. "Why are you defending him? The man just took our children away from us, and we may never see them again. Do you understand that?"

Kate set down the pot. "Yes, Ethan. I understand that." She walked over to the counter and pressed both palms on the top of it.

Ethan exhaled loudly and pushed back his chair, the legs scraping along the wooden floor. He went to her and slid his arms around her waist. "I'm sorry, Kate." She turned around and he pulled her to him. "I'm not helping, I know. I just feel so useless." He glanced over at Meryn. "I apologize, Meryn. This isn't your fault, and I guess it isn't Jesse's, either, not really. I'm sure he has to do all kinds of things he doesn't want to do. It can't be easy, living a double life like that."

"It isn't. I don't know how much longer he's going to be able to do it."

Ethan sat down and wrapped his hands around his mug. "Maybe I'm being too hard on him, I don't know."

"I was pretty hard on him tonight too." A slight stabbing pain shot through her chest, an echo of the terrible pain she'd experienced that night in the woods. She pressed the heel of her hand to the spot. "He gave me a necklace right before Caleb messaged him, and when he wouldn't agree not to take your kids tonight, or even to let me warn you he and Caleb were coming, I threw it back at him. He won't have any idea where we stand now, after everything that's happened."

Kate sat down beside Ethan. "Where do you stand?"

"I'm not sure."

"Still ..." Ethan's eyes hardened. "If anything happens to the kids, or if he isn't able to get them back, I mean what I said. I will hold him responsible."

"He'll hold himself responsible. He's a man of his word, and he'll do everything he can to make this right."

"Maybe. I just hope that's enough. You never know anymore. If this thing does go before a commission, I don't see how he'll have any control over what happens."

Silence blanketed the kitchen.

The bleak truth, that the Canadian Human Rights Commission had the power to make decisions that destroyed the lives of people they had never seen and who hadn't had an opportunity to speak in their own defence, was terrifying.

The i-com in Meryn's pocket vibrated and she pulled out the unit. *Jesse?* She scanned the message and looked up.

Both Kate and Ethan were watching her.

She shook her head. "Sorry, it's Brendan. He's freaking out that I'm not home yet and wants to know where I am. I guess I better call him and let him and Shane know what's going on. Then, if you don't mind, I'll sleep on the couch tonight, and one of them can come and get me in the morning."

"I'll bring you a pillow and some blankets."

"Thanks, Kate." Meryn picked up her mug and took it with her into the living room. She couldn't believe she had to call her brothers and tell them yet another story with Jesse cast as the villain.

Even though he'd saved her life when she was sick, their gratitude might only extend so far. They loved Matthew and Gracie as much as she did.

If anything happened to them, Ethan wouldn't be the only one standing in line to take out his fury on Jesse.

Chapter Twenty-Four

Jesse drove along the city's waterfront in silence, heading for the base. Emotions churned through him until he couldn't take it anymore. Pulling up to the curb, he jammed the vehicle into park and pushed open the door. "I need some air."

"Or you could just roll down the window and ..."

Jesse caught Caleb's loud exhalation of breath just before he slammed the door shut. His friend climbed out of the jeep and followed him as he strode across the grass-covered knoll leading down to the boardwalk. The lights of the houses lining the shore twinkled like stars on the lake. Jesse stopped under a lamppost, picked up a stone, and hurled it into the water as hard as he could, shattering the still, glassy surface. So many thoughts whirled through his head, it took him several minutes to reel in one of them.

Caleb waited in silence beside him.

"I used to love being a soldier."

"I know."

"I mean I loved everything about it, even the hazing and the five a.m. drills and the forty-kilometre hikes. What I loved most was feeling as if I was actually doing something to make a difference in the world, fighting terrorism and injustice, and protecting innocent civilians. I believed that we were actually doing something noble, you know?"

"And now?"

Jesse whipped another stone into the water. It landed with a plunk, sending rings rippling out over the water. "There is nothing noble about ripping innocent children out of the arms of their loving parents and handing them over to strangers."

Caleb didn't respond.

"I need to talk to them."

"Who?"

"The commission. Is that possible?"

Caleb pursed his lips. "I don't know. I could look into it. Are you sure you want to do that?"

"I haven't heard about other parents losing their kids for telling them a few Bible stories, have you?"

"No."

"So this is a precedent-setting case. If they take Matthew and Gracie away from Kate and Ethan, that will open the floodgates. Hundreds of children in this city alone will be vulnerable to the same treatment. The ramifications on a national level are mind-boggling. The public outcry, the cost to an already overloaded child welfare system, the effects on the kids now and in the future—this will have far more devastating consequences than anything that has happened so far. Someone needs to stop this before it goes any further."

"If you go to Ottawa and speak up for the rights of Christians, you'll be putting a lot at risk. You could lose your career, or worse."

"I don't care. If I don't go, and Kate and Ethan don't get their kids back, I'll lose a lot more."

"Meryn, you mean."

"Possibly. I'm not sure she'd want anything to do with me after that. And I'd lose other people I care about too."

Caleb studied him. "No guarantees, but I'll see what I can do."

"Thanks."

"Don't thank me. As I said, it's a huge risk, but I guess this is the sort of thing we signed up for when we decided to stay with the army, isn't it?"

"I guess." Jesse focused on the shimmering lights reflecting off the lake.

"What is it?"

He sighed. "I've been thinking a lot lately about not staying."

"Why is that?" Caleb didn't sound surprised.

"Because it's getting harder and harder to do the things we're being ordered to do, like taking kids away from their parents."

"And?"

"And arresting innocent people and enforcing a ridiculous curfew and having to pretend to be something I'm not. Or, to be more accurate, having to pretend not to be something I am."

"And?"

He tore his gaze from the water to look at his friend. "Aren't those good enough reasons?"

"Yes. I just want to hear you admit the real one."

He threw up his hands. "Fine. I want to be with Meryn. I'm tired of sneaking around and meeting in secret and worrying about being discovered all the time. And I'm desperately tired of stealing an hour or two with her and then having to walk away. I can't keep doing it."

"Do you want to marry her?"

That stopped him. He hadn't really thought that far down the road, but now that Caleb mentioned it … "After tonight, I'm not even sure we're together anymore. But if, after all this is straightened out, she agrees to have me, then yes, I'd marry her in a second."

Caleb picked up a stone and tossed it into the lake. It skipped across the surface several times before disappearing.

Jesse studied him. "What?"

"Have you thought about what would happen if you left?"

"I could have a life."

"Yes, but I mean what would happen at the base, and in this city."

A dark shadow fell across Jesse's plans. "Gallagher would move up."

"Very likely. With the army having so many new bases, there are no available higher-ranking officers to take over here. Some bases don't even have anyone above the rank of lieutenant on them yet, although they're moving people up a lot faster these days to compensate. So we're on our own here. Either I'd have to work closely with Gallagher or, if I left too, he could be promoted and put in charge. I hate to say it, Jess, but you and I might be the only ones preventing an evil, power-hungry fool from gaining control of the city."

"Can't you report him to Headquarters?"

"I've discussed him with the general before. Somehow Gallagher has everyone there fooled. They love him because he does everything they tell him to do and brings them all kinds of dirt on people, often without us knowing. He might even have been the one to supply them the information about—"

"Matthew on the playground." Jesse's fists clenched.

"Possibly. That information went straight to Headquarters. If it had come to me, I could have handled it differently, maybe even made it disappear, but someone went over our heads. I can't prove it was Gallagher, but even if it wasn't him this time, he's given them enough to ingratiate himself to them, even the general, which isn't easy to do."

Jesse's stomach churned. Somehow he'd been so focused on what he would be going to, he hadn't given much thought to what he'd be leaving behind. "So there's no way out."

"I didn't say that. You could still leave."

"And abandon you to deal with Gallagher."

"I've fought deadly enemies before. I'd just be doing it on home territory this time."

"And facing him alone. You wouldn't do that to me."

Caleb shoved his hands in his jacket pockets.

Jesse blew out a breath. "Tell me what to do."

"I'd never do that."

Jesse snorted.

Caleb offered him a wry smile. "Okay, I won't tell you what to do about this. It's something you have to decide for yourself. All I ask is that you don't make the decision lightly. Either way this is going to have a profound effect on both our lives, so give it a lot of thought. And pray about it."

Jesse shot him a look.

"What? I'm not a complete heathen, you know. I do believe in God. I even pray myself sometimes."

"That's news."

"How do you think I've been able to put up with you all these years? It's taken a lot of divine assistance, my friend."

"So what are you saying, that you're a believer now?"

"That might be a bit strong, but I told you when you became

a Christian that I'd have to figure out what I believe, and I have been working on it."

"Can I help?"

"Probably. I'll let you know. At the moment, you need to concentrate on helping your friends and then figuring out what you're going to do with the rest of your life."

"Is that all?"

"For the next few days, yes. After that, we'll see."

"I won't turn my back on you. We've been through too much together."

"Even so, you have to do what you are compelled to do. Just make sure you know what that is before you act."

"I will." Jesse held out his hand, and Caleb grasped it. Jesse pulled him closer for a brief hug. "We'll get through this, Cale, together."

His friend grinned. Caleb had said the same words to Jesse more times than he could remember, but this was the first time he had made the promise to Caleb.

Now Jesse just had to hope and pray that it would prove to be true.

Chapter Twenty-Five

The next morning, Meryn called Shane and Brendan to let them know they didn't need to pick her up after all, since Ethan had asked before he left for work if she could stay with Kate.

Her brothers came anyway.

"How is she doing?" Shane inclined his head toward the stairs as they went into the living room.

"She's devastated. But she was amazing last night, really strong. Ethan lost it and almost got himself arrested, which I couldn't blame him for, but Kate did what she had to do, even though it was obviously tearing her up."

"Will she want to see us?" Brendan dropped down on the couch. A small pink doll lay on the coffee table, and he picked it up in both hands and studied it.

Uh-oh. Brendan appeared calm, but sometimes it was hard to see the heat building inside that dormant volcano until suddenly the whole thing erupted.

"I'm sure she will. I'll go see if she's awake." Meryn went upstairs to Kate and Ethan's room. The kids' bedroom door was open and the sight of their little beds, still unmade, deepened the ache in Meryn's chest. She knocked softly on Kate's door before pushing it open.

Her friend was staring at the window, where bright sunlight streamed into the room and pooled on the beige carpet. She didn't turn toward Meryn when she came and sat down on the bed beside her.

Meryn touched her shoulder. "Morning, Kate."

For a moment Kate didn't move, then she drew in a shuddering breath. "This is the first time in five years that I have no idea where my children are. Did she give them a good breakfast? Matthew only likes toast and Gracie needs a sippy cup and I forgot to send hers ..." Her hands fisted around the cream-coloured duvet.

"I'm sure she did, Kate. Matthew can tell her what they like. And Gracie can drink out of a regular cup if she has to. You have to trust that Jesse found a good place for them. It's just for a couple of days."

Kate turned her head on the pillow and stared at Meryn, her eyes dull and listless. "We don't know that for sure, do we? Maybe they'll never be back. And as long as they're gone, I have no reason to get up. No one to get dressed or take to the park or draw pictures with or read books to." She let go of the duvet and rubbed her temples with the fingers of both hands. "I just want to go to sleep and wake up when all of this is over. Can I do that?"

"I'm afraid not, sweetie. Shane and Brendan are here, and they want to see you."

Kate deflated a little against the pillow. "I don't know if I can, Mer. If I see them, Brendan especially, I don't think I'll be able to hold it together."

Meryn squeezed her shoulder. "That's the great thing about being with family, Kate. You don't have to."

She sighed. "All right. Give me a few minutes, and I'll come down."

"Good." Meryn climbed off the bed and shut the door behind her. She straightened the sheets and blankets in the kids' room, then went down to the kitchen and began breakfast preparations, even though she knew Kate wouldn't want anything and Meryn didn't think she would be able to keep anything down, either. It helped to keep busy, to not stop moving. When she heard footsteps on the stairs, she flipped the power button on the coffee maker and followed Kate into the living room.

Brendan didn't say anything, just held his arms open, and Kate went to him. Although she had shed a few tears the night before, she hadn't broken down completely. Now she wept as though her heart were being torn in two. Meryn understood Kate's reluctance to see him. There was something about Brendan, a deadly combination of a deeply sensitive heart inside a strong, tough-guy body, that broke down all defences.

Shane slid an arm around Meryn as they waited. What would she do without his quiet strength and presence?

When Kate pulled a tissue from the pocket of her khaki capris to dab at her cheeks, Brendan's eyes, dark and angry, zeroed in on Meryn.

"What?" Meryn gripped the back of the couch. "Why are you mad at me?"

"I'm not mad at you. But your *boyfriend* is really starting to push it."

Shane tightened his hold. "Leave her alone, Brendan."

"Yeah, come on." Kate tugged on Brendan's sleeve. "That's not helping."

He stepped around her and walked toward Meryn. "Speaking of helping, what is he doing to get Matthew and Gracie back now that he's taken them away?"

"I don't know what he's doing exactly. I haven't spoken to him since last night. But I'm sure he's doing everything he can."

"He'd better."

"All right." Shane let go of Meryn and took a step toward his brother. "Enough."

Meryn shook her head. "It's fine, Shane, really. I understand. I'm going to finish making breakfast." She spun around and strode to the kitchen.

Behind her, Shane continued to berate Brendan. "What is the matter with you? She's hurting as much as we are. She doesn't need you coming down on her."

Meryn grabbed a dozen eggs from the refrigerator and started cracking them on the edge of a frying pan and dumping them in.

A minute later, Brendan came into the kitchen and walked over to stand beside her.

She ignored him as she grabbed a lifter from the ceramic holder on the counter and scrambled the eggs.

"I'm sorry, kid."

"It's all right." She jabbed at the eggs with the end of the lifter. "I can't even be upset with you, because I was angry at Jesse last night too."

He gave her a few seconds, then nudged her shoulder. "You know, for someone who can't be upset with me, you're managing to come off as pretty upset with me."

Her brother sounded so sheepish, Meryn's anger slipped from her grasp. She pressed her lips together to keep from smiling.

Brendan pointed a finger at her. "I saw that." He wrapped an arm around her. "Look, I know Jesse's in an impossible situation, and that he's doing the best he can. I also know that what he's doing, he's doing at great risk to himself. I really do admire that."

She looked up at him. "You'll lay off him?"

He grinned. "I didn't say that."

"Then will you stop calling me kid?"

"I can't promise that, either."

Meryn sighed and rested her head on his shoulder.

"I will try to think more before I speak. How about that?"

"It's a start, I guess." Meryn lifted her head and checked to see if the eggs were done.

"It's the best you're going to get today." Brendan dropped his arm. "Here." He reached for the bread and dropped a couple of slices into the toaster.

Kate stopped in the kitchen doorway. "All clear?"

Meryn smiled. "All clear."

"Good." Kate took four plates out of the cupboard.

Shane pulled open the silverware drawer and grabbed knives and forks for everyone. By the time the table was set, the toast and eggs were ready.

As Meryn had suspected, Kate only picked at her food. Her eyes were red and swollen, but she smiled once or twice when Shane or Brendan made a joke or teased her about something.

After scraping his plate clean, Shane set his fork down. "Brendan and I have to head out this morning to a new job site. This one's just outside town, though, so we'll be home tonight."

Meryn picked up his plate and slid it under her own to carry them to the sink. "That's good. I'm glad you won't be far away."

"Me too." Shane followed her over to the counter with their mugs. "What are you two going to do today?"

She walked back to the table and rested her hands on the back of a chair. "I haven't had a chance to ask you this yet, Kate, but I wondered if you wanted to come to the store with me. I've been thinking about opening it back up again, and today seems like a good day."

Kate didn't answer.

Meryn studied her. Did she not feel up to going, or did she want to be home in case the kids showed up? "Jesse will message us if there's any news."

Kate's slim shoulders relaxed as her hazel eyes met Meryn's. "All right then. Let's do it."

Shane touched Kate's arm. "Why don't you and Ethan come stay out at the farm for a couple of days?"

"Yeah. I'll check with him, but I'd like to be out there with all of you. Better than sitting here staring at the walls and waiting for the i-com to go off."

He squeezed her arm. "Brendan, we better get going."

Brendan dumped a handful of silverware into the sink beside Meryn as Shane and Kate went out into the hall. He crooked his finger under Meryn's chin and lifted her face until she was looking at him. "We're okay?"

The corners of her mouth turned up slightly. "Yeah, we're okay."

"Good." He winked at her. "See you tonight."

She followed him down the hallway to the front door.

Both of her brothers hugged Kate before going outside.

Meryn reached for her hand. "See? That wasn't so bad."

Kate rolled her eyes. "It was exactly what I thought it would be." She drew in a deep breath. "If we're going to the store, I'll have to go up and change."

"All right. You do that and I'll take care of the dishes, and when you're ready we'll head over."

"Sounds good." Kate touched the sleeve of Meryn's blouse. "Mer, I want you to know that, whatever happens, we'll all forgive Jesse. Eventually. Even Ethan admitted last night that none of this is really Jesse's fault."

"I hope so." Meryn offered her a weak smile. *Father God, please let Kate's words be true. Or better yet, help Jesse to bring the kids home, so there is nothing to forgive.*

Chapter Twenty-Six

Bells jangled as Meryn pushed open the door of the store and stepped inside. The building smelled a little musty. Not surprising, since she hadn't been here in weeks.

"Uh, Mer?"

She glanced over her shoulder.

Kate stood on the sidewalk, looking up. "How long has *that* been there?"

Meryn came back outside.

A silver fish symbol, about six inches long and three inches high, had been screwed into the brick wall above the door.

"I've never seen it before." Swinging around, she looked up and down the street.

Two other stores had fish symbols above their doors.

Meryn pressed a hand to her stomach. "They're marking the Christian businesses."

"Just like they did the Jewish businesses in Nazi Germany."

Meryn swallowed hard. The comparison was terrifying. "I guess so." She started to head back into the store but froze instead.

A woman walked down the sidewalk toward them, clutching the hand of a young child.

Meryn stared at the little girl's strawberry-blonde curls as the two of them drew even with her and Kate.

When they had passed by, the girl craned her neck to look back at Meryn. Their eyes met and the girl smiled. She tugged on the woman's hand, and the woman stopped walking and crouched down in front of her.

"What is it, darling?"

The little girl pointed at Meryn. "The lady."

The woman straightened up and turned around. For a moment, she studied Meryn and then her mouth formed an *O* shape and she walked toward them.

Meryn came down the stairs.

The woman stopped in front of her. "It was you."

Meryn's throat tightened. She nodded.

The eyes that met hers glistened. "I'm Alison Crawford."

"Meryn O'Reilly."

"Meryn." The woman reached for her hand. "How can I thank you? You saved her life. Her father had already gone into the hospital. When I got sick, I stayed home. I couldn't leave Ruby. Then she got sick, and I tried to take care of her, but I …" Her voice broke and she let go of Meryn and reached into her pocket for a tissue. After dabbing her eyes, she drew in a deep breath. "I lost consciousness, and she got out of the house somehow. Looking for help, maybe." Alison grasped Meryn's elbow. "Thank God she found it. Found you."

"I'm glad I was there." Meryn covered the woman's trembling fingers with her own and lowered her voice. "Your husband?"

The woman shook her head slightly.

A pang shot through Meryn. "I'm sorry."

"Thank you."

Ruby leaned her head against her mother's leg.

Alison rested a hand on the little girl's curls. "I don't know what I would have done if I had lost her too."

"I'm so happy to find out that she recovered. I've thought of her often since that day."

"And we've thought of you. And wondered who you were." She looked down at the little girl. "What do you say to the kind lady, Ruby?"

The little girl tipped back her head. "Thank you."

Meryn lightly brushed the dimpled cheeks, pale pink now instead of angry red, with her knuckles. "You're welcome."

Alison met her eyes again and nodded. Then she took her daughter's hand, and the two of them turned away. Just before they disappeared around the corner, the little girl looked back and waved.

Meryn lifted her hand before slumping against the door frame.

Kate touched her arm. "I'm glad you saw her."

"Me too." Meryn tore her gaze from the street corner and went into the store. She wouldn't have changed anything that had happened, but knowing the little girl hadn't died made everything she had gone through worth all the anguish she and Jesse and her family had suffered.

Kate swept the creaky wooden floors and dusted the shelves with a blue feather duster.

Meryn unpacked an order in the back room. Emptying the boxes reminded her of the shipments of books she'd accepted with Bibles hidden throughout. Her thoughts drifted back to the day she'd been arrested. Jesse had been furious. He'd begged her to avoid trouble, but instead she had sought it out. And it had cost her.

She didn't regret it, though. A small smile played around her mouth. More than thirty people had received a Bible, most of whom had never read one before. Although she'd been sentenced to a flogging, she'd also spent seven days in Jesse's quarters, and once he'd gotten over his anger, that week had changed both of their lives. Her smile faded.

Where was he now? Was he getting anywhere in his quest to bring Matthew and Gracie home?

She grabbed an armful of books and headed back into the store. Just as she reached the historical fiction section, the bells above the door jangled. Meryn looked over.

Drew shut the door behind him. His face lit up when he saw her, and he waved.

She set down the stack of books and headed over to him. "Hey, Drew."

"Hi, Meryn." He kissed her on the cheek. "Good to see the store open again."

"I thought it was time. I was starting to go a little stir-crazy at home."

Drew smoothed down his red-and-blue-striped tie. "You're looking better than the last time I saw you."

"Thanks."

"Not that you looked bad that day. Far from it. You looked beautiful, as always. Just a little pale. Of course you'd been ill, so that's not surprising. But you look good now. Even better, I mean ..."

Meryn laughed. "It's okay, Drew. I look better than I did. Got it."

His face was a little red, but he smiled back. "Sorry. It's just ... good to see you."

A slight movement on the other side of a shelf behind Drew caught her eye.

Kate, eyebrows raised, peered at Meryn through the space between two books.

She shot her a warning look before looking back at Drew. "It's good to see you too."

He lifted his wrist to check his watch. "I need to get to work. But listen ..." He reached for her hand. "What about that dinner you promised me? Are you free tonight?"

"Um, I ..." Would it be so wrong to spend a little time with him? Like Kate said, it was better than sitting around waiting for the i-com to go off. "I'm having dinner with my family tonight, but I'm free tomorrow evening. Does that work?"

"Sure. I'll come by here around five? That should give us plenty of time before it gets dark."

"Sounds good."

"Okay then." He squeezed her hand. "I'll see you tomorrow."

She followed him to the door. When he had gone, she turned and almost banged into Kate. Meryn jumped and pressed a hand to her chest. "You scared me."

"Are you sure that's fear?"

"What else?"

"I don't know, guilt maybe?"

"What are you talking about?" Meryn stalked back to the pile of books she had set down.

Kate followed her.

Meryn grabbed *Nineteen Eighty-Four* off the top of the pile and shoved it onto the historical fiction shelf.

When she reached for another book, Kate grabbed the pile and clutched it to her chest. "I'm talking about the fact that you just agreed to go on a date with someone who isn't the man you're seeing."

Meryn reached for the books.

Kate swung sideways, moving them out of her reach.

Meryn planted both hands on her hips. "It's not a date. Drew's an old friend, and we're grabbing dinner together. It's perfectly innocent."

"You think Jesse would be fine with you going out with another man?"

"Why are you so concerned with what Jesse would think? Last night in the kids' room you were furious with him."

"Is that what this is about, then? Getting back at him?"

"Of course not." Meryn threw both hands in the air. "This doesn't have anything to do with him. It's dinner with a friend. Why are you giving me such a hard time?"

Kate sighed and set down the books. "It's just that you and Jesse are so good together, but you've had to face challenge after challenge this past year. I'd hate to see you adding any more to the list, especially when he's fighting to get our kids back."

"I won't. Drew and I will have dinner, and that will be it. If he asks me to do anything with him again, I'll say no and make it clear there can't be anything between us."

"Will you tell Jesse you went out with him?"

"Of course. And he'll be fine with it. He knows Drew and I are friends."

"He knows *you* think you are."

Meryn's forehead wrinkled. "What does that mean?"

"It means I saw Jesse's face when Ethan suggested Drew come with us to pick you up from the base that day. He's well aware that Drew doesn't think of you as just a friend. And you know that too."

"I told Drew that's all we could be. He's accepted that."

"Come on, Mer, you heard him trying to talk to you today. He sounded like a flustered teenager asking his crush to the prom."

"That's ridiculous. He ..." The i-com in her jeans pocket vibrated. Meryn pulled it out and looked at the screen. "It's from Jesse."

Kate's face paled. "What does it say?"

"The kids are fine. They're with a couple who have a dog, and Matthew was excited about that. The hearing has been set for Thursday morning at eleven. Caleb arranged for Jesse to speak to the commission directly, so he's going to Ottawa tomorrow afternoon to get ready for the next morning."

Kate backed up and sat down on a brown leather armchair tucked into a recess between two shelves of books. "That's good, I guess."

Meryn replaced the phone, then crouched down in front of Kate and rested her hands on Kate's knees. "It's really good. Now you know the kids are okay and that someone will be there to speak on your behalf on Thursday. I'm sure Jesse will be able to convince the commission to let them come home. Matthew and Gracie could be back in their own beds by Thursday night."

"Are you going to send a message back? You could tell him about your dinner with Drew."

Meryn stood up. "No, I try not to message him, since I don't know whether or not the line is secure. He only risks sending me a message when he has something urgent to tell me. Besides, he has a lot on his mind right now. I'll tell him when all of this is over."

"Okay, Mer, you're an adult. I can't tell you what to do. I can give you some advice, though. Be careful. Make it clear to Drew again that you only want to be friends, and don't keep anything from Jesse. If he finds out on his own, he won't be happy."

"I'll be careful." The promise sounded a little hollow. Meryn picked up the stack of books and continued shelving them around the store, but her mind wasn't on the task. Maybe Kate was right and it was a bad idea to go out with Drew.

Meryn shook her head. She had nothing to worry about. Jesse would understand.

Chapter Twenty-Seven

Meryn's parents were both home. Not surprising, since it was after curfew.

Jesse stood on the sidewalk, looking up at the brightly lit window where one or the other of them passed periodically.

They were just as Meryn had described. Her father was tall and dark, dominating the room like Brendan did. Her mother was tall too, and slender, like Meryn and Annaliese.

As far as he could tell, they were alone. Jesse waited until a car passed by and then headed up the front walk. The doorbell cut through the quiet evening air, and he looked around furtively.

No one else was in sight.

Meryn's mother pulled open the door. Her cheeks blanched at the sight of his uniform.

He held up a hand quickly. "Everything's fine. We're just canvassing this neighbourhood as a follow-up from the Reds pandemic, making sure everyone is okay and no one needs anything." It was weak, but he thought it would be better if they didn't know who he was. At least until he found out if Meryn had ever mentioned him.

Meryn's father came up behind his wife. "Who is it, Isabelle?" He pulled the door open wider. His face darkened slightly when he saw Jesse on the front porch.

His wife patted his arm. "It's all right, Hugh. He says they're just checking on everyone to make sure they're okay now that the pandemic is dying down."

"Oh." Hugh O'Reilly studied him. Something flashed across his face, and he shot a look up and down the street. "Why don't we talk inside?" He moved back as Jesse came into the house.

The smells of apples and cinnamon filled the air.

Hugh closed the door behind him.

Isabelle motioned toward the living room. "Come in and sit down. Can I get you a cup of tea?"

"Just a glass of water, thank you." Jesse hesitated. It broke protocol to take off his boots when in uniform, but this was a private call and he couldn't bring himself to tromp through Meryn's parents' home while still wearing his shoes. He pulled them off and followed Meryn's father into the living room.

Hugh waved him toward the couch and took the big, chocolate-brown armchair by the gas fireplace. Shelves of books lined the walls behind Meryn's father, and Jesse scanned the titles.

Hugh tapped his fingers on the arm of the chair. "Booklover?"

"Yes, actually."

"Who's your favourite?"

"Dickens. *A Tale of Two Cities*, specifically." Jesse almost laughed at Hugh's look, the exact one that had crossed Meryn's face that night in her bookstore when he'd given her the same answer. "Is it the idea of me in particular or soldiers in general enjoying the classics that surprises you?"

"Do you really want me to give you my opinion on soldiers in general?"

Jesse's smile faded. "No, sir, I guess I don't."

"Hugh, behave yourself." Meryn's mother came into the room carrying a glass of ice water. "Soldier or no, the man is a guest in our home."

"It's all right." Jesse took the glass from her. "I understand."

Isabelle sat down on the armchair on the other side of the fireplace and crossed her legs delicately at the ankles. "So, Jesse, why don't you tell us why you are really here?"

He blinked and looked over at Meryn's father, whose expression hadn't changed. Jesse sighed and set the glass down on a coaster on the coffee table in front of him. "How did you know?"

"For starters, you're not a very good liar, which, in my opinion, is a point in your favour." Isabelle smiled. "Of course, the fact that Meryn sent us a picture of you a while ago helped. And the kids have told us quite a bit about you, including the fact that you recently saved our Meryn's life."

He shook his head. "That was more thanks to all of your prayers and to Meryn's own strength than anything I did."

Hugh's face creased into a proud grin. "She's a fighter, all right."

Yeah, she's fighting me pretty good right now. "Yes, she is, thankfully."

"We're hoping to come to Kingston soon to see her." Isabelle sighed. "We don't get there as often as we'd like, since my health isn't the best, I'm afraid."

Hugh reached over and squeezed her hand before turning back to Jesse. "What we didn't expect, though, was you showing up at the door on your own. Is this about our Katie, then?"

Jesse didn't miss the fact that they made no distinction between the two girls. "So, you know what's happening?"

"Meryn called to tell me. Our i-com hasn't been working very well, so I heard the story in snatches, but I believe I got the gist of it." Anger laced Hugh's words and his fists tightened on his knees.

Hopefully one of the snatches of conversation they'd missed was the part he'd played in the story.

"Seems little Matthew and Gracie were pulled from their beds and taken away in the night, and now a commission who knows nothing about them or their parents will determine whether or not they're allowed to go back to their safe, loving home. Is that about the sum of it?"

"I'm afraid so. That's why I'm in Ottawa, actually. I'm planning to address the commission in the morning, hoping to persuade them it would be a terrible mistake to take the children away permanently."

"What time will you be speaking?"

"Eleven."

Isabelle nodded. "We'll be praying."

Some of the weight lifted from Jesse's shoulders. No doubt the two of them on their knees made a formidable force, and he needed all the reinforcements he could get.

Meryn's mother rose, the movement as graceful as every other one she made. "I baked a pie this afternoon. You'll stay and have a piece."

Jesse wasn't about to argue. The warm, cinnamon-laden aroma was far too enticing, especially since he couldn't remember the last time he'd had a piece of fresh, homemade pie. He looked at the wall of books and snapped his fingers. "James Joyce."

Hugh cocked his head. "Pardon me?"

"I should have said James Joyce, shouldn't I, when you asked my favourite?"

Hugh's booming laugh was identical to his younger son's. "It wouldn't have hurt you any. Of course you'd have done equally well with Jonathon Swift or Oscar Wilde, or even Sam Beckett. Still, for future reference, I always prefer to hear the truth, so you did just fine."

"Sounds like the two of you are hitting it off nicely." Isabelle carried a tray with the pie and a pile of plates and forks on it into the room and set it down on the coffee table. She lifted a piece onto a plate and handed it to Jesse.

"Thank you." Jesse inhaled the pungent aroma. "This smells incredible."

"Go ahead and try it." Hugh accepted a plate from his wife and waved a fork at him. "I challenge you to tell me you've ever tasted a finer pastry."

"Hugh." Isabelle's cheeks flushed as she settled onto her chair.

Jesse took a bite.

Meryn's parents watched him closely.

Given the fact that he couldn't fool them, the pressure was on, but he was quite happy to tell the truth. "This might be the best pie I've ever tasted."

"Didn't I tell you?" Hugh cut into his own piece with the side of his fork.

"You did. And you were right." Jesse shovelled another bite into his mouth.

Isabelle sat back in her chair, looking pleased. "How are my boys doing?"

"They're good." Of course he hadn't seen them since he'd taken Matthew and Gracie from Kate and Ethan, and didn't relish the prospect of facing Shane and Brendan if he returned home without the children, either. Or maybe even if he did. "Meryn's thrilled to have them in town."

"So are we. Although Meryn can take care of herself, it makes us feel better knowing the boys are there to look out for her."

"Oh, they do that."

Hugh grinned. "Put you through the ringer, have they?"

"They have. On more than one occasion." The pie seemed to have disappeared from his plate.

Before Jesse could set down his fork, Meryn's mother had lifted out another piece.

He kept quiet and took another bite. He did lift a hand when he finished that piece and she looked as though she was about to cut him another. "I can't, thank you, but it really was fantastic." He set his fork on the empty plate and returned both to the tray. "How are things going here in Ottawa?"

Hugh lifted his massive shoulders. "Sounds like they're pretty much the same here as they are in Kingston and the rest of the country. It's taken some getting used to, having a curfew like a teenager again. And losing our Bibles was a real blow. But other than the odd bit of graffiti, no one's bothered us at church. We've a good congregation. Everyone looks out for everyone else, so we're managing to muddle along."

"That's good."

"Yes, it is." Isabelle's bright-blue eyes looked troubled. "It does seem to be getting a little more difficult to buy things, though. That's the reason we still haven't replaced that old i-com. We've been to three different stores, and as soon as they see the bracelets, they suddenly appear to have run out of stock or some other such excuse."

Jesse shook his head. "I don't think that's happening much where we are, but I did hear a rumour that it might be starting to go on here in the capital. It's not legal, but if they come up with a legitimate-sounding reason, like they've run out of product, it's difficult to prove." He reached into the inside pocket of his jacket and pulled out a small box. "I hope you don't mind, but I wondered if that might be the case, so I brought a new one along with me."

Isabelle's eyes widened. "Did you really?"

"I know how important it is to Meryn that she's able to communicate with the two of you. She worries when she doesn't hear from you or can't have a good conversation." He reached across the coffee table and handed the box to Hugh.

Meryn's father slid the thin silver device out and gave a low whistle. "She's a beauty." He looked up. "How much do we owe you?"

"I'd be happy if you'd accept it as a gift." He cleared his throat. "The thing is, your family is very special to me. They've welcomed me and made me feel a part of them, and I can't tell you how much that has meant. If I can give some small thing back, help in any way, I'm honoured to do it."

Hugh fixed his dark eyes on Jesse, lips pursed. After a moment, he gave a nod, as if he'd made up his mind. He lifted the device. "Well, we're grateful. Thank you."

Jesse pulled a card from his shirt pocket and set it on the table. "Please don't hesitate to contact me if there's ever anything you need. I have a few friends here in town I can call." He picked up the tray. "I should get going. I want to make sure I'm fully prepared for tomorrow."

Isabelle rose and took Hugh's plate.

Jesse followed her out of the living room and into the kitchen.

When he set the tray down on the counter, she picked up the pie and slid it into a small box. "I want you to take the leftovers." He started to protest but she shook her head. "You need it, from the looks of it. You're too thin. I'm sure that army food doesn't begin to fill you up. You need some good home cooking."

His throat tightened.

Meryn's mother set the pie down and touched his arm. "What is it?"

"It's just ... my mother used to say the same thing to my brother and me."

Her head tilted. "Used to?"

"She and my father died in a car accident a few years back."

Sadness washed over her face. "I'm so sorry, Jesse. What about your brother? Is he stationed in Kingston with you?"

"No, ma'am. He died too, seven years ago, in Somalia. His best friend, Caleb, is my commanding officer at the base. He's like a brother to me."

"Good. No one should be alone in the world. Especially not these days." She lifted both her hands to his face. "But you have more family than that now. You have all of us."

"I appreciate that, but ..."

"She'll get over it." Isabelle patted his cheeks before she dropped her hands.

His forehead creased. "I'm sorry?"

"Meryn. You were about to tell me that things are a little strained between you and my daughter at the moment, weren't you?"

Uncanny. "I didn't think you were the Irish one in the family, but you do seem to have the Second Sight."

Isabelle laughed, Meryn's lyrical laugh that he loved so much. "I'm not Irish, but heaven knows I've been surrounded by enough of it over the years that a little of it certainly might have rubbed off. Even so, I don't need it at the moment. I know my daughter. She told me you were the one who had to take Matthew and Gracie away, and I'm sure she didn't make that easy for you. She loves those little ones like they're her own, you know."

"I know."

"But they're not the only ones she loves. I realize she has a temper. Goodness knows where she got that from." She threw a pointed look in the direction of the living room, and Jesse grinned. "But she has also inherited her father's heart of gold. If she truly cares about you, and I know she does, she'll forgive you."

"Even if I don't bring Matthew and Gracie home?"

"She'll know you did everything you could. It might take some time, but yes, even then."

"I hope you're right."

"When it comes to my children, I usually am." Sorrow flickered in her eyes as if she was thinking of Annaliese. "Not always, but usually."

"In this case, I truly hope you are."

"Me too." A soft smile crossed her lips. "I very much hope to see you back in this house, and soon."

"I'd like that too."

She walked him to the front door.

Hugh came out of the living room and held out a hand. "Good to meet you, son."

Jesse gripped it. "You too, sir."

"As Isabelle said, you and Matthew and Gracie and all the family will be in our prayers until this is over."

"I appreciate it." Jesse tugged on his boots. "Please take care of yourselves."

Hugh clapped him on the arm. "You too. We know it isn't easy, the life you're living there on the base. We'll keep you in our thoughts."

"Yes, we will." Isabelle handed him the box with the pie and gave him a hug. The faint scent of rose perfume drifted from her.

His mother had worn something similar, and his chest clenched. "Thank you both. For everything." Too moved to say anything else, Jesse turned and left the house.

Meryn's parents had been all that he'd expected and more. He wanted to spend time with them, celebrating holidays and making memories. Would he and Meryn ever bring their children here to visit their grandparents? The thought made him ache.

Jesse shoved his hands in his pockets as he walked. *Time to stop daydreaming and start focusing on the task at hand.* If he failed to persuade the commission in the morning, being a part of Meryn's family might always be just that—a beautiful dream that had slipped through his fingers and disappeared.

Chapter Twenty-Eight

Ever since her conversation with Kate in the store, Meryn had been nervous about this evening. The scent of the single pink carnation in the vase on the table, the flickering light from the sconces on the wall, and the soft classical music playing in the background coaxed most of the tension from her tight muscles, and she relaxed against the back of her chair.

"That's better."

Meryn looked up.

Drew watched her, a small smile on his face.

"Sorry, there's a lot going on in my life right now. I needed a night out, I think."

"Lucky for me."

She studied him as he perused his menu.

Drew's light-brown hair with streaks of gold, his dark eyes, and smattering of freckles across his nose were definitely an attractive combination. He had a successful career with the bank and was a really nice guy.

Why hasn't anyone snatched him up yet?

He looked up suddenly and his lips twitched. "What?"

Her cheeks warmed. "I was just wondering how it is that you're still single? You must have had a lot of women interested in you over the years."

Drew laughed. "Thank you for that. I suppose there have been a few, but none that have captured my interest." He closed the menu and set it down, his face suddenly serious. "That's the problem with having your heart stolen early on by someone you think is the perfect person for you.

Even if those feelings aren't returned, it kind of ruins you for any other relationships."

Meryn reached for her glass of water. Kate was right. It had been a terrible mistake, coming here.

Drew touched the back of her hand. "Sorry. Don't mind me. I know the rules. We're here as friends. You gave me an opening there and I took it, but that's it for tonight, I promise."

For tonight? Meryn sighed. "Look, I know I brought up the subject, but ..." She took a sip of water and set her glass down. "Drew, if I have ever led you on or made you think there was something between us, I apologize."

He shook his head. "You've never done that. This has always been a classic case of unrequited love. Or deep like, anyway." His jaw had tightened slightly, but he sounded sincere. "You've been good at letting me know where I stand with you. Which is why, in spite of everything, I still want us to be friends."

"Me too."

Though Drew was easy to talk to and made her laugh several times as they reminisced about the past and discussed their families, the uneasy feeling that she shouldn't be there niggled in her stomach. Every time the door opened, she glanced over, even though Jesse was out of town. The last time she and Drew had gone out for dinner, Jesse and the major had walked in and caught them together. Although that was before she and Jesse had started seeing each other, and she had just told him there couldn't be anything between them because of their differences in beliefs, the evening had been ruined for both of them.

Meryn shifted in her seat. *He likely wouldn't be any happier to see Drew and me together tonight.* She was relieved when their server returned and set her chicken piccatta down in front of her.

Drew tried to keep the conversation going, but after her sixth or seventh one-word answer to a question he'd asked, he finally set down his fork. "What's going on, Meryn?"

"What do you mean?"

"I thought we were going to relax and enjoy ourselves tonight. And you were with me for a while, but now you're so far away you might as well be back home. Did I do something wrong?"

"No, it's not you. It's me." Meryn sighed. "Remember when you came to see me after I'd been sick?"

"Yes. I brought you flowers, which was very thoughtful of me."

She laughed. "Yes, it was. You also asked me a question, and I didn't give you a completely honest answer."

"What question?"

"You asked if I was seeing anyone, and I didn't lie to you, but my response was fairly evasive."

He pursed his lips and studied her. "You are seeing someone?"

"Yes. I have been for several months now."

"Sounds serious."

"It's complicated. But yes, the relationship is very important to me. In fact, if I seem uncomfortable tonight, it's because I convinced myself he wouldn't mind if I went out with you as a friend, but now I'm not so sure. I probably shouldn't have come."

"Does he know you're here?"

"No. He's out of town at the moment."

"Will you tell him?"

"Yes."

Drew picked up the burgundy cloth napkin from his lap and wiped his mouth. "Can I know who this man is?"

"I'd rather not say, actually. As I said, it's complicated."

He searched her face. "It's the captain, isn't it?"

She blinked. "Why would you think that?"

"The last time we had dinner and he walked in, you had a very strong reaction to seeing him. I knew then that if something wasn't going on between you, it had been. If you're involved with him again, then I can see why you would consider that situation complicated."

"Drew, I—"

He held up a hand. "It's okay. You don't have to tell me. I guess it's really none of my business, even if we are friends. I just hope this relationship, whomever it's with, isn't putting you in any danger."

"I don't think it is. And I don't want to do anything to put *it* at risk. So I'm sorry, but after tonight I can't go out with you alone again."

Drew dropped the napkin back in his lap. "Like I said, other than evading that one question, you've always been honest with me about us, and I appreciate it. But I'll be honest too and tell you I'm disappointed. I've only ever wanted you to be happy, though, and if he makes you happy, then I'm glad." Something that she couldn't identify flickered in his eyes.

Do you really mean what you're saying?

"He's a very lucky man, Meryn. Whoever he is."

"Thank you." She wiped her fingers on her napkin and set it on the table. "And I hope you give the next woman who has the sense to be interested in you a chance. I want you to be happy too."

"Maybe I will." He looked around for their server. "Why don't I ask for our food to be packaged up, and I'll take you home?"

"That sounds good."

His eyes, unreadable now, met hers. "I hope he appreciates you."

Maybe not so much at the moment. "I think he does."

The server came to the table.

Meryn reached for her purse.

Drew held up his hand. "Please." When she nodded, he handed the server his credit card, and within minutes their food had been returned, packaged up in two separate bags. He held the door as she stepped out into the cool evening air.

Neither of them spoke much on the way to the farm. When they pulled into her driveway, Meryn reached for the door handle. "Thanks, Drew."

"It was good to see you."

"You too." She climbed out of his little black sports car and, balancing her food container in one hand, shut the door behind her.

Drew pulled away, tires spinning as he turned out of the driveway.

A shiver rippled through Meryn, and she shook her head. What was the matter with her? Everything that was going on with Jesse and with Matthew and Gracie must be getting to her. She crossed the yard.

She should have listened to Kate. Meryn's relationship with Jesse was too important. *He* was too important.

And if they were able to work everything out when he got back from Ottawa, and she told him what she'd done tonight, she prayed he would believe that was the truth.

Chapter Twenty-Nine

The National House of Prayer in Ottawa was a beautiful, old stone edifice located just down the hill from the Parliament Buildings. Trying to clear his head, Jesse had gone for a late-night walk. Without making a conscious decision, he found himself in front of the building he'd heard about but had never visited.

Light poured from the windows and the glass on either side of the door, fitting for a building dedicated to prayer for the country and its leaders. Four stately columns rose from the front porch at the top of a wide stone staircase.

Jesse tipped back his head to take in the sight of the illuminated cross on top of a spire on the roof. *I wonder how long they'll leave that there.*

The thought, and the cynicism, saddened him.

He contemplated the hearing he would attend the next morning. *God, help me. How can anything I say make a difference?* He'd thought the neighbourhood was deserted, but a movement down the sidewalk caught his attention. He stuck his hands in the pockets of his jeans and pretended to study the building in front of him as a man approached.

"Captain Christensen?"

Jesse blinked in surprise. "Yes?"

The man moved to stand beside him, their shoulders almost touching, pointing to the building as if the two of them were discussing its merits. Lowering his voice, he said, "My name is Michael Stevens. I'm one of the commissioners hearing the child abuse case in the morning."

Jesse's head jerked. "Child abuse?"

"Yes, that's the official charge. They're contemplating classifying teaching the Bible to children as child abuse." He glanced up and down the street again. "Let's get out of sight, shall we?" He motioned toward the dark shadows along the side of the building.

Jesse's interest was piqued. How did the man know who he was? And why would a commissioner risk everything to meet with a witness before a hearing?

Stevens started across the side lawn toward the building.

After a second's hesitation, Jesse followed him.

When they were out of sight of any passing vehicles or pedestrians, the commissioner turned toward Jesse. Everything about the man was neat, from his impeccably trimmed hair and goatee to his tailored navy suit. "I got word you'll be testifying at that hearing."

"That's right."

"Why?"

"Excuse me?"

"I mean, what is your particular interest in this case? Why would an officer in the Canadian Army come all the way to Ottawa to address a hearing on behalf of Christians charged with a hate crime?"

Jesse glanced at the man's wrists. They were bare. "Is this an official inquiry, commissioner? It seems like a strange setting for one. I'd be happy to explain my reasons in the appropriate venue tomorrow."

The man shot him a look. "Do you really want to be confronted with this line of questioning in public?"

"I prefer my dealings to be done in the light, yes."

"Some dealings are more safely carried out in the shadows, as I suspect you are aware, or you wouldn't have followed me here."

"Why don't you just ask me what you want to know?"

"All right. Are you a Christian?"

There it was. The question Jesse had anticipated for months now. He'd wondered often how he would respond when it was posed to him, particularly in a situation where the consequences of giving an honest answer could be deadly. "Why do you want to know?"

In the soft light spilling from the windows of the House of Prayer, the corners of the man's mouth turned up. "I guess that's my answer."

"What do you mean?"

"If you were not a believer, you wouldn't hesitate to respond in the negative. These days, not denying the charge of being a Christian is an affirmation in itself, Captain."

"What difference do my personal beliefs make to you, Mr. Stevens? I'm not the one on trial."

"I just wanted to be sure you could be trusted."

"With?"

"This. I'm a believer too." The commissioner glanced toward the street as a car drove by. "We don't have a lot of time. If anyone sees us together, you will be disqualified as a witness, and I will be removed from the commission, possibly permanently, so please listen carefully."

Jesse contemplated him. He might have convinced Michael Stevens he could be trusted, but so far the man hadn't returned the favour.

"I know you have no reason to believe me. All I can do is promise you I'm telling you the truth and hope you can take me at my word. As I mentioned, the commission will be contemplating labelling parents who teach their children the truths of the Bible as child abusers. I don't need to tell you that will have far-reaching and devastating ramifications. I am as anxious as you are for the decision to have those children removed from their home overturned."

"What do you want me to do?"

"You'll need to make some very solid arguments. The most impactful one, as always, will be the economic one. Child Services is already overwhelmed with cases. A sudden onslaught of children in need of foster care will require more offices and case workers, temporary shelters for children when families are not available, and an increase in the budget needed to supply those children with essential needs such as food and clothing. I estimate that approximately forty to fifty million dollars will need to be poured into the system in the first few months following an upheld ruling. Here." Stevens reached into the pocket of his jacket and pulled out a folded sheet of paper. "I have a breakdown of all the numbers."

Jesse took the paper and glanced down at it. "That's a powerful argument."

"It will get the commission's attention, I promise you. The government has never kept a tighter lid on the nation's finances. Any ruling that promises to take a direct hit at those coffers will not be looked on favourably by Ottawa. The other thing we have going for us is that this is an election year. Since we are still technically a democracy, in spite of the ongoing martial law, the other powerful argument you can make will be that of public opinion. If you can convince the commission that the outcry against a ruling like this will be swift and strong, they will think twice before ordering it to be carried out. Although only about forty percent of the suspected Christians on the government's list accepted an identity bracelet, that's still a lot of votes. And votes are the most highly valued currency around here."

"Anything else?" Jesse stuck the folded piece of paper into the back pocket of his jeans.

"It's impossible to tell how these things will play out, but if you make those two arguments forcefully, there's a chance the vote will go in our favour. There are eight commissioners. At least five of them will have to vote for the ruling in order for it to be upheld. I won't, of course. Two others on the commission are, if not sympathetic toward Christians, at least willing to keep an open mind. You should be able to sway them, so if we can get just one more on our side, we can close the book on this case and prevent any others like it from being opened. If not, an ominous new chapter of our country's history will begin."

Jesse exhaled. "So, no pressure."

Stevens clapped him on the arm. "You won't be alone. I'll be there and I suspect there are many others offering up prayers on your behalf as we speak. We'll do our best and leave the outcome in God's hands, which is the only way we can live our lives now."

"That's true. You must find yourself in some dangerous situations these days."

"No more than you, I'm sure. If you ever need a friend in Ottawa, you know who to call."

"And you, if you need someone in the military."

Michael Stevens lifted his hand. "I should go. You take care, my friend."

"You too."

The commissioner walked across the grass to the corner of the building and looked out at the street, then strode to the sidewalk and disappeared from sight.

Did that just happen? Jesse pressed his palm to the cool stone of the building. The suggestions Stevens had made weren't revelations. Jesse had been planning to make the case for the economic, social, and political fallout already. Still, having numbers to back them up cemented his arguments. It was as though he had been heading into battle armed with a dagger to face a well-equipped platoon, and had suddenly been handed a C7A2 rifle. As they had when he was on the front lines, the feel of a weapon in his hands and, even more, the knowledge that the person beside him was watching his back, filled him with confidence.

The building in front of him represented the most powerful weapon of all. Jesse closed his eyes for a moment, soaking in the feel of the place, the peace and the power that radiated from its very walls.

Chapter Thirty

Jesse shifted on the cold, lime-green leather seat outside the chamber where the commission was assembled. He'd worn his full dress uniform, including the four medals he'd earned in combat in the Middle East, hoping it would give him, if not an intimidating presence, at least a creditable one.

He glanced at his watch. They'd made him wait almost two hours. He'd used the time to pray and to rehearse the arguments in his head, but now he just wanted to get in there.

Finally the heavy wooden door beside him opened, and a young man in a suit and tie motioned for him to come inside. "They're ready for you, sir."

Four men and four women, all impeccably dressed in business attire, sat around three sides of a large, gleaming table. A podium had been set on the fourth side, at the head of the table, and the young man led Jesse to it.

The eight commissioners regarded him somberly. Michael Stevens was the only one to meet his eyes, and then only briefly.

A woman in a pin-striped business suit sat opposite Jesse at the other end of the table. She dipped her head in his direction. "Welcome, Captain Christensen. I am Judith Colson, the head of this commission. We have been debating the issue before us, the charge of child abuse against"—she glanced down at the screen embedded in the tabletop in front of her—"Ethan and Kate Williams, for several hours now and are nearing a verdict. As you may or may not be aware, it is somewhat irregular to have a witness speak at one of our hearings. Our standard procedure involves reviewing the facts of the case as laid out for us in a written report and arriving at a verdict without the often muddying effects of personal opinion. As the request to allow you to speak came from high up, we have agreed to hear what you have to say. We would, however, in the interest of expediency, ask you to be as brief and coherent in your presentation as possible."

Nearing a verdict? Had some of the commissioners already made up their minds? The way she'd said *personal opinion* wasn't promising either. "Thank you. I appreciate that you agreed to hear me out. As you know, this is a precedent-setting case, the outcome of which will have far-reaching and potentially devastating effects on the entire country. May I?" He pulled the i-com from his shirt pocket and pointed it at the white screen on the wall.

She nodded curtly.

Jesse ran a finger over the device, and light flashed from one end. The numbers Michael Stevens had supplied him with the night before flashed up on the screen. Jesse walked them through the breakdown of the anticipated overload to the system and corresponding projected costs to the government, should the charge against Kate and Ethan be upheld. He cast an occasional glance at the commissioners, but most of the faces remained impassive.

Were the numbers having any kind of impact?

When he finished with the information on the economic ramifications of their decision, Jesse projected a second slide onto the screen. "Although there has been a steady decline in Canadian citizens listing Christianity as their religion, from sixty-seven percent in the 2011 census to just twenty-five percent in 2051, that percentage still represents five to ten million eligible voters in this country, at a minimum. Factoring in those who do not claim to be Christian but who will be opposed to a government that demonstrates a willingness to strike at the family—still largely considered the heart of society—without just cause, the numbers could be considerably higher. In short, Commissioners, the economic and political fallout of a ruling that allows authorities to tear children away from safe, loving homes will be devastating to the government, and to the country as a whole." Jesse slid the i-com back into his pocket as he turned to face the commissioners.

One of the men leaned forward. "The numbers are admittedly

compelling, Captain. Still, the fact remains that Kate and Ethan Williams were teaching their children from officially classified hate literature in defiance of the law."

"I personally carried out the order to remove the children from the home and conducted a search of the premises. The Williamses did not have a Bible in their possession, only a book of children's stories, which we confiscated. Incidentally, those stories have been shown to have a positive impact on people by teaching them values and morals that contribute to the well-being of the general population. Typically, children raised in religious homes are instilled with a morality that enables them to become healthy, contributing members of society."

"Until they start blowing up buildings and killing people, you mean," muttered another one of the commissioners, a young man wearing a blue button-down shirt and thick, black-rimmed glasses.

Laughter rippled around the table.

"Commissioners, you stated at the outset that you preferred to make your decisions based on facts alone. The belief that the 10/10 bombings were carried out by a radical Christian group is based on one unsubstantiated claim by an unknown caller, a claim that cannot be treated by any rational person as fact. If you genuinely wish to make your decision in this case on facts alone, that comment, and the recent, baseless view of Christians as terrorists, cannot be taken into account when you make your ruling."

The laughter stopped.

One of the women raised a hand. "What is in this for you, Captain? Why are you coming down on the side of the Christians on this?"

"I'm not coming down on the side of Christians, Commissioner. I'm coming down on the side of justice. I cannot see how removing children from a secure, loving home can possibly be considered just or a benefit to society. And I am coming down on the side of peace. The task that I have been charged with is to maintain peace and stability in my territory in a world where peace and stability have become as scarce as the resources of oil and water. A ruling that removes children from their homes will inevitably result in civil unrest and conflict, making it extremely difficult for the military to carry out its mandate."

"Why does a soldier want peace? Wouldn't that be working yourself out of a job?"

The question brought smirks to several of the faces around the table.

Jesse gripped the sides of the podium. "First of all, given the current global conflict situation, I don't see unemployment for trained military personnel as an imminent threat."

More smiles, this time possibly in his favour.

"Secondly, before I am a soldier, I am a Canadian. Canadians have always put the pursuit of peace over the pursuit of conflict and war. We have only ever fought to preserve the rights, freedoms, and values our country has always held sacred. For the nearly two centuries of our existence, my fellow soldiers have fought and died for the freedoms of speech and religion, and the right to peace and security for ourselves and our families. I believe my record shows that I, too, am willing to fight and to die for peace and for freedom, values that I am deeply concerned to see rapidly eroding in this country."

The room grew quiet.

Are they actually listening to me? Jesse leaned over the podium. "For most of the 1990s, Canada was ranked first on the United Nations' Human Development Index for highly developed countries. By the 2010s, we had slipped out of the top ten, and last year we ranked twenty-sixth on the list. This decrease in status is largely due to global concerns about our degenerating human rights record, a tragedy given that, historically, Canada's human rights record has been highly regarded worldwide."

Several of the commissioners nodded.

"We have often fought on behalf of other country's citizens when their human rights were being violated, since we believe so strongly in the fundamental rights and freedoms of all human beings across the planet. As human rights commissioners, you are in a unique position to slow this erosion and to safeguard the rights of the citizens of this country. In doing so, you will go a long way toward restoring our country to its former, well-regarded status, and you will honour those who have fought and died to preserve those rights."

When he finished, there was silence in the room for a moment.

Then the head of the commission stood up. "Well, Captain, I will give you that you were coherent, at least, if not brief."

There were chuckles around the table.

Michael Stevens smiled and inclined his head to Jesse so slightly that if he hadn't been looking for it, he would have missed the movement.

"Thank you for coming to speak to us. You will be notified of our decision later on today."

Jesse nodded. "I appreciate your time and attention, Commissioners." Stepping away from the podium, he walked back up the aisle and out of the room, leaving the fate of Kate and Ethan and their children, and countless other families in the country, in the hands of the eight men and women gathered there.

And, far more importantly, in God's.

Chapter Thirty-One

Jesse strode down the grey marble-tiled hallway to the lobby.

A heavy-set man in his sixties, dressed in a blue security guard uniform, shoved himself away from his desk and meandered over to the glassed-in counter. "Can I help you?" He bent down closer to the opening in the glass and propped both elbows on the counter.

"I'm wondering if you can give me some information on how these human rights commissions work." Jesse leaned a hip against the desk, trying to look casual now that the need for intimidation had passed. Maybe.

The man's bushy eyebrows rose. "Depends."

"On what?"

"What exactly you want to know. Could you be a little more specific?"

"Okay. I was just called to testify before one, and they told me I would be informed of their decision at some point today. Do you know how long it usually takes for a commission to reach a verdict?"

He pursed his lips. "Depends. The more complicated ones take longer, of course. You here about the child abuse case?"

"Yes."

"Well, that certainly qualifies as a complicated one. They've already been deliberating longer than usual, but I wouldn't be surprised if we don't hear anything for a couple more hours." He turned his arm to look at his watch. "Longer if they break for lunch."

"Do they usually?"

"Depends. Sometimes they do and sometimes they don't."

Jesse bit back a frustrated retort and worked to keep his features even. "You said 'if *we* don't hear anything.' Does that mean information about the verdict will come here?"

"Depends."

He counted to five slowly in his head. "On?"

"Whether or not there's a form to fill out. In this case there will be." He tapped a stylus on the counter. "The verdict will come here, to me, so I can fill out a requisition to either remand the minor children into the custody of Child Services or release them to a representative of the military to be returned to their parents." He looked Jesse up and down, appearing to take in his uniform for the first time. He pushed himself away from the counter and straightened up. "That would be you, I take it?"

"I assume so."

"When the results come back, your name will need to be included in the paperwork for authorization. If it is, and you can show me appropriate ID and sign the form, I can forward the requisition to your device. After that, you will be responsible for delivering the children to their home."

"So, it's best if I stay here and wait for the verdict to come through?"

"It will expedite the process, yes."

"Okay." Jesse half-turned and pointed to a bank of chairs along the wall in the corner of the lobby. "I'll wait over there. When you get the results, could you please let me know right away?" *Do not say "depends" again, or I won't be responsible for my actions.*

"Will do." The man dipped his head before turning and shuffling back to his desk.

Jesse crossed the expansive, cherry-paneled lobby and settled onto a chair between a man in a suit with a briefcase at his feet and a harried-looking mother attempting to keep a wriggling toddler under control. Several times she pulled the squirming child back onto her lap until he wailed in protest and the mother looked near tears.

At least you have your child with you. Be grateful for that.

He offered her a sympathetic smile that she tried valiantly to return. When they were finally called into another room, he wasn't sure who was more relieved—the mother or the man sitting on the other side of him.

A large clock hung on the wall above the front desk.

Jesse tried not to watch it, but his gaze repeatedly strayed back to it as the big hand made its way torturously around the face. After it had made one complete rotation, his stomach rumbled. He'd only had a cup of coffee for breakfast, and it was now well past lunch. Bracing himself for more frustration, he approached the front counter.

The same man ambled over to talk to him.

"Anything yet?"

"Nope."

"Is there a cafeteria in the building?"

"Yep." The man pointed in the direction Jesse had come from earlier. "Down that hallway to the very end, turn right, and you'll see it ahead of you a ways."

"Thank you. I'll just be a few minutes." Jesse followed his directions and found a typical government-building cafeteria, complete with orange plastic trays that had to be moved along rollers past cellophane-wrapped sandwiches and pieces of fruit covered in patches of brown. It didn't really matter. He just needed something to fill the void and give him the strength to face the rest of the day. He chose a sandwich with wilted lettuce and what looked like roast beef, grabbed a carton of milk, and pushed his tray to the payment machine located at the end of the rollers. After setting each item on the scanner, he opened the credit app on his i-com and held it in front of the screen. As soon as the light blinked green, he picked up the tray and looked around for an empty table.

In ten minutes he had tossed out his garbage, which easily could have included the food he'd just purchased, and made his way back down the hallway. He stopped at the front desk again.

The man didn't bother to get up from his desk, just held up a hand. "Nothing yet."

Repressing a sigh, Jesse turned and headed back to the hard leather chair clearly designed to discourage loitering in the front lobby. He could message Meryn, but he had already risked contacting her once this week. Besides, it would be cruel to send her a message telling her that nothing had happened yet just because he wanted to hear from her. He'd wait until he had some news to share, then send a message to Kate or Ethan that he could pass off as official notification, if questioned. He shifted in the chair. Crossing his arms over his chest, he closed his eyes, more to keep himself from watching the clock than anything.

The shrill cry of a baby woke him up. He immediately zoned in on the time. Almost seventeen hundred hours. It had been over three hours since he'd left the room where the commission was meeting. How late would they deliberate? Was it possible they would adjourn for the day and he'd be stuck in town overnight, staring at the walls of his hotel room?

"Hey."

A smacking sound drew his attention to the front counter.

The man in the security guard uniform brought his palm down on the counter again.

Jesse jumped to his feet when the man motioned to him. "Have you heard anything?"

"Yep." The man picked his i-com up off the counter. "Verdict's in."

"And?"

"Took them long enough. Might even be a new record."

Jesse tamped down his impatience. "What did they decide?"

The man squinted as he peered down at the device. "Says here they ruled in favour of the parents."

Relief surged through Jesse so thick and strong that for a few seconds he couldn't breathe.

The man in front of him didn't seem to notice. "Don't know what side you were arguing for, so not sure if that's good news for you or not, but there you have it. ID?"

Jesse fumbled in his pocket for his wallet and pulled out his military identification card.

The man glanced at it, then back down at the screen. "Captain E.J. Christensen. That's right. Sign here and you can go pick up those kids and take them home"—the man glanced around before lowering his voice—"where they belong, if you ask me."

"Me too." Jesse took the i-com and stylus the man held out and signed his name with shaking fingers before handing the unit back.

"Here." The man touched the screen, then held the i-com out again. "Scan this page. You'll need to present this to the child services worker before you can take the kids."

Jesse held his i-com up to the one the man held out and touched the button to scan the information. He double-checked that the transfer had been successful before dropping the device back into his pocket.

"Excuse me." Another man walked up to the front desk, lightly bumping Jesse as he set a briefcase down on the counter. "I just need to sign out for the day. Do you mind?"

It was Michael Stevens. "Sure." Jesse gestured for him to go ahead.

The security guard pulled a tablet-sized electronic device off the hook on the wall and handed it to the commissioner.

Stevens slid the stylus out of the holder on the side and signed his name. "Thank you."

He glanced at Jesse, then down at the briefcase as he picked it up from the counter.

A small piece of folded paper lay beneath it.

Jesse covered it with his hand and slid it into the pocket of his jacket before the man behind the counter could finish hanging the tablet up and turn back.

Stevens met Jesse's eyes briefly before making his way to the front door and disappearing into the crowds of people going up and down the stairs at the front of the building.

Jesse turned back to the security guard. "I'm free to go?"

"Depends."

Feeling almost giddy, Jesse actually laughed. "Depends on what?"

"If you have everything. Got your ID?"

"Yes." Jesse patted the wallet in his pocket.

"Requisition?"

"Got it."

The man checked his own screen again. "And I have your signed form. Yep. You're good to go."

Still smiling, Jesse turned and headed for the door of the courthouse. On the wide concrete veranda, he stopped for a moment, leaned against a pillar, and typed a message into his i-com. Then he bounded down the stairs and jogged the two blocks to where he had parked his vehicle. As soon as he climbed behind the wheel of the jeep, he glanced around, then pulled the piece of paper Stevens had given him out of his pocket and read what looked like a hastily scrawled note.

> *Deeply concerned before you arrived. Majority leaning heavily toward upholding the ruling. Afterward, a great deal of heated debate, instigated by one commissioner, clearly not as objective as he has sworn to be. Not that I can say too much about that. In the end, seven of eight couldn't cause the upheaval you described. Strongest point—no conclusive evidence found to link Christians to the 10/10 bombings. If, as representatives of the law, we are going to deal in facts, we cannot base our rulings on unsubstantiated claims. That sobered everyone, as this has clearly been done in the past. You may have managed to ensure it is done less often in the future. Patriotic angle didn't hurt, either, especially coming from someone who has clearly earned his stripes. Commission also ruled to submit a recommendation to the House to pass a law protecting children from being taken from their homes again, except in cases of clear abuse or neglect. So, well done, my friend. I sincerely hope we meet again one day.*

Jesse folded up the paper and stuck it back in his pocket before starting the jeep. *I hope we meet again too, just not under circumstances like these.* With a grimace, he pulled out onto the street and started for home.

Chapter Thirty-Two

The tension at the farm hung in the air like thick smoke, making it hard to draw in a breath. Meryn curled up in an armchair in the living room and tried to read, but the words scrambled themselves on the page, and she couldn't make any sense of them.

Brendan had gone to his gym in the barn shortly after he came home from work, and Shane was stretched out on his side on the floor by the train set, absently pushing an engine back and forth on the tracks. The television was on and Ethan and Kate sat on the couch in front of it.

Meryn glanced over at them periodically to see how they were holding up.

From the looks on their faces, what was playing on the screen made as much sense to them as the words on the page did to her.

When the clock on the mantel chimed once, everyone's heads swivelled toward it.

4:30.

Kate stood up abruptly. "I'm going to make dinner." She headed for the kitchen.

No one spoke until she was gone, then Ethan's eyes met Meryn's across the room. "She's going crazy."

She set the open book, spine up, on the arm of the chair. "I know. I don't blame her."

"Me neither. It's been five and a half hours. Do you think it's a bad sign that it's taking them this long to decide?"

Shane let go of the train and hauled himself to his feet. "It could be a good sign. Obviously it's not an easy decision for them. Hopefully the longer they talk about it, the more clear it will become that it would be ridiculous to rip two happy, healthy kids away from their parents."

Ethan sighed. "I hope so." He stood up and held his neck as he stretched his head from one side to the other. "Guess there's nothing to do but wait. I'll go help Kate with dinner."

Meryn nodded, knowing it would help both of them to keep busy.

Shane crossed the room and propped an elbow on the mantel above the woodstove, facing her. "How are you doing, kid?"

She pushed her hair from her face with both hands. "Not great. It's terrible to just sit around waiting to hear what's going on. I go back and forth between praying the i-com will go off and praying it won't if it's bad news. At least, until we know for sure, we can keep hoping everything will work out."

"I know what you mean. This is exactly what it was like when you were sick. We had no idea where you were or how you were doing. Every time we heard that buzzing sound, we all just froze, desperate to read the message but terrified to look at it at the same time."

"I'm sorry I put all of you through that."

"We survived it. And we'll survive this too, with the help of God and each other."

"I hope so. Did you know they're marking the Christian businesses downtown with fish symbols above the doors?"

"Really?"

"Yeah. There was one on the store when Kate and I went to open it this week."

A troubled look crossed Shane's face. "That can't be good. Maybe it's time to think about selling the store."

Meryn frowned. "Sell the store? What would I do all day? How would I live?"

"Brendan and I can support you. Or you could find another job, one where you aren't so ... vulnerable."

"I don't feel vulnerable there. I know all the business owners around me, and we look out for each other."

"But none of them were able to stop some punk from throwing a rock through your front window, were they?"

"No, but to be fair, most of them weren't around, since it was late on a Friday evening."

"That's true. That probably is the most dangerous time for you."

She rested a hand on her book. "I could think about closing by five every day, so I'm not downtown alone at night."

"It would make me feel better if you did."

Meryn's eyes narrowed. "Is that what you were trying to drive me around to this whole time?"

He grinned. "You'll never know, will you? But I am glad you got there, with or without my help."

"Brat." Meryn pulled a small, needlepoint pillow off her chair and threw it in his direction.

He chuckled as he caught it and tossed it back at her.

She tucked it down between her leg and the arm of the chair. "Speaking of brats, should someone check on Brendan?"

"Hey." Brendan strode through the doorway of the living room, his dark hair damp and curling around his ears and the base of his neck. "What are you calling me names for? I'm not causing any trouble."

"For a change." Meryn and Shane spoke at the same time.

When they both laughed, Brendan scowled. "You two are a riot." He sat down on the coffee table in front of Meryn. "Ethan and Kate are looking pretty grim in the kitchen. She was attacking a carrot with a knife. Ethan was hovering over her as if he was prepared to jump in if it looked like she might lose a finger. I take it there's no news yet?"

Meryn shook her head. "Not yet. They must still be deliberating. Jesse will contact us as soon as he has anything to tell us."

"I hope so."

"How was the workout?"

"Great. Gave me time to think."

Shane came over and dropped onto the armchair beside Meryn's. "About what?"

"How much things are changing. And how good it is that we have each other to lean on. Which got me thinking about all the people who don't have someone. There are quite a few new people at the church whose families are giving them a hard time for converting to Christianity. Some have even kicked them out of their homes. I was thinking we should do more to offer them support or assistance, whatever they need."

Shane tapped a knuckle against his chin. "It's a good idea. Up until now, we've all been focused on our own families and dealing with each new development as it comes along. It's time to get more organized. Meryn was saying they're marking the Christian businesses downtown with a fish symbol. The bracelets are already starting to make it harder to buy things, and the symbols could start making it more difficult to sell things too. We are definitely going to have to band together to help each other through."

Meryn's heart pounded. Since she'd had to stop distributing Bibles, and she wasn't needed at the hospital anymore, the feeling that she was doing very little to help had bothered her. What her brothers were talking about might be the opportunity she'd been looking for. She leaned forward. "Once this thing is settled with Matthew and Gracie, let's get together with Pastor John and discuss it. He'll have a better idea of what the needs are."

Brendan and Shane exchanged a look.

Her eyes narrowed. "Don't even think about it."

Shane gave her an innocent look. "Think about what?"

"Telling me you don't want me to get involved. I've survived a flogging and the Red Virus. I think I've proven that I'm willing to take risks and, if necessary, to face the consequences. The two of you are not going to start trying to shelter me now."

Her brothers looked at each other again, and Shane shrugged. "She's right, Brendan."

Brendan didn't appear convinced. "We'll see how things pan out. It's too early to know how any of this is going to go. We don't have to decide tonight who is going to do what."

Meryn pointed a finger in his face. "However it goes, we're all in this together. Got it?"

Brendan grinned as he grasped her finger and shook it. "Got it. For now, let's just concentrate on helping Kate and Ethan get through today."

"Yeah, I guess that's enough to think about at the moment."

"Dinner's ready." Ethan stood in the living room doorway, a dish towel flung over one shoulder.

Shane stood up and held out a hand to Meryn. When she grabbed it, he pulled her to her feet, and he and Brendan followed her into the kitchen.

Kate set a big bowl of salad on the table.

Meryn grabbed both her hands and held them up for inspection. "What are you doing?"

"Checking to make sure all your fingers are still attached. Brendan said he was worried about the way you were attacking those carrots."

"Oh yeah. Vegetable chopping. Very cathartic. Usually." Kate's eyes met hers. "Although I'm not sure how much it helped tonight."

"I know." Meryn squeezed her hands. "I'm sure we'll hear from Jesse soon."

"I hope so."

They all gathered around the table, and Shane reached for Meryn's hand. "Let's pray." He grasped Brendan's arm.

Kate and Ethan completed the circle as they bowed their heads.

"Father, it's been another tough week for this family. It's so difficult sometimes, knowing that what is happening is out of our control. We do know that what is going on with Matthew and Gracie is not out of your control, though. We know you love them, even more than we do. So we trust them to your care, and we pray that your will may be done, in this situation and in all those that are to come. Amen."

The tightness in Meryn's shoulders eased slightly. God *was* in control, she knew that. And with the world going crazy and chaotic, she was deeply grateful for that truth. She glanced at Kate. The lines etched on her forehead worried Meryn. If only Jesse would contact them ...

The food smelled delicious, but Meryn barely tasted the couple of bites she managed to get down. When she couldn't stand the silence another minute, she set down her fork. "Thanks for making dinner, Kate. Everything's—"

An i-com buzzed.

Everyone froze.

When it buzzed again, Kate pulled a unit out of her back pocket with shaking fingers. "It's mine." She started to touch the screen, then stopped and looked at Ethan. "I can't."

Ethan took the device from her. He covered her hand with his as he scanned the screen. After a few seconds, he lifted his head.

The look on his face sent joy and relief coursing through Meryn, even before he uttered the three words she'd been praying for days to hear.

"They're coming home."

Chapter Thirty-Three

Jesse drove from Ottawa to Kingston, a trip that normally took two hours, in just over an hour and twenty minutes. He made one stop at a service centre along the 401 Highway, so he could change out of his uniform and pull on jeans and a steel-blue T-shirt. Technically he should wear a uniform to pick up the kids, but he wouldn't have an opportunity to change after that, and he wanted to show up at Meryn's in civilian clothes. The fewer reminders the family had that he was a soldier, the better.

He contacted the child services worker as he drove and asked her to meet him at the Charletons' house. Knowing what Ethan and Kate had been through the last few days, he didn't want them waiting a minute longer than necessary before being reunited with their children.

Matthew and Gracie looked clean and happy when Mrs. Charleton brought them to the door. After showing Emily the form he'd scanned, he took Gracie from Mrs. Charleton and shifted her to one arm as he grabbed the suitcase Mr. Charleton handed him. "Did everything go all right?"

"Oh yes, we had a wonderful time." Mrs. Charleton touched one of Gracie's curls wistfully. "Such a sweet little thing."

"I'm glad to hear it. Matthew, can you bring Gracie's car seat?"

Mr. Charleton kept his head down as he handed Matthew the pink seat.

Jesse studied the man for a moment but didn't detect any guilt, only the sense that the man had been a little cowed by him. *Good.* "Thanks for taking care of them."

When he opened the jeep door, Matthew slid onto the backseat. "Are we going home?"

"I'm taking you out to your Aunt Meryn's farm, because that's where your mom and dad are. I'm not sure how long you're staying there, but when your parents are ready to leave, then yes, they'll take you home."

The boy still looked troubled.

Jesse slid the suitcase onto the floor and strapped Gracie into her car seat. After walking around to the other side of the vehicle, he opened the back door and crouched down. "What is it, Matthew?"

"It's just ... do we have to come back here?"

"Why? Didn't you like it here? Did something bad happen?"

"No, it was fine. I liked playing with Chief, and Mr. and Mrs. Charleton were pretty nice. It's just that I missed my mom and dad."

"They missed you and Gracie too. A lot. And you don't have to come back to the Charletons' house. You can stay with your mom and dad from now on."

Matthew's face brightened. "Really?"

"Really."

The boy leaned back in his seat, and Jesse closed the door. Obviously Matthew wasn't happy about being taken from his home, but at least it sounded as though the kids' stay at the Charletons' had been okay. Jesse wasn't sure he would ever have been able to forgive himself if something had happened to them, and he was quite sure Kate and Ethan wouldn't have been able to.

The drive out to Meryn's farm seemed to take as long as the drive from Ottawa to Kingston. Jesse tapped his fingers impatiently on the steering wheel at every red light, tempted to switch on his lights and siren and get there as quickly as possible. He preferred not to draw attention to himself, though, so he drove as fast as the law would allow, thankful when they left town and there were no more lights.

Finally he drove up Meryn's lane and stopped his vehicle at the end of the walkway. Since he was here on official business this time, he didn't bother hiding the jeep. By the time he climbed out, Kate and Ethan were halfway across the yard. Jesse opened the back door and unsnapped Gracie's seatbelt, then moved back as Kate dove through the opening and pulled her daughter into her arms.

Her eyes met Jesse's over Gracie's shoulder. "Thank you."

Jesse nodded, his throat tight.

Ethan came around the front of the vehicle with his arm around Matthew's shoulders and the suitcase in his hand. Still clutching Gracie with one arm, Kate knelt down and pulled her son to her with the other. For a moment she just held them, then she straightened and Ethan reached for Gracie. Matthew took his mother's hand, and the four of them crossed the yard to meet Meryn, Brendan, and Shane on the porch.

Jesse watched the joyful reunion for a few minutes, until it moved into the farmhouse.

Meryn was swept along with her family, but she did turn her head to look back at him and nod toward the house before she disappeared inside.

That was all the invitation he needed. Jesse set the car seat down on the porch and opened the screen door. The party had moved into the living room. He stopped in the doorway.

Kate came over to him. "I was just going to come out and get you. I'm sorry."

"No worries." He waved a hand through the air. "I don't want to intrude."

"Intrude? You just brought our children home to us." Her hazel eyes glistened as she stood on her tiptoes and kissed him on the cheek. "How can we ever thank you?"

"You don't have to thank me, Kate. I'm just glad everything worked out."

"So am I."

Ethan walked up to stand behind his wife. "This is it? They can stay?"

"Yes, they can stay. The commission overturned the order to take the children away. And they're recommending the House pass a law preventing other kids from being removed from their homes, except in cases of abuse or neglect."

Kate touched his elbow. "That's such good news. We're incredibly grateful for everything you did to make that happen."

"I was happy to do it."

Ethan pointed to the doorway. "Can I speak to you for a minute?"

"Sure." Jesse followed him out of the room and across the kitchen. When Ethan waved him on ahead, he went out onto the porch and turned around to lean back against the railing.

Ethan stopped in front of him. "Quite a relationship you have with this family. We alternate between threatening to rip you apart and begging for your forgiveness."

Jesse grinned wryly. "To be honest, I'm not sure which I'm less comfortable with."

"Me neither. But I do owe you an apology."

"No, Ethan, you don't. You were protecting your family. I can't fault you for that."

"Even so"—Ethan stuck out his hand—"I'm sorry I was so hard on you when you were just trying to help us the best way you could."

Jesse grasped his hand. "It's done. Forgotten."

"Thank you."

"I want you to know, that was one of the hardest things I've ever had to do."

"I know." Ethan's lips twitched. "That's why I went with the begging forgiveness option instead of the other one." He clasped Jesse's arm like Shane had done the night he'd brought Meryn home. "Look, it's obviously difficult for you to spend any amount of time with us, but I really am hoping to get to know you better."

"I'd like that."

"Good." Ethan let go of him. "Now I'm going to go spend some time with my children."

Jesse smiled. "You do that."

"I think there's someone else who'd like to talk to you before you go. I'll send her out." Ethan disappeared into the house.

Deeply grateful for the way things had gone today and the healing of the rift with this family that had begun, Jesse offered up a silent prayer of thanks. Then, as the screen door opened again, he added one for strength and the right words to say to heal the relationship that was most important to him.

Meryn came out onto the porch. She wore a black, short-sleeved shirt over fitted black jeans.

Jesse's breath caught as she walked toward him, an uncertain smile on her face.

"Hey."

"Hey." He hated that he had no idea where he stood with her. The only thing in the world he wanted at the moment was to pull her into his arms. He shoved his hands into the front pockets of his jeans.

"Are you holding court out here?" A look of amusement flitted across her face, which eased his apprehension a little.

"Apparently."

She stopped a couple of feet in front of him. "So I had a beautiful, crystal-clear conversation with my parents earlier this evening."

"Is that right?"

"Yes. They told me some kind stranger showed up at their door last night bearing an unexpected gift for them."

He met her eyes. "That was for you."

"Which makes it all the more remarkable, given how poorly I treated your last gift." The amusement vanished. "I'm so sorry about that."

He lifted his shoulders. "All broken things can be fixed, Meryn, if they mean enough to you."

She searched his face intently, but when she spoke, her voice was light. "What about us? Can we be fixed?"

It took everything in him to match her tone. "I guess that depends. How much do we mean to you?"

Emotions played across her face. They settled into something so intense his pulse sky-rocketed.

"Everything."

Jesse let out the breath he'd been holding. Now that was an answer. The corners of his mouth turned up. "Then yes, I'd say there's definitely hope for us."

"My mother thinks so, anyway."

"Does she, now?"

Meryn grinned. "My father's rubbing off on you already. That sounded decidedly Irish."

"Well, I could do worse." He circled his finger in the air. "Now back to what your mother said about me."

She laughed. "All right, she said, and I quote, 'Meryn O'Reilly, you'd be a fool to let that boy go, and I did not raise you to be a fool.'"

"I knew I liked your mother."

"She liked you too. They were both taken with you."

"And I with them." Slowly he pulled his hands from his pockets. "Close your eyes."

"Why?"

He smiled faintly. "Can't you just trust me, lady?"

The blue eyes that met his held the intense look he'd seen there a moment earlier.

Jesse gripped the porch railing to keep from reaching for her.

"I can. And I do. I'm sorry that I forgot that for a while. I won't forget again."

"Good. Then close your eyes and turn around."

When she complied, he swept her hair to one side and fastened the delicate gold chain that he'd had fixed before he went to Ottawa around her neck again. He had planned to behave himself this time but couldn't resist leaning down and pressing his lips to the soft curve of her neck.

Meryn was smiling when she turned to face him. "Can I open my eyes now?"

"Not yet." Jesse cupped the back of her head and pulled her closer, so he could kiss her behind one ear and then the other.

"Now?"

"No. It will do you good to trust me a little longer." He took her face in his hands. Her dark hair flowed over his fingers, and he breathed in the lavender scent of it. Head spinning, he leaned in and trailed kisses along her jaw until he reached her mouth.

Meryn moved closer to him, her hands resting on his hips.

For a long moment he lost himself in the taste and feel of her. When their kiss ended, she laid her head on his chest, and he wrapped his arms around her and held her tight. This last week had been one of the most difficult of his life, and he needed the warm, soft comfort of her against him.

"Now?" Her voice was muffled against his T-shirt.

He laughed and kissed the top of her head. "Now."

Still in the circle of his arms, her fingers found the gold heart. Meryn lifted it and gazed at it for a moment.

When she tipped back her head to look up at him, tears sparkled in her eyes. "Thank you for fixing it, Jesse."

Are we still talking about the necklace? Part of him wanted to ask her if their conversation would have gone the same way if he had not been able to bring Matthew and Gracie home. He couldn't bring himself to spoil the sweetness of the moment, though. "You're welcome."

"I'm so glad everything worked out in Ottawa."

"Me too. I had a little help. One of the commissioners, Michael Stevens, came to me last night. He's a believer too, and he gave me some hard numbers to feed the commission. I'm sure those had a big impact on their decision."

"That's so great. Knowing someone there was on your side probably helped a lot too."

"It did."

Meryn rested a hand on his chest. "Kate and Ethan are having a few people here on Saturday night to celebrate the kids coming home. Mostly just us and a couple of other friends she trusts. She wanted me to see if you could possibly stop in. I know it's difficult, but I told her I'd ask you. She'd really like the major to come too."

Jesse contemplated the invitation. Somewhere in the recesses of his mind, distant memories stirred, of being invited to hang out with friends on the weekend, going to play pool or see a movie. He'd taken for granted then how easy it was to be with people, just relaxing and having fun. Now he took a huge risk every time he tried to spend time with the ones he cared about the most. "I'm not sure if we can swing it, but we'll come by if we can, okay?"

"Okay."

"So what did you do all week?"

"I opened the store back up. And last night I went out for dinner with Drew. The rest of the time, I was just hanging out with the family, waiting to hear from you."

Jesse's stomach tightened. "Wait." He took her by the arms and eased her away from him. "What?"

"Which thing?"

His eyebrows rose. "Pretty sure you know which thing."

She sighed. "I had dinner with Drew. You remember him?"

"Oh yeah. I remember him. And the way he looked at me the last time I saw him. If his eyes had been lasers, I would have been a pile of ashes on the floor."

"Well ..." She sounded a little flustered. "We've been friends for a long time, and he stopped by the store on Tuesday when Kate and I were getting it ready to open. He asked if he and I could go for dinner, just to catch up, so we went last night." She wrinkled her nose. "You're not happy about that."

He tried to find a softer way to put it. *Nope, that's about right.* "I guess I'm not."

"Jesse, we're just—"

"Friends, I know. But let me ask you this. If I had a female *friend*, and you knew she had feelings for me and the two of us were going out for dinner together, would you be perfectly fine with that?"

"Of course."

He looked at her.

Her shoulders slumped. "All right, no, I guess I wouldn't be."

Jesse let go of her arms. "The thing is, I can't compete with him."

She let out a shocked laugh. "What are you talking about?"

"I'd like to be with you all the time, every day. But I can't be right now. Drew, though, he can come out here or drop by the store or take you for dinner in public any time he wants."

"You're right, there's no competition. But it's Drew who can't compete with you." Meryn reached for his hand and turned it over, palm up. "Close your eyes."

"Why?"

The corners of her mouth turned up. "Because it's time for you to trust me now."

He closed his eyes.

Meryn set something cold and hard on his hand. "There's no competition, because you have this."

Jesse looked down. A metal heart the size of a silver dollar rested on his palm.

"I know we can't see each other as much as either of us would like.

But even when we're not together, I want you to know that you have my heart too."

He brushed her cheek with the back of his fingers. "That might have been the most perfectly timed gift in the history of gift-giving."

Her smile broadened. "Then here's another one. I told Drew we couldn't spend any more time together, because I was involved with someone."

"For future reference, lady, that would have been good information to lead with."

She laughed. "So we're good?"

"We're good. We're very good." He slid the heart into the pocket of his jeans and tucked a strand of her hair behind her ear. "Want to know my four least favourite words?"

Her smile faded. "If they're the same as mine, I think I can guess. You have to go?"

"Yes, and as much as I hate them, unfortunately they're true."

"All right. If you and the major don't make it Saturday night, I hope you know how grateful we all are, to both of you."

"I'll pass that along to him."

"Good. This you can keep for yourself." She slid her hand behind his neck and pulled him down for one last kiss.

Jesse grinned when she let him go. "Yeah, I won't be passing that along." He rested his forehead against hers. "I'll really try to make it Saturday, okay?"

"Okay."

"See you soon." Jesse headed down the walkway. When he got to the jeep, he opened the door and looked back at Meryn.

She stood at the top of the stairs, leaning against the post, the soft glow of the porch light behind her haloing around her head.

He swallowed hard and lifted a hand before sliding behind the wheel.

As hard as it was leaving her, Jesse couldn't stay. Not yet. Just last week, he and Caleb had been able to help one of the Christians who had been arrested for breaking the new terrorist laws. It was Gallagher's day off and he'd been away from the base when the man was brought in, so they were able to let him go with a warning. As long as the two of them could continue to help without getting caught, it was worth staying in the army a little longer.

Besides, unless things changed at the base, he couldn't abandon Caleb to the company of Lieutenant Gallagher. His fingers tightened around the steering wheel as he drove down the lane.

Gallagher had made Jesse's life difficult for years, and clearly derived great pleasure from it. But Gallagher was clever. He'd made friends with all the right people, and managed to keep from them the kind of person he truly was.

All Jesse could do was watch him carefully and hope and pray the man would make a mistake that would reveal him for the despicable human being he was and cost him his career.

Only then would Jesse be free.

Chapter Thirty-Four

Meryn carried her coffee out onto the porch. An overnight shower had filled the air with the pungent aroma of leaves and dirt, and brought a welcome coolness to the wind.

Kate looked over from the porch swing where she'd been watching the kids blow bubbles in the front yard. "I can't take my eyes off them."

"I don't blame you." Meryn sat down on the Muskoka chair beside her and watched the kids giggling and chasing the rainbow-tinged bubbles. She took a sip of her coffee and set the mug down on the arm of her chair. "What would you have done, Kate?"

"If they hadn't come back?"

"Yes."

Kate didn't answer for a moment, then she exhaled. "I'm not sure. I know in my head they aren't ours, that they belong to God. Still, the whole time they were gone, I felt like this empty shell walking around, as if everything inside me had been carved out. Today I'm so filled up I could burst. Would I eventually have filled back up, or would I have spent the rest of my life a hollow shell? I don't know." Kate pushed her bare toes against the floor of the porch to move the swing. "People do it. They survive unimaginable loss and horror, but I just don't know how it would have gone for me or for Ethan. If we would have survived individually. If we would have survived as a couple. I hope so." She tore her gaze from Matthew and Gracie and turned to Meryn. "What about you and Jesse? Would the two of you have made it through if he hadn't been able to bring them back?"

"I don't know, either. I thought he might ask me that last night, but he didn't. Maybe he didn't want to hear the answer. I did know, even when it was happening, that it wasn't his fault they were being taken, that there was nothing else he could have done. I think that would have helped us to get past it eventually."

"Did you tell him last night about the other man?"

"Which one?"

Kate grinned wryly. "Either, I guess."

"We didn't have a lot of time, so I only told him about Drew."

"And?"

"And you were right. He wasn't happy about it."

"Uh-oh."

"Until I told him I used the opportunity to tell Drew I couldn't spend time with him anymore, because I was involved with someone else."

"Nice save. So everything's good with you two?"

"Better than good."

Her friend flicked a finger toward her. "I like the necklace."

Meryn fingered the gold heart around her neck. "Me too."

Kate stopped the swing and studied her. "Have you told him?"

"I just said I didn't have a chance last night."

"I don't mean that. I mean that you love him too."

"Kate."

"Forget it, Mer. Don't even try and deny it this time."

Her shoulders slumped. "No, I haven't. I can't. Not until he knows everything."

"No, I guess you can't." Kate lifted her feet to let the swing start rocking gently again.

"What is it?"

"I was just thinking about that day in the church, when Jesse pulled back the door and pointed a gun at you and Gracie. Who would have ever thought we'd end up here?"

"Not me, that's for sure. Not that day or for months after. I really tried not to let myself fall for him, you know."

"Oh, I know. I was there." Kate smiled. "It was kind of fun watching you fight what was clearly a losing battle."

"Happy to be such a source of amusement for you." Meryn picked up her mug, then set it down again without taking a sip.

"What is it?"

"I don't know." She shook her head, impatient with herself. "I feel restless today. As if something big is about to happen."

Her friend's eyes dropped shut. "Please, God. Nothing big. I can't handle that right now."

"I guess we don't really know what we can handle until it happens to us, do we?"

Kate opened her eyes. "I agree with you about that. None of us knows what we're capable of until we're put to the test. I truly believe that, if the worst happens, God will give us the strength to get through it." Her shoulders relaxed. "So that's the answer to the question you asked me earlier. I would have made it through, and Ethan would have too. Because if the worst did happen and we lost every single person in the world we loved, we still wouldn't be alone."

A refreshing coolness, like the breeze brushing past her face, flowed through Meryn's chest. "You're right. And we can't live our lives worrying about what might or might not happen in the future." She looked over at the kids in time to see Gracie turn a somersault on the lawn and land, arms and legs splayed out like a snow angel, on the thick, green grass.

Kate followed her gaze and laughed. "Exactly. So let's just enjoy today and be grateful. Maybe God will have mercy on us and we'll have a few weeks or even months of peace."

"I hope so."

A slight uneasiness still niggled deep inside, but Meryn pushed it back. It *was* a beautiful day. Warm rays of sun glinted off gold-tipped leaves. Birds flitted and trilled through the branches, blissfully unaware that the world was crumbling into chaos around them. And God had answered the family's prayers and brought Matthew and Gracie back to them.

And maybe he would answer Kate's plea too, and grant them a time of peace.

Chapter Thirty-Five

Jesse dropped the wooden bar across the barn doors and smoothed down his black T-shirt.

Caleb followed him across the driveway. "One hour, okay?" He pointed a finger at Jesse.

"Okay. Thanks for doing this, Cale."

"I'm happy to come in and see everyone, but I need you to remember that we're taking a huge risk here. Even an hour is pushing it. We can't stay a minute longer than that." Caleb glanced at his watch. "We're out of here at twenty-one hundred."

"Got it." Jesse rapped on the door frame.

Ethan called out, "Come in."

Jesse opened the screen and Caleb followed him into the kitchen.

Kate was dumping potato chips into a bowl, but she dropped the bag and brushed her hands off as she crossed the room toward them, a smile lighting up her face.

Ethan set a tray of drinks down on the kitchen table and followed her to the door.

"Jesse, I'm so glad you came." She hugged him briefly. "You too, Major."

"It's Caleb, please."

"Caleb." Kate touched his arm. "Thank you for arranging for Jesse to go to Ottawa. I'm so grateful to both of you for all you did for us."

He nodded.

Ethan motioned toward the hallway. "Go on in. We'll be right there."

Jesse led the way through the kitchen and into the living room. He scanned the room, looking for Meryn. She stood in front of the woodstove, talking to a man and woman. Their backs were to Jesse, but he recognized them immediately and elbowed Caleb. "Meryn's parents are here. I'll introduce you."

Meryn looked up as they approached. Her smile weakened his knees.

Jesse touched the small of her back lightly and returned her smile. "Mr. and Mrs. O'Reilly, good to see you again."

Meryn's dad grasped his hand. "Jesse. Good to see you too. We were thrilled and relieved to hear how well everything went in Ottawa."

"Me too."

Her mother rested a hand on his arm. "We never doubted it."

Jesse nodded at Caleb. "I'd like you to meet my friend and commanding officer, Major Caleb Donevan."

Caleb shook both their hands. "Just Caleb is fine."

Kate walked by them, carrying two bowls of chips.

Isabelle watched her. "If you'll excuse me, I think Katie could use some help."

Hugh rested a hand on her elbow. "You won't overdo it?"

She squeezed his hand. "No, I won't. I'll just help for a few minutes and then sit down."

"Good." His eyes followed her as she crossed the room. When he turned back, tiny lines of worry still creased his forehead, but he clapped Caleb on the shoulder. "Do you happen to know your way around a dart board, my friend?"

Caleb grinned. "I've been known to toss the sticks on occasion."

"Then let's go show those boys of mine how it's done."

Matthew jumped up from the floor where he'd been playing with the train set. "Can I come, Grandpa?"

"Of course." Hugh held a hand out to him. "I'll teach you some tricks, so you can beat your Uncle Brendan and Uncle Shane every time, okay?"

Matthew grasped his hand, and the two of them headed for the basement stairs.

Caleb raised his wrist in Jesse's direction and tapped his watch.

"I know."

Meryn rested her head against his shoulder. "The major doesn't know what he's in for, I'm afraid. My father takes his darts pretty seriously. As far as I know, he's never lost a game."

"He may have met his match this time. Caleb is the undisputed darts champion on the base. I've watched him play for years, and I've never seen him lose, either."

"Hmm. That could get interesting. My brothers usually give up fairly quickly, so I'm sure they'll be back here soon. Maybe Caleb will keep my father busy for a while." She lifted her head. "I'm glad you were able to get away. And the major."

"Me too. I thought I'd have to come on my own, but Caleb pointed out that it actually might look less suspicious if the two of us went together, since most of the time I do go out alone. I hope he's right."

"When do you have to leave?"

"Nine o'clock. We do patrolling in three-hour shifts, and the territory's pretty large. We'll have to cover a lot of ground in two hours as it is. We can't do it in any less time than that."

"An hour's better than nothing." Her smile held a hint of sadness, but she pushed back her shoulders. "Have you met our pastor?" She pointed across the room to a tall, lanky man, quite a bit younger than Jesse had expected, with reddish hair and beard.

"No, not yet."

"Come on, I'll introduce you."

Jesse followed her. One of the things that bothered him the most about having to keep his faith a secret was not being able to go to church. Other than the day they'd stormed Meryn's, it had been years since he had darkened the door of one. For most of his life that had been by choice. Now that he would give anything to go, circumstances prevented him. He was definitely interested in meeting the man who led the congregation he would gladly become a part of, should things change for him.

The pastor turned toward them as they approached, his eyes as warm as his smile.

Meryn let go of Jesse. "Pastor, I'd like you to meet Captain Jesse Christensen. Jesse, this is Pastor John MacLeod."

Jesse held out his hand. "Good to meet you, Pastor." The man's grip surprised him. Good. The pastor was even stronger than he looked. He'd need that strength to guide his people through the days to come.

"John, please. And it's good to finally meet you as well. I've heard your name often. I believe there's several in the church who owe you a debt of gratitude, which means I do as well." His voice held a faint lilt, as though he'd grown up around people with a strong accent or had lived in Scotland as a child.

"I've been happy to do what little I can to help, although I am sorry I'm not able to worship with you on Sundays."

The pastor waved a hand through the air. "God knows we all do what we can. And he sees the price we have to pay to do it. Thankfully we can all worship him wherever we are, any time we wish to, but of course, should you ever be able, you'd be most welcome to join us."

"I certainly hope to one day. In the meantime, please don't ever hesitate to let me know if there is anything I can do for you. Meryn knows how to get a hold of me."

"I appreciate that. And, as we all fight our battles in our own way, you should know that you are on my list of people to pray for daily."

"That means more to me than you know."

The pastor nodded. "You take care, Jesse. Meryn." He headed over to the table where Kate and Isabelle had set out coffee and cold drinks.

Brendan's laugh boomed through the living room.

Meryn looked at Jesse and grinned. "See?"

Jesse glanced over. "Yep. You called it. Your brothers are back but no Caleb yet. He must be holding his own."

Brendan and Shane stood with Kate and Ethan behind the couch on the other side of the room. Brendan said something to Kate and mussed up her hair.

She smacked him on the chest with the back of her hand, and he grinned.

Jesse pointed to the group. "Should we join them?"

"Sure."

Meryn's mother sat on the couch, Gracie in her lap. Jesse winked at the little girl as they went by, and she gave him a shy smile and snuggled against Isabelle.

What a hole would have been ripped in this family if he hadn't been able to bring those kids home. His stomach clenched at the thought.

Shane smiled at them as they approached. "Jesse. The man of the hour."

"It's true." Kate rested her hand on Ethan's back. "Our hero."

"Hardly that." Jesse waved off the praise. "All of your prayers had a much greater effect than anything I had to say to the commission, I'm sure."

"Lucky for you they did." Brendan's dark eyes gleamed. "I don't know anyone who lives as close to the edge as you do, Christensen. That's the third time you have narrowly escaped a massive butt-kicking. One of these days your luck is going to run out."

"I fully anticipate it will."

Brendan flexed the fingers of one hand before curling them into a fist and cracking his knuckles. "Too bad too, because it's been a long time since I laid one on a date of Meryn's."

"Brendan!" Meryn's cheeks flushed pink.

Ethan laughed. "You really punched one of Meryn's boyfriends?"

"More than one, when they started to get a little handsy. Although most of them weren't actually boyfriends."

"None of them were," Meryn said dryly. "You never let any of them stick around that long."

"I always figured if they were going to be scared off that easily, they didn't deserve you. It was a test."

"Designed so everyone would fail, of course." Shane took a swig from a can of cola.

"Of course." Brendan crossed his arms over his chest, looking pleased with himself.

"He kept a pretty good eye on me too, when Kate and I were dating." Ethan punched Brendan lightly on the arm. "There were times I could have sworn he was lurking around in the bushes, just watching us."

"I was. Bushes, upstairs windows, the backseat of cars, whatever it took. With Meryn's guys too."

Jesse shook his head. "And none of them stuck around very long. Go figure."

"No, they didn't. Not until ..." Brendan stopped and shot a look at Meryn.

Jesse looked at her too.

The flush on her cheeks deepened, but she didn't meet his gaze.

Until what? Or who?

"Until recently," Brendan finished lamely.

"Hey." Kate clapped her hands together, breaking the awkward silence. "I just remembered your parents brought pies. I'll go get them and set them out on the table in here, and you can help yourselves, okay?"

"I'll help." Ethan backed away from the group and followed her out of the room.

Should he push Meryn on it? Jesse shook his head. *Let it go.* This wasn't the time or the place.

Shane poked her in the arm. "Can I get you anything, kid?"

"No thanks, I'm good. If you really want to do something for me, you can stop calling me kid."

He grinned at her.

Jesse draped an arm around her shoulders. "Why do you hate that so much? It's a pretty typical nickname for the youngest sibling in a family, isn't it?"

Brendan snickered. "She hates it because she knows that's not why we call her that."

"Brendan." Meryn levelled a warning look at her brother.

A huge smile crossed his face. "It's because of the goats."

Jesse's forehead wrinkled. "The goats?"

Meryn ducked out from under Jesse's arm. "Okay, fine. You guys enjoy yourselves; I'm going to find some actual grownups to talk to."

She started to turn away, but Jesse took a step toward her, hooked an arm around her waist, and pulled her back to his side. "Oh no, darlin'. I need to hear this, and I really want you with me when I do."

Meryn shook her head as Brendan turned to Jesse. "We call her that because, from about the time she was ten years old, she had these gangly legs that were way too long for the rest of her. She looked like the goats we had on the farm when they were first born and trying to walk. Between that and the fact that she was the youngest in the family, we really didn't have a choice. It had to be *kid*."

Meryn shut her eyes and blew out an exasperated breath.

Shane and Brendan laughed.

Jesse reached over and tilted her chin up to face him. "Sorry, Meryn. I just had to know."

She glared at him. "I don't think you're sorry at all."

He gazed at her calmly until she rolled her eyes.

"All right, fine. Do you want a piece of pie?"

"I'd like some pie," Brendan said.

Meryn gave him a dirty look. "You can get your own pie."

"Hey, why are you mad at us and not him? He's the one who brought it up, you know."

"But *he* didn't laugh at me."

"Well, he's not stupid. He has a lot more to lose than either of us does."

Meryn looked at Jesse.

He lifted one shoulder, conceding that her brother had a point.

She shook her head. "You know what? The three of you are on your own. I'll see you later." She stalked over to the dessert table and grabbed a scoop to help Kate drop ice cream onto plates.

Jesse turned to Brendan and raised both hands.

"What?"

Shane dug an elbow into his ribs. "You threw him under the bus, you big goof. What was with that?"

Brendan grinned. "She'll get over it. Meryn's got a trigger fuse, but the heat fizzles out pretty quickly. I'm sure you've experienced that before."

Jesse exhaled. "I guess I have. More than a few times." His gaze lingered on her.

Shane nudged him. "You've got it pretty bad, don't you?"

For the millionth time, he wished he was better at hiding what he was feeling. Of course, Meryn's brothers were pretty highly tuned to anything anyone was thinking about her, so that might not have helped him, anyway. "Yeah, I do. She's the most amazing woman I've ever met. Not sure why she's with me, but I'm really glad she is."

"Knowing Meryn, I'll bet it wasn't easy to win her over."

He let out a short laugh. "You have no idea. She pushed me away for months, because she said she couldn't be with anyone who didn't share her faith. Even after I became a believer, there still seemed to be something holding her back, but I ..."

A look passed between the two brothers.

Jesse narrowed his eyes. "What was that?"

Brendan appeared to have developed an intense interest in the blanket hanging over the back of the couch. He picked at it, not looking at Jesse. "What was what?"

"That look you two just gave each other."

He shrugged. "We're thinking about going to check out the dessert table, that's all."

"That wasn't a 'let's go get dessert' look, that was an 'I guess she hasn't told him yet' look. Is there something I should know?"

When Brendan didn't answer, Jesse swivelled to face the other brother. "Shane?"

Shane looked as uncomfortable as Brendan, but he did look Jesse in the eyes. "Look, Jess, it's not our place to tell you. It's Meryn's. But you should ask her about it."

"Oh, believe me, I will."

"Good. In the meantime, I think we should go check out the selection before everything's gone. You want a piece?"

"I'll grab something in a minute. You guys go."

Shane grasped Jesse's shoulder. "Don't look so concerned. This is something the two of you can work out. I want you to remember one thing when she does tell you. I've seen the way my sister looks at you. I truly believe she loves you."

Jesse managed a small smile. "Thanks. That helps."

Shane nodded before heading over to the table.

Jesse leaned back against the wall and watched Meryn. *What are you keeping from me?*

As if she could read his thoughts, she turned to him, and their eyes met. An uncertain look crossed her face.

What will things be like between us, after? When I know, finally, what it is that stands between us like an electric fence, harmless-looking enough until one of us wanders too close to it and it stings and jolts? Jesse mustered a smile. As soon as the two of them had a moment alone, he would ask her what it was she hadn't told him.

It was time for him to know the truth.

Chapter Thirty-Six

Jesse pushed himself away from the wall when Meryn set down the scoop.

She said something to Kate, then came around the table. When she reached him, she stopped and searched his face. "Is everything okay?"

"I'm not sure, actually."

Her forehead wrinkled. "What is it?"

Jesse glanced around the room. Way too many people. "I have to go soon. Walk me out to the jeep?"

"Okay."

He took her hand and guided her through the living room and into the kitchen.

Empty chip bags and pop bottles littered the counter. The aromas of spices and warm pastry wafted through the room, the familiar comfort clashing with the uneasiness churning in his gut.

Jesse held the screen door open for her.

It wasn't quite dark, but already a harvest moon, full and yellow, hung just above the roof of the barn.

He tightened his grip on her hand, cool and trembling in his, as they went down the stairs and crossed the yard. They reached the barn in silence, and Jesse let go of her so he could lift up the bar. He rested it against the side of the building and swung open both doors.

Meryn walked into the barn. The interior of the building was dimly lit by a lamppost outside the door and moonlight streaming through the cobweb-covered windows that lined the wood-plank walls.

Jesse stopped in front of her when she reached the jeep.

The smell of dust and hay hung thick in the air.

Meryn's eyes, when she looked at him, were large and questioning.

Leaning down, he sought out her mouth. Her lips were soft on his, her skin like satin beneath his fingers.

Meryn's arms circled his neck, and she drew him closer.

Jesse held up both his hands.

Her fingers warm on the back of his neck, she pulled back, a smile playing across her lips. "What are you doing?"

He glanced up at the hayloft. "I just got thinking, if Brendan happens to be watching us from behind those hay bales up there, I don't want him to think I'm getting *handsy* with you."

Meryn laughed. "You don't have to worry. I checked to make sure he was in the living room and deep in conversation before we left."

"What made you think to do that?"

Her eyes sparkled. "Years of practice."

"Hmm."

"What?"

"Although I'm benefitting from all that practice tonight, I'm wondering what your ditching Brendan freed you up to do over the years."

Her smile widened. "You don't have to worry about that, either. I give Brendan a hard time about chasing away all those guys, but the truth is, there weren't very many that I really wanted to stick around. Ditching Brendan was far more about driving him insane than trying to get away with anything. I usually sent the guys off myself, then settled back to watch him come charging out of the house to try and find us."

Like a bull out of a chute. Jesse chuckled. "Thanks for clearing that up, at least."

"What do you mean *at least*?" Her arms slid from his neck, and a sudden coolness shivered across his skin. "Is there something else you'd like me to clear up?"

"Actually, there is." He drew in a steadying breath. "Meryn, is there something I should know about your past?"

Her face went so pale her skin glowed in the moonlight. "Why? What did my brothers tell you?"

"Nothing. I mean, I was telling them about how you pushed me away for a long time, and that even now there seems to be something holding you back. They gave each other this look, as if there was something you hadn't told me. When I pushed them on it, Shane said it wasn't their place to tell me; it was yours."

She bit her lip. "He's right. There is something I need to tell you. I've tried to, several times, but we kept getting interrupted, or it just wasn't the right moment."

The screen door slammed. Heavy footsteps thudded down the porch stairs.

Jesse winced. "You mean like that? Because that's Caleb."

"Exactly." Her voice was strained. "Can you meet me next week?"

He reviewed his schedule quickly in his head. "I can't get away before Thursday."

"Thursday, then. Nine o'clock. I'll tell you everything."

"Thursday."

"Yes."

Jesse grimaced. "That's fine. I didn't really need to sleep this week, anyway."

She squeezed his arms. "Please don't look so worried."

The words might have been comforting if she didn't look so worried herself.

Gravel crunched beneath Caleb's hiking boots. In ten seconds he'd be at the barn doors.

Jesse cupped the back of her head in one hand and pulled her to him. His kiss wasn't gentle this time. When he lifted his head, her breathing was shallow and her lips had parted. If Caleb's shadow hadn't fallen across the barn floor at that moment, he would have kissed her again and staked his claim even more firmly.

Her gaze shifted to the doorway.

Jesse dropped his hand.

Caleb came into the barn. "Sorry, Jess. We need to go."

"I know. It's okay."

Caleb turned to Meryn. "It was good to see you, Meryn. And to meet your family. Your dad plays a mean game of darts."

"Who won?"

"I don't think I better say."

Her eyes widened. "Are you telling me the king has been dethroned?"

"By a sheer-luck, triple-twenty, come-from-behind shot."

"If you beat my father, then it wasn't luck—it was pure skill. I'm impressed." Meryn stood on her tiptoes to wrap her arms around his neck. "Thank you, Caleb."

Caleb met Jesse's eyes as he hugged Meryn. "I didn't do much. Jesse did all the work."

"I don't just mean for that. I mean for all the times you cover for him so he can see me. I know that's risky for you, and I hope you know how much I appreciate it."

He cleared his throat. "You're welcome."

Jesse caught her hand and led her out of the barn. As soon as they were out of Caleb's sight, he stopped, reached for her other hand, and pulled both to his chest. "Meryn, you need to know, whatever you tell me Thursday night, nothing could change the way I feel about you. Nothing."

Meryn nodded and pulled one hand from his to reach up and rest the back of her fingers on his cheek.

She had done that before. When was that? The memory crashed through his mind. Right before her flogging. Not a good sign. His chest tightened.

She dropped her hand. "I'll get the doors. You go."

He nodded and, once again, turned and walked away from her.

When he and Caleb drove out of the barn, Meryn lifted her hand.

Caleb gave him a minute, until they were out on the road, before he rapped his fist against Jesse's arm. "That was fun. I'm glad we went."

"Me too."

"You don't sound glad. Did something happen?"

"No. Not yet, anyway."

"Not yet? What does that mean?"

Jesse sighed. "There's something in Meryn's past she hasn't shared with me. We're supposed to meet on Thursday night, so she can tell me about it."

"Are you worried?"

"Yeah, I guess. A little. I'm sure we can work it out, though, whatever it is."

"I'm sure. Unfortunately, you're on your own for a cover story for Thursday."

"Why?"

"I've been appointed part of the Canadian contingent helping to provide security at the G7 Summit. I'm heading to Germany on Wednesday, and I won't be back until Sunday. I just found out today, or I would have let you know earlier."

"It's unusual for them to appoint a base commander as part of a security detail, isn't it?"

"Yeah, it is, but this came straight from Headquarters. Germany must have requested additional security, not surprising with the threats that have been levelled against this summit."

"That's all right. I'll figure something out. Sounds like an interesting trip."

"It should be. I'm interior security, so I have clearance to be at some of the high-level talks." Caleb drummed his fingers on the steering wheel. "You'll keep an eye on Gallagher, right?"

"Sure. Other than Thursday night, I'll stay at the base and make sure he isn't up to anything."

"Good. I feel better about leaving, knowing you're there." He blew out a breath. "Sorry. I've been trying not to say things like that."

"Why?"

"Because it's self-serving. I want you to make the decision to stay or leave the army on your own, without any pressure from me."

Jesse shook his head. "You haven't pressured me, don't worry. I made the decision all on my own."

Caleb glanced over. "You've decided?"

"Yes. After I brought the kids back Thursday night, I realized I couldn't leave. I mean, what would have happened to them if you and I hadn't been there to fight to get them back? Not to mention that, as you've said, we're all that is preventing Gallagher from taking over the city, which would send things spiralling out of control pretty quickly. I can't leave you to deal with him on your own. We're a team. It would be selfish of me to leave just because I want to be with Meryn. So I'm staying."

"I'm not going to lie and tell you I'm not happy about your decision, Jess, even though I am sorry you and Meryn won't be able to be together."

"And I'm not going to lie and tell you that part of it isn't ripping me apart. Still, it's the right decision. For now."

"Have you told her?"

"Not yet. After we talk on Thursday, I'll see if it's the right time to break that news to her."

"Sounds like the two of you have a lot to deal with. I'm sorry I won't be there for you next week."

Jesse shrugged. "You can't turn down an assignment like that. I'm sure everything will work out. To be honest, as much as I'm dreading the conversation, I'm looking forward to everything finally being out in the open. Once we work through it, there shouldn't be anything keeping us apart anymore. Except for the ongoing threat of imprisonment or death if we're caught together, of course."

Caleb grinned. "Every relationship has its challenges."

Jesse rested his head against the seat. The thought of Caleb being an ocean away sent an unexpected wave of apprehension swirling through him. It was only for a few days, though. And Jesse would keep a tight rein on Gallagher and his little cronies, make sure they weren't up to anything they shouldn't be.

Everything would be fine.

Chapter Thirty-Seven

Although dark clouds hung low in the sky, blocking the meagre light of the moon, the night vision goggles helped Meryn make her way through the woods quickly. Now that she could see where she was going, she didn't crash through the trees like she used to, but made her way almost silently over and around logs and bushes.

She clambered over one last tree root and headed for the clearing.

The silhouette of the cabin loomed just ahead. The green army jeep was parked around the back of the building.

Her pulse jumped. *Jesse.*

Tonight was the night. The secret she had carried around for so long would no longer be a secret.

Meryn quickened her steps. A few feet from the cabin, she froze.

Jesse wasn't alone. Voices drifted through a crack in the door.

She scanned the yard. The hood of a sports car extended past the far corner of the cabin. *No.* The blood running through her veins turned to ice.

Annaliese.

Meryn crept to the side of the cabin. How had her sister found them? Now that she had, would she turn them in? Meryn strained to hear what she and Jesse were saying, but blood pounded in her ears so loudly she couldn't make out the words.

Stay where you are, Meryn.

She slid off the goggles and dropped them on the ground, then sidled around the corner of the building and leaned closer to the door. Through the crack, she could see the two of them.

Annaliese stood with her back to the door, long blonde hair shimmering down almost to her waist.

Jesse faced her, eyes cold, arms crossed over his chest. "Why can't you just leave Meryn alone?"

"I'm her big sister. It's my job to save her."

"I believe she would consider herself already saved."

Annaliese let out a cold laugh. "You don't believe all that garbage, do ...?"

Meryn bit down on her lip until she tasted blood on her tongue. *She knows.* Everything they had built so carefully was crashing down around them. She could picture the sly smile that always crossed her sister's face when Annaliese had someone cornered, trapped like an animal. Meryn had seen that look more times than she cared to remember.

"You do, don't you? She's turned you. Unbelievable. Their lies spread like poison through water, destroying all who taste even a drop. How could you betray your country like that?"

"How could you betray your sister like that?"

She drew herself up. "That's not a denial."

"Of what?"

"That you're a believer now. Which is very interesting information for an *informant* to have. What do you suggest I do with that, Captain?"

"Keep it to yourself. For the sake of the sister you claim to want to help so badly."

"Meryn has made her own bed, and now she has to lie in it. The question is"—she tilted her head—"who is lying in that bed with her?"

Meryn gritted her teeth.

Jesse took a step toward her, hands tightening into fists.

Meryn's breath caught. *Don't do it, Jesse.* She couldn't imagine him hitting a woman. Still, her sister had an uncanny ability to push people to do things they normally would never do.

He stopped inches from Annaliese. "Do you know your sister at all?"

"Define *know.* I can rhyme off her vital statistics, but I have never, my whole life, been able to understand her."

"No, you wouldn't, would you?"

Annaliese moved closer to him. When she spoke, her voice was soft and sultry. "I do know her well enough to know that, if you are with her, you must be feeling pretty ... lonely these nights." Her hands moved slowly up and down his arms.

Heat roared through Meryn. *All right, enough. I'm going in there.*

Before she could move, her sister pressed her mouth to Jesse's.

He grasped both her elbows and thrust her away from him. "Get out of here, Annaliese. The Canadian Army no longer requires your services."

"That is a mistake, Captain." Her voice carried slivers of ice. "Your superiors will not appreciate losing such a valuable source of intelligence."

"I'll handle my superiors. You just get out of my sight. And don't go anywhere near Meryn ever again."

"You can't keep me away from Meryn. I'm her sister."

"You are *not* her sister. Kate is her sister. Family is not just an accident of birth. You have to earn your right to belong. You lost the privilege of being part of your amazing family the day you locked your terrified little sister in that chicken coop. Now get out of here."

Meryn backed around the corner of the building quickly as the door to the cabin flew open and light sliced through the blackness of the yard.

Grass swished beneath her sister's high-heeled black boots.

Meryn held her breath until a car door slammed, hard enough to rattle the window above her head.

The loud roar of an engine broke the silence of the country night.

She turned her head toward the road. When the lights of the sports car disappeared in the distance, Meryn exhaled.

Behind her, the door of the cabin opened and the porch creaked. "Meryn?"

She rounded the corner of the building. "I'm here."

Jesse bounded down the steps and met her at the bottom. His arms circled her waist, and he lifted her off her feet. For a long moment he held her, face buried in her shoulder.

Meryn clung to him, pressing her lips together to hold in the sobs that rose in her throat.

Finally he lowered her to the ground. His hands cupped her face. "I was afraid you'd come into the cabin."

"I almost did. I was so focused on seeing you I didn't notice her car at first, but then I got closer and heard voices." She gripped his arms. "What was she doing here? How did she find us?"

"I don't know. Although I'm sure she's been keeping an eye on you. Or has hired someone else to."

Meryn drew in a quick breath. "Is that why I sometimes feel like I'm being watched out at the farm? Do you really think she would stoop that low?"

He cocked his head.

She sighed. "You're right. Of course she would."

A drop of rain landed on her cheek.

Jesse looked up. "We shouldn't stay here, now that Annaliese knows where we meet. Why don't you go? I'm just going to grab a few things that could connect us to this place."

"No, I'll help you so we can both get out of here faster." Heart pounding, Meryn followed him up the steps. Her chest squeezed when she walked into the room, softly lit by the floor lamp Jesse had set up. This place had felt so safe to her, a refuge against the rest of the world. Now the world had stormed in and destroyed the illusion. They could never come here again.

Jesse grabbed a plastic bag from a drawer in the kitchen and started stuffing the few items they'd brought here into it.

What had he just said? It had sparked something in Meryn, a warning she needed to give him. She snatched the portable heater up off the floor and started winding the cord around it. Urgency clouded her thinking, but she waded through the swirling fog until she found it. "Be careful, Jesse. Annaliese must be furious. Trust me, you don't want to make an enemy out of her."

Jesse stopped his frantic packing. "Meryn, she hurt you. She couldn't be anything *but* my enemy."

A warm tingling sensation spread through her abdomen. She crossed the space between them, set the heater on the kitchen counter, and threw her arms around his neck. The world retreated again as she kissed him, demanding more from him than she ever had before. If she couldn't tell him how she felt, not yet, she could show him.

When he lifted his head, the jade eyes that probed hers were dark and liquid. He pulled her to him. His heart pounded, strong and steady, beneath her cheek. "We better go."

"We still need to talk."

"I know. I'll drive you home."

"All right. I—" She froze at the sound of a vehicle pulling into the driveway.

Jesse let her go and stalked toward the window. He lifted a corner of the black paper he'd taped back up after Meryn had been ill and peered out.

A door slammed.

He spun around to face her.

Meryn pressed a hand to her stomach. "What is it?"

"Army jeeps. Two of them."

He strode back to her and gripped her shoulders. "I'm sure they're coming for me, not you. If I go with them peacefully, everything will be okay. I haven't done anything seriously wrong, not that they know about, anyway. If there's any justice left in this country, they won't hold me long."

Footsteps thudded up the porch stairs.

Jesse gripped her tighter, face grim. "Just do what they say, Meryn. I'll go with them, straighten this out. When it's safe to meet again, I'll send you a message. Okay?"

"Okay."

"Remember, whatever happens, God is in control. We have to trust that." Jesse lowered his head and kissed her. "I love you."

A fist pounded on the door before she could answer. "Army. Open up."

He took a step toward the door, but it crashed open, banging against the wall.

Lieutenant Gallagher stood in the doorway, gun drawn.

Jesse moved to stand in front of Meryn.

The lieutenant strode into the kitchen, a mocking smile spreading across his face. "Well, well, Captain Christensen. Imagine finding you here." Four more soldiers followed him into the room.

"You need to come with us, Captain. We have a warrant for your arrest." Gallagher flashed his i-com in their direction. He motioned toward Jesse, and the two soldiers who had come through the door last brushed past the other three men and came over to him. "Hands out."

He held them out.

Meryn bit back a cry as the handcuffs snapped around his wrists. The soldiers took him by the arms and directed him toward the door.

When he reached Gallagher, Jesse stopped. "I don't know what strings you pulled to get that warrant, Lieutenant, but my arrest won't hold up. I haven't done anything wrong."

"Is that right?" Gallagher's gaze flicked to the bracelet on Meryn's wrist and back to Jesse.

Meryn's stomach tightened. Getting involved with a Christian was enough to earn him a prison term now, or worse.

"You can take it up with the commission. From what I hear, you're good at that. I'm just following instructions to get you and bring you in."

"Well, you have me. Let's go."

Gallagher's eyes narrowed. "You're not the one giving the orders around here anymore, Christensen. I'm in charge now." He nodded toward the door. "Put him in the back of one of the jeeps and stay with him."

Meryn's breath jammed in her throat. Neither Gallagher nor the two men who had come through the door right after him made a move to leave. One of them was Private Whittaker, the soldier who had come into her store with Lieutenant Bronson the day she had received her first shipment of Bibles.

The other man leered at Meryn as he spoke to Private Whittaker. "They know to take him back to the base and not wait for us, right?"

She sucked in a breath. Images from the night she was attacked in Jesse's quarters slammed through her mind. The pistol, her wrists duct taped together behind her back, the bed, the knife, the stinging pain. And the mocking words.

There is no safe place. We can get to you anytime we want. Maybe next time we won't be in such a hurry.

She didn't recognize the second man with Gallagher, but she knew that voice.

Was this the next time?

Jesse looked back at her as the men holding his arms directed him toward the door. "Meryn? What is it?"

He must have seen the terror on her face and, after glancing between the two men with the lieutenant, understood what it meant. He struggled with the soldiers. "What's going on, Gallagher?"

"Get him out of here." Gallagher waved a hand toward the exit.

The two men holding Jesse dragged him outside.

The lieutenant followed them to the door.

For a moment, Meryn thought he might leave and call for his men to come too, but instead, he slammed the door and slid the lock across.

When he turned around, her eyes met his hooded ones across the room. His gaze raked over her body.

Cold shuddered through her. "You are a sick, evil man."

He let out a short laugh. "My reputation precedes me, I see. Good. It will save time if you already know that about me and I don't have to prove it to you." He gestured to the other two men. "What about my friends here? Do they need to show you how sick and evil they can be?"

Meryn pushed back the fear threatening to clog her throat. "No. If they're hanging around you, I already know they're loathsome bottom-dwellers."

His smile disappeared as his eyes went as hard as stone. "That's where you're wrong, gorgeous. We don't dwell on the bottom. Not anymore. We are rapidly clawing our way to the top over the crushed bodies of whoever tries to stop us. As your *boyfriend* is about to find out, that is never a good idea."

Meryn swallowed hard. "Why? What are you going to do to him?"

"Same thing we're planning to do to you. Figuratively, anyway."

One of the other men laughed.

Horror coursing through her, Meryn backed up. *Father, help me. Please help me.* No other words would separate from the tangled mass of frantic thoughts buzzing through her mind. Her gaze darted to a knife in the holder on the counter, and she snatched it up. She had a weapon at least. This time. Turning toward the men, she held the knife out in front of her.

Gallagher stuck his gun back in the holster and crossed his arms over his chest, a grin crossing his face as he watched.

Meryn concentrated on the two soldiers advancing slowly toward her. When they got close, she swiped the knife at Private Whittaker.

He yelped and snatched back his arm, a line of red soaking through his torn sleeve.

Meryn turned to the other one when he moved closer and slashed at him, but he jumped back, then grabbed her wrist and twisted until she cried out in pain and dropped the knife.

He shoved his forearm under her chin and slammed her back against the refrigerator.

Meryn gasped for breath as his arm pushed against her throat.

"We told you we could get to you any time."

The fear that had gripped her dissipated as anger rose to take its place. Meryn kicked out hard. The heel of her hiking boot connected squarely with the man's shin.

He grunted and his arm fell from her throat as he bent down and gripped his thighs. When he straightened up, the back of his hand smashed across Meryn's cheek.

Furious, she spun back to face him. She raised a clenched fist, but Private Whittaker stepped in front of her and closed his fingers over both her wrists, lifting her arms above her head.

He pressed his body against hers.

The first man straightened up and reached past Whittaker, grabbing her shirt and yanking on it until the cloth tore.

Meryn struggled to free her hands, but the private's grip only grew tighter. She bit her lip to keep from giving them the satisfaction of hearing her scream in frustration.

The wooden frame splintered as the door crashed open behind Gallagher.

Before the lieutenant could move, Jesse had lifted his cuffed hands over Gallagher's head and shoved his arm against the man's throat. He tightened his grip until the lieutenant's face turned purple and his eyes bulged.

The two soldiers who had taken Jesse out of the cabin appeared in the doorway.

He lunged backward to stand against the cabin wall, dragging the lieutenant with him. "Call them off, Gallagher."

Meryn's heart pounded in her chest. *Help us. Help us. Help us.*

The man who'd been pulling on her shirt spun around and yanked out his gun, but he couldn't shoot without taking the chance that he'd hit Gallagher. He took a step toward the two men.

Jesse glared at him. "One step closer, Smallman, and I'll break his neck."

The man stopped.

Private Whittaker didn't loosen his grip on Meryn, but he did look back to see what was going on.

Jesse leaned in close to Gallagher's ear. "Call them off and let her go, or when I get out, I will hunt the three of you down, one by one, slit your throats, and string you up by the ankles to bleed out like the rutting pigs you are."

Gallagher coughed and sputtered, but when Jesse's arm started to tighten again, he choked out, "Let her go."

The private waited a few seconds, then released his grip on her wrists. Meryn planted her palms against his chest and shoved him away.

He raised his fist, but lowered it at Gallagher's sharp, "Don't!"

Meryn bent down to pick up the knife on the floor. Gripping it in both hands, she skirted around the two men and made her way on trembling legs toward the doorway.

"Meryn?" Jesse's voice was urgent. "Are you all right?"

"I'm fine." Talking sent sharp pain stabbing up and down her throat.

"Go home now. Quickly. And lock your door."

Meryn hesitated. She couldn't leave him.

"Please, Meryn. Everything will be okay. Go."

The hand of one of the soldiers in the doorway edged toward his gun.

Jesse jerked Lieutenant Gallagher backward. "Don't do it."

The soldier dropped his hand to his side.

There is nothing I can do to help, and I'm only making things harder for him, being here. I have to go. But what would they do to him if she left? She met Jesse's eyes.

He inclined his head toward the door. "Trust."

Both of the soldiers moved out of her way as she started for the porch.

Behind her, Gallagher spoke, his voice jagged and raw. "Resisting arrest? Assault? Uttering death threats? Not very *Christian* of you, Christensen."

Her heart sank. So Annaliese had told them that too. That was going to make things a lot worse for Jesse. What else did they know?

With one last glance back, Meryn brushed past the soldiers and went out into the cold night. Her hands clenched into fists at her sides as she stumbled through the woods.

Right or wrong, her sister had just become her enemy too.

Chapter Thirty-Eight

Jesse gave her as much of a head start as he could.

Letting go of Gallagher was going to be like opening the door on a caged lion. The man was coiled, ready to spring.

Jesse braced himself for what was coming as he loosened his grip and lifted his arms over the lieutenant's head.

Gallagher whirled around and drove a fist into Jesse's stomach.

Pain shot through his abdomen as he bent forward, gasping for breath.

Whittaker and Smallman each grabbed an arm and hauled him upright.

Gallagher looked over at the two soldiers still standing in the doorway. "Go back to the base. We'll bring the prisoner."

Neither of them moved.

Jesse studied them.

Fear and uncertainty flickered on both their faces.

They were good men, men he had worked with and trained with and broken bread with. Would they help him? Make sure Gallagher did this by the book?

The fear won out. One of the soldiers nudged the other in the arm, and they turned and left the cabin.

Jesse was on his own.

Gallagher stalked over and shoved the door closed behind them, as far as the splintered frame would allow. When he got back to Jesse, he drew back his fist again. And stopped. A hard glint entered his eyes.

Uh-oh. Getting beaten up out here by the three of them would no doubt be preferable to whatever evil scheme had just planted itself in Gallagher's demented mind.

The lieutenant dropped his arm.

The disappointment of the two men at Jesse's sides was palpable.

Under different circumstances, he would have laughed.

"I have a better idea." Gallagher spun on his heel and headed for the door. "Bring him."

Smallman limped across the yard.

Jesse glanced down at the private's left leg. What had happened? He didn't remember the little rat limping when he first came into the cabin.

They reached the jeep. Smallman opened the door and shoved Jesse onto the backseat as Whittaker went around to the other side.

They rode in silence for a few minutes.

Jesse's heart pounded and he breathed deep, trying to bring his trepidation under control. He needed to stay calm and keep a cool head if he was going to be able to deal with whatever was about to happen.

The growing patch of crimson soaking into the sleeve of Whittaker's camouflage jacket caught his attention.

"What are you looking at?" The private sneered.

"You're bleeding."

"What was your first clue?"

Jesse pressed his lips together. He'd stopped playing that game in seventh grade. If the guy wanted to bleed to death, that was his business. Before she'd left, Meryn had picked a knife up off the floor. She must have slashed Whittaker's arm when he came after her. So maybe she stabbed Smallman in the leg too. Jesse glanced down.

No blood.

Kicked him, then. With those hiking boots she would have been able to do some damage. So she'd given both of them a souvenir of the evening. *That's my girl.* He repressed a smile. If Gallagher or the others thought he found anything amusing, things would get a lot worse for him fast.

The clicking of the turn signal brought his head up. Where ...? His chest clenched. *No. He wouldn't ...*

Gallagher showed his identification to the man in the guard house, and the large gates slowly opened. The lieutenant drove into the parking lot and wheeled into a spot marked *Reserved* near the door of the old Kingston Penitentiary.

The prison had closed in 2013, but the army had reopened one wing when they moved into town. The men they sent there had not been convicted under the terrorist act but were violent offenders, arrested mainly on gang and drug charges when the military cracked down on both.

"Gallagher ..."

The lieutenant ignored him and jumped out of the vehicle. "Let's go."

Smallman and Whittaker looked at each other.

Jesse jumped on their hesitation. "You can't let him do this. I don't belong here. I should be taken to the base. All three of you are going to end up being court-martialled, or worse."

Smallman pushed open the jeep door. Whittaker came around to stand behind him as he hauled Jesse out of the backseat. They both took him by the arms again.

Jesse's gaze locked on Gallagher's. "Lieutenant, you cannot leave me here. I've put half these guys in this place." He worked to keep the rising panic out of his voice.

"How nice for you. It'll be like old home week, won't it?"

"They will kill me."

"Then we'll have saved the taxpayers the cost of a hearing." Gallagher strode toward the front doors.

The two privates dragged Jesse toward the entrance.

Gallagher stood in the shadows of the large stone pillars, waiting to be let in.

Jesse muscled his way toward him. "If I'm being charged under the terrorist act, I should be held on the base."

Gallagher tipped back his head to reveal his throat, reddened and already darkening with bruises. "We'll deal with the assault and attempted murder charges first. If you survive those, then we'll take care of the terrorist offences."

"When the major comes back, you'll be done."

The dark eyes narrowed. "That's what you don't get, Christensen. I'm not the one who's done around here. You are."

A buzzer sounded, and Gallagher yanked open the heavy door and held it as Smallman and Whittaker hauled Jesse inside. "Wait here." Gallagher stalked toward a window, where a large, bald man in a blue shirt, patches of rosacea flaming across his cheeks, sat at a desk. "We're delivering a prisoner for you to process."

The man leaned forward to look around the lieutenant.

Jesse wished he were wearing his uniform. Surely then the man would inform Gallagher they'd brought Jesse to the wrong place.

The man regarded him somberly for a moment, then sat back in his chair. "Do you have the form?"

Gallagher entered the information into his device and held it up for the man to scan.

He read it over before looking up. "Are you the one pressing charges?"

"Yes."

"Tip back your head." The man held up his device and took several pictures of Gallagher's neck from the front and from both sides. "Any other injuries?"

"No."

The man pushed a button on the wall. Thirty seconds later, a guard opened the door to the left of the window and came out into the waiting area. A second guard stopped and held the door open.

Gallagher crossed his arms over his chest, looking triumphant.

The two privates let go of Jesse's arms, and Whittaker shoved him toward the guard as he approached.

"Let's go." The nose of the large, burly man had obviously been broken more than once. He either had a penchant for fighting or prisoner uprisings were commonplace here.

Neither of those scenarios boded well for Jesse. He sent a last, heated look at the lieutenant.

A cruel smile on his face, Gallagher lifted one hand and waggled his fingers.

The two guards each grabbed an arm and led Jesse down a long, grey hallway. Behind them, the heavy metal door slammed shut with a clang that echoed off the walls.

Chapter Thirty-Nine

Meryn hadn't taken time to grab the night vision goggles. Halfway through the woods she was bitterly regretting that decision. She lost track of the number of times she tripped and fell on tree roots and jutting rocks.

Misty rain drifted in the air, and jagged sobs tore at her tender throat. Would they come after her? How long would Jesse be able to hold them off? And what would they do to him when he let the lieutenant go?

Intense hatred for the man coursed through her. Why was he out to get Jesse? And why were Gallagher and his men so determined to destroy her life?

Meryn pushed back the questions and concentrated on getting home. It seemed to take forever, but finally the dim glow of the lights in her farmyard broke through the screen of branches in front of her. She kept her eyes fixed on the light as she burst out of the bush and into the open grassy area.

Moonlight danced on the surface of the water at the bottom of the hill. A crane rose slowly into the air, long wings barely moving as it glided over the pond. The serenity and beauty of the scene contrasted starkly with the ugliness of everything that had happened in the last hour. Meryn looked away. She scrubbed her hands together to brush off some of the mud as she made her way across the yard and up the stairs to the porch. Twisting the handle, she stumbled through the door and into the kitchen.

Shane and Brendan sat at the table, a pot of coffee between them. Their heads whipped toward the door as she came through.

"Meryn!" Brendan shoved back his chair so hard it crashed to the floor behind him. He left it as he covered the space between them in three strides and grasped her by both arms.

Meryn rested her forehead on his soft denim shirt until the pounding in her chest gradually subsided. She lifted her head.

Brendan held her out at arm's length. Concern darkened to rage as his gaze travelled the length of her.

Meryn looked down. She was covered in mud and grass stains, and the front of her shirt was ripped. She gathered up the torn cloth in one hand and held it to her chest.

Brendan reached out and touched the spot on her cheek that still stung from the slap she'd taken. "Did someone *hit* you?" His voice was thick with fury. He took her by the arms again. "Meryn, who did this to you?"

"Here." Shane tugged her out of Brendan's grasp and slid an arm around her shoulder. "Give her a second." He led her over to the table and directed her onto a chair. Crouching in front of her, he took her hand in his. "First of all, are you hurt?" He turned over her arm to reveal a thick smear of blood across the underside of it.

Still clutching the front of her shirt, Meryn shook her head. "That's not mine."

Shane took her chin in his fingers and tipped her head to the side. "Your throat is red."

"I know. He ... they ..." *Where do I begin?*

Brendan had been pacing back and forth between the door and the table, his eyes wild. He stopped and spun toward her. "Who's *they*? Who did this?"

Shane waved a hand in his direction. "Let her think."

She drew in a long, quivering breath. "I went to the cabin tonight to see Jesse. When I arrived, Annaliese was already there, talking to him."

Brendan's fists clenched. "Did she do this? Did she hurt you?"

"No. She never saw me. I waited outside until she left. She must have told someone Jesse was there, because a few minutes later two army jeeps drove up."

"I'll kill her. I swear, this time I'll kill her with my bare hands."

Shane threw him a look. "Brendan. Not helping." He turned back to Meryn. "What happened when the soldiers got there?"

"There were five of them, including Lieutenant Gallagher, who hates

Jesse for some reason. He arrested Jesse and ordered two of the soldiers to take him out to the jeep."

Brendan's eyes narrowed. "What about the other two?"

"One of them pushed me up against the fridge, and the other one grabbed my shirt and ripped it, while Gallagher stood there watching."

Her eyes met Shane's and a shudder rippled through her.

Normally calm, his eyes reflected the heat radiating from Brendan in waves. Shane squeezed her hand, his jaw tight. "Then what?"

"Before ... anything could happen, Jesse burst back into the cabin. He choked the lieutenant from behind until he ordered his men to let me go."

Shane expelled a breath, as if he'd been holding it in. "You got away."

"Yes. I didn't want to leave Jesse, but he told me to go home." She pressed her fingers to her mouth. "Gallagher was already out to get him. Who knows what he did to Jesse after I left." Her voice broke.

Shane rubbed his hand in circles over her back until some of the cold gripping her eased. "Should we call Rick to come out and take a look at you?"

"No. I'm fine." She sat up and looked around the room. "Where's Brendan?"

Before Shane could answer, Brendan strode back into the room, a shotgun in each hand. He handed Shane one of the guns, then pulled a box of ammunition out of his pocket and tossed it onto the table.

Shane reached for the box.

Meryn's chest tightened. "Brendan, what are you doing? You can't go after those men. They're trained soldiers and likely already back at the base."

He shoved a round into the chamber of his shotgun. "I'm not going after them, kid. But if they come after you, Shane and I will be more than happy to be the welcoming committee."

Chapter Forty

The guards directed Jesse to a small room and processed him quickly. When he had pulled on the orange jumpsuit they tossed to him, they cuffed him again and led him out of the room.

The same cold, clammy presence that seeped from the walls and rose from the floor in the warehouse where he had met with Scorcher swirled around him now. *Even though I walk through the valley of the shadow of death, I will fear no evil, for you are with me.* He clung to the words, repeating them over and over in his mind.

There was evil in this place. The unspeakable horrors that had occurred inside this historic building over the two hundred and twenty years of its existence permeated the air, leaving it heavy with a fear and despair he could almost taste.

He ignored the catcalls as the guards directed him past several cells filled with prisoners. They stopped in front of the last cell.

The guard with the crooked nose pulled a black baton from his belt and gripped it in his right hand, then tugged a metal canister from his pocket and held it in his left hand. He nodded at the guard on the other side of Jesse.

The second guard entered a code before placing his thumb on the pad by the door.

The lock clicked open.

Three sets of bunk beds lined the wall. Inmates reclined on five of the six beds. None of them were asleep, and each one watched the entrance to the cell with interest as Jesse was pushed inside.

The door clanged shut behind him. "Hands through the opening."

Jesse didn't like the idea of turning his back on the men, several of whom had sat up when he entered the cell, but he liked even less the idea of facing them while still cuffed. He stuck his hands through the small slot in the door and waited as the guard unlocked and removed the handcuffs. As soon as his hands were free, he spun around and pressed his back to the door. The sounds of the slot sliding closed and the retreating footsteps of the guards sent apprehension pouring through him, but he pushed it away.

The power of the men in front of him would rise in correlation to the level of fear they sensed in him.

He met the gaze of each man steadily.

Three of the five were men he had arrested himself, which was not good. From the looks on their faces, they recognized him too.

The biggest of the men, Hernandez, a tattoo-covered gang leader with a shaved head, swung his legs over the side of his lower bunk and stood.

Jesse refused to look away as the man approached him slowly, drawing out the moment like a wild cat advancing on its prey.

"Well, well, well. Looky here, gentlemen." Hernandez stopped in front of him and ran a finger down the side of Jesse's face. "We have ourselves our very own soldier boy to play with."

Jesse's jaw tightened. Everything in him longed to slap the man's hand away. He kept his hands firmly at his sides. If security cameras were aimed in their direction, he didn't want to be accused of instigating whatever was about to happen.

Springs creaked as the other men in the cell got up. Two of them hopped down off their top bunks. All four ambled over and stopped in a semicircle behind Hernandez.

What had he done to establish himself as the alpha male of the group? Jesse shoved away the thought. *I really don't want to know.*

"Not so high and mighty now, are you, *Captain*?" Hernandez's hand dropped down to the zipper of Jesse's jumpsuit and he toyed with the pull tab at the top. "I had a really good thing going out there, but you just couldn't keep out of my business, could you?"

"Not when your *business* was destroying people."

A cruel smile crossed the gang leader's face. "That is my specialty, destroying people. Want to see a sample?"

Not particularly, no. Jesse clenched his teeth. *Don't say it. Being a smartmouth is not going to help you any.*

Hernandez lifted his hand to cup Jesse's chin. "Such a pretty face. Seems almost a shame to …"

That's it. Getting hit was preferable to being pawed at. He jerked away from the other man's touch.

Hernandez's eyes hardened. He drew back his fist.

Jesse ducked.

The big man's fist smashed into the metal door. Fire leaped into his eyes as a string of curse words, English and Spanish tangling around each other, spewed from his mouth.

Not the most intelligent move. Jesse had no time to rethink his strategy as the other men were on him in an instant, dragging him away from the door. He managed to put two of them on the ground before a solid punch from Hernandez landed just below his left eye.

The world darkened and tilted.

Before it could right itself, two of the other guys had grabbed his arms and yanked them behind him.

Brendan, you were right. My luck just ran out.

The next blow caught him in the abdomen, and he bent forward, working to suck in oxygen. More punches came, landing on his ribs on both sides. Helpless to protect himself, Jesse concentrated on staying on his feet. As soon as his legs gave out, the kicking would begin. *God, help me.* He called on every anti-torture strategy he'd ever been taught in order to block out the screaming pain. *Meryn.* He tried to focus on a picture of her in his mind, but what was happening to him was too real. The shock of it sent rage, helplessness, and agony billowing through him in wave after wave of red.

From somewhere far away, the sound of wood clattering against metal slowly pulled him out of the mist swirling through his brain.

"All right. Enough!" The broken-nosed guard dragged his black baton across the bars of the cell. "Knock it off."

Hernandez landed one more blow to his gut before the two guys holding Jesse's arms let go.

He dropped to his knees. Air had become a precious commodity, and he gulped for it greedily. After a moment, he struggled to his feet, grasping two bars in an attempt to keep himself there as the room spun around him.

The guard stood in front of him. He looked almost bored. "You want to file a complaint, Christensen?"

Yeah right. Slide your i-com and stylus through the bars, and I'll get right on that. "No." Even that much talking sent tongues of fire shooting across his cheek from the tender area below his eye.

The guard shrugged and rapped his baton on the bars again before pointing it in the general direction of Jesse's cell mates. "Any more and you're all in the hole. Got it?"

Silence greeted him, which appeared to be good enough for the guard, who meandered off down the hallway.

Jesse turned around and slid his back down the bars, gingerly lowering himself onto a hard, metal bench. It was slightly safer than stretching out on the empty bed, and either way, he wasn't about to sleep.

His cell-mates slowly made their way back to their bunks.

Hernandez's black eyes stayed riveted on him for what seemed like hours, but finally he turned over and faced the wall.

Jesse leaned back against the bars. Thundering pain continued to roar through him, tightening every muscle as if he had gotten caught in the grip of a giant vice. Every breath required effort and pinballed against the sides of his windpipe. Amazing how something that was usually done without conscious thought could become such a torturous chore.

In the dim, artificial light in the cell, it was nearly impossible to determine the passage of time. Gradually, though, the light creeping past the cell from the windows located far down the hallway heralded the arrival of morning. A new day. What would it bring him?

Jesse shifted on the bench and stifled a groan at the fresh onslaught of pain the movement caused him. Whatever the day brought, it couldn't be worse than what he'd just been through. Could it?

Gallagher. The man had given himself the night to come up with new and devious ways to torment Jesse. No doubt the man had used every minute of it to his full advantage.

Jesse winced. It might have been better for him if the guard hadn't interrupted what had been going on in the cell last night. If he had just let the inmates finish the job and end Jesse's life. By now, all this would have been over.

He pulled one foot up on the bench and rested his chin on his folded arms. *God, you hold the power of life and death—Hernandez and Gallagher don't. You know the number of my days, and obviously that number was not up last night. If it's up today or tomorrow or whenever you choose, that's in your hands. All I ask for is the courage to finish well and honour you. And that, whatever happens to me, you watch over Meryn.*

Two guards, different men than the night before but equally brawny and intimidating, marched down the hallway and stopped outside the cell.

"Christensen," one of them barked.

The sound reverberated through his throbbing head. "Yes."

"Get up."

He dropped his foot to the ground and stood, trying not to let the blistering pain show on his face. His eyes met Hernandez's dark ones, which were fixed on him intently. Jesse turned toward the exit.

The slot door slid open. "Hands out."

He shoved his hands through the opening. Cold steel closed around his wrists again.

"Stand back."

He moved away from the door as it opened.

One of the guards motioned him through. "Let's go."

They took him back to the small room where he'd been processed the day before and handed him the jeans and T-shirt he'd worn to see Meryn at the cabin.

Jesse stripped off the orange jumpsuit, biting his lip to keep from crying out at the dagger-like pain that blurred his vision. His stomach lurched as he pulled on the T-shirt and jeans and did up the zipper and button.

After taking a moment to catch his breath, Jesse walked into the hallway ahead of the guards. Now what? Was this move a good sign or a bad one? It all depended on who waited for him at the exit. If Caleb happened to find out what was going on and either got back himself or sent someone for him, he might have a chance to ...

The door to the front lobby swung open.

Gallagher and his followers stood on the other side. The smirk on the lieutenant's face told Jesse everything he didn't want to know.

This wasn't over yet.

Chapter Forty-One

Jesse fought the urge to look down as Gallagher and the privates dragged him across the parking lot and through an endless maze of corridors at the base. Many of the soldiers they passed—most of whom he knew—stared openly as they strode by. He forced himself to hold his head high, but his cheeks burned by the time the four of them reached their destination.

All six cells in the new wing of the jailhouse on the base were empty. Jesse hadn't been in this part of the building yet, as it had only been completed a couple of weeks earlier. The smell of the sterile white paint that covered the floors, walls, and ceiling still wafted in the air. He'd asked Caleb what kind of prisoners it would be used for, but even he didn't know. The large *Restricted Access* signs in the hallway leading to the wing and on the big metal door at the entrance increased Jesse's trepidation.

Smallman gripped his arm and directed him to follow Gallagher and Whittaker through the door and down the walkway, past several cells with nothing but bars separating them.

Jesse contemplated the setup as he walked past each one. Why the lack of privacy? Did the army not think the prisoners here deserved any? Or was it that they wouldn't be here long enough to need it? Nausea welled at the thought.

Gallagher unlocked the door of the fifth cell, the second one from the end, and pulled it open. The cell was bare except for a small sink and toilet in one corner, and a hard metal bench, similar to the one in the penitentiary cell he'd just left, along the back wall. Smallman pushed Jesse inside and removed his cuffs. Whittaker waited in the walkway, and Smallman retreated to his side, both men hovering in the doorway.

Gallagher stood in front of Jesse. "Are you going to thank me?"

Jesse gaped at him. "*Thank* you? For what, arresting me? Almost having me killed?"

"For dropping the charges against you. I could have left you in there to rot, you know."

Jesse pressed his lips together to keep from telling Gallagher what he thought of him and his *magnanimous* gesture.

The lieutenant held all the cards at the moment.

Except the ace. If Jesse could survive long enough for Caleb to return, Gallagher would be dealt with once and for all. Holding his tongue made that prospect more likely. Slightly.

Gallagher gave him a few seconds before he shrugged. "All right, then. If you don't appreciate my efforts, I guess I'll stop trying to help you."

He started to turn away, but Jesse grabbed his arm. "Wait."

Whittaker and Smallman started forward.

Gallagher held up his hand to stop them.

"If you dropped the charges against me, why am I still in jail?"

"I dropped the assault charges. Unfortunately there's nothing I can do about the terrorist charges." Gallagher's tone was mocking. "Your case is already before the CHRC as we speak."

His words drove into Jesse's gut like hard fists had the night before. "How is that possible?"

"Let's just say certain friends of mine in high places share my concerns about one of our own turning against his country in such an egregious way." He yanked his arm out of Jesse's grasp. "I've told them about everything you've been up to here. It wasn't hard for me to make it sound like your actions are a dire threat to national security. As you know, since 10/10 the government takes those kinds of threats very seriously."

Impotent rage tidal-waved through him. Jesse lunged for Gallagher.

The two privates were on him in an instant, hauling him off the lieutenant and pinning his arms behind him.

Gallagher stepped closer to Jesse and lifted up the bottom of his T-shirt.

Jesse gritted his teeth.

The lieutenant let out a low whistle. "The boys were in a nasty mood last night, I see." He dropped the shirt. "And yet, here you are, just begging for another beating. Is that seriously what you want? Because if it is, I would be more than happy to oblige you." When Jesse didn't answer, Gallagher's eyebrows rose. "Well?" His hand closed into a fist.

Jesse exhaled. "No."

"I didn't think so." The lieutenant's fingers uncurled. He reached out and gripped Jesse's shirt at the neck, pulling him closer. When he spoke, his breath was hot on Jesse's face. "I know you're waiting for the major to swoop in here and rescue you, but I have taken great pains to ensure that he has no idea what is going on. When he gets home in a couple of days, it will be far too late for him to do anything about it. For once, you are going to have to stand on your own two feet, Christensen."

Gallagher was a couple of inches shorter than Jesse, barely six feet, but somehow the lieutenant seemed taller at the moment. Jesse had read studies about the phenomenon, that a prisoner often perceived a hostile, aggressive captor as bigger than he actually was. He deliberately lowered his head to meet Gallagher's eyes, determined to cut the man down to size.

The lieutenant tightened his hold on the T-shirt. "If I were you, I'd stop wasting what little time I have left wishing and waiting for something that isn't going to happen, and use it to reflect on how your past choices and actions have brought you to this point. As much as you'd like to hold me responsible for all of this, you have no one to blame but yourself. And that's a burden you'll have to take to your grave." He let go of the shirt abruptly and jerked his head toward the opening of the cell. "Let's go."

The privates released him and followed the lieutenant to the door. None of them looked back as they went out into the walkway, and the door clanged into place behind them.

I will never get used to that sound. Jesse ran his hand over his head. "Gallagher."

The lieutenant turned to face him. "What?"

"Why are you doing this? What did I ever do to you?"

The hard glint he'd seen in Gallagher's eyes earlier sparked in them again. "You committed the cardinal sin, Christensen. You got in my way."

Jesse didn't move until the three men reached the end of the walkway and the door slammed shut behind them. Then he slumped against the bars of the cell.

Was it true? Did Caleb really have no idea what was going on? If so, and if Jesse's case was being pushed through that quickly, the lieutenant could be right. By the time Caleb got back on Sunday and found out what was happening to Jesse, it might be too late to do anything to help him.

Jesse's throat burned. When was the last time he'd had anything to eat or drink? He shoved himself away from the bars and crossed the cell to the sink, but nothing happened when he turned the handles. On the way back to the front of the cell, something clunked beneath his running shoe, and he looked down.

A drain. In the middle of the floor. *Odd.*

He checked the cells on either side of his.

Both of them had a drain too. If it weren't for the small sink and toilet in the corner, the drain could have been a primitive sanitation system. Otherwise, he had no idea why it would be there.

A few feet outside his cell a dark-green hose lay coiled beneath a dripping tap. The sight of the drops of water sliding down the wall and pooling on the floor only intensified the dryness in his throat. His eyes narrowed. Why was there a hose lying in the hallway of the jailhouse? He sank down on the floor and reached through the bars as far as he could. The hose still lay a good foot beyond his reach. He scanned his cell, but there was nothing in it he could use to close that gap. He smacked the bars with both palms before resting his head against them.

A thin ray of sunshine filtered through the barred window up near the ceiling. Jesse watched it creep slowly across the floor, trying to estimate how long he'd been sitting there.

Water continued to slide down the wall and fall into the puddle on the floor. *Drip. Drip. Drip.*

No wonder Chinese water torture was so effective. His sanity was slipping from his grasp at the same rate, one small drip at a time. After a couple of hours, the door at the end of the hallway crashed open and he gripped the bars and pulled himself to his feet.

Whittaker marched down the hallway. Smallman trailed along behind him, carrying a tray with both hands. Tendrils of steam rose from a plate.

Jesse's gaze lasered in on a bottle of water on the tray.

The two men stopped outside his cell. Neither of them looked as cocky as they did when their dark lord stood in front of them like a shield.

Jesse smiled grimly.

Whittaker clanged the same metal canister the guard at the penitentiary had held in his hand against the metal bars. "What's so funny?"

"Just thinking about the two of you and how Gallagher has you both running around doing all his dirty work for him, like his own personal servants. He'll turn on you too, you know. Eventually."

"Shut up, Christensen." Smallman held the tray in a white-knuckled grip.

Clever. The flicker of uncertainty on Smallman's face encouraged Jesse. "He uses people to get what he wants. And he's not about to share it once he has it. He'll leave you floundering in the muck behind him like he does everyone else, and you'll have nothing."

Whittaker held the canister up and aimed it at Jesse's face. "He told you to shut up. We're just here to deliver your dinner. Do you want it or not?"

Jesse glanced down at the tray. Meatloaf, maybe. Or tuna casserole. It was usually difficult to tell. Still, it looked hot and it might replenish some of the strength rapidly draining from his body. "Yeah, I want it."

Whittaker lifted the slot in the door.

"He's not going to turn on us." Smallman's words were tentative, more of a question than a statement.

Jesse seized the opening. "Yes, he will. Or, more likely, he'll be brought down, and you'll be dragged down with him. He's breaking every possible rule to get what he wants, and the army isn't going to put up with that much longer. If you turn him in before he's caught, you'll be the hero. Instead of a court-martial, you'll be looking at a promotion. You don't want to be a private forever, do you?"

"That's it." Whittaker slammed the slot shut, then held up the can and pushed the button.

Jesse whirled away, but not before a small squirt of pepper spray caught him. Stinging pain shot through his left eye, and his vision blurred immediately. He clamped a hand over his eye.

"Let's go, Smallman. If he's not gonna listen, he's not gonna eat."

Still holding his eye, Jesse spun back and shot his other hand through the bars to snatch the bottle of water before Smallman could pull the tray away.

"Hey." Whittaker reached for the security pad by the door.

Smallman let go of the tray with one hand and grabbed his arm. "Don't. The lieutenant said not to open the door for any reason."

Whittaker glared at Jesse. "Fine. Choke on it, Christensen. It's better than you deserve."

The two of them stormed down the hallway.

Jesse twisted the cap off the bottle and tipped back his head to down half the water. He forced himself to stop drinking and replace the cap. He had no idea how long he'd be sitting in this cell or when he might see food or water again. Better to conserve, even if his body cried out for more fluids.

Jesse sank onto the metal bench. Pulling up his left knee, he rested his elbow on it and covered his eye again. It still burned, as if there was sand under the lid digging into the cornea. It would take more water than he had to make any difference, so he wouldn't waste any by trying to relieve the discomfort that way. Thankfully, Whittaker hadn't sent too big a spray in Jesse's direction and he'd been able to turn, so most of it missed his eye, but what had gotten in was bad enough.

Would the commission find him guilty?

Probably, given that Gallagher's version of events was all they had to go by.

What would his sentence be? Thirty lashes?

He could handle that. Meryn had withstood fifteen without begging for mercy, and she didn't have his training. Of course, she'd had divine help, but he'd have that too.

What if it was more than thirty? Forty was the most they could administer at one time, but he'd heard of people being sentenced to a hundred or more and the sessions broken up over days or weeks.

The thought that had been hovering around his periphery since they'd left the cabin drifted into stark focus now. They *could* give him the death penalty. He had a hard time wrapping his mind around the possibility, but it did happen.

Jesse sighed. No use speculating until he knew for sure. There was nothing he could do here, locked up, except wait and pray.

And watch the dying sunlight as it made its way slowly across the cell floor.

Chapter Forty-Two

The sun had sunk below the roof of the barn as Meryn paced back and forth on the porch. The waiting was driving her mad. Especially since she didn't really know what she was waiting for. Would Jesse send her a message? Show up at her door? If something happened to him, would anyone let her know? Caleb would, but she'd called the base a dozen times asking for him, and all they would tell her was that he was unavailable to take her call.

The porch light flicked on. Shane pushed open the screen door and poked his head outside. "Meryn? Brendan and I are going to put on a movie. Want to join us?"

Meryn stopped pacing. "I don't know if I can concentrate on a movie." She clenched her fists against the sides of her head. "It's driving me crazy, not knowing what's going on."

Shane sighed and came outside, letting the screen door slam shut behind him. "I know it is. We're all concerned. But it's only been twenty-four hours. No doubt you'll hear from Jesse soon, and he'll tell you that everything's fine."

You didn't see the look in Gallagher's eyes when Jesse was holding him. She repressed a shudder. "I hope you're right."

The sound of tires turning into their gravel driveway sent her pulse rocketing. *Jesse.* She bent over the railing to peer down the lane, trying to make out the vehicle in the fading daylight. Her shoulders slumped.

It wasn't him. No one she knew drove a fancy Lexus hybrid like that.

Meryn glanced back at Shane.

He shrugged and shook his head. No one he knew, either.

The car stopped at the end of the walkway. A man in a navy suit with dark hair and a goatee climbed out of the vehicle.

Had something happened to Jesse?

Meryn's hand fluttered to her throat as the man strode up the walkway. When he started up the stairs, she moved back from the railing.

Shane came up beside her, fingers reassuring on her back.

The man reached the porch. "Meryn O'Reilly?"

"Yes."

"My name is Michael Stevens. Could we talk for a moment?"

Fear tingled through her. She searched the man's eyes. They were serious, but that seemed to be in keeping with the suit and the car. Clearly his job, whatever it was, was an important one.

Shane stepped forward. "I'm Shane O'Reilly, Meryn's brother. Why don't we sit down?" He gestured toward the Muskoka chairs on the front porch.

Stevens held out his hand for Meryn to go first.

She supported herself on the railing as she walked over to one of the chairs and sat down.

He took the one opposite her and clasped his hands between his knees.

The screen door opened again, and Brendan came outside. "Is everything okay?"

Meryn waved him over. "Come join us. Mr. Stevens, this is my other brother, Brendan."

He half-rose from his chair to shake Brendan's hand.

Shane settled onto the porch swing.

Brendan leaned back against the railing and crossed his arms over his chest. His eyes dropped to the man's bare wrists, and a shadow flitted across his face.

Meryn studied their visitor. *Why does that name sound familiar? I'm sure we've never met.* "May I ask what this is about, Mr. Stevens?"

"Michael, please. Major Caleb Donevan asked me to come."

She bent forward slightly, trying to retrieve a breath. This was about Jesse, then.

"You know who that is?"

"Of course. He's the commanding officer at the base."

"Yes. Listen, I know you have no reason to trust me, but—"

A puzzle piece dropped into place in her mind, and her eyes widened. "Yes, I do."

All three men looked at her.

"You're the commissioner, aren't you? The one who helped Jesse convince them to overturn the order to take Kate and Ethan's children away. He told me about you."

"Yes, that's right."

"Then you're a believer."

"Yes, although, as you have already noted"—he held up both wrists—"that is not public knowledge. Yet. I'm hoping to be able to keep working with the Canadian Human Rights Commission as long as possible, to use the position to do a bit of good before I'm found out, like Jesse had been doing with the army."

Had been. Past tense. What did that mean? "Is the message from the major about Jesse? Has something happened?" She knotted her fingers together in her lap.

"I'm afraid so. He's been charged with a crime under the terrorist act. His case is before a human rights commission right now." He glanced down at his watch. "The hearing should be over any time. I found out about it when I was reviewing the docket this morning and came across his name. I tried to get on the commission hearing the case, but unfortunately I wasn't able to, not without arousing suspicion that would put both of us in jeopardy. Instead, I spent the next several hours pulling every possible string I could until I found out the major was in Germany, providing security for the G7 Summit. Which, incidentally, is a highly irregular assignment for the commanding officer of a base. I'll be recommending an investigation into how that came about as soon as I get back to Ottawa. But I was able to reach Major Donevan on a secure CHRC line and explain what was going on."

Meryn's palms were damp, and she wiped them on the legs of her jeans. No wonder she hadn't been able to contact the major. And no wonder Gallagher had been able to push this as far as he had. Heat poured through her. No one had been there to stop him. "Is there anything he can do about this?"

"Not from Germany. When I spoke to him a couple of hours ago, he was trying desperately to catch a flight home. The way this case is being pushed through, I don't know if there is anything he will be able to do, even if he is able to get back here, but he's certainly going to try."

Shane reached over and covered her hand with his. "What crime has Jesse been accused of?"

"Treason."

Her heart stopped beating. Treason. They couldn't find him guilty of that. What had he done that could possibly be considered a betrayal of his country? She fixed her gaze on Michael Stevens' face. "You know the law. You don't seriously think they have enough to convict him of treason, do you?"

Bumps rose on her arms as she waited through the silence that greeted her question. *This isn't happening.* Was it only last night they had met at the cabin? *I can still feel his arms around me, his mouth on mine.* Meryn touched her fingers to her lips.

Stevens shifted in his chair. "It's always difficult to know how these things will go, but I'm praying they will rule in his favour. I came to Kingston hoping to speak with him, and let him know the major's trying to get back."

She leaned forward. "Did they let you see him? Would they allow me to?"

"No, I'm sorry. He's being held in a restricted area. I showed them every credential I had, and they still refused to let me in. They said only immediate family could see him. Do you know if he has any family around?"

Meryn shook her head. "No, he doesn't."

The commissioner nodded. "He won't be allowed visitors, then, not until ..."

"Until what?"

"Until he's either acquitted and released or convicted and his sentence is carried out."

Meryn pressed a hand to her abdomen, trying to ease a sudden, searing pain.

Stevens cleared his throat. "The major knew you'd be worried, so he asked me to let you know what's going on while I was in town. I promised him I would, so as soon as I hear—"

An i-com buzzed.

Stevens reached into his jacket pocket and pulled out the silver device. His face paled as he scanned the screen.

Shane's fingers tightened around hers.

The commissioner looked up.

Meryn's eyes met his and her body went cold. "They're going to kill him, aren't they?" The words came out in a raspy whisper.

Brendan uncrossed his arms and came over to crouch down at her side. He wrapped his arm around her shoulders.

Michael Stevens nodded. "They've given him the death penalty, yes."

Chapter Forty-Three

The clicking wouldn't stop. Jesse groaned. The fitful sleep he'd finally fallen into had been a reprieve from everything that was happening to him. *Apparently the reprieve is over.* He lifted his head.

Darkness had fallen over the jailhouse. Pot lights recessed into the ceiling every six feet draped a dull fluorescent glow over the head and shoulders of a man in the walkway.

Jesse sat up on the metal bench, blinking to clear the last of the blurriness from his left eye.

Click. Click.

He squinted into the dimness of the cell.

Gallagher stood on the other side of the bars. He held a pistol in his hand and aimed at a point down the hallway. Every few seconds he pulled the trigger, advancing the empty chamber.

"New toy?" Jesse rubbed a hand over his face.

"New assignment, actually."

He sighed. *Really not in the mood for his games right now.* "And what assignment would that—?" He zeroed in on the gun in Gallagher's hand.

The room banked sharply and Jesse planted both palms on the bench in an attempt to recover his equilibrium.

I'm the assignment.

Gallagher lowered the weapon, reached into his jacket pocket, and pulled out his i-com. He touched the screen and light flashed from the unit. "Do you want to hear it from me, or would you rather read the official pronouncement?"

"Official would be a nice change." Jesse's voice sounded thick in his ears.

Gallagher propped the device up on the security pad by the door.

The projector app flashed a large, red maple leaf up near the ceiling. Underneath the symbol, words danced across the whitewashed walls.

Jesse squeezed his eyes shut and opened them until the letters gradually settled into place. The *Order to Carry out Sentence* form from the Department of Justice was familiar. His name at the top sent a fresh surge of dizziness washing over him. The only other words on the wall that would register in the midst of the thick fog muddling his thoughts were *Execution Warrant* and the signature of Serena Leblanc, the current Justice Minister, scrawled across the bottom.

I will never see Meryn again.

Numbness set in. His brain activity slowed to a crawl. A hypothermia-like deadness started in his fingers and toes and crept up his arms and legs. *Better than feeling.* "Do I get to know what I've been convicted of?"

Gallagher leaned a shoulder against the bars. "Officially? Treason."

Jesse let out a cold laugh. "I fought for this country. I would have gladly died for her."

"You're about to get your chance."

His head weighed a hundred pounds. He rested it against the wall behind him. "When?"

"Tomorrow night. Twenty-two hundred hours."

One day to live. The glacier creeping through him slid into his chest. As if he were already leaving his body. "Not taking any chances, are you?"

Gallagher's eyes narrowed. "On what?"

"On the major coming back. Or somebody figuring out that you've gone insane and turning you in."

A sneer twisted across his face. "If I'm rushing things, it's because you cannot be wiped off the face of the planet soon enough for me. Unfortunately, by law, we have to wait a minimum of twenty-four hours between the time the signed order arrives at the base and when the sentence is carried out."

"And we both know what a stickler you are for the law."

Gallagher laughed. "I can be, when it suits me. And in this case it suits me to give you the full twenty-four hours to sit here and think about your wasted life, knowing there's a bullet waiting for you at the end of it."

Jesse's head snapped up. "A bullet?"

"Yes, didn't you know? That's how they carry out executions in this country now. Old school. Fast, cheap, and remarkably effective."

The fire that ignited in his gut melted some of the ice that had been drawing him into a blissful oblivion. *Not good.* "When do I go to Ottawa?"

Gallagher held the pistol up to the light and racked the slide. "You don't."

"What do you mean *I don't*?"

"Until now, all executions have been carried out in Ottawa, that's true. But they're finally starting to allow them to be done by the commanding officers on the bases. And with Donevan out of the country and you out of commission, so to speak, I am currently the commanding officer."

Heaven help us. How had he and Caleb failed to grasp just how deep Gallagher's connections to those higher up the chain of command went? He knew far more about what was going on in the country, even on their own base, than either of them did. And if he was that strongly connected, he could do anything he wanted to and it was unlikely anyone would intervene.

Jesse's stomach lurched.

They'd fallen into the hands of a madman.

Gallagher waved the gun around at all of the cells. "What did you think they were building this new wing for? It's our very own death row, Christensen. And you get to be the first-ever resident. This is a historic moment. Or will be, once we *christen* the place tomorrow night." He chuckled at his own wit as he pulled a cartridge out of his pocket and held it up. "I think this is the one I'll use. I've carried it around for years, kind of a lucky charm. But the luckiest moment of my life will be the one where I put a bullet in your head, so it seems only appropriate to finally break it out."

Jesse followed the movement of Gallagher's hand, hypnotized by the gleaming gold cartridge. Could that really be the instrument of his death? *Maybe I'm still asleep and all of this is just a terrible dream.* Sitting on the hard bench, though, a death sentence literally hanging over his head—he glanced over at the form still splashed across the wall—the grief writhing through him at everything he was about to lose was all too real.

"Was it worth it?"

Gallagher's voice called him back from far away.

"Was what worth it?"

"The decision you made to believe. To cast your lot in with the Christians."

For the first time since Gallagher had woken him up, he had something solid to grasp hold of. "Yes."

The lieutenant cocked his head. "You don't regret it? You wouldn't renounce it all, even to save your life?"

"No. Never."

"But you chose death."

"For my body, maybe, which is nothing. But I chose eternal life for my soul, and that's all that matters."

Gallagher's eyebrows drew together, as if Jesse were speaking a foreign language. "Still, I win."

A small smile crossed Jesse's lips. "For now. But not in the end."

"Whose end?"

"Everyone's. The end of all things. What's happening here isn't justice, and even you have to know that. But in the end there will be real, true justice. And if you don't fall on your knees and repent of every evil thing you have ever done before that day arrives, everything you fought so hard for, that you thought was so desperately important, will crumble like dust in your hands, and you will have nothing."

"You're talking in riddles. I have no idea what you're saying."

"Then I'll pray that God will help you understand, because that's the only way you can."

Gallagher snorted. "Don't waste your prayers on me. I'm not the one in need of prayer here."

"Aren't you?" *Are you absolutely sure which of us is the prisoner here and which of us is free?* The question Meryn had asked him that day in his quarters when he was wrestling against God with everything he had, drifted through his mind. He hadn't understood what she was saying that day any more than Gallagher understood him now.

And you were every bit as in need of my grace and mercy then as he is at this moment.

The truth of those words travelled through him as if on a current of electricity. If they penetrated his heart, he might be able to let go of the hatred he felt for the man standing in front of him, the one holding the bullet that could very well end Jesse's life. He might even be able to forgive him. *But only with your help. I can't do it on my own.*

Gallagher grabbed his device off the security pad and powered it down before shoving it back in his pocket. "Enjoy your last night, Christensen. I know I will." He tossed the cartridge toward the ceiling. It spun end over end before he snatched it out of the air and set it down on the small wooden shelf above the dripping tap. "A little something for you to remember me by until we meet again tomorrow night." He turned to face Jesse, slowly and deliberately lifting the gun until it was pointed at his face. "Sweet dreams."

Jesse locked onto the dark, stone-cold eyes staring straight at him.

Click.

Chapter Forty-Four

Legs trembling, Meryn made her way down the walkway, Michael Stevens behind her. When they reached his vehicle, she stopped and held out her hand.

He enclosed it between both of his. "I'm truly sorry, Meryn. I deeply admired ..." He drew in a breath. "Admire Jesse. I had hoped we would become friends."

"He would have liked that too. He appreciated your help in Ottawa so much."

"I'll be praying for you both." He let her go and opened the door to the Lexus.

Meryn watched him as he circled around the farmyard and drove down the driveway. When he turned onto the road, she headed for her car. She only managed to pull the door open a couple of inches before someone reached past her and slammed it shut. She whirled around.

"Come on, Meryn. You can't go over there. The commissioner said you can't see him."

"Shane, I need to go." Her voice broke. "I have to try."

"If you show up there, the first soldier who sees you will arrest you for being out after curfew."

"At least I'd be on the base."

"But you still wouldn't see him. He's in a restricted area. And you'd be facing another flogging. That wouldn't help anyone, especially if Jesse heard about it, and I'm guessing this lieutenant"—his mouth contorted as though the word tasted bitter on his tongue—"would be only too happy to tell him."

"At least he'd know I tried to see him."

Shane's face softened. "You don't have to prove anything to him. Jesse knows you love him."

"Does he?" Tears welled in her eyes, but she blinked them back and lifted one shoulder. "I never told him."

"I did."

She blinked. "You did?"

"Yes. At the party Saturday night. I told him that I'd never seen you look at another man the way you look at him and I was sure you loved him."

"I do."

"I know." He rubbed his hands up and down her arms. "I'm so sorry about all of this."

"I can't believe it's happening."

"Let's go inside."

Brendan waited for them at the bottom of the porch stairs. When they got to him, he pulled Meryn to him.

The ground felt unsteady beneath her feet, as if tectonic plates shifted below the surface. Her brother was strong and solid, and she gripped his shirt with both hands.

"You're shaking." He tightened his hold.

"I'm freezing."

"What can I do?"

"Nothing. There's nothing any of us can do." She let go of him. "I'm going to take a bath." It wouldn't help to melt the ice forming inside her. But the last time she'd been frightened and hurting, Jesse had drawn a bath for her. Maybe remembering all the good moments they'd shared together would help a little. *As long as I don't think about how there will never be a moment like that again.* Meryn swayed on her feet.

Brendan grasped her arm. "Here. I'll walk you up."

Nodding woodenly, she let him lead her into the house and up the stairs to her room.

"Will you be okay?" He stood on the round, multicoloured area rug in the centre of her room. Shane hovered in the doorway.

"Yes."

Neither of them looked too certain about leaving her, but Meryn turned away and slipped into the washroom off her room. She couldn't convince herself she'd be fine. She certainly didn't have the energy to try and convince them.

Meryn sat in the tub until the last of the bubbles evaporated and the water turned cold. The tips of her fingers broke the surface. She could just slide under the water. Stay there where it was cool and quiet. Drift off to a place where nothing would hurt anymore. Where no one deliberately ripped the life from someone good and young and strong, someone who had fought for justice and peace and sacrificed his own freedom and safety for the sake of others. Who had given everything up for his God. *Do you see what is going on here? He's suffering. In your name. Do you care?* She pressed her palms against her forehead, the pain suffocating. *I know you see. I know you care. Help Jesse to know you're with him. Give him courage.* The prayer took everything from her, and she slumped back against the cold enamel tub.

"Meryn?" Brendan rapped on the door.

She didn't have the strength to answer him.

"Are you okay?" The near panic in his voice roused her.

Meryn pushed herself upright. "I'll be out in a minute." She towelled off quickly and pulled on Jesse's royal-blue T-shirt and flannel pyjama bottoms. They'd always comforted her, but tonight the sight of them sent daggers shooting through her chest. She pulled open the washroom door.

Brendan sat in the rocking chair in the corner of her room.

"I'm just going to sleep. You don't have to stay."

"Who's going to move me, you?"

Since he was twice her size, it wasn't likely. "Fine. Suit yourself." His presence in the room did help, a little anyway. She stopped when she got to him and squeezed his shoulder. "Thanks, Brendan."

He covered her hand with his. "I'm here if there's anything you need."

"I know." She tossed him the blanket from the end of her bed before she crawled under the covers, shivering from the cold deep inside her and crawling across her skin.

Shane pushed open the door. "Meryn?"

"Yeah?"

"Do you want me to call Mom and Dad?"

She thought about it. "I guess we should let them know what's going on. But tell them not to come, that there's nothing they can do here. Just ask them to pray."

"Okay. I'm right across the hall if you want me." He kept the door open a few inches when he left.

Sleep wouldn't come. What was Jesse doing? Could he get any rest? How could anyone sleep knowing it was the last ... She pressed her knuckles to her mouth to stifle a sob.

Wind moaned through the branches outside her slightly open window, sending dark, spindly shadows dancing across the ceiling, like fingers reaching up from the grave.

Meryn flung an arm over her eyes. *Father, help us both.*

Chapter Forty-Five

In the darkness of the jailhouse, Jesse rested his head on his folded arms and stared at the ceiling.

Water dripped in the walkway, the only sound to disturb the thick silence in the building.

During his tours, he'd often stretched out on his cot, contemplating the day to come and wondering if it might be his last. The awareness of his own mortality, of the fragility of life, was woven throughout everyday existence in a part of the world where life was considered of less value than ideology, and martyrdom was something to be longed for.

Jesse winced. His faith was more important to him than his life too, but martyrdom—if that's what his impending death could be considered—didn't feel like something to be sought after. Life was too precious, too much of a gift.

He shifted, trying in vain to get comfortable on the narrow metal bench.

What is Meryn doing right now? Did she know what was happening to him? If Caleb didn't know yet, she likely didn't, although she had to be concerned that she hadn't heard from him. Was it possible he could be gone from the earth for a day or more before she even knew? Would she feel it, the sudden departure of his spirit from this realm? Would the loss echo deep inside of her even before she understood why?

I didn't tell her I loved her often enough. The thought sent a pang through him. Sure, she had never said the words to him in return, but she did love him. The way she had slowly let down her guard and allowed him in, the look in her breath-taking, ocean-blue eyes when they met his, the soft touch of her fingers on his cheek, the intensity of her last kiss. All those things told him more than her words ever could.

He winced as he leaned over and grabbed the bottle of water he'd nursed all day. Tipping it back, he drained the last few drops, then tossed it across the cell.

It clattered off the bars.

He followed its movement as it hit the floor and spun around. The most entertainment he'd had all day. His cynical smile faded as his gaze lifted.

The bullet sat on the wooden shelf, mocking him with its presence. How could something so small, beautiful even, contain within its tiny gold cylinder the power to destroy so many lives?

Not that the idea was a revelation. He knew as well as anyone the destructive power of a bullet. One of them had stolen his brother, Rory, from him. And Jesse had aimed his weapon at an enemy soldier and pulled the trigger more times than he wanted to remember. Stealing another man's brother, a father's daughter, a wife's husband, a child's mother. Every one still haunted him, especially ...

Jesse swung his legs over the side of the bench and sat up. *Not what I want to spend my last few hours thinking about.* He slumped against the wall behind him. *God, I said I'd pray for Gallagher and I'm trying to, but I can't seem to come up with any petitions regarding him that don't contain the words* smite *or* lightning bolt, *which I doubt is what Jesus had in mind when he told us to pray for our enemies.* The words stuck in his throat when he tried to say them, not because he didn't believe God's mercy could extend even to someone like Gallagher, but because he knew it could. The truth was, he didn't want to pray that Gallagher would turn to God and all would be forgiven. He wanted to pray that the man would burn in hell for all eternity. *So you'll have to give me the words. And you'll have to change my heart if you want me to say them.*

He thrust his hands into the pockets of his jeans. His fingers brushed against something cold and hard, and he pulled it out.

The silver heart Meryn had given him.

Jesse lifted it to his lips. Meryn. She was all he wanted to think about. Her, he could pray for. Clutching the metal heart tightly, he closed his eyes. *Help her. Give her the strength to face the days ahead. And since I can't tell her myself, help her to know, deep in her heart, how much I love her. How much joy she brought me. And that her face was the last image in my mind and her name the last thought in my head when my time on earth came to an end.*

CHAPTER FORTY-SIX

It helped Meryn to be surrounded by family. Kate and Ethan came over late Saturday morning. Meryn played outside with Matthew and Gracie all afternoon, throwing the ball and picking wildflowers and chasing the kids around the pond. Running and running but never quite able to leave behind the thought that screamed through her mind, haunting her every second.

Jesse will die tonight.

At lunchtime, she made sandwiches and salad for everyone and insisted on doing the cleaning up herself. Late afternoon, she headed back into the kitchen and put together a dinner of spaghetti and meatballs. She couldn't stop moving. Couldn't stop doing. If she did, she would collapse on the floor in the foetal position, with her hands over her ears, trying to block out the words.

Meryn set the bowl of pasta on the table and went back over to the kitchen counter.

"What can I do to help?"

Kate's concerned voice startled her. She jumped and almost dropped the four glasses she'd grabbed from the cupboard.

Brendan took them from her hands and carried them to the table. One or the other of her brothers had been within arm's reach all day. They hadn't said much. Still, their constant, silent presence helped a bit. If anything could.

Meryn shoved her hair behind both ears with shaking fingers. "I don't know, Kate. Maybe you could slice the bread?" She turned back to the counter and pulled open the silverware drawer.

"I will do that, but that wasn't what I was asking."

She exhaled loudly. "I know. But there's nothing. Really. There's nothing anyone can do." She turned to lean back against the counter. Wrapping both arms around her waist, she pressed her lips together to hold back the sob that rose in her throat. *Meryn O'Reilly, you will not cry.* If she started, she might not be able to stop.

Kate slid her arms around Meryn. "I'm so sorry, Mer."

Meryn rested her head on Kate's shoulder for a few seconds before straightening up. "Supper's almost ready. If you want to bring the kids in and wash their hands, we can eat."

Kate gazed at her, as if she wanted to say more, then she nodded her head. "All right."

A look passed between her and Brendan as she left the room.

Meryn ignored it and went to retrieve the knives and forks. They were worried about her. And frustrated by their inability to help. She didn't blame them. If any one of them were in the same position she was, she wouldn't have a clue what to say or do, either.

"Meryn." Brendan's voice was edged with concern.

She shook her head. "Can you tell Shane and Ethan that supper's ready?" Meryn felt her brother's gaze on her, but she didn't look over. The compassion she knew she'd see in his eyes would undo her.

With a sigh, he left the room.

Meryn closed her eyes and reached out a hand to steady herself on the counter. *What is Jesse going through at this moment?* What thoughts went through someone's head in the hours and minutes before his life would end? Was he thinking about her? Did he know how desperately she wanted to see him but wasn't allowed to?

She opened her eyes. She had avoided looking at the clock all day, but her gaze fell on it before she could stop herself. Six o'clock. Four more hours until ...

"Aunt Meryn!" Gracie ran into the room, cheeks pink from the sun.

Meryn dropped the silverware onto the table with a clatter and scooped up the little girl. Chubby arms circled Meryn's neck, and she rested her cheek on the top of the soft curls. She carried Gracie to the table and sat down. Around her, Kate and Shane set more food on the table and spread the cutlery around, but their actions barely registered in her mind. Still holding tightly to Gracie, she helped the toddler with her supper. Meryn moved the food around her own plate, trying to look as if she were eating something so her brothers wouldn't give her a hard time.

No one talked to her. If they spoke at all, their voices were hushed and muted, as though they were at a funeral. When Brendan started to clear the table, she couldn't take it anymore. "Leave them, Bren. I'll do it."

He hesitated.

She met his eyes for the first time that day. "Please. I need to."

He set the pile of plates back down and sat. "Okay."

Meryn lifted Gracie off her lap. An intense pressure was building inside her, and the last thing she wanted was to explode in front of the kids. "Kate, Ethan, I appreciate you being here, I really do. I don't know if I could have made it through this day if you hadn't been. But you should go now, get the kids to bed." She braced herself on the table as she got up.

Kate stood too, and reached for Meryn's hands. "Are you sure? We could spend the night, be here if you need us."

"No, don't. You'll sleep better at home. I'll message you if I need you."

Kate's shoulders slumped. "All right." She kissed Meryn's cheek. "We're praying."

"I know." Meryn picked up Gracie in one arm and reached for Matthew's hand. She followed Kate and Ethan to the door and squeezed Gracie before handing her over to Kate.

Kate's hazel eyes brimmed with tears. She shifted her daughter onto one hip and grasped Meryn's elbow. "You and Brendan and Shane come for lunch tomorrow after church, okay?"

"Okay." She crouched down in front of Matthew. "I love you, buddy. You know that, right?"

He threw his arms around her. "I love you too."

Meryn held him for a moment, then straightened up and ruffled his light-brown hair.

Ethan didn't speak, just pulled her into a hug. When he let her go, he kissed her forehead, then guided Matthew out onto the porch.

Meryn shut the door behind them. When she turned around, Brendan and Shane still sat at the table, watching her.

Brendan drove both hands through his dark hair. "This is ridiculous, knowing what's going to happen and not being able to do anything about it."

"Brendan." Shane's voice held a warning

"No, Shane, he's right." Meryn snatched the pile of plates off the table and stalked to the counter. She set the plates down hard. "It's crazy to just sit here." She picked up the pile and banged the plates down again. "Doing nothing but waiting to hear that Jesse is ..." Helpless rage poured through her, and she slammed the pile of ceramic plates against the counter again and again until they smashed into pieces.

"Meryn." Shane's hands covered hers, and he pulled her away from the dishes. "You cut yourself."

"I'm fine." She tried to tug her fingers from his grasp.

He held on and sought out her eyes, his dark-Irish ones filled with sorrow. "You're not fine. None of us are. But the cut we can do something about."

"Here." Brendan reached into the cupboard above the fridge and pulled out the first-aid kit. "Do you want to sit down?"

"No," she said curtly. A memory crashed through her mind, of Jesse doctoring her wounds after she'd been cut by flying glass when a brick was tossed through her store window. That was the first time she'd realized her feelings for him had changed from irritation and hostility to something much more confusing. Much more difficult to handle.

"All right." Still holding on to her, Shane reached for the roll of paper towels and ripped off a couple. He wrapped them around the cut and squeezed gently.

Stinging pain thrummed along her palm. Meryn was glad. It was easier to deal with that than the ache deep inside of her. "This is all my fault."

Shane's eyes narrowed. "What are you talking about?"

"I'm the one who asked him to stay in the army. He was going to leave so we could be together. I convinced him to stay. If I hadn't, he wouldn't be facing a death penalty right now."

"And Kate and Ethan wouldn't have their children." Shane slid a finger under her chin and lifted her face until she met his gaze. "Jesse's been able to help a lot of people by staying in the army. He wouldn't regret the decision to stay—the decision that he made himself, by the way—for a moment, even with everything that's happening now. He's too good a man to be that selfish."

Meryn blew out a breath. "I guess he wouldn't."

Brendan tore the paper and the backing off a large square Band-Aid. When he came up beside her, Shane removed the paper towel, and Brendan covered her palm with the bandage. "Come here." He pulled her close and pressed her head to his chest.

His tenderness severed the tenuous grasp she had on her emotions. Meryn buried her face in his shirt and sobbed. Grief over all she and Jesse were about to lose and all that would never be, and rage over the senseless, mind-numbing theft of a life that held such promise, such love, overwhelmed her, and she wept until she had no tears left. Brendan's arms around her, and Shane's warm, strong hand rubbing her back, gradually brought her back from the brink. She wiped the tears from her cheeks with both hands. "I'm sorry."

"Don't be." Shane brushed the hair from her face. "What do you need?"

Besides seeing Jesse's face one more time? Nothing. "I'd like to sit in the living room for a while. Would you put on a fire?"

Relief at having something concrete to do flickered across his face. "Sure. I can do that. Brendan, why don't you put the kettle on and make tea? If she's not going to eat"—he sent her a pointed look—"she should at least drink something. I'll start the fire, then come back in here and help you clean up."

Meryn winced at the mess on the counter. "Sorry about that."

He rested his hand on her back and guided her toward the door. "Don't worry about it. You only did what all of us felt like doing, believe me." He waited until she had curled up on one of the brown, leather armchairs in front of the woodstove, then draped a knitted blanket over her and went to get the fire started.

When flames leaped behind the glass of the woodstove, Shane left her to go back to the kitchen.

Meryn rested her head against the back of the chair, listening to the crackling of flames and trying not to think.

Dishes clinked and cupboard doors opened and closed. After a few minutes, Shane came back out and turned on a movie.

Brendan followed him into the living room and handed Meryn a steaming cup of tea, then settled onto the couch a few feet away.

She felt his eyes on her, but Meryn gazed at the screen, at characters speaking words she couldn't comprehend, carrying out movements she couldn't follow.

Finally the credits rolled.

The clock above the mantel chimed. Nine o'clock.

"Here." Shane had made a fresh pot of tea and he refilled her mug and set the pot on the table beside her.

Meryn took the mug and wrapped both hands around it, pulling it close so she could feel the warmth of it against her.

What would she do without her family? She would have lost her mind sometime throughout this long day. Still, she felt a deep, driving need now for everyone to go. *Jesse's alone.* It didn't seem right to be surrounded by people who loved her, when all that surrounded him were thick metal bars. At least they could spend his last hour on earth in shared solitude, even if he didn't know it.

"Is there anything else you need?" Brendan slid to the front of the couch.

"Actually, there is." They wouldn't like it, but she had to convince them to respect her wishes. "I need to be alone for a while. Neither of you slept much last night, I know, so go get some rest, okay?"

Shane shook his head. "I don't think that's the best—"

She held up a hand. "I won't do anything rash, I promise. I just need some time to think, and to pray. It's the only way I can get through the next few hours."

Brendan chewed on his lower lip. "You'll call us if you need us?"

"Yes."

"Where's your i-com?"

"In the kitchen."

Shane turned and left the room.

Brendan crouched down beside her and gripped her arm. "Are you sure, Meryn?" He inclined his head toward the couch. "I could sleep there. I wouldn't bother you."

"I'm sure. But thanks."

He squeezed her arm and pushed to his feet. "If that's what you want."

"It is."

Shane came back into the room. He set the device on the small wooden table beside her and bent down to cup her face in his hands. "You will message me if you want anything. I don't care if it's four in the morning. Understood?"

"Understood."

"All right." He didn't look too happy, but he let her go and straightened up.

Brendan rested his hand on her head. "You try to get some rest too."

"I will."

But she wouldn't. Even if Jesse was gone in an hour, she would keep her vigil all night long, praying for him, for all of them, and for the country she loved but didn't even know anymore.

Chapter Forty-Seven

Jesse sat on the bench with his back against the wall, both knees drawn up to his chest. He pushed a hand against his aching stomach. No one had come to his cell all day. *So much for a last meal.* It did seem a little pointless, eating at this stage of things, but he still wouldn't have turned down a good steak dinner. If he'd been about to receive a flogging on an empty stomach, he would have been more concerned. *At least it doesn't require a lot of energy to take a bullet to the head.* He managed a grim smile. He was descending into black humour. Not good.

He had no way of knowing what time it was exactly, but the diminishing wall of sunlight stretching across the floor told him it had to be well past dinnertime, maybe close to twenty-one hundred hours. Shivers prickled across his skin. *Almost time.*

Jesse propped his elbows on his knees and dropped his face into his hands. *God, give me strength. Help me to honour you by facing death with courage and dignity.*

The clanging of the door at the end of the hallway brought his head up sharply. *Already?* He got up off the bench.

Gallagher and the two privates marched toward him.

Jesse's eyes narrowed.

Whittaker and Smallman each gripped the arm of another prisoner, a man with a white cloth bag over his head.

Jesse swung his gaze back to the lieutenant, who had stopped at the cell beside his and pulled open the door.

The privates directed the man, hands cuffed in front of him, into the cell.

Jesse strode to the wall of bars between them. "What is this?"

Gallagher sauntered over. "Brought you some company. I thought the two of you could spend his last hour together."

"*His* last hour?"

Gallagher's face twisted into a smirk.

Jesse gripped the bars tightly to keep from reaching through them and punching the look off his face. A terrible apprehension settled into his gut like a rock. "What's going on here, Gallagher? I thought I was the one who was supposed to die."

"A death sentence was handed down, yes. Someone has to die. It's just not going to be you. Not this time, anyway. You'll be free to go, with a dishonourable discharge, of course."

"You're letting me go."

"Yes."

"Why?"

"Because I want you to live with this." Gallagher spun on his heel and strode toward the man standing quietly in the middle of the cell. "Meet the man who *is* about to die for your crimes, Christensen." He grasped the top of the white hood and pulled it from the man's head.

The sight of his best friend hit Jesse in the gut like a two by four, and he bent forward slightly. *This isn't happening.* He straightened up and gripped the bars even tighter. "Gallagher, don't do this. Caleb hasn't done anything wrong. He doesn't deserve to die. Is there still a functioning legal system in this country or not?"

Gallagher's laughter was mocking and echoed off the hard stone walls of the prison. "Might I remind you that the crime you have been convicted of is *treason*? That makes you the last one with any right to lecture anyone on the way the country is being run. In any case, the decision has been made, and it is now out of my hands. Donevan will die tonight." The lieutenant nodded at Caleb.

Smallman removed Caleb's handcuffs, and the privates and lieutenant left the cell.

When the door at the end of the hallway slammed shut, Caleb walked over to Jesse, rubbing his wrists. He stopped when he reached the wall of bars and dipped his head. "Sundance."

Jesse's chest squeezed. Was this really them, going out in a blaze of glory like the famed outlaw and his partner? "Cale, I'm so sorry."

"Don't be. It's not your fault."

"I had no idea Gallagher would pull something like this."

Caleb let out a short laugh. "Really? I'm not surprised at all. This is classic Gallagher." He sighed. "It's a different world, Jess. And it started changing a long time before the bombings. That just gave the powers that be the excuse to legalize the persecution. Guys like Gallagher hate Christians, and the new legislation has handed them the power to get rid of as many of us as they can."

"But this is still a democracy. There must be—" Jesse's head jerked. "Wait, *us*?"

Caleb grinned. "I've been figuring things out, taking a close look at this Christianity thing, like I told you I would. And I've been watching you and seeing how different you are. I finally ran out of excuses to keep fighting against it."

"Wow." Jesse slid down the bars until he sat with his side resting against them. "When?"

Caleb sat too, facing Jesse with his shoulder against the metal. "In Germany." He shook his head. "It was bad, Jess. The world is in an unbelievable mess. The EU is falling apart because several of their members have declared bankruptcy and pulled out. And Africa? AIDS had already decimated them, then they were slammed by the Red Virus. A bunch of countries there are either extinct or on the verge of extinction. Life expectancy has dropped in Asia because of pollution levels. And things aren't much better here in North America. At least six American states have run out of water. Everyone is fighting over resources, and quite a number of hostile countries have turned their sights on us because we have oil and water. Drought and other natural disasters are rampant, especially earthquakes. It's as if the entire planet is imploding."

Jesse rested his head against the bars. It was too much for him to take in.

"The mood hanging over the summit was complete hopelessness. The leaders spent the majority of the time just looking at each other as though they had no solutions to offer. One night I couldn't take it anymore. I went out for a walk and passed one beautiful, old church after another. Even though they're mostly empty now, there still seems to be a power emanating from them. I found one that was open and went in. I sat in the pew and started praying, and suddenly everything changed for me, like a light going off. Or flowing in, I guess."

Jesse lifted his head. "And Gallagher found out."

"Yeah. Michael Stevens contacted me yesterday to let me know what was going on. I managed to get a flight out late last night. I was heading over to see you this morning when Treyvon Adams stopped me. Do you know him? He was transferred to the base about three months ago."

"Yeah, I know him. We've talked a few times. Seems like an okay guy."

"Keep that in mind. He'd heard about you being arrested, of course. That took about thirty seconds to spread through the ranks. He figured that, since the two of us are close, I might be able to answer some questions he's had about Christianity. We got talking, then Gallagher and his two cronies started walking toward us. They were being loud and obnoxious, like usual, and I'm sure they didn't hear anything, but the second Adams saw them, he panicked and started singing like a bird. He accused me of proselytizing, insubordination, sedition, inciting hatred, everything he could think of. He stopped just short of telling Gallagher I'd been selling classified military secrets to the Russians, although I think he may have even hinted at that at one point. About ten words in, there were three pistols pointed at my head, and by the time he finished and shut his mouth, they had more than enough to arrest me and toss me into a holding cell."

Jesse's fist tightened around a bar. "So, not an okay guy."

"Reserve your judgment until you hear everything. I think Gallagher's first thought was that he would try and fast-track a death sentence for me too, get rid of us both in one fell swoop, but even he couldn't manufacture enough evidence to push that through so quickly. At some point he realized it would probably be a more effective punishment for you if they killed me in your place."

"Which is true."

Caleb shrugged. "After he came to that conclusion, it was a simple matter of removing your name from the paperwork and inserting mine.

He even managed to get the general's signature on the revised execution warrant, but he may not have needed it. The death of one imminent threat to national security is pretty much the same as another these days, so Gallagher's banking on the fact that no one will have the time, resources, or desire to follow up on this case. And he's probably right about that."

"He told you all this?"

"No, actually. Adams snuck in to see me this afternoon. He came to apologize, and I have to give him credit for that. I really didn't think he'd have the nerve to face me after what he did. He seemed genuinely remorseful, so he may be okay after all, just skittish. He told me what Gallagher was planning, which I appreciated, because otherwise I wouldn't have known until you did what he was up to."

"Gallagher has lost his mind. How does he think he can get away with all this?"

"He *is* getting away with it. He's building his own empire here, and after I'm gone and you're out of the army, nothing will stop the little weasel from crowning himself king. You and I were the only ones with the authority and the backbone to stand up to him, and now he's getting rid of both of us. Everyone else around here is already too scared to question anything he does, and that's just going to get worse after today." His eyes narrowed as he studied Jesse. "What?"

"Nothing."

"Come on. You're busting to contradict something I just said. What is it?"

Jesse's gaze dropped to his hands. "It doesn't seem like the best time to pick an argument with you."

"It's the perfect time. First of all, you may never get another chance."

Jesse flinched.

"Secondly, I'm kind of in need of a distraction here, Jess. And as you know, my favourite distraction is picking apart your ill-conceived and poorly executed arguments."

A stab of pain shot through Jesse's chest. For as long as he could remember, Caleb had been part of his life, always there when he needed him. There was no one he respected more, no one, other than Meryn, that he loved or trusted more. *I've already lost Rory. What will I do when Caleb is ...?* Jesse bit his lip to keep from groaning. "Okay, fine. Emperor."

"What?"

"The head of an empire is an emperor, not a king. Like China and Rome and ..." He fished for another good example. "... Star Wars," he finished lamely.

"Star Wars? That's what you've got?" Caleb tilted his head to one side, the corners of his mouth twitching. "You really have to let that movie go, man. It's like a hundred years old."

"It's nothing like one hundred. Seventy-five, maybe."

"Same thing."

"If you were a seventy-five-year-old man, you wouldn't think so."

"Apparently I don't ever have to worry about that, so it's a moot point."

Jesse drew in a deep breath. "Any chance you could quit tossing out glib comments about what's about to happen?"

Caleb smiled, but for the first time Jesse detected a hint of sadness in it. "Sorry. Laughing's a lot more appealing than the alternative at the moment."

"Lucky for you I'm about to make an impassioned argument on behalf of one of my brilliant theories. Those usually have you rolling on the floor," Jesse said dryly. "Star Wars may be theologically questionable, but it's still relevant as a reflection of culture, now more than ever. We're essentially living out the premise as we speak: a tiny band of social outcasts trying to stand up against the seemingly overwhelming power of the dark side, led by the evil *emperor*."

Caleb gave him a wry grin. "All right. Remarkably, you've made your point. In any case, it doesn't really matter. Gallagher can give himself the culturally relevant title of Grand Poobah, for all I care. The bottom line is he's setting himself up as supreme ruler in this little corner of the world." He reached through the bars and gripped Jesse's arm. "So grant a walking dead man his last request. When you get out of here, gather your little ragtag band of rebels together and don't let him get away with it. Stand up to that guy whenever and however you can. Be the proverbial thorn in his side. After all, you have nothing to lose. To die is gain, right?"

Jesse's eyebrows rose.

"What? My mother gave me this New Testament when I joined the army." Caleb tugged a small red book from his shirt pocket. "I've carried it around with me for years, and a few months ago I realized it might do me more good if I opened it up and actually read it." For a moment he flipped through it silently, then his head shot up. "Britain."

"Britain?"

"Yeah, the British Empire. They had kings and queens, right? Not emperors."

Jesse held up both hands in surrender. "I stand corrected. You win."

"What?" Caleb pressed a hand to his chest. "*You* are conceding defeat in an argument? Now I'm more glad than ever it's heaven I'm about to go to. Things must be exceptionally cold in that other place right about now."

Jesse mustered a weak smile.

Neither of them spoke for a moment, then Caleb said, "I feel like we should be singing or something. Unfortunately, I don't know any hymns."

Jesse snorted. "Just as well. I've heard you sing. Not how I want to spend our last ..."

Caleb punched him lightly in the shoulder. "It's all right. Our last few minutes together. You can say it."

"It's not right that you're the one who has to pay the price for what I did."

"It is right." Caleb gripped the New Testament in both hands. "In light of the new laws, I'm as guilty of treason as you are, and just as worthy of death. Remember the night we were on our way to Meryn's and you told me you were going to stay in the army, that helping the Christians was your purpose for being on the planet? Well, this is the task laid out for me, I know it. And I have it easy. All I have to do is close my eyes and go see Jesus. And Natalie. Your work isn't finished yet, my friend."

Jesse glanced up at the window, at the darkness on the other side of the glass, and swallowed the lump that had risen in his throat. "I don't know if I can do it without you."

"Yes, you can. You know where your strength comes from, and it's not me. And Meryn will be at your side. That should help."

A lock clicked open at the end of the hallway. Caleb grabbed a bar and pulled himself to his feet, and Jesse followed suit.

Gallagher and his two henchmen tromped down the hall toward them.

Caleb straightened to his full height and grasped Jesse by the forearms. "Here's my final order: fight the good fight, my brother. Finish strong. Rory and I will be watching you and cheering you on."

Jesse nodded, unable to push any more words out of a throat that had gone tight.

The door of Caleb's cell crashed open, and Gallagher stepped inside. "Let's go, Donevan."

Caleb squeezed Jesse's arms and slid one hand down to his friend's, pushing something into his palm before he let go.

Jesse glanced down at his hand, then slipped the small red New Testament into the back pocket of his jeans. He sagged against the bars as Whittaker and Smallman grabbed Caleb and dragged him to the middle of the cell. Whittaker yanked his arms behind his back and snapped handcuffs around his wrists.

Shoving his hand into the front pocket of his jeans, Jesse found the silver heart and gripped it so hard that the metal dug into his skin.

Gallagher moved to Caleb's side. "On your knees."

Caleb sank down, his eyes not leaving Jesse's.

Some of the horror leached from Jesse at the look of peace on his friend's face.

Gallagher held his pistol to the base of Caleb's neck. "Any last words?"

"Listen to the Christians, Gallagher. They're telling the truth. You have to—"

The loud crack of the pistol firing drove the last of the strength from Jesse's knees. He let the heart fall to the bottom of his pocket and gripped the bars of the cell with both hands so he wouldn't slump to the floor along with Caleb. Closing his eyes, he pressed his forehead to the cold metal. For a few seconds, he concentrated on drawing in one shaky breath after another.

Then the door to his cell flew open.

He opened his eyes and spun around.

Gallagher stood in the opening, his uniform splattered with blood.

Jesse choked back the bile that rose in his throat.

"A present for you, Christensen." Gallagher dangled a grey identity bracelet from one finger.

Jesse let go of the bars and lurched toward the door.

Gallagher grabbed Jesse's right arm and snapped the bracelet around his wrist, then planted a hand on his chest and pushed him up against the doorframe.

Jesse's fists clenched.

"A word of advice for you, *Captain.* Either get as far away from here as you can, preferably out of the country, or stop those Christians from spreading their garbage around here. I will be watching you. If I see you in here again, nothing will give me more pleasure than putting a bullet in your brain and sending you to hell to join your friend over there." He waved a hand in the direction of Caleb's cell.

Tendrils of hatred snaked through his chest. *God, help me.* Jesse met Gallagher's gaze. "Caleb's not in hell. He found out the truth in time." He leaned in closer. "And a word of advice for you, *Lieutenant.* Listen to what he said, before it's too late."

Gallagher gestured to the star shapes on his shoulder. "That's *Major* to you." He sent a pointed look toward Caleb. "The mighty have fallen, but there are always those with more might ready to rise up and take their place. I'm the one with the power now, Christensen. And if you're smart, you won't forget it." He slammed Jesse against the doorframe again. "Now get out of my sight."

The only thing Jesse wanted more than to wrap his hands around the man's throat and hold on until life had ebbed from his body was to see Meryn.

Jesse brushed past Gallagher and made his way down the hallway, trying to block out the sound of water gushing from a hose behind him as he made his way toward the exit and freedom.

Chapter Forty-Eight

Meryn counted the low bongs of the grandfather clock on the mantel above the woodstove.

Ten. Eleven. Twelve.

She squeezed her eyes shut. Two hours had passed since Jesse's life had ended. And hers.

That isn't right. Somehow she would have to find the strength to go on. Right now, though, that task felt like climbing Mount Everest on her hands and knees. It took everything she had just to keep breathing in and out. Anything more than that was inconceivable.

Her eyes had riveted on the clock at 9:55, and she didn't looked away until a quarter after ten. She hadn't felt a sudden, gaping emptiness inside her like she thought she would, only an unbearable ache that would deepen in the hours and days to come.

The fire Shane had started had burned down to embers. With a deep groan, Meryn flung off the knitted blanket and made her way to the box of wood. Her fingers shook as she gripped a piece and pulled open the door of the stove.

"What did I tell you about locking your door?"

She jumped and dropped the wood onto the floor with a thud. Heart pounding, she whirled toward the voice.

Jesse stood in the doorway. His face was gaunt and bruised. Blood had dried over a cut below his left eye, but unless her mind was playing tricks on her, he was alive.

"Jesse?" His name came out like a sob. Ever since Michael Stevens had told her the news, she'd been afraid she would lose her mind. *Now*

I have. Still, if there was any chance the figure in front of her wasn't a hallucination … She stumbled toward him.

Jesse caught her halfway across the room.

Only when she felt his strong arms around her did she allow herself to believe that what she was seeing might not be an apparition.

"Meryn." He pressed his lips to the top of her head, then, when she looked up at him, covered her face with kisses before finding her mouth.

When he finally lifted his head, she gasped for air and clung to him to keep her trembling legs from giving out beneath her. "You're alive."

"Against all odds." He pulled her close.

She rested her head on his chest, still not able to believe he was real, even though his heart thudded erratically beneath her cheek. Gradually the fact that he was shivering uncontrollably registered in her mind and she looked up. "Did you walk all the way here?"

"Yes."

"Why didn't you call me? I could have come and gotten you."

"I didn't want you anywhere near the base. Terrible things are happening, Meryn." A shudder moved through him.

She took his hand. "Come and sit. I'll put more wood on the fire."

Jesse sank down on the couch.

Meryn stoked the coals and added pieces of wood until flames flickered behind the glass of the woodstove door. She sat down on the coffee table in front of him and reached for his hand. It was as cold as ice, so she rubbed it between both of hers. "What …? How …?"

He sighed. "It's a long story. I'll tell you everything, but first I really need to take a hot shower, if you don't mind."

"I don't think I'll mind anything you do ever again."

Jesse tapped her on the nose. "We'll see how long that lasts." He moved to the front of the couch.

She tightened her grip.

He glanced down at their clasped hands and back up at her. "What is it?"

"I thought you were dead. I didn't think I would see you again. Now I'm afraid this is a dream and if I let you go it will end."

Jesse smiled faintly. "I would hope, if you were dreaming about me, you'd imagine me looking a lot better than this."

"You couldn't possibly look any better to me than you do in this moment."

"That's the shock talking." He blew out a breath. "Look, I know you're overwhelmed. So am I. But I promise you this is real. I'm here, Meryn. And I'm not going anywhere. I never thought I'd see you again, either, and I have no desire to let you out of my sight. In fact, I'd take you with me, except that it would be wildly inappropriate, and frankly, I just don't have it in me to take on your brothers tonight."

She studied him. "No, you don't look like you do. When did you last eat?"

His forehead wrinkled, as though he was trying to remember. "I grabbed a snack before I saw you last."

Her eyes widened. "That was two days ago."

"Believe me, I know. Although it feels like a lifetime."

"Yes, it does." She let go of his hand, reluctantly. "I'll warm up dinner for you while you're gone. And I'll leave some of Shane's clothes outside the door. There's a new toothbrush in the cupboard too."

"Thanks. I won't be long." Jesse got up and crossed the room, supporting himself on the furniture and the wall as he passed by.

Her chest ached. *What has he been through the last forty-eight hours?*

When he disappeared down the back hallway, Meryn grabbed a long-sleeved navy T-shirt and grey track pants from Shane's pile of clean clothes in the laundry room and dropped them outside the washroom door.

Water ran in the shower.

This must be real, then. Or a very elaborate illusion. She held her hand against the door for a moment before she went to the kitchen. After pulling the pasta and sauce out of the fridge, she heated up a plate of spaghetti for Jesse and fixed him a salad. Her fingers trembled as she plugged in the kettle and took two tea bags out of the canister on the counter.

"Meryn?" Shane stood in the opening between the kitchen and hallway. "What's going on? I thought I heard voices."

"You did." She dropped the tea bags into the pot and spun around, clasping her hands in front of her. "Shane, you won't believe it. Jesse's here." Saying the words out loud helped them feel more real.

His eyes widened. "What? I thought ..."

"I know. He hasn't told me what happened yet, but they must have let him go."

"Unbelievable." A smile spread across his face. "That's amazing, kid." He walked over to her. "I'm happy for you. Both of you. I'd love to hear his story."

Meryn nodded. "Me too. But do you mind waiting until tomorrow? He's starving and exhausted."

"Of course." He wrapped his arms around her and hugged her. "I'll tell Brendan what's going on." He let go of her and stepped back, a wry grin on his face. "He won't love it, but we'll give the two of you some time together. Talk to you in the morning, okay?"

Meryn nodded. When her brother had left, she reached for the kettle and poured water over the tea bags in the pot.

Jesse's arms slid around her waist.

Meryn smiled and set the kettle down. "You weren't kidding."

"About not wanting you out of my sight? No, I wasn't." He touched his lips to the curve of her neck.

She turned in his arms. "I meant about not being long, but being in your sight sounds good too." Her smile faded as she brushed the back of her hand over the bruise below his eye. Who had done that to him? His short, dark hair was damp, and he smelled like soap. Meryn took a deep breath, inhaling the sight and scent of him. "What happened, Jesse? Did they let you go? I thought ..." Her voice shook. "Michael Stevens said they sentenced you to death."

A shadow crossed his face. "They did hand down the death sentence. Only Gallagher didn't kill me. He killed someone else in my place, right in front of me."

Horror slashed through her. She didn't want to know. "Who?"

He let go of her. His fingers rasped over the stubble on his cheeks.

Her chest clenched at the pain swirling through his eyes, the same pain she'd seen in them the night he'd told her about his brother's death.

"Caleb."

Meryn sucked in a sharp breath. For a moment she couldn't speak. "Jesse ... I'm so sorry. That must have been horrible."

"It was. But it was also powerful, somehow. He believed, Meryn. And his death was miraculously peaceful, given the circumstances."

She rested her forehead against his shirt. "I'm so glad."

Jesse held her tightly against him. When she lifted her head, he swiped his thumbs over her cheek to wipe away the tears.

Meryn cupped his face in her hands and kissed him.

He pulled her close again and rested his chin on the top of her head.

I could stay here forever. He needed food, though, and rest. "Come and eat something." She handed him the tray of food and grabbed the teapot and a mug before following him back to the living room.

Meryn didn't speak while he ate, content to watch him, to feel him next to her, to touch his arm, brush back his hair, anything to convince herself that he was really there and that he wasn't going to disappear again. When he finished, she moved the dishes onto the coffee table.

Jesse stretched out on the couch, his head resting on a cushion in her lap. He caught her hand and turned it over. "What happened?" He ran a finger gently over the Band-Aid on her palm.

She grimaced. "It was a long, terrible day. By suppertime I'd had enough, and I took out my frustration on a pile of plates."

"Are you okay?" He pulled her hand to his mouth.

Warmth tingled through her. For the first time since Michael Stevens had left the house the day before, she wasn't freezing. "I am now." She fingered the grey bracelet around his wrist, and the warmth intensified. *No more secrets.*

He let go of her. His eyes dropped shut as he bent his arm above his head. The bottom corner of Shane's navy T-shirt slid up a couple of inches, and she caught a glimpse of discoloured skin.

Meryn gasped and lifted the shirt.

His abdomen was covered in splotches of black and blue.

"Jesse! What did they do to you?"

"Oh yeah. Gallagher thought it would be fun to toss me in a cell with a few of the guys I'd put in prison over the last few months."

Her insides twisted. "They could have killed you."

"They gave it their best shot. They would have done it gladly, but a guard came and ended things before they could."

"And I've been grabbing you and holding on to you since you walked in the door. Why didn't you stop me?"

He opened one eye and squinted up at her. "You're kidding, right?"

Meryn would have laughed if she hadn't felt so sick, and if a white-hot anger, laser-focused on Lieutenant Gallagher, wasn't sweeping through her. "I'll ask Rick to come out in the morning and make sure none of your ribs are broken." She didn't have the energy to try and keep everything she was feeling out of her voice.

He fixed his eyes on hers. "We have to let it go, Meryn. The rage. And the hatred." He reached up and trailed a finger down the side of her face. "If we don't, it will destroy us."

Aren't we destroyed already? She sighed. "Have you?"

"Not yet. Not even close. But with the grace of God I'm going to try." He closed his eyes again.

Meryn pulled his shirt higher, so she could inspect the bruises. She ran her fingers lightly over his ribs.

Jesse drew in a quick breath and caught her fingers in one hand while tugging the T-shirt back down with the other. "I swear, lady, you're the only person on the planet who could make me forget how tired I am and how much pain I'm in at the moment."

She bit her lip, her cheeks warm. "Sorry."

He smiled, eyes still closed. "Don't be. It bodes well for the future."

Her chest constricted.

Without looking at her, he squeezed her fingers. "Don't."

"Don't what?"

"Panic. Withdraw. Whatever it is that you do."

"If you behave yourself, I won't."

"If *I* behave myself? You're the one undressing me."

She choked out a laugh. "I was *not* undressing you. I was checking out your injuries."

"Potato, potahto. The point is, you're the one who needs to behave."

Meryn pressed her lips together. "I'll try to restrain myself."

"I hope so. If not, I'll have to call Brendan down here and tell him *you're* getting handsy, see what he does with that."

More laughter bubbled up in her throat. Meryn covered her mouth with her hand to try and hold it in, but that only made it come out as a kind of laugh-snort, which got Jesse laughing. Once they started, neither of them could stop until he drew a knee up on the couch and held a hand against his ribs, and she realized how much this must be hurting him. That sobered her quickly. The laughter had helped, though. The intense ache deep inside of her eased.

She shook her head. "How can you make jokes after everything you've been through?"

"I have to, Meryn. Yeah, it hurts, but physical pain is all I can deal with right now. Caleb was cracking jokes too, while we were waiting for them to come for him. Now I get it. As he said, laughing is preferable to the alternative."

She stroked his face, the lines gradually smoothing out as he relaxed. Then she asked softly, "Do you want to talk about it?"

"Yes. But not tonight. Tonight I just want to be here, with you."

"Okay." She pulled a blanket over him. For hours she rested her hand on his arm and watched him sleep, unable to drift off herself until, sometime in the early morning, the shivering she now knew had nothing to do with his long walk in the cold, finally subsided.

Chapter Forty-Nine

Jesse sat up on the couch. His stomach roiled, and he concentrated on taking in slow, deep breaths in an attempt to settle it.

Rick opened his leather briefcase and dropped the stethoscope inside. "Do you want me to give you something for the pain?"

"No, I think I'm okay. The ribs don't hurt as much as they did. Until someone starts poking and prodding them, of course."

"Sorry." The doctor's smile held sympathy. "Good news is, none of them appear to be broken. Bruised, of course, and possibly one or two cracked. It will help that I've wrapped them, but you'll have to take it easy for a couple of weeks. I don't see any evidence of internal damage, but if you start to feel worse or have any unusual pain, let me know right away."

"I will. Thanks." Jesse winced as he got to his feet.

"You don't have to get up."

"That's okay. I'll walk you out." He followed the elderly doctor into the kitchen.

Meryn stood at the stove, scrambling eggs with a lifter. She wore a light-blue sweater that brought out the incredible colour of her eyes, and her hair was pulled back in a sleek ponytail.

His breath caught at the sight of her.

She turned to them with a bright smile that did far more for the pain than any prescription could. "Is everything okay?"

"Looks worse than it is, Meryn." Rick patted her arm. "A little TLC, and he'll be good as new."

She met Jesse's eyes over the doctor's shoulder. "I can do that."

Warmth flooded through him, and he winked at her.

Rick turned and headed for the door. "I'll leave you to it, then."

"Thanks for coming by, Rick." Meryn followed him and watched through the screen door as he picked his way across the front yard to his car.

Jesse came up from behind and wrapped his arms around her, inhaling the scent of lavender. "Where are your brothers?"

"They left early to go to church and then over to Kate and Ethan's. We're supposed to meet them there for lunch."

"I didn't even hear them come down. Must have been pretty out of it."

She leaned back against him with a sigh. "Are you really okay?"

He tightened his hold. "Physically, I'll be fine. I can't think about what happened to Caleb yet, but I'm grateful to be alive. And my head is whirling with everything I have to do."

"Like what?" The doctor drove past the end of the walkway, and Meryn lifted her hand.

"Now that Gallagher's taken over, I'm worried that things are going to get worse fast. We need to start working together, supporting each other."

She nodded, her hair soft against his chin. "Shane and Brendan were saying the same thing recently. We should talk to them about what they're thinking."

"Sounds good. I have a few ideas too. I'd like to put a plan in place to get food and supplies if they become hard to buy, make sure we have lots of water, plan the wedding, and set up an underground system for books and Bibles. We—"

Meryn stiffened in his arms. "What did you say?"

"Set up an underground system for books and Bibles?"

She pulled away from him and whirled around. Her face had gone pale. "Not that one. The one before that."

"Oh. You mean plan the wedding?"

She crossed her arms over her chest.

Not a good sign. Should he have given her a little more warning?

"Whose wedding are you thinking of planning?"

"Well, ours, of course." He wrinkled his forehead. "Who else's wedding would I want to plan?"

"I wasn't aware that we had a wedding to plan."

He tilted his head at the sudden shakiness in her voice. "We do, if you'll have me." Jesse reached for her hand. "Marry me, Meryn. The last couple of days, thinking I would never see you again, were the worst ones of my life. I love you with all my heart, and I never want to be apart from you. But I can't stay here if we're not married, so I thought ..."

Meryn pulled her hand from his. "Jesse. You've been through a lot. You're not thinking clearly."

She felt suddenly miles away from him. *What is that about?* "I have been through a lot, but I've never seen things so clearly in my life. If I learned anything from what happened with Caleb, it's that life is a precious and fragile thing that can be taken from us at any time. We live in a crazy world that is getting crazier every day. I have no idea how much time we have left, but I do know that I don't want to waste another minute of it. I want to do all of those things I mentioned, but more than anything, I want to marry you and start our life together. Please say yes."

Meryn stepped back.

The same glacial numbness that had crept through him when he read his death sentence started in his extremities again. *I can't lose her too.*

"This is all just too ... I need more time. Yesterday I thought you were dead, and suddenly you want to marry me. It's too much to process."

He studied her for a moment, then shook his head. "Don't lie to me, Meryn. Please. Not after everything we've been through together. This is about what you were going to share with me in the cabin, isn't it? Why don't you just tell me what you've been keeping from me, so we can deal with it once and for all?"

She bit her lip. "You're right. You deserve to know. The truth is, I've been married before."

The words ripped through him like the sound of the gunshot had the night before. For several long seconds he couldn't move. Then heat surged through his chest. "So you're what, divorced? Separated?"

She shook her head. "Widowed. At least, I think so."

He closed his eyes, praying for calm. When he opened them, he forced himself to speak slowly, deliberately. "What does that mean, you think so? How could you not know whether or not you are a widow?" A sudden revelation struck him, and he waved a hand around the room. "Is that why you live way out here all by yourself? You're waiting for the husband you may or may not have to come home?"

Meryn winced and he breathed in slowly in order to push back the rising fury. *Hear her out.*

She pressed a hand to her abdomen. "My husband was a soldier too. A peacekeeper. He was stationed in the Middle East."

Jesse started.

Her eyes narrowed. "What is it?"

"It's just ... I'm starting to realize how much we don't know about each other. I was in the Middle East for a while too. What happened to him?"

"That's the problem. I don't know. He's been missing for almost four years."

His fury evaporated and he sank onto a kitchen chair. A husband. She had a husband. It took the last of his rapidly waning energy to lift his head and search her face. "Did you love him?"

Meryn sat down beside him. "Yes, I did. Very much. He'd had a difficult life. His mother died when he was really young, and his father never got over it. When I moved in, this house was like a time capsule. Everything had frozen in place when she passed away. Even the pictures on the walls never progressed past that awful day, as though his dad refused to acknowledge that time had gone on, that life should be going on." She smoothed the plastic tablecloth with the side of her hand. "In spite of that, he turned out to be this amazing guy, kind and funny and strong. We met when I was in my last year at Queen's, and he was at the Royal Military College. Then we both graduated and he went through basic training and left for his first tour. When he came back three years later, he had changed. He had this new awareness of how brief life could be, how important it was to make the most of every moment."

Jesse slumped against the back of his chair. *Not sure I want to hear any more of this.* She seemed to need to get it out, though, so he didn't speak, just gave her time to gather her thoughts.

"He was home for a few months, then he got called up again. Just before he was to leave, he came to me with a marriage license. He said he didn't want to go away again without everything being settled between us, so we went to city hall and got married. He promised me he would give me a ring and a big wedding when he came home, do it right. But it felt right to me. We had a wonderful few days together, and then he left and never ..."

Under the table, Jesse's fingers dug into his thighs.

She lifted her shoulders. "He never came back. Four months after he was deployed, he went missing. Last year the army sent me his death certificate but wouldn't tell me anything about how he died. I wrote all these letters, even went to Ottawa twice, but if they gave me any information at all it was vague and generic. It made me wonder if they even knew for sure that he was dead. Maybe he was still just missing, but they wanted to close the book on him, tie up all the loose ends, so they decided to say he was gone." She met Jesse's eyes. "Could that happen? Could they have made a mistake, or lied about what happened?"

He exhaled. Anything was possible, especially when it came to that part of the world. Everything was so crazy there, so surreal. But going missing in the Middle East, being taken prisoner, was pretty much equivalent to being dead. He didn't know anyone who'd come back from that. Jesse shook his head. "It's not impossible, but it's not likely, either. If he's been missing that long ..."

She clasped trembling fingers together on the table. "You're right, I was waiting for him. I thought I would wait forever, but then I met you. And I tried to push you away. But finally I couldn't anymore, and I started to think that maybe everyone was right. It was time to let him go and move on. That last night in your quarters, I realized that my life had become a time capsule too, frozen and waiting for something that was never going to happen. So I did. I moved on. But somewhere, in the back of my mind, it was still hard to let go, to give my heart to you fully, when I didn't have absolute proof that he was dead."

This cannot be happening. "I was transferred back to Canada about that time. I may be out of the army, but I still have friends I can call. I could look into it for you, see if I can find out anything about your ... about what happened to him. What was his name?"

"Corporal Logan Phillips."

The sick feeling in his stomach swelled to a nausea he had to swallow back. "Logan Phillips?" *It can't be.* "Was he blond? About six feet?"

"Yes." Meryn's eyes widened. "Did you know him?"

"Do you have a picture?"

"Yes, in my wallet. I'll get it."

While she was gone, Jesse concentrated on drawing in one deep breath after another, but it didn't ease the pounding in his chest. *The little blond boy in the pictures in the hall.* The thought struck him like an unexpected blow to the gut. He'd looked familiar ... He lowered his forehead onto his hand.

When Meryn came back, he sat up and reached for the photograph she held out.

Her fingers touched his and stilled as she probed his eyes. "You're shaking again." She lowered herself slowly onto the chair beside him, her eyes not leaving his. "What is it?"

He glanced down at the picture in his hand, although he didn't really need to. The last of the warmth drained from his body.

"You did know him." She whispered the words.

"A little. We weren't in the same unit, but our paths crossed a few times. He was a good kid. Everyone liked him."

"Do you know what happened to him?"

"Yes." He dropped the picture onto the table and reached for her hand. It was cold, but his was the same, so he couldn't do anything about it. "Meryn, I'm so sorry. He is dead. I know that for sure."

She pulled her hand from his and crossed her arms as though to ward off the pain of his words. "How could you?"

"Because I'm the one who killed him."

Chapter Fifty

Jesse pushed back his chair and stood up, unable to handle her blue eyes searching his face so intently. He strode to the window. The plans he'd just been making flashed through his mind. He choked down the lump in his throat. His plans were all meaningless now. "We were out in the desert one afternoon. The sun was beating down so hard you could see the heat shimmering above the ground, like something you could reach out and touch. Tensions were running high, like they always are in that part of the world. Twelve Canadian soldiers had just been blown up in a convoy, and three others had been picked off by snipers over the last week. Every time we went out, we felt like sitting ducks because we could be hit by a missile or the ground could explode beneath our tanks at any minute."

He wanted to turn, to see her face and know how she was doing, but he kept staring out at the patches of shade, at the blades of grass still glittering with morning dew, and remembering that stifling, unbearable heat.

"We'd stopped for a break and were all standing around, drinking warm cola and shooting the breeze, when suddenly someone yelled, 'Bomber!' I spun around and saw a man running toward us. None of us ever went out alone. We stuck together, because it gave us at least a small sense of security, knowing there were others there to watch our backs or, too often, pick up the pieces. The sight of one man alone running toward a bunch of soldiers was never a good thing. We yelled at him to stop, but he kept coming. He was shimmering too, and blurry, as he passed through the waves of heat and dust. I would have thought I was seeing a mirage, except that everyone else saw him too. I was in the best position to get a bead on him, so I grabbed my rifle and set my sights and, when he got close enough, pulled the trigger." He summoned every ounce of courage he had left and turned to face her.

Meryn's hands were fisted together against her mouth. Tears glittered in her eyes.

"He went down right away. Four of us went to make sure he'd been taken out. He was lying face down in the sand, so we were ten feet away from him before we saw it: the maple leaf on the shoulder of his uniform. I knew right away I'd just done something that would change my life forever. I reached him and turned him over, desperately hoping he would still be alive and we could do something to help him, but I'd aimed high in case he was wearing a suicide vest, and the bullet had gone through his neck. He was gone. They buried him that night, quietly, and proceeded to cover up the whole thing. The death of an Allied soldier by friendly fire would have been big news, and an even bigger hit to a morale that was already incredibly shaky. That's why the army wouldn't give you any details about what happened. That would have been admitting they knew more about it than they wanted anyone to believe."

Jesse crossed the room and sat back down on the chair. He clasped his hands together tightly to keep from reaching for her. "I lost it after that. I couldn't deal with what I'd done, couldn't handle being there one more day, surrounded by killing and blood and fear. They sent me to a military hospital in Austria for three months to recover from PTSD, as if such a thing were possible. Caleb had been injured, and he asked to be sent to the same hospital. Without him I don't know if I would have survived. Especially when we both came down with Reds and almost died. We managed to come through it, I'm still not sure how. God's mercy, I guess, although I definitely didn't feel as if I had any right to that at the time."

A noise came from Meryn, more jagged and soul deep than a sob.

The sound cut into him like a blade, but he had to keep going, had to tell her everything. "When I was about to be released from the hospital, I requested a transfer back to Canada. I still think about it all the time, still sometimes see him so clearly in my dreams running across the sand because the rest of his platoon was under fire and he was just trying to get help. Those are the nights I wake up shaking and drenched in sweat. Including ..." He looked at her.

"That night in your room." The horror in her voice drove into his chest. "You said 'stop.' You were talking to him, weren't you? You were talking to my husband."

"Yes. Only, the thing is, it isn't always the thought of him that wakes me in the night. The few conversations we had, he always mentioned you. He didn't say your name, but the way he said 'my wife,' well, it was obvious he loved you very much. My first thought, when we turned him over and I realized he was dead, was of you, what you would go through now because of me. You're the other one who's haunted my dreams for years now, even before I ever saw your face." Jesse lifted a palm into the air. "I've never been able to forgive myself, so I don't expect you to forgive me, but ..."

Meryn's chair scraped across the floor as she stood up. "I need you to go."

"Meryn ..." A desperate panic gripped him, and he stood too. He started toward her but stopped when she shook her head and stepped back.

"No." Her voice was emotionless, detached. She had already left him. "You were wrong. Some things are too broken to be fixed."

When he didn't move, she pointed to the door, hand trembling. "Go. Now. And don't come back."

He struggled to find the words that would change her mind, that would convince her to let him stay so they could work this out, find a way to be together, but they wouldn't come. The shock he'd felt that day in the desert and for months afterward, the way he'd moved through the mundane tasks he needed to accomplish—as though nothing around him was real or held any meaning—slammed into him as strongly as it had then. He turned and made his way to the door. When he reached it, he looked back, fresh pain spearing him at the sight of her face, gone so pale there was almost no sign of life there. "I'm sorry, Meryn."

The words, like his plans, were meaningless, and dissipated in the air as he pushed open the door and stepped outside.

Chapter Fifty-One

A cool wind swooped down from the north and blew through Jesse's navy T-shirt. His ribs protested every thud of his running shoes against the hard ground. He embraced the suffering, welcoming every piercing stab in his sides, like a friend shielding him from a much worse pain. *I deserve this. I deserve this.* The thought pounded through his brain with every step.

He ran until the knife-like agony slicing through his lungs made it nearly impossible to suck in oxygen. Then he slowed to a jog, working to drag one ragged puff of air after another through his windpipe. Sweat trickled down his back. His heartrate gradually slowed. Shoving both fists against his hips, he trudged down the gravel shoulder of the road. *Where am I going?*

His left foot dropped into the long grass at the side of the road, and he went down hard on one knee on the sharp gravel. Shock reverberated through his body.

A few feet ahead of him, the rotting trunk of a tree lay across the ditch.

Jesse hauled himself up and stumbled toward the tree. When he reached the trunk, he collapsed in front of it, dug both elbows into the soft wood, and dropped his face into his hands.

I have nowhere to go. You've stripped everything from me. I've lost Meryn. And Caleb. I have no family, no friends, no career, no home. I have nothing left for you to take. I have nothing left to give.

No sounds disturbed the quiet of the countryside. Even the birds had gone still. *Have you left me too?* The silent cry of anguish echoed through the hollow carved out inside him by everything that had happened the last few days.

A truth blew through him like the wind riffling through the branches above his head. A tear slid down his cheek. He wasn't alone.

All right, then. If you can use a completely broken man with nothing to offer you, I'm yours. Do with me what you will.

Pain still vibrated along every muscle and deep down inside his heart, but the peace that flooded through him dulled it to an ache in the background. An ache he'd have to learn to live with.

An approaching vehicle drove him to his feet as he wiped the moisture from his face. His stomach clenched at the sight of a green army jeep. *Really? That's what you've got for me? Another confrontation with a soldier?*

The jeep slowed as it passed him, then pulled over to the shoulder. Jesse braced himself against a branch.

A man in khaki-green camouflage jacket and pants exited the vehicle and started back toward him. When he drew closer, Jesse's hands curled into fists. Treyvon Adams. Other than Gallagher or his henchmen, the last person on earth Jesse wanted to see at the moment.

Adams made his way through the long grass of the ditch and stopped in front of him. "Captain." He inclined his head.

Jesse's jaw clenched. "Just Jesse is fine."

"Jesse, I've been looking for you."

"Is that right?"

"Yeah. I'm sure you have some things to say to me, or maybe you'd just like to punch me in the face. Either way, I won't try to stop you, so go ahead." When Jesse didn't move, Adams met his gaze. "I mean it. Take a swing at me. I deserve it."

His own thoughts coming back to haunt him. *I guess we all deserve it, don't we? You haven't given me what I deserve, thankfully, so I guess I can pass along that favour to someone else.* The rage surging through him like adrenaline dissipated. "I'm not going to hit you, Adams."

"It's Trey." He lifted his cap and ran a hand over his tight black curls before replacing it. "And I came to tell you how sorry I am. I didn't mean for anything to happen to Major Donevan. I panicked. I never dreamed they'd kill him."

Jesse's legs were weak and he sank down on the log. "Neither did I.

A lot of things have happened the last few days, the last year really, that I never dreamed were possible."

Trey rested a boot on the trunk and crossed his arms over his knee. "Me too. It's made me think about my life, you know? What I believe and what's important. That's why I wanted to talk to the major, to see if he could answer some questions I had about God and Christianity and whether there's anything to it."

"He told me. I don't have all the answers, but I can discuss it with you anytime."

"I appreciate it. And I will come talk to you." Trey dropped his foot. "For now, though, you look all done in. Can I take you someplace?"

Good question. Where could he go? The answer came to him. There really only was one place. "I'd appreciate a lift into town."

"Sure." Trey turned to climb back up to the shoulder of the road.

Jesse followed him to the jeep and swung into the passenger seat. *Still can't drive.* The thought brought a sad smile to his lips.

Trey nodded toward the backseat. "Gallagher asked me to empty out your quarters so he could move in. I brought a few things I thought you might want."

Jesse shot him a sideways glance. How closely was the man working with Gallagher?

Trey looked over at him. "I shouldn't say this about a superior officer, but something about that guy makes my skin crawl. However, it occurred to me that it might be helpful for us if he thought I was on his side, so I'm trying to play along."

"Us?"

"Yeah. I'm guessing you're going to work against Gallagher from out here, and I want to be part of that. If you need a friend on the inside, I'm your man."

Jesse studied him. Could he trust the man? Trey had betrayed Caleb and cost him his life. Was it possible the impact of that had changed Trey enough that he was now willing to risk his own life? It was hard to believe, but the eyes that met Jesse's steadily seemed earnest enough.

"I know you have no reason to believe me, but I hope you'll give me the chance to earn your trust. I owe it to the major to make up for what I've done."

Jesse pursed his lips. It really would be helpful to have someone still with the army helping him out, undermining Gallagher's attempts to make the Christians' lives miserable whenever possible. The skittishness worried him, but only time and circumstances would tell whether or not Trey could hold up under pressure. *I have nothing left to lose.* Might as well take a chance and pray it turned out okay. "All right. I might take you up on that."

"I hope you do." Trey reached into his shirt pocket and pulled out an i-com. "I grabbed this for you. And here's my card. Message me if there's anything you need."

Jesse took his device and the card Trey held out. "I will." A couple of blocks past Kate and Ethan's place, he gestured toward the curb. It was one thing to put himself at risk. Until he knew for sure whether or not Treyvon Adams could be trusted, there was no sense in putting his friends in danger.

Trey pulled to the side of the road.

Jesse pushed open the door and climbed out of the jeep.

"Here." Trey reached over the seat, grabbed a green military-issue duffel bag, and hauled it to the front. "Your stuff."

"Thanks." Jesse winced as he reached back into the vehicle for the bag and hefted it over his shoulder.

"I really am sorry, about everything. I hope someday you can forgive me. In the meantime, I meant it when I said I want to help. I'll wait to hear from you." Trey held out his hand.

Jesse hesitated a couple of seconds before he gripped it. "I'll be in touch."

"Take care."

Jesse slammed the door. When the jeep disappeared down the street, he turned and walked in the opposite direction. He pondered the conversation he'd just had as he approached Kate and Ethan's house. It had been a surprise, finding out that Trey Adams might be on his side.

Now he was about find out if anyone else was.

Chapter Fifty-Two

Jesse rapped on the front door and waited, his stomach in knots. Memories of the last time he'd shown up at this house didn't help ease his mind any.

Ethan opened the door. "Jesse!" He gripped both his arms. "Good to see you, my friend. Shane and Brendan told us you were alive, and we're all anxiously waiting to hear the story."

"Thanks, Ethan. Where are they now?"

"Out in the back with the kids. I'll let them know you're here, so we can—"

"Jesse?" Kate came up behind Ethan. He stepped back as she pulled the door open wider. "Come in." She pulled him through the door and hugged him. "I can't believe you're here." She peered around him. "Where's Meryn?"

"She's still at home. Can you do me a favour? Would you go see her? She really needs you right now."

"What happened? Is something wrong?"

"It's a long story. She can tell you when you get there."

Ethan pulled a set of keys out of his jeans pocket and handed them to her. "Go. I'll take care of lunch."

Kate slipped between them and headed for her car.

Ethan grabbed Jesse's elbow. "Everything okay?"

"Not really. Can I talk to you and Shane and Brendan?"

"Of course. Let's go out to the back deck, so we can keep an eye on Matthew and Gracie."

Jesse dropped his duffel bag at the front door and followed him through the house. The laughter and excited squeals of the kids in the backyard brought a sad smile to Jesse's lips. He'd almost forgotten what innocence sounded like.

Shane sat on a lawn chair on the deck, a glass of iced tea in his hand. A Frisbee landed at his feet, and he picked it up and whizzed it back toward his brother.

Matthew and Gracie both clapped when Brendan leaped up in the air and grabbed it.

"Brendan?" Ethan planted his hands on the railing of the deck. "Can you come up here for a few minutes?"

Shane set down his drink and pushed to his feet. He crossed the deck and held out his hand. "Jesse. I can't tell you how good it is to see you." When Jesse took his hand, Shane pulled him close and slapped him on the back a couple of times.

Will he be as glad to see me when he finds out the truth? Jesse worked to keep his features even as Shane let him go. "It's good to see you too."

Brendan bounded up the stairs and punched him in the shoulder. "I can't believe you're here. What happened?"

Where do I even begin?

Ethan gestured toward the picnic table. "Let's sit down and you can tell us everything." He looked out at the yard. "Matthew, take Gracie to the sandbox, okay?"

"Okay. Come on, Gracie." The two of them wandered past a large outbuilding, heading for the back of the expansive, fenced-in yard.

Jesse lifted one leg and then the other over the wooden bench, crossing his arms in front of him on the table.

Ethan touched his shoulder. "Can I get you a drink or anything to eat? We've been waiting for you and Meryn to get here, so we could have lunch."

"Just some water, thanks."

Ethan disappeared into the house as Shane and Brendan settled onto the bench across from him. When Ethan came back out, he handed a glass of ice water to Jesse.

"Thanks." He sipped the cool liquid before setting the cup down on the table. The ice rattled in the glass, and he pulled back his hands and folded his arms again.

Ethan dropped down beside him. "So, what happened? We heard you'd been given a death sentence."

"I was." He drew in a long breath, then told them everything that had happened on death row.

When he finished, the other men sat in stunned silence for a moment, then Shane clasped his arm. "I'm sorry, Jesse. I know you and Caleb were close."

Jesse's throat was tight. "We were. He was like a brother to me. The scary thing is, Gallagher succeeded. He was able to get both of us out of his way and get himself promoted to major in the process. He's taken over the city, which means that things could get worse fast for Christians. We need to stick together, now more than ever. The most important thing is to make sure we have access to food, water, and supplies."

Brendan nodded. "Shane and Meryn and I have been talking about the same thing. We've largely been operating on our own until now, taking care of our own families. That has to change, especially with what's going on at the base."

"I agree. Just before he died, Caleb asked me to pull together what he called a ragtag band of rebels, a group of people who will do everything they can to make life difficult for Gallagher, to keep him from setting up his own little kingdom here where he can do whatever he wants without opposition. It will be dangerous, but someone has to stand up to him."

Brendan's fists clenched on the table.

When he started to speak, Jesse held up a hand. "Don't commit to anything right away. You need to pray about this. Banding together to fight Gallagher could cost us everything, including our freedom or even our lives. You have to think about how much you're willing to risk." He shifted on the bench. "Ethan, you have a wife and kids. Talk to Kate. If you decide you can't get involved, I'll completely understand."

Ethan had been gazing out over the backyard, watching Matthew and Gracie dump pails of sand beside each other to make a castle. "Kate and I have been talking. These are dangerous times, and we can't hide away and try to stay safe, as much as we'd like to. If we don't stand up to Gallagher and others like him, what kind of world will we be leaving the kids? So yeah, we will think about it, and pray. If I do get involved, Kate will want to as well."

Shane sighed in resignation. "So will Meryn."

"Well, she might not now." Jesse cleared his throat. "Shane, Brendan, there's something else you'll have to consider before you throw your lot in with me. Your sister and I are ... not together anymore."

All three men stared at him.

Brendan spoke first, his dark eyes wide. "What? How did that happen? I thought the two of you were inches from the altar."

"So did I. In fact, I proposed to her an hour ago."

Shane cocked his head. "What happened?"

"I did something I don't think she will ever be able to forgive me for."

Brendan's eyes narrowed. "What did you do? Did you hurt her? Do Shane and I need to take you out and teach you a lesson?"

Jesse let out a strangled laugh. "I almost wish you would. It might make me feel better." He studied the glass in front of him, mesmerized by the liquid trickling down the sides. Like drops sliding down a whitewashed wall ... "Four years ago, when I was stationed in the Middle East, I killed a man."

Ethan frowned. "I'd have thought you'd killed a lot of men."

"I did, but this one was different." He rubbed his fingers along his jaw. "A guy appeared out of nowhere in the desert one day, running straight for my platoon. We thought he was a suicide bomber. I took him out before I realized he was a Canadian soldier. What I did has haunted me for years—it's the reason I requested a transfer back home. I didn't think that situation could get any worse, but today, when I was talking to Meryn, we realized that the soldier I killed wasn't only on our side, he was her husband." Jesse looked up at the shocked faces staring back at him. "So, I didn't mean to ..." He shook his head. "I would have rather cut off my own arm, but yes, I did hurt her. Far more than I can ever make up for. And if you don't feel that you can work with me, knowing that, I won't blame you."

"Wow." Shane glanced toward the house before turning to Ethan. "Where is she now?"

Brendan looked at Ethan too, as though Meryn was no longer Jesse's business.

Which, he guessed, with a stab of pain in his gut, she wasn't.

"At her place. Kate went to be with her."

Shane blew out a breath. "You're right, Jesse, that's a lot to think about. We'll pray about it too, and discuss it, and let you know what we decide."

"That's all I ask." Jesse studied the faces of the men around the table. They'd become friends to him over the past few months. More than friends. Brothers. He'd gladly go into battle against the deadliest enemy with any one of them at his side.

Something ignited deep inside him, something he thought had been torn from his grasp when Meryn ordered him to go.

Hope.

Joining him wasn't a decision he wanted his friends to make lightly. They had to know beyond any doubt, like he did, that it was what God was calling them to do. But he'd seen the fire in their eyes, all of them, including Meryn and Kate. Even after what had just happened with Meryn, he had every confidence they would all stand with him when the time was right.

And when it was ... Jesse drained the last of the cold water and smiled grimly as he set the glass down on the wooden table with a thud.

When it was, then they would go to war.

Sara Davison is the author of the romantic suspense novels The Watcher and The Seven Trilogy. She has been a finalist for eight national writing awards, including the Word Award for Best New Canadian Christian author, a Carol, and two Daphne du Maurier Awards, and is a Word and Cascade Award winner. Sara has a degree in English Literature and currently resides in Ontario, Canada with her husband Michael and their three children, all of whom she (literally) looks up to.

www.SaraDavison.org

Acknowledgments

I continue to be grateful to so many who are travelling this journey with me.

To Michael, my anchor, my safe place, and the love of my life. I could not do what I do without your encouragement and unwavering support. Thank you from the bottom of my heart.

To Luke, Julia, and Seth, three of my greatest blessings from God. Thank you for your patience, and for always stepping up when I need you to help out, or give me some peace and quiet, or make me laugh. My life is infinitely richer because you are in it.

Endless love and gratitude to my family members—by blood and marriage—who have been my biggest fans and supporters from the beginning. If we chose our family in this life, I would have chosen each one of you.

Thanks, as always, to each person in my writer's groups and book clubs. Your advice and encouragement make me a better writer and your wisdom and friendship make me a better person.

And to Sherrie and Christina and all the amazing people at Ashberry Lane Publishing. I am in awe of how hard you work, and how deeply committed you are to producing excellent books that glorify God and bring readers joy and hope. You are kindred spirits and family, and I am so grateful that we are taking this journey together.

Discussion Questions

1. There may come a time when Christians in North America will have to take a stand for or against Jesus Christ, like Meryn and her family did when they accepted their identity bracelets. What are the costs and benefits associated with both choices? Has making it known you are a Christian ever cost you anything? How high a price would you be willing to pay to pledge allegiance to Christ?

2. Matthew's teacher gives him a hard time for talking about Jesus at school. If you have children or grandchildren, how would you advise them to respond if they are laughed at for their beliefs? Can you think of a Bible verse, passage, or story you could give them to help them deal with a situation like that? How else can you support or equip them to face a society increasingly hostile toward Christianity?

3. Meryn risks her life to help a sick child. What do you think you would you do in a similar situation? Consider Meryn's assertion that "the child's life wasn't worth more than her own." Can you draw a comparison between this situation and sharing the gospel with someone in the face of personal risk?

4. Gracie's faith is so simple and yet so powerful. What can adults learn from this? In Matthew 18:3, Jesus said, "... Truly I tell you, unless you change and become like little children, you

will never enter the kingdom of heaven." What do you think Jesus meant by this?

5. The night before he speaks to the commission, Jesse calls prayer the "most powerful weapon of all." Do you believe this is true? Have you personally witnessed the power of prayer? Describe the experience.

6. Matthew 5:44 says, "But I tell you: Love your enemies and pray for those who persecute you." Jesse tries to pray for Gallagher the night before Gallagher plans to execute him. What do you think Jesus had in mind when he told believers to pray for their enemies? In what ways can we show our enemies love? What are some possible results of us being able, with the help of the Holy Spirit, to do these things?

7. After Meryn sends him away, Jesse cries out to God, saying, "*I have nothing left for you to take. I have nothing left to give.*" Have you ever felt this way? Did you learn anything about God through this painful experience? About your faith? About yourself? Can you relate to Jesse's words, "*If you can use a completely broken man with nothing to offer you, I'm yours. Do with me what you will.*" Can God use someone like that? What examples from the Bible can you use to support your answer?

Don't Miss the Rest of the Seven Series!

The End Begins
Book One

One of them is a prisoner and one of them is free.
The Same One.

The Morning Star Rises
Book Three

In the midst of all the fear and confusion,
only one thing is clear ...
This isn't over yet.

CPSIA information can be obtained
at www.ICGtesting.com
Printed in the USA
LVHW092054110722
723221LV00033B/1123